Happy Accidents

A Finding Maisy Novel

By K.D. Elledge

This is a work of fiction. Names, characters, places, and incidents either are the product of the author's imagination or are used fictitiously. Any resemblance to actual persons, living or dead, events, or locales is entirely coincidental.

Previous books by K.D. Elledge:

Finding Maisy

Out of Time

Dear Finley

Available on Amazon,
Audible, and iTunes

Happy Accidents Apple Music Playlist
https://music.apple.com/us/playlist/happy-accidents/pl.u-11zBP5aF89PxNpp

For Happy Accidents Aesthetics,
follow my Pinterest link
https://pin.it/6DZbWQFt3

TikTok Handle
@authork.d.elledge

Facebook Page
Author K.D. Elledge

Follow me on Goodreads @
https://www.goodreads.com/user/show/179285346

This book is dedicated to my work fam…my Radiology peeps…my friends…to our book club, adequately named…the Cliterature Club. You inappropriate, vulgar, and absolutely iconic group, keep me going. Never change ladies!

CHAPTER 1

Novalie

Love is bullshit. Love is a trap that snares your soul like a frantic hare and cages it for its own guilty pleasures. It leaves you blind and blissfully unaware of your own fleeting, inconsequential existence. You bask in its glorious radiant light, unaware that it's really just a magnifying glass, burning a hole through you.

Would I burn for it all over again if I could turn back time? That's the real question. Would I choose to have known love in that way…just once, knowing what I know now?

Was it worth it?

My hand races across the off-white paper of my journal—jotting down the torrent of thoughts warring inside my mind. My normal picturesque handwriting became nothing but chicken scratch with each frantic stroke of the pen.

I pause writing as a memory moves to the forefront of my mind…Levi asked me how I could possibly feel comfortable writing with a pen in my journal. Wouldn't I be worried about making mistakes, he'd laughed. I recall giving him a haughty look and stating, matter-of-factly, that there are *no* mistakes in life…only happy accidents. A quote I'd stolen from my favorite artist, Bob Ross.

I use that quote often to justify the things in life that happen and change your path for the better.

The pen quivers in my hand as I shove away the memory and let my anger writhe like a dormant beast ready to unleash hell. With a curse, I sling the journal across the room with enough force to knock over several items along my antique white dresser. A glass vase of lilies smashes against the hardwood floor, bits of glass shards flying about wildly. Good riddance. I never want to see white lilies again in my life. The death flower, as I like to call it. My house is littered with the vile things.

I watch the water from the vase spread and realize with *horror* that a picture of Levi is among the shattered bits on my floor. My body is moving faster than my heart can keep up. I snatch the broken frame off the floor and slip the picture free, wincing as a jagged piece of glass slices my index finger.

"*Fucking hell*," I swear as I rush to the bathroom sink and let the tap water mix with the red of my blood. With my other hand, I slip the picture of Levi into the corner groove of the mirror, scanning his handsome face with a mix of emotions roiling through me. But I can't do that for more than a few seconds before I look away. The blood from my finger drips into the clogged sink, spreading with the water in a crimson swirl. Nausea rears its ugly head, and I take deep breaths to ward it off.

I startle and gasp when a voice behind me comes out of nowhere. "*Nova*...you okay? I heard something crash." Through the mirror, I watch my brother Ian sidestep the mess of glass and water and inch toward the open bathroom door. His solemn brown eyes move to mine in the reflection, and he pauses as his gaze drops.

His voice is but a whisper as he asks again, "Are you okay?"

It's odd to hear that soft tone coming from him. Our usual banter consists of rendering each other speechless with insults. Ian moves a step toward me, but I subtly shake my head in a silent request for him to stop. He does so with a frown. His tall, lanky form is taking up too much space, making it hard to breathe.

"I'm fine...get out." My voice is strained, but firm.

His lips purse as he nods once, running a hand through his short, reddish-brown hair that's a few shades lighter than my own. The black suit he's wearing today looks strange on him. My brother's normal attire consists of his immaculate police uniform five days a week and workout clothes on the weekend. This suit looks forced, which *it is.*

He interrupts my cold surveying of his current state of dress. "Everyone's here now...they're all waiting on you. Mel's here too. Can I at least clean up this mess and look at your finger?"

"No. I'll be out soon."

Ian leaves after a noticeable hesitation, and I breathe a sigh of relief. After wrapping my finger in gauze and tape and cleaning up the mess I made, I put away my damp, leather-bound journal. I debated tossing it in the trash but stopped myself, even though I'm certain I'll never be able to stomach reading it or writing again.

Walking over to the wrought-iron mirror hung on my bedroom wall, I do a quick check of my appearance, finding it much as I expected. Swollen hazel eyes, rimmed in red, sallow skin made even paler by the high-necked black dress. Even my normally vibrant dark auburn hair is dull and lifeless in the half-assed chignon I managed this morning.

I hear a tap on the bedroom door and Ian's muffled voice stating the obvious. "It's time to go."

Walking toward the door, I realize I'm barefoot and quickly slip on some low black pumps. Then, I make one last stop in the bathroom, snatching the picture of Levi from the mirror and tucking it into the pocket of my dress.

Reaching for the door handle, I pause. A tear slides down my cheek, and I want to scream. I haven't even made it through the door. I *can't* do this. I slam my hand against the wall, hoping pain will push back the misery in my heart enough to get through this one *fucking* day, but the glint from my ring pierces my eyes. Rolling my fingers, I watch the sparkles created by the diamond's many facets.

I squeeze my eyes shut and whisper to a ghost, "How *dare* you do this to me?"

Am I truly insane? Scolding a dead man. With my shoulders back, chin up, I wipe away the dampness on my cheek and open the door.

CHAPTER 2

Novalie

A never-ending blur of faces and regurgitated 'sorrys' follows me around our…no, my small house. Claustrophobia shouldn't be an issue in my own home, but here I am, struggling to rein in the panic I feel crawling up my throat. My best friend, Melina Templeton, is a step behind me like she'll catch me if I fall…and her worries are warranted. I would like to fall and never get up. Her dark brown curly hair is thick and bounces with her steps as she greets a few of Levi's work buddies. Her tan skin is complemented by the black dress edged in teal lace. She's fierce-looking and collected as usual.

That's something I can always count on—her strong, take-charge demeanor. It's helpful on days like this.

Lemon drop shots line the entryway table with a photograph of Levi in the center. They were his favorite guilty pleasure shots, but being a health-nut, it was rare he indulged. Still, his friends and family wanted to share memories and, to do that, they all agreed that they needed liquid courage. I take the final step to the table and throw back a shot, relishing in the tangy lemon flavor and sharp sting of liquor, then stare at the picture in front of me. Tears burn behind my eyes when they meet his large brown ones. I always told him he had puppy-dog eyes. His five o'clock shadow was showing that day, which was unusual for him. He liked being clean-shaven and in a sharp suit.

Tears spill over in big rolling blobs down my cheeks, and a shuddering rattles me to my core. Out of habit, I begin aligning the shot glasses in a more pristine pattern. Someone grasps my elbow and hauls me toward the hallway bathroom. It takes me a moment to realize it's Mel. My back hits the wall when she releases me inside, and my body slides down until I'm hugging my knees on the floor. I hear the soft click as she locks the bathroom door.

Melina's too-big golden eyes are shiny with unspent tears of her own when she drops down to her knees in front of me. "If you want to leave…we'll leave right now. Screw the wake."

That's what I love about her…Mel doesn't give a shit what people think. I always care too much about other's opinions. If I'm being honest, it's the thing I hate most about myself. My head shakes subtly as I bury my face in my lap and mumble, "I need to be here. People expect me to say something." A sob hitches in my throat.

"I'll do it for you if you want. I can do your speech," she offers.

Lifting my gaze back to hers, I shake my head. "I'll do this. I just don't know how I'll make it through the words."

She reaches for the toilet paper and pulls some free for me to clean my face. "Get it out in here. Let it all out, Nova. Then we'll slam a few more shots and get this fiasco over with. I've got you the whole way." Nodding, I sit a little straighter when she adds, "Say whatever it is you need to say now…the stuff that you can't say out there."

Tears fall so fast and constant that the toilet paper is unable to keep up. I squeeze my eyes shut and whisper, "I'm fucking furious at him…for leaving me, for…" I trail off. I feel ashamed of that. We were supposed to grow old together. My watery eyes meet hers. "What am I supposed to do now? How can I move on? I don't think I'll survive this." My face hits my knees again as I shake with emotion. "I loved him so much. It hurts." I press my palm into my chest. My fingers curl as if I could rip out my broken heart. "I'm just so fucking angry," I grind out through gritted teeth.

"I know, honey, but you have so many people who love you, and we'll help get you through this. You're not alone." Mel's hand squeezes my shoulder.

As nice as that sounds, I want to be alone. I want it so badly right now. We both shift our heads when we hear Levi's mother speaking on his behalf through the thin bathroom walls. Standing on shaky limbs, I give Mel a curt nod. "Let's get this over with."

We make a beeline for the shots and down two each before turning to listen to a few others speak about Levi in the past tense. Levi was a good man. Levi was a hard worker. Levi was…ugh…it's sickening. Every time someone drifts near me, Mel shifts a little more in front of me, using body language to keep them away.

A few more speeches and boom, it's my turn.

Mel squeezes my hand, and it gives me just enough gumption to move my legs as she whispers, "You're a supernova; never forget it." Her words squeeze my heart. She's called me that since we were teenagers.

Mine and Levi's living room is small…quaint. We purchased this house because it was affordable and adorable, plus we didn't have children and, therefore, didn't need much space. The room seems minuscule now with all these people in a veritable sea of black hovered around me like vultures. I focus on the fireplace lit with candles across the mantle and several pictures of the two of us together. Reaching up, I fix a crooked photo and scoot a candle over so that it's more centered.

The room is quiet, and it takes me a few seconds to realize it's because I'm just standing there. Swallowing the panic and lump climbing my throat, I pull out the notes I'd written last night on a tear-dampened napkin. I think my chest may burst from the forceful beats of my heart as I look over the smeared mess of words.

I adjust my stance to face the crowded living room. "Uchumm." I clear my throat. "Thank you all for being here. I'm sure Levi would appreciate it." A sniffle breaks free, and I think I'm going to lose it already. Mel nods toward me encouragingly. "Levi—" I break off. I can't say was.

My eyes dart around nervously, landing on Levi's mother, Polly. She shifts her eyes away from mine as if she can't stomach facing me. In fact, that's the impression I'm getting from several of the grievers. It makes my stomach churn with unease. Finally, my eyes land on a picture of the two of us hanging across the living room. I anchor my gaze there. We were horseback riding on the beach in the Outer

Banks. His brown hair was tousled in the breeze, and if I try hard…I can almost feel the softness of his locks gliding through my fingers when he'd laid his head on my stomach that night. We had an amazing vacation that year. If only I could reach into that photo and pull myself through.

Deep breath in, and I begin again. "Levi loved adventure. He incorporated that into his home life as well as his work life. While I like being curled up with a book, he liked being on the move. He also loved helping his community, as many of you well know. He donated not only supplies but his time and aid to several local charities."

A lone tear streams down my cheek when my gaze shifts to my mother, who's crying in my father's arms. I spew more boring facts to stifle my emotions a while longer. I talk about his good deeds with the animal shelter, his accomplishments as a psychiatrist, his drive for perfection in everything he did. When I run out of facts, I walk away from the fireplace without another word. People's eyes rove over me at the unexpected pause and exit. Ignoring the glares and whispers, I snatch several shots, almost spilling them, and lock myself away in my bedroom.

I don't speak to Mel, to my parents, to his parents, to his siblings, to my sibling…I just leave.

I down the shots one after another, then hold my face tightly against Levi's pillow, and I scream.

CHAPTER 3

Novalie

Six months later…

Dust particles invade my nose, and a squeaky sneeze whooshes out of me. Dragging the box of books, I back-step until I reach the new shelves lining the far wall. When I heard about an estate auction last week, I never imagined I'd find so many sought-after collectibles. Reaching on my tiptoes, I clean the top shelf first, preparing the books for their new home.

Two swipes in and my phone goes off with a ting. Huffing, I toss the cloth into the soapy water and walk over to my office desk, my heels clacking on the old hardwood floor. Three missed messages from Mom greet me, but the latest is from Melina.

Mel: Call me back hussy. I've tried your cell for days. If you keep ignoring me, I'm arranging an intervention!

Turning off the phone, I shove it into the desk drawer, rattling everything atop it when I slam it shut. Raking a hand over my face, I exhale forcefully. It's then that I catch sight of the open sign in the large glass window at the front of my shop. I forgot to turn it on this morning. I curse under my breath as I race over to flip the switch. Neon green illuminates my face as the sign crackles and comes to life. Propping the front door open with a rickety wooden chair, I drag out the shelf I use for free books. It's something I've been doing for a month now. Sometimes people donate books, and sometimes I buy them for kids and leave them outside during the days I'm open…which is *every* day.

One month after Levi died, I packed up and left our country home and moved into the apartment above this bookstore. It's a small, one-bedroom space that has an open, industrial feel to it. The money from selling the house paid for the apartment but not the store, so I financed the rest even though I was highly discouraged from friends and family. I get it. They didn't want me moving away, and they were afraid that I couldn't afford this place, but I've managed. It's *also* why I work seven days a week.

The *truth* is everyone thinks I've disassociated. They believe that's why I left and sold everything the two of us had together except for a very few trinkets like a box of clothes, and my wedding set. Their worries are valid but pointless. I like it here in the hidden mountain city of Asheville, North Carolina. And while I don't see my family as often due to the distance, I talk to them when I can. I can't help that they're needy and expect me to call every week.

I pick a few dead leaves out of the flowers lining my windows and straighten a large potted fern that sits atop my fat cement frog. It's gaped open mouth is just begging for some succulents to be added there. I'll make a note to get some soon.

Breathing in the crisp morning air, I glance to the sign above my front door that reads, *Nova's Novel Garden.* It's cheesy, but I thought it would incorporate the plants I sell along with the books.

Once inside, I go back to cleaning the back shelves for the new editions. Yelling at my Alexa to play Stevie Nicks, I bend to sink the rag into the water again and hear the clinking bells that hang from the front door. I wring out the rag and yell over a shoulder, "Welcome. I'll be around shortly if you need any assistance."

No one responds.

Wiping my hands on my green, floor-length layered skirt, I squinch my brows and stand, leaning around a bookshelf to peer toward the front. I frown, not seeing anyone, then turn to clean the second shelf. Squeezing the rag again, I start scrubbing. Rocking side to side, I sway and sing to *Rhiannon* while I work.

That's what I love the most about being here…the peace this bookstore brings me. I have solitude, quiet, and all the books I could read.

I spend the next ten minutes finishing up the shelves and then start the process of stacking the new books in alphabetical order. The sound of a shoe scuffing the ground has me pausing. I stop and again lean around the bookshelves toward the front entrance but, like before, I see no one. With a shrug, I turn back to the task at hand, picking up another book.

A hand clamps down over my mouth, the book drops, clattering to the floor as my peaceful reality is shattered into a million pieces. My eyes flare wide as my body is dragged backward.

It all happens too fast to comprehend. A scream breaks free from me, but it's muffled by the large palm clamped over my lips. My heart beats wildly as my heels clatter and scrape across the floor and my fingernails dig into the flesh of his forearms instinctively, trying to gain purchase and freedom. I flail in the arms of my assailant. Panic sucking the very life from me.

Suddenly, my back is pulled flush against the man holding me, and my chest is pressed into the far wall of a hidden reading nook, smooshing my face to the side. *I can't breathe.* My thundering heart is threatening to beat its way right out of my chest.

I feel hot breath against my cheek before hearing a gravelly voice whisper into my ear, "Do *not* try to scream again…understand me?"

I crane my neck and shift my eyes toward the voice, but he pushes me into the wall harder and I nod, self-preservation kicking in. Tears prick my eyes as raw fear drags its meaty claws through me. A sniffle comes out of my nose with my choked sobs straining to be set free.

"You live here…upstairs, right?" the man asks quietly. I don't deign to answer until his fingers tighten on my face, causing me to nod. He breathes what sounds weirdly like a sigh of relief. "Do you live here alone?" he asks, his breath against my ear making the hair rise on the back of my neck.

I nod again, knowing he'll make me answer anyway, and I can't exactly lie and bank my hopes on someone waltzing in here to save me.

"Good. I'm going to tie your hands..." I squirm against him and try to mumble pleas through his fingers, but he tsks and says, "Just long enough for us to have a little chat. Now, don't scream...I don't *want* to hurt you."

But he *will*...that's the implication there. The obvious, looming threat. I squeeze my eyes together as tears roll down my cheeks to land on his hand. Very slowly he releases my mouth, but I don't move an inch. Dragging in a tattered breath, I cough. It's then that I feel a cloth wrapping around my hands behind my back—twining them together. He cinches them unbearably tight, and it draws a soft cry from my lips. Before I can gather my wits, he spins me to face him. One hand rests on my shoulder, keeping me braced against the wall, while the other grips my jaw firmly, forcing me to tilt my head back and look up.

Gray-blue eyes hold me captive in their murky depths. Sweat dots the man's brow and mixes with smudges of dirt and grime...and *blood.* My gaze travels the rest of his features fast and assessing. His dark hair, almost black, is short with the top being a little longer and sticking out haphazardly. His sharp jaw is covered with a five o'clock shadow. There's a semi-fresh cut across the bridge of his nose—a nose that looks as if it's been broken before—and some dried blood dots his face in splotches. As my eyes drop, I notice the weathered snap-button shirt he's wearing that's clearly a size too small. My brows furrow more at the snug jeans, none of which match the vibe of this man's rising tattoo that covers the front of his neck and peeks from his shirt sleeves that don't reach his wrists.

He looks *familiar*, but I can't place why.

My eyes snap back to his and take in the strange look he's giving me. Confusion bolts through me. He's scanning me too, brows furrowed and mouth set in a tight line. With a subtle shake of his head, as if to clear it, he leans in close to my face, baring his teeth as he says, "You're going to do as I say. I'm shutting this place down, and *we* are going upstairs."

My mouth pops open with a sputter of pleas. "I…I can't, please. What do you want? Is it money? I can get you money." Tears rain down my cheeks.

His eyes follow those drops of sorrow and fear pouring from me, and his jaw tics. "Don't make things harder than they have to be. *Just cooperate*."

My knees start to give way, but he holds me firm in place. Before I can swallow my pride and beg again, he's yanking me from the wall and spinning me away from him. He grabs my bound hands from behind and directs me forward, my heeled feet stumbling along. A sob racks my chest as we make our way toward the shop entrance.

I plead *again* for my life. "*Please*…whatever it is you want…just tell me." I can't let him make it upstairs.

He pushes me enough to make me pick up speed. "*Keep walking*."

Bile threatens to rise in my throat, acid coating my tongue as I stand by the door and watch him lock the entry and then flip the open switch off. My feet move mechanically as he aims me toward the door in the back of my shop that leads to the staircase and the rear entrance. In a blink, we're facing those stairs, and I freeze.

I can't let him in. If I do, I'm a dead woman. I feel it resonate inside me.

Adrenaline finds me in that moment, and a part of me that I didn't know existed rears its head. I kick backward, my heel coming in contact with a shin. He grunts as I lunge forward, causing his grip to loosen. The moment I feel the release, I shift and run. My only option is my apartment upstairs as his body is currently blocking the rear exit door. Taking the stairs two at a time, I push forward. I make it halfway up before he slams into me from behind, and we smack the staircase.

His heavy body is pinning me down as his fingers lace into my hair beneath the high ponytail and yank my head back. His voice seethes into my ear. "*Not very smart.*"

"I'm s-s-sooor-ry," I stutter and wince with pain from my tied arms behind my back being crushed with his weight.

"Let's try this again…civil-like," he hisses.

Pulling me to my feet, he doesn't wait for me to move. Instead, the breath is whooshed out of me as he lifts my body with ease and tosses me over his shoulder like a sack of potatoes. My squeak of protest is lost on his ears as he bounds the steps. The door creaks open and then slams as we enter my home.

The finality of it robs me of sanity. This *can't* be happening.

CHAPTER 4

Novalie

The strange man shifts me forward until I'm cradled in his arms and then places me on one of my kitchen island chairs. My body shakes with tremors as he moves silently behind me and secures my hands to the wooden slats of the high-back chair. I refrain from speaking; words are lost to me anyway, caught like a fly in a web. How can this be real? Surely, this is a nightmare. A gut-wrenching feeling swarms my insides like wasps. Is this how people feel when they know they're going to die? Sheer panic that you'd give *almost anything* to escape.

Closing my eyes, I pray for a miracle.

He moves with silent grace around my apartment, rifling through my things. I watch as he pulls a pair of scissors from the knife block. I suck in a breath and squirm, but he ignores me and moves past where I sit. My brows pinch together until I realize what he's doing. He snips the cord of the old landline phone I've kept for nostalgia.

"Where's your cell?" he demands.

"It's..." I debate a lie.

"Don't fuck with me right now...*where is it?*" he growls.

My voice cracks. "It's in the shop. My desk drawer."

I watch as he backs away slowly. "Do not move," he demands. For a large man, he moves with preternatural grace.

The moment the door clicks shut, not giving myself a moment to reconsider, I stand awkwardly from the chair forcing my arms back painfully, but then I grip the wood slats with my bound hands, lift the chair, and rock my body side to side. With momentum, I begin slamming the chair into the island over and over until I hear splintering. Heart racing, sweat pouring from my temples, I hold the chair from behind and slam it one last time into the bar and hear the satisfying crack as part of the chair snaps. My hands are still tied, but free from the chair as I bolt to the door and spin with my back to it. Fumbling with the handle, I find the lock and lift onto my tiptoes to get a better feel for it. Just as my fingers graze the lock, the door opens, smacking me in the back. My body hits the wall before I crumple to my knees.

I scream then—let it screech from my parched lips.

It only lasts a second before a hand is once again garbling the sound. "Shut up. *Shut the fuck up*!" he whispers forcefully into my ear. Suddenly, his hand is gone from my mouth. I hear the distinct sound of cloth ripping at the seams right before my mouth is snagged with it. He ties the gag tightly around my head and yanks me to standing. *This time* when he ties me to something…it's a metal industrial pipe that snakes along the walls of my apartment.

He's making certain I can't break loose again.

His massively tall frame stands over me, assessing; for what…I don't know. Then he kneels before me and runs his thumb over my knee, marring it red.

He takes a long, ragged breath and shakes his head in aggravation before storming away. I watch as he pulls my cell from his pocket. He comes back over, drags the gag away briefly asking, "What's the code?"

My entire body slumps in utter defeat. "1201," I say, my voice coarse and ragged.

The gag is replaced, and he's moving again, punching in the code and nosing through my cell. He makes a face at something he sees and then his eyes dart back to me, but whatever gave him the look is gone fast. Closing my eyes, I lean my head back against the wall.

A sting drags me back to the present and, to my utter shock, the stranger is sitting before me dabbing alcohol into the wound on my knee. A bandage lies beside me. His eyes linger on my face for a beat as he cleans the wound. "No more trying to escape. I'm going to remove this gag…I need you to be on your best behavior. You understand?"

I nod solemnly.

With one hand he releases the knot behind my head, and the gag falls away. I hate that my lips tremble like a child's when I ask, "Why are you doing this?"

An odd smile graces his lips but doesn't reach his eyes. "It's a long story; one I don't care to rehash all at once. Let's start with this. What's your name? And before you decide on a creative lie, remember that I can just as easily read your mail, or go through your phone."

Licking my dried lips, I say, "Novalie Rhodes."

He nods once as he bandages my knee. "Is that a maiden name or married name?"

I give him an incredulous look, but then it hits me. His face when he looked at my phone. All the old photos of Levi and me are still in there. I swallow hard. "Married."

He freezes, his whole body tensing. He looks to be contemplating that as he cranes his head around to my bound hands and eyes my bare ring finger there. "Thought you lived alone? When will he be home?"

I don't know why the truth rolls out of me so fast, but it does. "Never." A fresh wave of tears stream down my cheeks.

"Ah," he says, and I swear there's a bit of actual sympathy in his tone briefly before he continues his interrogation. "When did he die?"

"Six months ago."

"What's your middle name?" he asks casually, as if I'm not kidnapped and tied to a damn pipe.

"Are you serious? What does it matter who I am?" My hackles rise with the aggravation of the situation I now find myself in.

His eyes narrow on me like a raging sea…that's what they look like, a raging sea of gray and blue—a storm. "What is it?" he asks again, unperturbed by my question.

"Annie."

"Novalie Annie. That's…*different.* What was your maiden name?"

"Sawyer," I whisper with confusion still blanketing my face at the absurdity of having a normal conversation with this lunatic.

"Novalie...does everyone call you that?" he asks as he stands and moves to wash his hands in the kitchen.

My eyes trail after him, and for the first time I notice his bare feet. His boots are discarded by the door as if he has no intention of leaving. I'm not sure when he did that. And now, I'm fairly certain I passed out for a bit. "No, they call me Nova," I reply.

"Okay, *Nova.* I'm going to shower. Do you happen to have any men's clothing?"

My mouth drops open as I scan his attire once more. It doesn't add up. The clothes look like they belong to someone else, and even the boots by the door look too small for his feet. Through my confusion, I say, "You're going to leave me like this...while you shower."

"Yes and no. You're coming with me," he says flatly. "Now do you have any clothes?"

My eyes threaten to bulge from their sockets. My words come out strangled. "*With you*?"

His brows rise along with one side of his cheek. "Not *in* the shower with me...but in the bathroom. You think I'd leave you alone after your attempts to escape? Clothes, do you have any?" he asks again.

"The box at the top of the closet has a few," I manage to say, the solid lump in my throat worsening.

The man drops to a crouch in front of me, reaching for the gag to replace it. My plea stops him as I ask, "What's your name then? I gave you mine." He looks as if he'll ignore me, gently replacing my gag. He unties me from the pipe, and rises, taking me with him. Walking to the bedroom, he says over his shoulder, "Soren Lee Marshall...Ren for short."

My brows pinch together, the name sounding as familiar as his face. He brings me into the bathroom, looking around as if he's deciphering what to do with me. I mumble, praying he'll remove the gag.

"Nice try," he says and then lifts my arms to the end of the shower rod, securing me there.

Suddenly my chest is rising fast again with the influx of panic when he disappears into my bedroom and I listen as the hangers move on the metal rod, as a box scrapes from the top shelf, as the tape is torn to open it. A few moments later the man…*Ren*, steps through the open doorway, his button-up shirt now off and tied around his waist. Sleeves of tattoos climb over his arms and more on his thickly muscled chest. I can't help staring at his rippling abdomen, littered with three rather nasty scars. The kind of scars that have a story behind them.

I shift my eyes from him the moment he catches me staring. Adjusting on my feet, I lean against the wall, keeping my focus there as I hear his clothing hitting the floor. Heat and fear move from my neck to my face. The steam from the shower seems to rid the room of oxygen.

I just have to keep breathing…stop panicking. Somehow, I'll figure out a way to escape.

What kind of lunatic kidnaps someone and immediately showers? What the hell is happening here?

CHAPTER 5

Soren

Leaning my head back in the shower, I let the scalding water shred through me, not even concerned with the burn as it enters each and every open gash in my skin. Between everything that's happened the last few days, I'm a disgusting mess, and nothing has ever felt as good as this shower. I take a glob of her flowery-smelling body wash and scrub for a second time.

The shock on her face when I started undressing was almost comical, but it was a clear sign for her to avert her eyes, which she did with a quickness I've never seen. She's got to be in her late twenties, but she blushes like a virgin teen. I'll admit, bathing with a woman tied to the shower wasn't exactly part of the plan, but she was slick in her attempt to get away earlier, so…now she's forced to listen to me shower.

And I *do* take my sweet time. An hour later, I step out of the shower into the thick steam. Nova is twisted so that her back is to me, but I can tell it must be painful for her arms.

Giving her a few more minutes to stew, I wrap a towel around my waist and rifle through her bathroom contents like a fucking creeper. I need to know who I'm dealing with here, and a good way to do that is snooping. I find no medications except for one—an unused bottle of Xanax. By the date on it, it was prescribed not long after her husband died. Slipping it into my pocket, I turn to see she's now eyeing me. I grab the towel as if I'll drop it, and she turns away fast.

Smiling, I drop the towel and look at the clothes I gathered. Gray sweatpants and a plain black tee will work…but I guess I'm going commando. Even if she kept some…I'm not wearing another man's boxers. The jeans in the box were too small, and the shirt, but it'll do. I dress and then find some of her deodorant that's been unopened and an entire drawer full of dental supplies, including several unopened toothbrushes, all of it neatly organized. "You mind if I use these?" I ask, holding up a blue-packaged toothbrush and the deodorant.

She's gone rigid, and I'm beginning to see a bit of fire in her eyes. She narrows them at me.

I smirk. "Didn't think you'd mind." I watch her bristle. Holding back a smile, I turn to the sink, swipe a spot on the mirror to clear the steam, then brush my teeth and use her swish twice. It's as euphoric as a shower. I find some liquid band-aid for the bridge of my nose and swipe some over it.

In the reflection, I catch her watching me. We lock eyes through the one clear streak on the mirror.

With an exhale, I finally go to her and untie her hands, pulling her along as I stride to the living room. I spin her to face me. Her eyes darken as they move over the clothes I'm wearing. Her late husband's clothes, no doubt. She looked like she wasn't wearing any makeup before…or very minimal, but streaks of faint black are smudged around her thick lashes from crying or maybe the shower steam.

I take in her hate-filled eyes, a multitude of hazel colors, and match them as I size her up. Giving her a once-over from top to bottom. From her thick reddish-brown hair hanging haphazardly from her ponytail to her fitted white tee cropped to show a teeny sliver of her stomach. Her long green skirt looks like it's meant to be worn to a Renaissance festival rather than casually. Her sharp, angular face is almost gaunt, as if she rarely eats enough. Her brown leather heels don't help her height much; she's *so* small…fragile, really.

Nothing, and yet *everything* I imagined.

I've been watching her for days now. Saying that in my head sounds as shitty as it is, but circumstances being what they are, I'll do what I must. I just hope I'm not wrong in my assessment of this woman.

Exhaling, I remove her gag completely this time, letting it hang on her slim neck. "No screaming?" I keep my voice low, demanding.

A curt nod from her, but still no words. I look to the right side of the living room and through the large glass doors there that lead out to the balcony. "It's getting close to lunchtime. You have food here, I assume?" I ask.

"Yes." Her dainty voice has my eyes dropping to her full lips that still have a slight tremble.

"I'll make lunch. You can get yourself cleaned up, but don't try any funny business. Don't try to scream, don't try to leave. Understand?"

Confusion washes over her face, but she nods primly. I untie her bound hands and watch as she rolls her shoulders and rubs her wrists, which I'm sure are aching. Her legs shake, and I grab her elbow as her knees give way, making her gasp.

We have a silent standoff, our bodies a few inches apart before I release her. "Take off those ridiculous heels; you can barely stand."

Her eyes widen, and the light catches the green and golden hues mixed with brown. "I can't stand because you left me tied in an odd position for over an hour! And hit me with the door, making me injure my knee!"

I smirk to infuriate her more, really enjoying this fire that's been hidden under her petite surface. All her sadness and fear are beginning to melt into molten fury. "Semantics. Either way, you're going to take them off, get cleaned up, and eat."

"Are you going to make me? Am I to do as I'm told without any explanation? Why are you doing this?" She backs a step away as she says it, attempting to place some kind of distance between us.

I step forward, robbing her of that distance, and crowd her as I lean down. "I'm in charge here, not you. Trust and believe I have a good reason for what I'm doing. Take off the damn shoes and get cleaned up."

"Trust and believe…*you*? That's insane. You know that, right? You're some *thug*, who's kidnapped me and yet you ask me to trust and believe you!" She scoffs.

Without another word, I pull a knife I found in her husband's belongings from the pocket of the sweatpants and flick it open. She flinches, but I'm faster. Bending down, I grab her leg with one hand in a vise grip and push the tip of the knife under the strap of her heel. She squeals, her hands bracing on my shoulders as I yank her foot to me. She tries to move, but the knife cuts the leather strap like butter, and I yank it off her foot. She watches in horror as I repeat it on the other side.

Standing, I close the knife, dropping it back into my pocket. "Do what I say, Nova; this will all go a lot easier."

Her hand is now hovering over her mouth, but she nods, regardless. I lightly push her toward her room, and she finally gets her bare feet moving. Once she disappears in there, I move her antique work desk to barricade the front door…in case she tries to run again. This will *hopefully* slow her enough for me to get there.

While she's gone, I toss the old prescription of Xanax in the trash and find some sourdough bread, lettuce, tomatoes, and freshly shaved turkey meat to prepare sandwiches with. My stomach growls the whole time. This will be the first real meal I've had since I got out. Next, I locate some cucumbers to slice up and douse with sea salt and pepper. Her entire fridge is immaculate. I've never seen such organization. Nothing outdated, all healthy ingredients organized and labeled.

It's unnerving.

After preparing the food and pouring two glasses of water, I nose through her kitchen some more. I see her out of the corner of my eye as she stands by her bedroom door, unmoving, but watching me like a hawk.

"Are you some sort of pervert?" she asks with a straight face.

I cock my head to the side and can't help the half-smile creeping up. "No. Are *you*?"

Her cheeks pinken as her eyes harden and turn to slits. Her face is cleanly washed, her hair now wrapped in a large thick bun. She straightens her shoulders as she grits her teeth. "Why are you here…Ren, was it? Why are you going through my stuff?"

I ignore her and open a cabinet, stepping to the side. I wave a hand at its contents, which are perfectly stacked, even with all labels pointing out. None are a *centimeter* out of place. I raise my brows at her and ask, "The real question is what are you undiagnosed with? What kind of '*Sleeping with the Enemy*' shit is this?"

She gasps. "Is there something wrong with being neat? You're probably a slob, and that's why this bothers you."

I snort and point for her to sit at the one island chair that still remains. The other is shattered in jagged bits on the floor. Her chin rises, but she does as I say reluctantly. "I'm not a slob," I tell her, "and you certainly have issues, lady. No one is this organized."

"Well, *I* am," she seethes.

I slide her plate over and watch as nervous energy replaces her haughty one. My mouth curves as I say, "I didn't poison it. Where would I even find poison around here?" Her brow raises in challenge, so I reach over the counter and snatch her sandwich up and take a large bite, then pop a cucumber in my mouth. "Thuuree," I mumble through a mouthful, "awll good."

Her little nose squinches up with distaste. "You *are* a slob," she says, watching a piece of lettuce fall from my mouth.

"*Eat.*" I jab a finger at the food and push over the water.

"What if I'm not hungry?" she counters.

I finish the bite with a lick of my lips and stare at her until she becomes uncomfortable. "You're skin and bones…*eat.*" Before she can throw a retort at me, I slam a hand onto the counter hard enough to get her attention. "Just…*eat.*"

I can't help but notice her throat bobs with a difficult swallow, but she relents and begins eating. She takes small bites and chews completely before taking the next. She's a pillar of perfected movements—holding herself regal as if she's royalty rather than the owner of a quaint bookstore.

We're silent for a long while. Then, she seems to be considering something. "You've watched the movie *Sleeping with the Enemy*?" she asks, her voice laced with skepticism.

"I grew up in a house full of women. There wasn't a single Julia Roberts film that they didn't watch on repeat."

She seems intrigued by that, but then her face falls. A tear slips down her cheek, and I don't want to think about how that affects me. She wipes it away and looks up. "You'll tell me your name, that you have a family…so tell me *why* you're here. I can't take the *not knowing*. Are you here to hurt me, Ren?"

Getting up, I clean away the dishes, slipping them into her dishwasher. I stop and lean across the counter, placing us closer together, and look down into her eyes. "I won't hurt you."

"Why then...why are you here?" she asks again. When I refuse to answer, she asks, "Are you an escapee? You're *him,* aren't you?"

My eyes drill into hers, point *one* for the OCD book nerd. I don't say anything—let her draw her own conclusions first.

"I thought I recognized you. You're the prisoner who escaped a few days ago. I overheard some of my customers talking about it. Are you *hiding* here then?" she asks.

Point *two.*

"Talk to me. If I'm meant to be held captive, at least tell me why." Another tear leaks down her cheek, and my hand moves of its own volition to wipe it away, but I stop myself midway.

Clearing my throat, I stand tall and lean back against the opposite counter, crossing my arms over my chest. "Yes...to both."

Her shoulders slump, but she takes a breath that seems calmer than before. "I won't tell anyone about you if you just let me go. I can get you some money, clothes, a car, whatever you need to disappear," she prattles on as I roll my lips into my mouth.

"No," I simply say.

"*No?*" One of her brows arches inquisitively.

"No, you can't leave, and neither am I."

"*Why not?*" she asks impatiently.

I walk around the counter to stand directly in front of her as she spins in the chair and tilts her head back. I can almost *feel* the fear that radiates from her every time I get too close. And why wouldn't it? I kidnapped her...sort of. It's her house, and I'm not some perv, but still, I've frightened her. It was a necessary evil, though.

I tilt my head to give a predatory glare. "*You* are going to help me in a different way."

Her body tenses, back stiff. "What? How?"

My jaw flexes, an exhale releases through my nose as I offer her the truth. "You, Novalie Annie Rhodes, are going to help me clear my name."

CHAPTER 6

Novalie

My mood has swung from terrified to enraged over the last two hours. I feel as though I have whiplash from it. But right now…I'm absolutely baffled. Ren…the asshole, dropped that bomb on me and then casually walked away, found my broom, and has begun sweeping the mess I made breaking the chair.

I'm at a loss for words…but only for a brief second before the questions come barreling out of me. "Why *me*? Why clear your name at all? Why are you not pressing toward the Mexican border by now or Canada?" He ignores me, and I slide from my chair and pace the living room, noticing he pauses, watching me whenever I near the door. Finally, he finishes sweeping and puts away the broom, turning to face me—him in the kitchen and me as far in the corner of the living room as I can get.

Agitation is clear in the rigidity of his jaw. His voice is deathly calm but laced with anger as he speaks. "*Why* would I want to clear my name? Let me ask you this, Nova…would you be okay if *you* were framed for murder?" My hand goes to my neck in shock, but he ignores my open mouth and adds, "Would you be able to just run away and let everyone believe you're a killer? Well, I'm not *fucking* running!" His voices raises. "Someone will pay for the life they took from me."

My back hits the wall, and I didn't even realize I'd backed up a step. "But why *me*?"

He runs a hand over his head and then clear down his face with exasperation and something else I can't quite figure out. "I needed access to amenities. Water, food, shelter…but more importantly, internet."

I consider that, and then a thought hits me. "Have you been *watching* me, Ren?" I ask, with chills sneaking up my spine.

He nods once, completely unashamed. "No offense, but you were an easy target."

My body goes rigid as I sling daggers at him with my eyes. "What is that supposed to mean?"

"You looked to be alone…above this old store. No one visits you from what I could tell, and if they do, it's not daily. You have groceries *delivered*…seems lazy and antisocial but whatever. You're secluded and don't have a life."

I cut him off right there. "You can call me anything but lazy, you…*jackass*! And I have…had a life until you walked into it!"

He shrugs as if my words mean very little. "Anti-social then and definitely a recluse with no *nightlife*. Either way, your place is the perfect hideout in plain sight."

My head shakes with aggravation. "You can't stay here…you can't! I do actually have a life. I have family and a best friend who likes to randomly barge in. And I have a—" My voice falters on the lie, but I say it anyway. "I have a boyfriend."

He's full-on smiling at me now with sickeningly perfect teeth and canines that are slightly longer, creating a quirky wolfish grin. His voice rolls over me as he says, "You *don't* have a boyfriend, Nova."

"And why would you say that so confidently? You know *nothing* about me." My nails bite into my palms as my fists clench.

"I know there's absolutely no evidence of a man ever having been in this house. No men's toiletries, no clothes other than your late husband's, no pictures hanging up. Hell, there's no sign of *you* in this home, let alone a man. No family photos," he tosses his hand around to the walls and shelves, "and nothing on your phone to indicate a boyfriend, and…" he grins wider, "no condoms here either."

Heat blooms on my face, and even my ears feel as if they are on fire. "You son-of-a—"

He interrupts me by continuing his assessment of my living situation. "I know you read romance novels in-between customers. I know you bite your lip or nails when you're nervous." He stares at my mouth, and I realize I'm doing it now. Abruptly, I stop. His voice lowers—becomes softer as he continues. "I know you're lonely, and at night. You sit up there on that balcony and stare at the moon."

Wetness gathers my attention, and I rake my arm over my face to wipe away the shameful tears and clear my blurred vision. "How can you possibly believe all that to be true from spying on me? You *don't* know me." My voice lacks the conviction I'm striving for.

"Tell me I'm wrong," he demands. "*Tell me.*"

I don't answer him. A perfect stranger stares back at me and sees right through my façade of a life. Does everyone see me as this broken widow who's *alive* but not living? I move the conversation away from my personal life and onto the situation. With a childish sniffle, I clear my nose to speak. "How do you expect to clear your name, and how long will something like that take? While I may not get a lot of visitors, you can't expect no one to *ever* show up. Someone will eventually come, and then what?"

Ren moves across the space between us, closing that distance, but moving slowly. When he reaches me, he gives me a confident look. "If you can learn to trust me and keep my being here a secret…we won't have any problems. I need time to do a little research—time to discover the truth. I can hide if someone shows up. But here's the thing, I need your word that you'll keep me a secret from *everyone*. Not a soul can know."

I take a deep breath and smell my Jasmine body wash coming from him, and that feels…*strange*. "How am I supposed to trust you?" I ask quietly.

"You're going to have to open your mind to the possibility that people aren't always what they seem. I'm innocent. That, I assure you." He steps closer—an intimidation tactic if I've ever seen one. "Will you help me, Novalie?"

The storm raging in his eyes has since settled, and now more blue shows than gray. I give myself a moment to contemplate his request. He bound my hands, tied me up, went through my belongings…he's a convict. A man charged with *murdering* someone.

The word 'but' is hanging there…tempting me to release it. *But* what if he's innocent? What would I do if I were in his shoes? How far would I go? Should he spend the rest of his life in prison if another murderer…the real one is out there? Am I simply lonely, as he said, and it's making my judgment off-kilter? Maybe the prospect of solving a murder is too tempting for a crime junkie like me. Or maybe my people-pleaser nature just can't help it.

I can't be seriously entertaining this…*can I*? From now on, I'll be adding finding a therapist to next year's calendar.

"Nova," Ren says quietly, watching my inner turmoil play over my features, no doubt.

"What if I say no to everything?" I throw at him. "Are you going to get rid of me?"

His smile is nothing but lethal, but then I can see the mischievous glint in his eye. "I'll tie you up and feed you, *bathe* you," his eyes darken on that one before he continues, "take care of you while I use your place without your consent."

I curl my lip in disgust. "*Bathe me*? You are a pervert, aren't you?"

I'm shocked when he laughs, and…it's *genuine*. The sound so odd inside my small space. "What's it going to be, Novalie Annie Rhodes?"

All sanity has left the building, and he holds all the cards in this game…however, I have two aces up my sleeve. My police officer brother, and my uncle, who's a retired detective.

I force myself to remain stoic as I say, "I'll help you…Soren Lee Marshall."

CHAPTER 7

Soren

Novalie pads across the floor and sits on the sofa, spreading out her long skirt and angling her feet underneath her. She's not subtle. It's clear she's creating distance from me. She's been quiet for a few minutes, as if she's processing everything…or *scheming*. More likely, the latter. I move to sit beside her, making her back go ramrod straight, but I plop down anyway and smile as her eyes narrow on me.

It's the most entertainment I've had in ages.

She flicks a manicured nail toward the adjacent camel-colored leather chair. "There's a perfectly good seat right there."

I give her a toothy grin. "I like this one. Besides, if I'm going to be living here…we need to get some things straight."

Her eyes move to the window, avoiding my gaze as she says lazily, "You're not *living* here and get what things straight exactly?"

"For starters, you need to put up a sign on your bookstore letting people know that you'll be closed for a few days." I'm rewarded with her undivided attention after the words leave my mouth. Her eyes widen ever so slightly, making me smile more before adding, "I need a few days to decipher whether or not I can trust your discretion. After that, you can run your shop as usual."

"No way." She doesn't let her eyes blink as she stares me down. "I've been closed once in five months for a dental cleaning. This place is my sole source of income and livelihood. People will notice if I'm closed, and God forbid my family rides by or my friend.

I don't miss the singular use of the word '*friend*' in that statement.

"Who's this friend?"

Her eyes roll, and it's cuter than expected. "It's none of your business who I'm friends with, but you should know that she's a bulldog when it comes to me."

"Sounds like a good friend," I say and she simply purses her lips and refocuses on the window as if she may leap from it at any moment, so I distract her again by demanding, "You'll text her saying you have the flu and that's why you're closing for a few days."

On cue, her eyes dart back to me. "I'm never sick, and it's May…the flu isn't exactly going around right now." When I don't back down, she goes on, "Then what, Ren? I close down my life for three days, then *what*? How long will you squat here searching for vengeance? What if you never find what it is you're searching for? Wha…"

"Honestly, I don't know how long this will take or *if* I'll find what I'm looking for. I know you have no reason to trust me, but I need you to try. All I need is a place to hide in plain sight, somewhere no one would even consider looking. It's the perfect cover. Eventually, the search will stretch away from here, and everyone will assume I've fled the country. All I need is a little time. Can you give me that?" Her uncertain eyes find mine, and I exhale. "I promise not to hurt you in any way. I'm not a murderer, and I'm *definitely* not a pervert."

I swear her cheek tugs upward slightly in an almost smile but vanishes fast. She rolls her pink lips into her mouth before huffing out a sigh and asking, "Besides my house, what do you need from me?"

I cock my head to the side and contemplate that. "We can order food, new clothes, and a few hats. I'm going to need a burner phone for later." I realize fast I hadn't considered her money situation, or lack thereof. "Do you have the money to spare for a few things? I can assure you I'll pay you back tenfold."

Pride has her looking offended. "I can handle those expenses."

Nodding, I continue. "For the first few days, I'm going to need time to research my own case…need to take a new look at it—find a new angle. There has to be something the police missed."

Her eyes move to the balcony door. "Even if you discover some hidden truth, what makes you think the cops will believe you? You're an escaped convict. It would take finding the actual killer and having a full-blown confession before they'd listen."

My cheek pulls into a side smile. "I haven't been *totally* honest with you."

Her attention once again flits to me, and she says sarcastically, "Do tell. I was just starting to believe in you."

I bite back a laugh. "Finding you wasn't *exactly* an accident." Her brows wrinkle together, and I lean closer. "I heard about you and your family. The famed Detective Sawyer, who solved the Maisy Murray human trafficking case and retired a mysteriously wealthy man. There was lots of talk about him on the inside."

Her face shows nothing as she mutters, "*So*, you know of my uncle…what of it?"

"I saw a picture of you in the paper one day…you were surrounded by all these flowers and books." I smile. "The paper's heading read, *Nova's Novel Garden's grand opening*. Underneath that, it labeled you the niece of Detective Jimmy Franklin Sawyer, and I'm sure you've seen the rest."

"What about it?" She fidgets with her hands in her lap.

"Two things…everyone knows that Detective Sawyer doesn't put up with shit. That man was a damn legend. I could use someone like him on my side at the end of this."

She gives a cynical laugh. "So, you knew my name all along. You saw a vulnerable woman living alone and preyed upon her all because of some misplaced desire to have the aid of her infamous uncle. You clearly don't know Jim. He's a recluse himself these days…very old, and *very* retired."

I just smile and nod. "Maybe, but it couldn't hurt to try."

"What's the second thing?" she asks with a stoic face. "About the picture in the paper."

I let my stare linger—intimidate her more than I should. "You weren't smiling."

Confusion contorts her features. "Excuse me?"

"You weren't smiling. It was your grand opening…and you looked…"

"Let me stop you right there." She storms off the couch in a whirl of skirts and marches a few feet away from me before spinning, a tendril of her burnt red hair escaping the bun to land onto her face. "You stalked me out in order to up heave my life for your little scavenger hunt; don't for one second think that you actually know anything about me or my family after an ad in the local paper!"

I throw up my hands in surrender. "Maybe you're right. Maybe I read you wrong, and maybe I chose the wrong family, but I'm not leaving, and you're in this whether you like it or not."

Her hands slide to her hips in a challenging way that's not at all unpleasant to witness. "And your trusting me is a mistake. I have no reason to help you and absolutely no reason to believe that you're innocent. If you're smart…which, that's *a stretch*, you'll flee now and find refuge elsewhere."

I move fast in her direction, startling her, and for every step I take, she takes one back until she hits the wall. Leaning into her coveted space, I whisper, "You're stuck with me, Nova. I'm not going anywhere and…" I slam my hand against the wall beside her causing her to flinch, "go ahead and test me…I dare you. Try to leave or rat me out." I leave the threat hanging between us like a black veil.

She needs to have a healthy fear of me—needs to be on edge.

Her eyes are glistening again but, to her credit, tears don't fall this time. "Well, then…seems I have no say in the matter."

"You don't." I let my voice penetrate deep, then push off the wall and stalk away from her.

It takes several moments for her to collect herself enough to stop using the wall for support and, on shaky limbs, she makes her way back to the sofa where she uses all her remaining strength to sit down gracefully.

Her silence after that is deafening. I almost want to make a joke just to rile something in her and bring about that fire I've glimpsed. As I sit at her olive-green desk, which is much like the kitchen…every single item has a place and not a single pen is out of sorts, I keep her in my peripheral vision. She's watching me as I open her laptop and turn it on.

After a few seconds, the lock screen appears, and before I can even ask, she says in a whisper, "1201."

I key in the number and cut my eyes to her. "Why that number…for both your devices?"

Her solemn eyes drift to the balcony door. Something far off and distant rages in them as she says, "It's the day my husband died."

CHAPTER 8

Novalie

It's been hours now. The sun is setting on this wretched day, and with it, any hopes I had of getting away from Ren and his ridiculous plan. He had me place the sign on the entrance to my bookstore earlier…stating I'd be open on Monday with my usual hours. Today is Thursday, and that means I'm stuck in this house with him *all* weekend.

He also kept his word and forced me to text my mother and Mel. After he scoured my phone…he realized pretty quickly that those were the only two people I messaged on a regular basis, and he didn't want anything to seem suspicious.

As far as they know, I now have the flu.

Ren used my mobile Walmart app to purchase food items and male toiletries along with Levi jeans, razors, plain

T-shirts, boots, boxers, socks…things like that. He spent most of the day on the computer researching his own case, which he refrained from enlightening me about. I took it upon myself to grab the nearest book on my TBR list and drown my brain in it.

Normally, reading fantasy smut books consumes me entirely, but my mind and body recognize that danger is close. And that's why I've read the same damn line four times now. I snap the book shut with a huff.

He pays me…his *captive*, no mind at all. Frustration is evident in his muttered curses about something he reads online. With his profile to me, but not his eyes, I take the opportunity to look him over. He has a strong nose and defined features. His skin is lightly tanned in a way that shows little time in the sun, not enough for much color. His five o'clock shadow looks to be four or five days past a shave. His hair, which is thicker on top, is dark brown…almost black. His arms are covered with network of geometric and mechanical-looking tattoos mixed with some colorful traditional pieces. They mix and mingle together seamlessly, moving onto his neck part of the way and then they fade into a mandala. Whoever did this work was really good. I can't imagine these are prison tattoos…so maybe he got them before. My eyes lower as my head angles, taking in his broad shoulders and drifting even lower to his tapered waist.

He's rough around the edges but would be handsome to anyone with eyes. Which I would never admit aloud. Watching him…it makes me even more curious about his charges and his life before them. I don't pry though…at least, not yet. I'll find a way around his threats, and I have a good idea of exactly how I'll do it.

Suddenly, I feel eyes on me. My cheeks burn as I'm caught gawking at him. Without a word, I leave the couch and his penetrating stare. I don't ask, nor do I speak as I snake past him and into my bedroom before disappearing into the bathroom. Shutting the door, but not all the way, I turn on the faucet and splash my face with cool water. I've tested him today—moved throughout the house to see if he watched me. He always did, but the more the day went on, the less he watched...especially if I went to the bathroom. Patting my face dry with a cloth, and turning off the faucet, I peer through the cracked bathroom door. He can't see into the bedroom from where the desk sits, so I tiptoe out, grateful now that I'm barefoot. He owes me a pair of leather Mary Janes...the bastard. Those were my favorite heels.

Ren wasn't the only one paying attention today. I watched as he scoured the house once more earlier, undoubtedly looking for hidden devices that I could use to message for help. What he missed was the top drawer of my side table, and the only reason he missed it is because it doesn't have a handle and doesn't appear to even *be* a drawer. I purchased this specific end table for that reason. You simply press it inward to release the drawer. Doing so now, I hold my breath as it pops open with a soft thud.

I exhale, albeit quietly, as I watch the bedroom doorway, but Ren must not have heard it. Sliding the drawer out carefully, a most devious smile tugs at my cheek at the sight of my Kindle. Pulling it out, I quickly click it on. Once inside my apps, I touch my Gmail square. In an instant, my mail is loading, and in another, I'm composing a fast email to my brother and Uncle Jim.

My fingers move deftly. I'm on the last sentence when the Kindle is jerked from my hands. A short, cut-off scream leaves me as my heart leaps into my throat and I clasp a hand over my mouth. My body trembles as I spin and back myself into the corner. Ren's face is a mix of anger and disappointment.

How the hell did he move that silently?

He stoically eyes the contents of the email. Then rattles it off in a jesting way. "*If you get this email…send help immediately. I'm being held hostage by Soren Marshall in my home. This is not a joke…*" He stops and looks at me a second before he takes the Kindle and cracks it over the side of the bedpost.

I press into the corner as if I could slip through the wall somehow. He may have promised not to hurt me, but right now he looks as if he could rip me to shreds. "I'm so…sorry." A tear rolls down my cheek as I struggle to remain standing—knees threatening to buckle.

Ren places his fingers over his mouth as if he has something to say but holds it back. He takes the broken Kindle and tosses it in the waste bin close to me. My body is pressed into the corner between the wall and the end table as if that will protect me. Ren stands a few inches away now and looks to me, then at the drawer. He begins rifling through it, looking for anything else I might be hiding in there.

His gruff voice is startling when he finally speaks again as he rakes his fingers through my belongings. "I thought we had an understanding, Novalie. I guess I can't blame you for trying." His brows raise in what looks like appreciation. "You're like a scared little frail thing but backed into a corner…your claws come out. You're a fighter, aren't you?"

"I'm no fighter," I whisper. "A survivalist maybe, but no fighter."

He smirks and stops looking through the drawer briefly and turns to me. Taking the last step toward me. He's close enough now to smell the jasmine scent of my own body wash on him again. "Oh, but you are Nova." Something foreign and yet familiar coils through me, but I shove it away as he goes on. "What can I do to convince you to trust me?"

"Shattering my Kindle like a caveman wasn't a good start." I bite my lip right after it leaves my mouth.

He gives a throaty laugh. "True, but I already have to keep you away from the computer and phone; I don't need other temptations lying around." Something plays across his features, and I can only decipher that it's akin to turmoil, as if he's battling some part of himself. With a slight shake of his head, he reaches up, almost as if it's against his will, and wipes away another fallen stray tear.

I'm shocked speechless as his calloused finger glides over my cheek. It's almost scarier than my predicament. He drops his hand and asks again, "What can I do? I wouldn't be here…doing this if I wasn't desperate."

I ponder that for a moment. My fear all but gone now with this new side of him. Leaning back to look into his eyes, I give him my own demands. "I want to know everything about your case…about your life. If I'm to keep you a secret, then I should have the chance to form my own opinion of your innocence or lack thereof."

"Deal," he says quickly. "What else do you want, Nova?" And the way he says it, all low and guttural, has me concerned about his intentions with that question.

"No more intimidation…no more breaking my stuff. Treat me kindly, and I'll do the same." I lift my chin a little higher, which probably looks ridiculous due to my short stature.

"Deal. And you won't tell a soul about this arrangement. You'll quit trying to run or get help."

"Deal," I say softly, and I swear, it feels like I actually mean it this time. I can breathe normally once he backs up a step and begins rifling through the last of my drawer's contents. "I don't have any more electronic devices," I admit.

He nods but looks anyway, unconvinced.

My eyes flare wide, and I take a sharp breath, suddenly remembering what *else* is in that particular drawer. That thought slaps me a moment too late. Before I can stop him, his brows rise, and I watch as his Adam's apple bobs several times as if he's working hard to swallow. Ren pulls his hand from the drawer—his hand that is now clutching my neon pink vibrator. Heat blasts my cheeks in a veritable inferno, and my hand covers my mouth in horror.

His heavy, stormy eyes fall back to me, assessing as his cheek is rising in a cocky grin that makes me want to punch him in the face. "Well, well, *Novalie Annie Rhodes*…seems I was right." His voice is even cockier than his blasted face.

I can't remove my hand from my mouth, so I whisper through it instead. "About what?"

"*You* are the pervert here." His laughter trails behind me as I dart past him toward the bathroom and lock myself inside.

CHAPTER 9

Soren

Night has fallen completely, and with it, Novalie finally emerges from her bedroom. She's been hiding out in there for two hours, showering, and well, just…hiding. Me finding her bedside toy has torn her out of her comfort zone.

For me, I wanted to plunge myself into a cold shower too. Seeing it, holding something so personal of hers and the thoughts of where it's been was almost too much to handle. Try as I might, it's been hard to think of anything else. I chalk up my creepy thoughts to the fact that I haven't been with a woman in a *very*…*very* long time.

I'm leaning against the counter beside two boxes of the best-smelling pizzas I've ever smelled in my life when she walks over, hair damp and woven into a thick braid along her shoulder, reaching almost to her waist. She's wearing flannel pajama pants with a green snug-fitting tank top that brings out the olive flecks in her hazel eyes.

"Hungry?" I ask as she leans against the counter.

"Sure," she says softly and then opens a box and takes out a slice.

She doesn't question my ordering pizza from her phone. I made sure to have them leave it by the door. She just eats in silence, probably in a state of shock given her circumstances. I decide I've had enough *silence* and break the ice in the room by saying in a too-chipper voice, "Sorry about the vibrator."

She chokes on her bite, coughing. I snatch a cup from the cabinet, fill it with water quickly and hold back my grin as she takes it and chugs down several gulps.

Her eyes flare with malicious intent. "You are a real piece of work. Do you have any manners at all, you pig!"

I nibble on another bite of pizza and then scrutinize her, unaffected by her words. "What's your deal? You're a grown woman. Why is it shameful to please yourself…everyone does it. Why are you so…*rigid* and a priss?"

She takes a bite, baring her teeth as if she is ripping into my flesh instead of a cheesy pizza. After swallowing, she clears her throat. "I'm not a *priss,* and since when is it a crime to be modest? What goes on in a woman's bedroom is private." Her cheeks pinken.

I just shrug to piss her off and then say through a mouthful, "It's okay…*really*. It's perfectly natural."

She glares me down. "Could you just drop the vibrator talk already? And don't speak with your mouth full."

My mind wanders of its own accord back to that drawer. Shaking my head, I exhale and get my shit together. "I guess," I say, faking sadness through another purposely sloppy bite of food.

She veers the conversation in a different direction quickly, rolling her eyes and wiping her mouth with a napkin. She asks, "How old are you?"

A smile tugs at my lips. "Growing an interest in me, huh? Thirty-two. And you?"

She gives me a mocking raised eyebrow, ignoring the first part of that. "You mean to tell me you didn't look at my license inside my phone case?"

I smile wickedly. "Of course I did. I'm just making conversation. You're twenty-six."

She gives an exaggerated eye roll, but after a few seconds, her curiosity starts nipping at her, and questions seem to flow easier now that we've gotten over the events from earlier. "Were you married…or are you married, I should say?" she asks.

My brows raise. "How have you seriously not heard the news reports?"

"I sink myself into work and reading and…I don't watch TV, like, *ever* really. I heard about an escapee, but that's about it," she admits.

"My wife's dead," I say bluntly.

Shock washes over Nova's face as she takes me in. "I'm so sorry. I had no idea you'd lost a spouse too."

My laugh is sarcastic and forced and takes her by surprise. "Oh, I didn't just *lose* my wife, Nova…I lost *everything*. It's her murder I'm being framed for."

Her face is suddenly leached of color. I watch with bated breath as she processes what I just said. How in the world does this woman not know anything that goes on around her…in her own town? "I didn't do it," I tell her again even though I know she can't one hundred percent believe that. She doesn't know me and *shouldn't* trust me.

She sips her water and then sets the glass down and wraps her arms around herself. A thousand questions roll over her features. She seems to settle on the most pressing one and finally asks, "What happened?"

I take a beat to read her body language. Her arms loosen. Her taut shoulders droop slightly. She's…relaxed. So I ask her one last time, "Are you willing to stick this out til the end? To help me no matter how bad the scene will sound?"

She doesn't answer right away…which gives me hope. If she'd blurted out her agreement, it would've been far from convincing.

She gives a curt but sure nod. "I'll help you…as long as you keep to your word. No harm comes to me or anyone I love in the process. *And*, when this is over, you're gone from here. No one will ever know of my involvement. Whether you get your answers or not."

"You have a deal, princess." I wink at her scowling face.

"Princ…"

I cut her off before she falls into another rant. "Around five years ago I woke up…covered in blood." Novalie's mouth is still open, paused. "My wife's name was Victoria Styles. I'd booked Vicky and I a cabin out in the mountains. Far enough away from the city, but close enough to visit the nightlife. It was our second anniversary, you see. I wanted to travel somewhere, but she didn't want to go far…she was a nurse and they were short staffed. She said she was afraid they'd call her in. So we stayed near home. Anyway, we went out on the town the first night. We both had too many drinks, hopping from one bar to the next. We took an Uber back to the cabin. It was late, like two in the morning or close to it." Swiping a hand over my face, I pause.

I'm shocked when I feel Nova's nearness and find that she's slid a little closer to me. "What happened next?" she asks softly.

I shake my head. "I don't remember everything, but…when we went to bed that night, it was *not* on good terms." I watch her face grow concerned. "I woke up the next morning…covered in blood. I panicked as anyone would and ran, yelling for her throughout the cabin. I couldn't find her anywhere. I called 911 at some point, but I'm not sure when. Everything after that was a blur. I was so distraught, and they wouldn't listen to me. I became…*combative*."

"They always look at the husband first," Nova says, not in a negative way, just matter-of-factly.

"And I wasn't doing myself any favors when I started swinging at the police officer who was being an ass to me."

"Okay, but they couldn't have arrested you on the blood alone, right? There had to be some other evidence…even if it was circumstantial."

Nova's eyes are alight with such intrigue that I can almost forget for a second that she's not choosing to do this…I'm forcing her. "Believe me, they had plenty more. There was a…trail of blood and drag-style marks that led toward the driveway."

Nova doesn't seem to realize it, but she's sidled up even closer and is a ball of nervous energy as she listens. Before I finish, I ask her, "You don't have a queasy stomach, do you?"

She shakes her head. "I watch crime shows to relax."

I tip my head to her and raise a brow. "Wouldn't have pegged the little prim princess to be into blood and gore."

She doesn't flinch at my statement, just grins, and it stuns me to my core. Little dimples bloom on her angular cheeks. "You don't really know me…like I said. Now, *go on.*"

"Very well." My lips form a thin line as the memory replays. "There was talk of the possibility that she was dismembered…and mind you, this is when they didn't have a murder weapon, and there was no body…*nothing.* They were just jumping to conclusions." I push off the counter and pace a few feet away, closing my eyes. The visions of that day flash through my mind like a goddamn nightmare.

"Are you saying they *never* found her body?" Nova asks.

I grunt. "If only. A week later…while I'm incarcerated, they tell me about…*pieces* of her found along with clothing and jewelry. It was in a makeshift fire pit about a mile out from the cabin. It was covered in limbs, and the ashes and contents of the fire were determined to have been set around the same night I was there with her. One of the tracking dogs found her severed finger near the firepit, under some leaves."

Nova stares at me puzzled, but unfazed at the gory details.

"What is it?" I ask.

"So they think you killed her, cut her into pieces, took her close to where you camped and just burned her right there…and went back to bed."

"That about sums it up."

"Did they find any weapons later on? Did they discover the spot she was most likely killed? Did they look into any other possibilities? Did they have any other suspects?"

My brows raise at her peppering of questions and at how she barely breathed through them. "No weapon, no location of death for certain, and the lead detective, Joe Sparks, looked into her past, looked into her job relationships, and said he found nothing. She didn't seem to have any enemies."

Nova's brows knit together. "What about your relationship? Was it so terrible that they could believe you did this without question?"

I hesitate, remembering the screaming matches between us, the broken glass, the hateful words. "It wasn't the best relationship," I admit.

"Oh, so you two fought a lot? Was it…*violent*?" I watch her creep back into her nervous posture with arms recrossing her chest.

"Not on my end. I know…given your situation, that's hard to believe, but I never laid a hand on Vicky."

Nova begins nibbling on a violet-painted nail. She catches herself and drops the hand, side-eyeing me. "I can see why they would think it's you," she says—more to herself than to me—indecision swimming in her eyes.

"But?" I ask, leaning closer if only to smell her scent. I'd almost forgotten how lovely the smell of a woman is, how absolutely mind-wrecking it can be. And more than that, hers seems to settle me, even during this awful retelling.

She turns her cat-like eyes to mine, long soft lashes curling upward after her shower. "It doesn't make sense. Several things don't align." Her voice is soft and thoughtful.

"Like?" I prompt her for more.

"Let me rephrase…they don't align because I have little information, but for one, did they find your own vehicle's tire prints near the burn pile? Was there significant blood found at the scene…enough to even indicate she was killed there? Was forensic testing done on your clothing and her nail beds? Or nail *bed*…the one found. Was there any theft involved?" A full smile crosses my face and makes the laceration across the bridge of my nose sting. Her cheeks pinken. "I'm so sorry…" She apologizes for her rapid-fire questions.

I wave off her apology. "No tire prints near the fire, some by the entrance to that trail, but there were multiple, so undetermined, no weapons found, no theft, and they believed a flattened area on the ground outside is where she was possibly dismembered, but that was never proven. The snow was clearly disturbed there. They believed six-mill plastic was used to put her on, but that was speculation. However, they did find a small, ripped piece there, near where she was dragged. My DNA along with hers was under her fingernail and on my clothes." She's angling her head at that. "That's to be expected…we were together all day…and I'm not sure about the amount of blood…that was on me. They said there was enough…that no one could've survived it."

She doesn't drop my stare, as if she's making a decision right here and now about whether I'm truly a killer or not. Her jaw tics. "Why would you dismember and hide the body, but stay sleeping in that bed covered in her blood? It's counterintuitive."

"My sentiments exactly." I roll my lower lip inward and watch her eyes flit there and back up. "You starting to believe me, princess? It's not very smart, you know," I tease her.

Her chin raises higher, which is cute considering she reaches my chest even with the head tilt. "You're right. It wouldn't be very smart. One more question."

"Anything." I hold her gaze.

"How can you talk so casually about the death of your wife?" Her eyes drill into me as she assesses my body language.

Exhaling through my nose, I say, "Innately, we judge those on trial based on their behavior, right? Do they look remorseful enough? Are they truly sad?" She braces herself when I grit my teeth, biting out the next words. "I grieved, cried, cursed God. I did all that. It's been five years and I can still feel her blood coating my hands." Nova's face pales slightly. "We were far from a happy couple and, in fact, heading toward divorce, no doubt, but she was still my wife. I loved her once. So, if I seem nonchalant now, it's because I've had five years to grow rancid inside with the need for vengeance. My life was taken from me…how would you react? I can promise you…you'd be surprised by how much your soul can change with trauma."

She swallows hard, and her hand caresses her neck nervously. Something like understanding washes over her features. I realize too late that she does have *some* idea about loss…albeit not like mine, but her former life was taken from her too with the death of her husband.

She nods almost imperceptibly. "I'll give you this weekend to convince me…you have til Sunday."

My eyes land on hers intensely. "You don't make the rules here…I do."

"We shall see." She grabs another slice of pizza, breaking up the serious moment we were having there. After she chews and swallows, she says, "You have til *Sunday,* Ren."

I smirk at this little haughty female pretending to be in charge. “And after that?”

“After that, if I’m not convinced of your innocence…I *will* find a way out of this, and you *will* be on your own.” Her delicate brow raises in what looks to be a challenge.

Okay. I’ll give the little minx a bone, let her feel in control. “It’s a deal, princess.”

CHAPTER 10

Novalie

Leaning over the bathroom sink, I splash ice-cold water onto my tired face, a poor attempt at rejuvenation. What was I thinking last night…blatantly agreeing to let that con sleep here, stay here, *and* agreeing to help him?

Of course I didn't sleep. How could I with him sprawled out on my living room couch? He'd demanded we get some rest after that conversation, and while I was more than happy to get some distance from him, it did me no favors. My mind stormed with all the decrepit things that could happen to me if he was indeed intent on hurting me. I briefly considered crawling out my window…but I'm certain that my clumsiness would have me sprawled on the street below.

Ren made sure to sleep with my laptop and phone beside him and the front door still barricaded to slow any attempts of possible escaping. His unencumbered view of the balcony door also removed that option. While he slept soundly, I listened to every noise creaking through the house, every car passing by, every single shift of his body.

My nerves are shot to shit today. Faint dark circles lie under my eyes like the bruised egos they are. Quickly, I brush my teeth and walk over to the closet to get dressed but stop in the entrance. The box of Levi's belongings sits crooked on the top shelf. I reach on tiptoes and right it, my throat tightening.

What would he think of this diabolical mess I'm in?

He'd probably tell me all the ways *he* would get away or talk himself out of it with his slick tongue. He was a very opinionated psychiatrist who could have the most insane person questioning their behavior. While the two of us were vanilla in the way we lived life, I was still the less rigid one. The only thing he hated more than disorder was spontaneity. I never had a problem with that, but there were times when I'd want to venture into uncharted territories. Levi would hate this…despise what I'm doing. But he has no voice anymore…so what does it matter?

Shaking away the unease I feel, I shift a few of my favorite skirts hanging in the closet but then remember that I have all weekend with this stranger and he's not allowing me to open my shop. No need to dress in my usual then. I slip on a pair of faded jeans and a cropped lavender tee with mushrooms clustered in the center of an open book on the front. Then, I French braid my long hair and create a bun at the nape of my neck.

The moment I open the door to exit my bedroom, I gasp sharply. Ren is standing on the other side, his stormy eyes intense.

"What the hell?" I scold him.

His hands fly up in innocence. "I was about to knock; you opened before I could."

Lifting my chin higher, I glower at him.

"I wasn't creeping at your door." His cheek pulls up to the side, which annoys me to no end.

"Sure you weren't." I ignore his brightening smile and ease around his massive form, heading straight for my French press. I peek over my shoulder to see he's facing my direction, casually leaning against the wall. "What?" I ask, annoyed.

"Mind if I get cleaned up?" He gestures to the bathroom.

I scoff. "You're asking permission now?" I laugh sarcastically. "You were fine with taking me hostage yesterday, bounding my hands, *bathing* beside me for fuck's sake."

He straightens to standing and cocks his head, his eyes dancing with merriment. "What a filthy mouth you have…oh, and don't forget the nightstand…add that to your growing list of outlandish things I've done."

I turn away from him and back to the task of making coffee, if for no other reason than to hide my burning cheeks. Grinding my teeth along with the coffee. "Pervert," I mumble. After a few seconds, I feel his presence and flinch when I realize he's beside me grinning.

How the hell does he move like that?

"What is that thing?" he asks, eyeing my new French press.

"It's a French press for making coffee, of course."

"Why not just use a regular coffee maker?"

"The press extracts more of the oils from the beans and trust me...it makes a difference. Once you taste my coffee...you'll see."

"Fancy...like you, princess." He chuckles as he saunters away.

I watch every step, unable to stop. Without asking me again, he disappears into my bedroom. I finish the coffees and bagels with cream cheese and I've almost got the fresh strawberries diced when I stop cold in my tracks.

He's left me alone. I'm fixing him breakfast and listening to seventies music on my retro radio...and *he's left me alone.* What the hell is wrong with me? I clutch the knife I'm holding tightly and listen to the water running from my bathroom sink. A few steps will have me to the door. I could unbarricade it rather quickly, but then I look to my balcony that is perched above the bookstore.

Is he testing me?

I begin to rapidly doubt everything, and some semblance of common sense drips into my mind. Here's my chance. I could at least try to climb down from the balcony and...I'm not sure about the drop, but I could *try*.

Knife in hand, I pad over to the balcony's sliding glass door and ease the lock backward and then shift the door open. Once I'm out, my nerves ratchet up several notches. The southern heat is already baking this morning and sweat beads on my brow. Looking over my shoulder, I don't see him. I lean over the iron railing and watch as a few bystanders waltz by...one even eyeing the closed sign on my door below. The drop to the awning over my bookstore's entrance isn't too awful far, but I would impact it enough to demolish the thing. My sweaty hand grips the knife harder as an internal war ensues.

Something absurd is curdling in me…like guilt. I told this man I would help him. What if he's telling the truth? Could I condemn him to a life in prison and live with that? What is wrong with me? I have the perfect opportunity to yell for help or shimmy over this damn railing right now. More people walk along the streets below, and one couple even glances up my way. I could do it. Leave…*jump*.

But I don't.

With my chest making a rapid staccato beat, I back away a few steps, throat gone dry. My back hits something hard, making me suck in a breath. A hand grips my wrist…the one holding the knife.

"You thinking of running again, princess?" Ren's voice is hard like gravel against my senses.

I release the knife and hear it clang to the floor. "I…I…" I'm sputtering and can't find the words.

Slowly Ren turns me to face him but doesn't say a word. He just stares at me as if giving me time to either be truthful or to lie. I decide on the former. "I'm sorry. The thought did cross my mind."

Disappointment flares in his eyes. "*But?*"

I look down, not able to meet his intense look a second longer. "But I changed my mind."

I flinch as his fingers press under my chin, forcing me to look up. "You're a smart woman. I don't blame you for doubting me, but if this is going to work. This can't happen again."

I nod, and for some reason my eyes sting. I'm not sure if it's from the loss of the chance of freedom, or for *betraying* my word to him and getting caught.

Amazingly, his eyes soften. "Don't get all mushy on me. I can't stand to see a woman cry. Be the annoying smartass.

Her I can handle." That sobers me entirely, and I give him a small smile.

A few minutes later, we sit in the living room nibbling on the fruit and bagels. The laptop is open, and Ren is reading several articles regarding his case. I watch when he lifts his coffee and takes the first sip. His eyes flare, and he actually groans. I don't want to think about what that sound does to me. The way I felt it more than heard it.

"Fucking hell, this is amazing," he says before taking another drink.

"Thank you."

After a few minutes of research, Ren pauses, his eyes still on the computer screen. "Tell me about your life, Nova…distract me enough to where this doesn't feel overwhelming."

This has me a bit surprised. Twisting my mouth to the side, I consider his request. "I'm not very interesting, I'm afraid." His eyes cut to mine as if to say…tell me anyway. I loose a breath. "Well, okay then. I grew up in Cleveland County. My mother, Helena, is a realtor. My father, Baron, is a lawyer." Ren's eyes meet mine, and I can see the wheels turning, but I ignore that spark of hope I see there. "I have a brother, Ian. He's three years older than me."

"What does your brother do for a living?"

My mouth drops open to speak, but I bite my tongue.

Ren catches the hesitation. "Don't tell me…he's a cop, isn't he?"

My shoulders slump and I nod gravely. "Yes. He is."

Ren continues his search as if he didn't just steal the last ace I had to play. "So you have a lawyer father, a cop brother, and a retired detective uncle? I'm not sure if that will prove serendipitous or my downfall, princess."

"My uncle's why you chose me, but I think you are relying heavily on a man you know nothing about."

"Yeah, not my most well-thought-out plan." He shrugs as if it doesn't matter either way. "Why the bookstore?" I shift my head at the question, so he clarifies. "What made you want to open a bookstore? You seem like an Ivy League type to me."

Crossing my legs, I lean back on the chair and sip from my mug. "I was always a little different growing up. I knew I never wanted to work for anyone. My parents did push me to go to college, so I went to Appalachian State." His brows rise, impressed. "I majored in English Lit, but along the way I met Levi."

Ren's eyes shift to me and then back to the screen. "What was he like…your husband…if you don't mind me asking?"

My breath becomes shallow, but I clear my throat and sit a little straighter. "Not at all. He enjoyed outdoor activities. I'd indulge him even though I much preferred museums, art, books, and things of that nature. He was a psychiatrist and loved his career. Levi was…a hard worker and…old fashioned, liked suits and for me to wear dresses. That man would have thrived in the fifties." I laugh a little. "Levi was charming, and everyone ate up anything he said like it was a delicacy." Ren's brows crease for some reason, watching me intently now. "He was a penny pincher and liked to keep his house along with his vehicle sturdy and reasonable, which was good because we were planning for a future. We saved and lived below our means most of the time. We even discussed children, but he wasn't quite ready." I swallow the lump in my throat threatening to form.

Ren stops completely and watches me carefully as he asks, "What did you do for work back then? Before the bookshop."

"Stayed at home, actually. I didn't work."

"Is that what you wanted?" he asks.

Leaning forward, I sit the mug on the coffee table and narrow my eyes at him. "What does that matter?"

"It matters, Nova." Ren's tense body doesn't soften.

My mouth hangs open. A slew of curses begs to stream from it, but I hold them back firmly. "What are you insinuating?"

"That you put your life on hold for your husband." My face reddens, but he continues. "Who finishes college and decides to stay at home twenty-four-seven that doesn't have children yet? Not to mention the 'old-fashioned' comment." Ren makes quotes with his fingers. "That sounds more like controlling to me."

I push off the couch and storm to the kitchen. Ren doesn't bother following as I sling my words over a shoulder. "You don't know a damn thing about me or my husband and have *no* right to make assumptions."

"I'm sorry. I have a habit of reading people." His voice is hard and unapologetic.

"You don't sound like you're sorry," I add as I drop my mug into the dishwasher.

"Well, I'm not actually, but can we just forget it and get back to working together?" He twists around to eye me from the sofa.

I roll my eyes with irritation but make my way back to him. He gestures for me to sit beside him instead. I hesitate, but he grabs my hand and has me plopping down anyway.

He releases my hand, but I can still feel the calloused grip there long after it's gone.

"I'm sorry," he says again. "I tend to give my opinions and observations freely. You want to go over some of the case details with me?"

I nod once and lean in beside his shoulder to read. His masculine scent hits me like a freight train. I forgot what it was like…that smell. The heady, comforting scent of a man around. We read in silence together and occasionally point out shady investigation details spouted by reports as the day drags on. I glance only once at the balcony door, but this time, I don't feel the pull toward it as I did earlier.

CHAPTER 11

Soren

We spent half the day looking for details of my incarceration until we needed a breather. There's only so much we can gain from news reports…we need case files and actual evidence.

There was no more talk about her life. I struck a chord with her yesterday, and even though I know I'm right, I've refrained from pushing her further. From the way she keeps her cabinets to the way she has zero signs of her personality anywhere in this space, I can see it. She's hiding in plain sight too. She's been kept silent for too long, and I fear losing her husband sent her over the edge. While she may hide it from the world, there is a hellcat under that prim surface that's been caged far too long.

Her braid has come loose, and tendrils of hair float around her face as she opens the packages that just arrived of the various things I ordered. Food was delivered too, and I helped put it all away while she went through the clothes. I made sure to create disarray in her cabinets and fridge. No more Miss Perfection. She's yet to notice. Laughing, I walk back toward Nova when suddenly there's a knock on the door.

Her face is as shocked as mine and is rapidly draining of color. "There shouldn't be any more orders coming in."

I get her meaning. "Nova, if it's the police…" I say, fear gripping me, but my words fall flat as I hear the distinct sound of a key being inserted into the lock and a muffled, agitated voice call out, "Nova…I know you're in there…I'm coming in!" My heart sinks into my stomach.

"Oh my God. " It's *Melina*," she whispers frantically.

"Is that your friend? What the *hell* is she doing here?" I say through gritted teeth.

"Yes…and *I don't know*! I did what you said and messaged her that I was sick."

The doorknob turns, and I dart for the bedroom, my entire plan disintegrating with each step. Nova has no reason to trust me and every reason to blow the whistle. Slinking into the shadows behind the bedroom door…I listen.

The sound of heels clacking on the wooden floors is what finds me first and then, "*Well*, you don't look sick! What's going on, Nova? Why aren't you answering my *calls* or *messages*…or your parents for God's sake?"

Nova's tone is exasperated when she replies, "I shouldn't have given you a key."

Her friend's heels move further into the loft, her voice softening a bit. "Answer me. Are you okay? At least tell me that."

"Yes, I'm good, promise. I…I've…"

Worry slithers down my spine as I listen intently. She could be gesturing to where I'm hidden. I shouldn't have moved the barricade from the door and wouldn't have if it hadn't been for the damn Walmart packages.

Nova's voice strengthens. "I decided to take a much-needed break from work to have a weekend to relax."

Her friend is silent…no doubt assessing the situation. Finally, she responds. "You don't need to *ever* lie to me. You're my best friend…*hell*, my only friend. I'm sorry I barged in on you, but it's been a hard six months, babe. Watching you distance yourself, move away, and then this."

"I'm not distancing myself." The strength seems to wane from her tone.

"Yes you are, but you don't have to. I'm here for you. You know that, right? And your poor mother is worried about you."

"I get it. I'm fine though, really." Nova's voice cracks with emotion.

I can almost feel her pain through the wall like sap leaching from a tree, and it's unnerving. I wasn't wrong in my assessment of her, that much I know. And now, to hear what her friend is saying…it just drives my point home. She's mechanical and broken.

They stay silent, far too long for my liking before I hear, "Well, I can understand needing time off, and you're a workaholic. If you want me to go, I will. Is that what you want?"

"It's not that I want you to go, Mel, it's just…"

Nova's cut off when Melina gasps and then makes a strange squeaky noise. "You dirty lying ho." My brows snap together and I shift my head as if that makes hearing them any easier. Pressing my ear as close to the doorjamb as possible, I hold my breath.

"That's not what it looks like…well…I." Nova fumbles for words, and my brain tries but fails to catch what's happening in there.

"Don't lie to me again, Nova," Mel demands. "Those are men's boots by the door. Whose are they? Is that why you're being weird? You don't need to feel ashamed for wanting to be with someone you know. It's been a long time. If you're dating…it's okay. But I need dirty details, so spill."

Nova sighs heavily. "You got me. I…I'm seeing someone, but it's new and a bit scary. I wanted to keep it quiet."

"Nova, that's great. I wish you'd told me. Is he hot? What's he like?" Melina asks, like a teen gossiping at a slumber party.

"Yeah, yeah. Don't get too excited; he's a slob and an annoying, brutish type. It'll likely go nowhere."

I roll my lips in to bite back a laugh at the audacity this little minx has.

"Ohh, just my type. But he's hot, right?" Mel laughs.

My lips twitch upward awaiting her response.

"He's alright I guess…in a lumberjack sort of way."

"So, he's built then?" I hear what sounds like a smack to the arm and Mel laughing. "Okay, okay…is he here? Can I meet him?"

My whole body seizes up right before Nova says, "*No*, he's stepped out for a bit. I'll make sure you meet him if this 'thing' we have even lasts. And I promise to make a day with you; now can you trust that I'm okay."

"I guess so. I love you, supernova. You know that, right?"

"Me too. Always." Nova sniffles.

After a few minutes of mundane conversation, the two say their goodbyes from the sound of it. As I hear the lock of the front door click into place, I walk back into the living room slowly, peeking around the doorframe first to make sure she's actually gone. Leaning against the wall, I watch as Nova wipes tears from her cheeks without looking at me. "Are you good?" I ask.

"*Sure.* I just lied to my best friend in the whole world. The one person who's been there for me through everything."

"I'm sorry." The words come out easily, and I realize…I *am* sorry. I've uprooted this woman's life, and while I'd do it all over again, it doesn't sit well with me. Her tears…I don't like them.

She tilts her head my way. "It's okay."

I can't stand the sadness lingering in her eyes, so I decide to lighten the mood. "So, I don't know who this boyfriend is, but he sounds just awful. Annoying, a slob, and a brute, huh?"

Nova giggles and sniffles at the same time. Wiping the remaining moisture from her face, she cocks an eyebrow my way. "Among other atrocious qualities, yes."

I push off the wall and come to stand before her. I'm not sure why I do it, but I brush a tendril of her hair away from her face, letting my fingertip drag across her cheek a bit too long. Her breath hitches, her lips part invitingly, and for a brief moment I see something in her eyes I haven't seen in a long time. Yearning maybe, for comfort, for another human's touch. I drop my hand as if it was burned, not wanting to bother with dreams of that nature. She's not in this situation by her own desire, and even if she was, she's far too good for me. Out of my league is an understatement.

I sigh and then grin. "Well, this hot boyfriend you have will have to take a hike…cause you'll be spending every day with me."

"He's not hot, and he might not like that." She grins fiendishly.

"I might not care, and *I think* that *you think*…he is hot."

"Are we going to continue talking about my nonexistent, hypothetical, un-hot boyfriend or are we going to solve your case?"

"No wonder your *handsome* boyfriend is a brute…he has to deal with your smartass mouth."

She gapes at me before smiling. "How did I get so lucky as to have been kidnapped and held hostage by such a *gentleman*?" she says sarcastically.

"You're one lucky lady. You get a handsome boyfriend and even hotter kidnapper."

Her eyes threaten to roll inside her head as she pushes past me and heads for the computer. "Come on, you delusional psycho. Let's get to work."

I watch her walk away, but I remain frozen for a few seconds…reflecting on the fact that she had the opportunity to climb over that balcony and another chance to tell her friend about me. She did neither of those things. In one day with her, she's allowed me into her life and offered me a safe harbor. She's not what I expected.

While I'm glad this has worked out in my favor, it's concerning—her willingness to jump into the fire with me so quickly.

CHAPTER 12

Novalie

Ren runs a hand through his hair in exasperation. "What if it was a random psycho that happened upon us in the woods?"

"That's impossible and improbable. They'd have killed you too, no doubt, and not to mention...they wouldn't have staged it to make you out to be the murderer. No random serial killer would've done that. And if it was a rapist or someone out to torture only women...he'd have kidnapped her, not killed her there."

Ren nods in agreement. "Yeah, I know. I just don't understand who could've done something so vile to her. They had to have a reason."

"What if they did it to *you*...not her?" He stares at me, so I reword that. "What if they wanted to hurt you and, to do that...killed her?"

He contemplates it, but not for long. "I can't think of *any* reason someone would do that either."

"You have no enemies then?"

"None that I know of," he replies honestly.

"Shocking," I mutter under my breath, making him give me a face. "Money is the root of most murders." My mouth twists with the thought as I say it, then another thought hits me. "Victoria's belongings? Where are they?" I ask, tapping my nail against the desk, while sitting beside him.

He turns to me, his thigh brushing mine, causing my eyes to drop there. "Why do you ask?"

I snap my eyes back to his and try to ward off the dangerous feeling that just sliced through me from a simple graze of our legs. It's more proof that I'm just a lonely fool. Swallowing hard, I say, "I used to write in a journal before...Levi died. There may be some clues in her stuff, especially if she kept any type of journal. She could've had secrets you knew nothing about."

He hums to himself. "Last I heard, her things were still in a storage unit. Her parents have most of it, but some was left in my old house and later put in storage when the property was sold. I had a friend of mine set up the billing for me so that the storage unit was paid for each month. He was in business with me."

That piques my interest. "You had your own business?"

"You really don't watch TV, do you?" Ren nudges my thigh with his. "I co-owned M&T Restorations."

My brows raise at that. I know the place well…more than well. I have a bit of history with it. "The classic car place? Marshall and Talon?" I ask, bewildered.

"That's the one," he says with pride. "We didn't just fix them and sell them; we built custom restomods too."

"That's amazing," I say quietly, my words barely audible, my head trailing back to a memory from several years ago—one long forgotten.

"That sounds an awful lot like a compliment." He drags me from the thought with a devilish grin.

I store that memory away for analysis later. Snorting, I say, "Gross. Anyways, can you trust reaching out to this friend? We need to see her things if they're still in there."

He has a crooked smile on his face. "Yes and no. Yes, I trust Micah, and no, we can't get him involved in this. I'm absolutely certain the police will be all over his phone lines and locations, knowing he's the one that has access to my life."

I blow out a breath. "Okay then…let me think. We need a way to gain access to parts of your life and hers. You can't be seen, but I can. I just need a good enough reason to be snooping about."

"Or we could just break into it." His voice and stead-fast eyes hold no humor.

"Like…walk into the storage place and snip the locks?" I scoff.

"Exactly. There's cameras, but if we disable the system…it's doable."

Nibbling on my lower lip, I groan. "I can't believe I even considered that asinine plan for a second. Don't you think it would look *really* bad if the one storage unit that's broken into is hers? That would alert police that you're still in the area."

Ren looks at me, considering. "Okay, princess, what do you suggest?"

"Stop calling me that." He cocks his head with arrogance as I continue. "What if I really *do* have a reason to be snooping?" I cock my head and give back an arrogant smirk to match his.

"Like what reason?" he inquires.

"What if I were taking notes to write a book on the life of Soren and Victoria? A non-fiction murder thriller." I catch how that sounds and add, "I'm sorry. I didn't mean that so flippantly."

Ren clears his throat. "It's fine. It's a good plan. Do you think you can use that to persuade your way into that storage locker?"

"Maybe. It's worth a shot. I mean…no one is looking for me or would find me as a threat, and I have no connections linking me to you." I pause and take him in briefly before a question stirs. "Are you so sure that I won't run to the police the moment my feet hit pavement?"

"Let's just call it instinct. I read people well, remember." He can tell I'm not buying that but doesn't elaborate. "Well, princess, are you ready to officially join the dark side?"

I give Ren a smug look. "I always did like Darth Vader best."

He smacks a hand over his chest dramatically. "A woman after my own heart."

Two hours later, I'm parked in front of Thompson Storage. My 1970 Chevy Nova SS is obscenely loud enough for a bystander leaving to stare in my direction. The moment I sat in my car after leaving Ren, the same tug of memory surfaced, the same as the first time I saw Soren. Only this time, I realized it wasn't because of his escapee status.

Although now is not the time to dwell on it. I'll revisit that hidden memory later.

Adjusting my sling bag and fluffing out my knee-length flower skirt, I square my shoulders and enter the main office. My white wedges barely make a sound as I make my way to the desk.

I wasn't nervous when I left Ren. Honestly, I was oddly excited to go on this 'mission' and quite proud of the double-take he did when I exited my bedroom in the little lace-trimmed pink crop top and flower skirt. It was nice to be noticed…*seen* again. But when I stepped outside…I'd be lying if the thought of fleeing didn't spark for a moment, but it was so faint this time.

For reasons I don't quite understand, I *want* to do this.

The man behind the desk is maybe in his fifties. I send a silent thank you to the universe that it's not a woman. I've never been the sensual, flirty type, but right now…I *need* to be. Leaning over just enough for a bit of cleavage to show, I ask softly, "Excuse me, sir." My eyes drop to the name tag.

"Mr. Thompson. I was wondering if I could have a moment of your time?"

The man tilts his face up to meet my eyes. His brown ones round noticeably before he clears his throat. "Yes ma'am. How can I help you today?" His clean-shaven face is doing him *no* favors as it accentuates his double chin, and the balding center of his head is covered by wisps of graying hair that he slicks over to one side.

I give him a delicate smile and pull out a leather-bound notebook from my sling bag and a pen. "My name is Novalie Rhodes. I own the bookstore in town."

Recognition lights his eyes. "Oh, yeah. I've seen that place. Near Ronnie's Barbecue, right?"

Of course he'd frequent the barbecue place. I nod and block out my snarky thought. "That's the one. I'm on a new adventure of sorts…aspiring to be an author and well…you could really be a huge help for me."

"How so?" he asks. Setting down his pen and documents.

I don't fail to notice his eyes lingering a bit too low on my neckline. My heart beats wildly, but I maintain eye contact. "This novel I'm writing is about the Marshall case."

His eyes flare with understanding. "I see."

I lean further down, placing my elbows on the desk so that my breasts are pressed together more enticingly. "This is going to be a huge bestseller. I just know it. Everyone is fascinated with the case…so anyways, I know Victoria's belongings are kept here in Storage Unit 42. I was hoping to have a look around just to get an idea of who she was as a woman."

His head shakes subtly, and I see my plan failing fast, so I add, "I'd be forever in your debt, and I promise not to touch anything. I just need to see what she was like, you know?"

"Miss…"

"Novalie," I say.

"Right." He leans back, causing the double chin to become a triple. "Novalie. I could get into a lot of trouble for that. It's against policy."

"Just ten minutes and I'm gone. Promise."

He shifts his head side to side as if making sure we are indeed alone. Then he leans forward, and his voice lowers. "You know I find it odd that someone keeps her stuff here anyways. She's dead, and her man…when they catch him…won't ever get out of jail, so why not trash it. It's been five years, and only once has anyone questioned looking inside."

My ears prick up at that. "Who came to look inside?"

"I can't say…sorry."

I store that knowledge away until a later date and say, "You're right…it's a waste, really. Stuff's probably worthless to anyone except her, and she's long gone." I wink at him and hope he gathers my meaning of 'no one gives two shits about this stuff and let me see it.'

He sighs and stands. His gray work shirt is half untucked, and a bulge of gut peeks out. "Alright. This stays between us, and you get ten minutes…don't touch anything. Okay?"

I clap my hands together like a child. "Yes, sir…lead the way."

I follow him to the end of the lot. Dead in the center of a long line of metal buildings, he stops and pulls out a master set of keys, fumbles through them and eventually finds the right one. The metal clangs as he unlocks it and rolls up the door.

"I'll wait over there." He points to a table and chairs set up near the entrance.

I watch him walk away only for a second before I step into the storage shed. Even though the day is bright, I click on my phone light to illuminate the area. The hair on my arms rises. I didn't even consider how creepy this would be, snooping through a dead person's belongings.

The first thing I notice is that there really isn't much in here. I was expecting a life full of odds and ends. But no…not here. There's no more than five boxes, an oak dresser with flower decals along the sides that looks expensive, a plastic bin with clothing, an antique grandfather clock, and a computer desk.

I waste no time in breaking my promise to Mr. Thompson. Clearing the computer desk and dresser first, I find them empty. Dragging out box number one, I sift through nothing but more clothing as I sneeze from a waft of dust. Box two is full of trinkets and room decor. I make sure to place each back where it was. As soon as I open box three, I freeze. A photo of Victoria and Soren on a beach somewhere has my heart aching painfully. He's in blue swim trunks, his thick, toned body sun-kissed as he leans against a pier railing. His hair is longer, and he's sporting a short beard. It's him but different. A world away from the hardened, scarred exterior waiting back in my home. Ren even has fewer tattoos than now. He's laughing at something or someone on the other side of the camera. Victoria has an impish grin on her face.

She's not what I imagined. She has dirty blonde hair and blue eyes, not gray-blue like Soren's…lighter and unamused if I'm reading the photo accurately. She's slim and tall…regal looking in a bright yellow bikini. On the left side of her abdomen is a butterfly tattoo with one wing in a swirling design of black ink only and the other, the same design, but in blue ink.

Slipping the picture into my bag, I move on. This box has very few photos, people I assume are family members of hers or Soren's. Nothing substantial is found as I dig—old school annuals, elementary grade trophies, things of that nature. Box four was a bust too, containing linens and an old vase.

Box five is much smaller than the others, a little larger than a shoebox. Popping the tape along the sides, I peel it back. A man might not realize what box he'd tapped into, but as a woman…I certainly do the moment I've opened it. This disarray of miscellaneous things amounts to what most women have in their nightstand. It's like whoever went through her stuff simply dumped the whole drawer in here. Pens, an empty notepad, a Band-Aid, a nail file, a sterling toe ring, an anklet of lavender beads…random girly things. No journal though. Not many women write in journals anymore, but it would've been nice to delve into her psyche.

I sigh aloud—frustrated. What did I think to find here? A bright arrow pointing to the killer. Plus, the police had to have gone through everything of hers, right? None of the things in here—other than those few pictures I saw—are worth even keeping. What happened to the rest of her life, because surely this is not all of it? Maybe family took her most precious belongings, like jewelry and such.

Looking down at my phone, I realize I have about two minutes before Mr. Thompson will be hovering. Putting the last box back neatly, I snap a few photos of the things around me, more for the ruse of a book I'm writing than anything else. I turn to snap one last photo of that old clock in the corner when a memory snags. My cheek pulls into a smile as the memory warms my heart.

My grandmother was an odd bird and very sneaky. She liked riddles and hiding things from Ian and me when we were children. One evening, we were being exceptionally naughty, and she, in her way of distracting us from killing each other, decided to hide something special inside the house, and we could have it as long as we worked together and solved her riddles. The first two riddles were easy enough…given that I was around five years old and Ian was eight. I don't remember what they were, just that we came to a conclusion quickly. The third riddle, I do remember clearly.

I stand still yet move all day…what am I?

Time. As we darted for that old grandfather clock, I remember my grandmother softly saying, *tick-tock, tick-tock*. Hidden inside was an old VHS movie, *Where The Red Fern Grows*. She was already popping popcorn before we had a chance to realize she'd duped us into sitting down and shutting up. We laughed though and cried at that damn movie.

Shaking off the memory, I dart over to the clock. Thankfully, someone left the key sticking right in the lock. Nostalgia hits me as the glass door rattles open. Reaching up behind the face of the clock onto my tiptoes, my fingers shift in dust and God knows what else. I can't see back there…I'm too short, but I reach further anyway. My index finger feathers over a piece of what feels like crinkling paper and cool metal atop it.

Footsteps sound from outside, making my heart ratchet up. Straining, I stretch my fingers, snagging the hidden items. Pulling them out, I don't have time to look; I shove them in my bag, shut the clock, lock it fast, and I'm sweating as I back away from the contents inside the dreary storage unit.

A second later, Mr. Thompson veers around the entrance, eyeing me and Victoria's things. "You get a feel for her? Was it useful in any way?" he asks, seeming genuinely curious.

"Time will tell." I smile.

He nods and looks nervous for a moment. "Um, could I give you my card…you know, in case you ever want to talk about the case or something?"

Not wanting to sound like an ass and say no, I simply nod curtly. His smile beams as he turns to head toward the main office, me on his heels. The moment we enter, I hear the TV mounted near his desk blaring the local news. He rummages through his desk drawer, pulling out a card. When he hands it to me, he says something, but my attention is now laser-focused on the news reporter.

Soren's face looks back at me as the reporter warns of his dangerous nature. She's interviewing one of the police officers on the case…the detective that was there the day it happened. She addresses him as Detective Joe Sparks. When she asks about leads, my heart nearly ceases to beat as well as my breath not flowing in or out of my lungs.

The detective smiles confidently, and says, "*Actually, we have reason to believe that the suspect is still local. Someone could be aiding and abetting him. I suggest everyone being vigilant and watching their surroundings carefully.*"

The interview goes on, but that statement chills me to the bone and lodges in my brain like a bullet.

CHAPTER 13

Soren

It's been fucking *hours* since she left. *Hours*! Dread pools in my gut, making me nauseous. Pacing around the house, over and over, I go through, in my head, *each* of our conversations. Was I too sure? Am I a fool to have so quickly let her out of my sight? *Shit*...what have I done?

Opening her fridge to get a water, I eye the twelve-pack of Coronas inside. I'd seen them yesterday but was not about to get buzzed and have her escape. Now today, I let her waltz right out the fucking door. Might as well have a beer if I'm to go back to prison. Taking one out, I pop the top and snatch a lime and knife off the counter.

Fitting an Appalachian State ball cap onto my head that I found in her closet, I drop the lime in my beer, stick my thumb over the mouth and slowly turn it upside down to infuse it, then head to the balcony. It's reckless to be out here in the open, but thankfully, dusk is settling and hopefully people can't see my face clearly from up here.

I pull the hat lower and eye the cars that pass. I realize then that I don't know what she drives to even watch out for her. The first sip of the Corona has me moaning. *Damn*, I missed this. It's hard to recall the last time I was able to sit on a porch and relax.

Another thirty minutes pass, but no sign of her.

Suddenly, I hear the rumble of an engine, a big-block 454 by the sound of it. I stand and lean over the railing. Less than a block away, I see a deep blue Chevy Nova with black racing stripes making a left toward the back alley. Even from here, I can tell who's behind the wheel. It's her. Petite little Nova…*drives a Nova.*

I'd laugh out loud if it wasn't for one fact that just punched me in the face. Worry and recognition pinch my brows together. I know that car. *Hell*, I built the engine for it amongst other parts. My mind reels as I try to stitch the memory together. It was years ago…maybe like six or seven.

I go back to the fridge, grab two more beers and a few slices of lime and a bowl of strawberries I'd washed earlier and head back to the porch…calmer now than before. Casually, I sit back in the wrought-iron balcony chair and kick up my feet. Sipping the beer, and smile as the memory, now fully there in my head, plays like a movie. It feels impossible…but it's not. I remember now. The saying 'It's a small world' couldn't be more true.

A few minutes later, I hear Novalie enter the house, but I don't move. I wait for her to find me. The nerves from earlier wash away with every soft tap of those odd, clunky heels she has on. I smell her sweet scent before I see her, as if she's watching me from behind.

I pop the top off the extra beer and hold it for her to come closer. "Want one?" I still don't look back at her.

"They're mine…so sure."

What a smartass. I smirk as she comes to sit beside me, smoothing her skirt in the back before sitting and crossing her legs. She takes the beer with a soft smile. I have to force my eyes to move from those perfect legs gleaming in the last rays of the sun.

Finally, I meet her eyes. "I was certain you went to the cops."

"Why did you stay here then? Wouldn't it have been smarter to run?" Her tone is playful.

I cut my eyes to her. "Nah, I decided to go down with this ship."

Her lips curl with humor. "Me being the ship?"

Now she has me grinning like a fool. "Yes…more like a fucking USS Destroyer…but I digress." Novalie laughs outright and, *damn*, it's refreshing. "Wanna tell me what happened today, or is it your desire to keep me guessing?"

She purses her lips after a long drink from the glass bottle. Her moan has me shifting in my seat and quickly trying to imagine something gross…because I barely know this woman and shouldn't be having any sort of thoughts no matter how long I've gone without the touch of a woman. And I don't want to decipher how excited I am to have her back here…with me.

Novalie turns her seat to fully face me. Her eyes are a mix of apprehension and humor still lying underneath it. "Can I ask you something first?" she implores.

"Anything," I say without hesitation.

"Do you remember a 1970 blue and black Chevy Nova? Specifically, one *you* sold some years back?"

It's a stretch to try and keep my features placid. So...she's remembered it too. Interesting. "I've worked on so many cars..." I feign ignorance to see what she recalls.

Her eyes say she's reading me like a fucking book, but she goes along with it. "I bought that car from *you.* I still drive it to this day. I think *that's* why you looked familiar to me. You don't remember?"

I shrug. "I'm not sure, like I said, worked on a lot of them. Sold a lot of them too."

She glares at me and downs another drink. "You're full of *shit,* Soren Marshall. You know *exactly* what I'm talking about. Her eyes drop to the column of my throat, and I swallow hard as she follows my tattoos there. "The crossed pistons at your throat, the gears and tools—I knew you looked familiar, but back then you didn't have these." She leans in, her fingertip barely grazes the skin of my throat over the tattoos, but I feel a jolt rush through me. Heat flushes my skin. She snaps her hand away as if she realizes how bold that was.

Swallowing hard, I say, "I remembered the moment I saw you down the road in that car. I can't believe you still drive it every day."

"Classic or no, she's not meant to be couped up in a shed somewhere," Novalie says, her voice changing, wilting with each word.

I lean forward, both of us now even closer. Her words seem to have a double meaning that I don't like at all. I want to tell her exactly why *she* shouldn't be couped up...shouldn't have been made to lie dormant. Her description of that car couldn't have hit closer to home for her. From the little I've gleaned of her husband…he sounded like a control freak. I'd place a bet on it that he's the reason her cabinets look like that—the reason there's no sign of her in this house—bland décor and nothing that screams Novalie other than her clothing. She's still under his control, even from the grave.

Shyly, she asks, "Do you recall *everything* about that day?"

My cheek pulls up. "How could I forget? *In fact*, I'm not sure why it took me so long to place you. Even in that newspaper article, I didn't realize it was you. But that was a long time ago." I laugh. "It'd snowed for three days, and the shop's heat went out the night before. You came bouncing into my shop with frosted-over glasses, some multicolored weird toboggan, and a coat that would fit three people inside."

"My toboggan was cute and…" she points to her eyes, "corrective surgery got rid of the glasses."

I wave her off as if the glasses mattered to anyone as gorgeous as she clearly is. "Anyways, you were demanding to buy the Nova parked out front, but the price was out of your range. You haggled with me for thirty minutes while I was trying to replace a transmission."

She grins. "And when you finally rolled out from under that car, you were covered in grease and had a beard, if I'm remembering correctly."

"Is that why you blushed the entire time…does the working man look excite you, princess?"

My reward is her incredulous face and cheeks turning pink instantly. "You were just as annoying and slobbish then."

"Uh huh." I ignore the dig and continue. "You managed to talk me down almost five grand on that car…and I never even got your name. I *may* have let the price drop…because you were *flirting* with me."

Her mouth makes an O before she lights into me. "I did no such thing. *You* were flirting with *me*!" She pauses. Her face blazes red now, and it does something wicked to me.

"And we were both *married* and didn't know it." I let that hang in the air between us. Her chest rises and falls a little too quickly. Does she remember it like I do? I'm certain she does if her blush is any indication. We bantered back and forth, which seems to still be our commonality. The power went off in the middle of our short encounter, and I used a flashlight to start the purchase contract, but my phone rang.

She interrupts my thought with one of her own, eerily finishing mine. "When your phone rang, and you left…your business partner helped me get everything settled. I never knew your name either, didn't see you again. I assumed you were either a Talon or a Marshall based on the shop's name. And in my defense of the flirtatious behavior, I had a really rough week and…things weren't great at home." Her shoulders seem to roll inward with that admission. I can't tell if it's shame or defeat.

This is the first time she's revealed any cracks in Mr. Perfect Levi Rhodes's picturesque image. I keep that to myself, if only because I don't want to taint the fluid conversation we are currently having. So I say, "Things weren't so great for me either." I tap my beer to hers, making her perk up. "Since you admitted to flirting, I can admit something too." Her mouth opens to retort, but I keep going. "I almost looked up your name." Her eyes bore into me. "I can't count the times I would open my mouth to ask Micah for your name, the times I opened the file cabinet and was tempted to scroll through it."

She surprises me by asking, "Why didn't you?"

"The obvious reason. Guilt. Even though my marriage was…rough at times, it was new, and I still felt like I could be a better husband. Maybe if I was a better man, tried harder, I could fix it, you know?"

She nods gravely as if she *completely* understands, and that doesn't sit well with me. We are silent for a few moments, finishing the beer, letting it carry away part of our worries. It sits there, in a hidden part of my conscious, the thing I can't say aloud. It would make me sound like a horrible person. But to myself…I can say it. I wish I would've left my wife. I wish I would've called the quirky girl who bounced into my shop, mouthed off, all to buy a car made in 1970. She was ridiculous and…perfect all at the same time. I have a good idea of why she bought that car, and it's really nothing to do with her name. It was a symbol of her independence, her free spirit that was being trampled. She didn't want the sturdy KIA or whatever shitty car Levi would rather her drive…no, she wanted something fast…something reckless.

And if I would've left Vicky…she'd be alive, maybe living a better life than the one I tried to give her.

The silence is broken when she sits her empty beer down and pulls a crumpled piece of paper from the bag beside her. She flattens it on her thigh. "The storage unit was not much of a success. There weren't a lot of belongings in there to start with, but definitely nothing that showed me her life in any way." My brows furrow as I wait for her explanation. She drops her head to the paper she's still hiding with her fingers. "After I found this," she turns the small, ripped paper to me, showing me a random phone number there, "I left the storage unit. I thought about having my uncle look up the number or my brother, but my brother wasn't home and my uncle didn't answer his call. It's not something I would want to text about, so I headed back this way. And before you ask, I was going to tell them the same story I told the storage unit owner, that I'm writing a novel about your case. That way they wouldn't be suspicious."

My head bobs with approval, and a grin tugs at my cheek. She hands me the paper, and I read it several times, not recognizing it. Nova reaches into her bag and pulls out two more items—a key and a box—then hands them to me, smiling. "This key was with the number I found."

She puts the small metal key in my hand and I recognize it instantly. Frowning, I say, "This is to my safe-deposit box. Well, mine and Vicky's. We always kept these hidden." Brows furrowing, I roll it around in my palm.

She interrupts my thoughts as she passes me the box she's holding and says, "I also took so long because I went to the techy shop downtown and found you a burner phone. I figured, before we go any further, you needed a way to reach me…just in case."

Emotions swirl inside my chest. She's fully invested in this…in *me*. I should feel guilty. For the mess I'm dragging her through…I should feel ashamed…and part of me does, but it's a necessary evil. "Thank you for this," I say quietly. "Not just the phone…but for trusting me when you didn't have to."

"Time will tell if I'm daft for doing so." She reaches to grab the bottles, but I halt her with a hand and jump up to get them myself.

When I return, she's staring at the moon, unbraiding her long hair now in waves. Her skin almost radiates in the moonlight. I hand her the beer and position my chair a bit closer to her before I sit.

"So the key being hidden is no biggie, I guess. If you guys kept those hidden, but do you recognize the number?" she asks.

I shake my head. "Not at all."

"Why would she have a number hidden in an old grandfather clock?"

My eyes shift to hers, and it's hard to concentrate on the damn number with her hair gleaming like burning coals under the moonlight and her catlike eyes soft with no sign of worry. She's relaxed around me tonight…completely. She catches me staring, so I blurt out, "I have no idea, but it can't be anything good. I…felt like she might have been unfaithful at times but could never prove it."

She inclines her head and then stands and waves me over to the balcony's edge. "I just thought of something. Now that we're in this together, we need a way to communicate if we get separated." I make a puzzled face, but she motions for me to lean over the railing with her. "You see that fern past the awning alongside my shop door?" I nod. "There's a cement frog with an open mouth underneath. If we ever get separated, I'll leave you letters inside it."

I chuckle lightly. "Why not just message? I do have the burner now."

"Because there may come a day when you don't have it. I used to love hiding things with my gran, and you just never know."

I nod, following her back to the chairs. We fall back into them, and then she shocks me to my core as she lays her hand on my thigh. My body stills with the touch, solid as stone. Her voice is soft as the night air when she speaks. "We'll figure this out, Soren…and get your life back."

I hesitate but then say, fuck it and place my large hand over her small one and squeeze once. The heat between our skin is unreal. Blowing out a breath, I say, "If not, I hear Mexico has some really nice beaches." She chuckles but doesn't move her hand from mine for several seconds before it slips away. I don't know what to make of it. Two lonely people reaching for any affection maybe…starved for human touch. Either way, I'll take the small gesture of kindness and hold it close.

Tilting her head and closing her eyes, Nova breathes in the warm summer night and then exhales loudly. "There's something else, Ren."

Dread threatens to ruin my good mood. My head lolls to the side to eye her. "What is it?"

"I saw the news today…they're saying that they think you *haven't* fled. That you're still in the area. That someone may be harboring you. I don't know why they think that, but…we need to be careful."

I work my jaw, feeling frustration rise like a tide in this harbor *I* created. "We will. No worries," I tell her, even though we most definitely have fucking worries.

"Also," her eyes shift to mine with such sympathy, "they have a reward out for your capture, and it's…substantial. If anyone sees you—"

"How much?"

Her brows rise. "Two hundred thousand dollars and rising."

"*Fucking hell*," I mutter.

"Right. So, you can *not* be seen, and my college ball cap isn't enough to hide who you are." She tips the hat in front with her finger for emphasis.

"Noted." I flick her nose, making her smile. "Anything else I should know about?"

"Just that you…aren't so bad, Soren Marshall."

"Is that a sincere compliment, princess?"

She shakes her head as if she immediately regrets giving it. She leans forward, slipping one more thing from her bag and hands over a photo of Vicky and me. I keep my face stoic as I look at the ghost before me. "Thought you might want at least one photo…sketchy marriage or not."

I look at it long and hard. Buried emotions threaten to claw through the grave and resurface. It's like the last five years drained it out of me, but it's still there. I toss it onto the table, enlisting a look of surprise but understanding from Nova. "I'm deciphering the past to regain my freedom but leaving it there…in the past where it belongs," I say to Nova as I tap my beer with hers again.

Novalie smiles, contemplating my words—letting them settle inside her, then says, "I'll drink to that."

CHAPTER 14

Novalie

The morning brings such clarity as if the light streaming in from the windows managed to open a crevice in my mind, allowing bright purpose to flow through. I quickly shower and dress in jeans, a white tank, and my favorite Vans with roses embroidered along the side. I'm pulling my hair into a high ponytail as I walk swiftly into the kitchen to make breakfast.

My mind tends to keep wandering back to last night. One question burns inside me. A question that can never be answered but burns just the same. Was it fated for us to meet again? It sounds ludicrous inside my head, but still. Was I meant to help this man? Or can this all be chalked up to coincidence? Or is this one of those happy accidents, as I love to call them?

I can't deny the feeling of purpose growing stronger inside me. I feel…*needed* again. Am I scared that this might end horribly…of course, but if there's a chance I can help him prove his innocence…what a wondrous thing that would be. He's still annoying and a slob, I smile, but also kind of fun to be around. Which I'll never admit to him.

My eyes dart to the living room couch and see the ends of Soren's legs hanging over the side, and I grimace. That has to be severely uncomfortable for such a tall man. Slowing my pace so as not to wake him, I grab the bacon and start it first, then carefully reach up to pull out everything I need to make blueberry pancakes.

As soon as the cabinet is open…all thoughts of Ren being *fun* evaporate. My mouth drops open, then a scowl quickly replaces the shock. A gruff morning laugh makes me jump, and I spin around to find Ren leaning against the bar, covering his mouth with a hand.

"Your face is priceless, princess." He laughs out the words.

I sneer, turning back to my cabinets. I peer inside each to find ingredients now in disarray in every single one. "You're an ass, Soren Marshall."

"What? Just trying to lighten your load. It has to be a lot to carry…all your perfectionism." Humor is bleeding from his tone.

Grabbing the syrup and pancake mix, I shut the door to the cabinet a little harder than I intended. Spinning toward him, I pin him with a glare. "As I've said before, there's nothing wrong with being organized!"

He throws his hands up in surrender while smirking. "Okay, okay…got it."

"Do you though?" I ask, unconvinced, as I prepare the batter. He doesn't answer, and there's a smile constantly pulling at his cheek. "You're insufferable." I push the bowl his way. "You're on pancake duty while I finish the bacon."

"Aye-aye, Captain!" He exaggerates a salute and lights the other burner.

Twenty minutes later, we sit at the island together, eating. His eyes keep finding mine, and finally I smile back, shaking my head. "You're infuriating, but I have to admit…these pancakes are to die for."

"Don't judge a book by its cover there, nerd. I'm a good cook and devilishly handsome. And…actually, I think I'm the most fun you've had in years," he retorts.

My fork pauses on the way to my lips. My thoughts from a few moments ago rush me, and my cheeks burn. Can he freaking read minds? I groan and roll my eyes. Clearing my throat, I take a bite. "I'd rather be a nerd than an illiterate. Changing the subject before he can respond, I say, "So, I have a few questions about the night you and Vicky went out…before she…"

"Died," he finishes for me.

"Yes." I bite my lip. "I thought we could begin searching through the details prior to that night. The bars you went to, the people you were around, and the conversations you had. Maybe there's something there."

He nods thoughtfully. "I've thought about them a lot." His voice grows solemn with that admission.

"Can you tell me about it?" I ask.

His brows raise, and he swallows a bite of bacon. "We went to Larry's Bar and Grill first, ate there and then ended up at The Watering Hole."

"What was she like that night?" I ask. "Did she act strange in any way…or *scared*?"

His head cocks as he watches me. "Yeah. I told the cops as much. She wasn't herself. I told them she seemed off."

"How so?" I ask, finishing my food and gathering up our plates to wash.

Soren stops me. "I'll clean this up."

It's on the tip of my tongue to stop him, but as he moves to the sink and begins washing the dishes, I simply slip up beside him with a towel and begin drying the rinsed ones.

His voice is stoic as he continues his assessment of that night. "She was arguing with me more than normal. She looked around the room a lot, which bothered me. Like she was being watched. I asked her what was wrong…a few times, but she would just get angry. I thought…I thought she was on something."

"Oh," I whisper. "Was she an addict?"

"She hid it well, even from me, but I know she had several prescription meds." Suddenly he looks embarrassed. His tone changes, wavering as he says, "Speaking of…I threw away the script you had for Xanax. Sorry…brought back bad memories."

My brows pinch together, mouth open. "I didn't take them anyways. It was an old prescription. It still didn't give you the right," I chastise him.

"I know…sorry."

My eyes travel across Ren's face, seeing regret there. "It's okay, I get it." He looks at me then, with a mix of emotions. Finally, I break the stare off and change the subject. "Why would she be angry with you on your anniversary?"

His hands slow on the soapy plate he's washing. "I had mentioned…a week before that maybe we shouldn't have married."

"Oh." The thought grips my heart. "That must've been hard for her to hear."

A slow breath leaves his chest. "Yeah, I'm sure it was, but I was also convinced she wanted the same. We were growing further and further apart. We weren't having…" he clears his throat awkwardly, "we weren't intimate for a long time. She thought I was cheating; I thought she was cheating."

The burn of anger and resentment clod in my throat from a long-ago memory, but I swallow the acrid bitterness down. Drying the last dish, I almost stop the words but let them grace my lips anyway. "Were you?"

Ren turns to me, and we're so close that I can smell his masculine scent. His head shakes once. "Never."

I nod, seeing the truth in his stormy eyes. "What else happened?"

"She didn't just argue with me; it was louder, more urgent. Bystanders tried to intervene at one point. I was sure that she was cheating, and I think I know who with."

My curiosity rises with my arched brow. "Who?"

"It was either a coworker or her ex. She was fond of this guy who worked with her at the hospital. She talked about him a lot…as a *friend*. But there was also her ex-boyfriend. They were real serious before Vicky and I got together."

"What happened with them?" I ask as we migrate to the living room and sit across from each other. I brace my elbows on my knees, listening intently.

"He was abusive." My mouth makes a shocked O as he continues. "It gets worse too." He pauses before saying,

"He'd tried to call her several times when we first got together. She blocked his number."

"Soren." My voice rises a little with the implications running rampant through my head. "What if it was him? Did the police interview him? Did they know about the volatile relationship?"

He shrugs. "They claimed they did a thorough check on the guy."

My head makes little bobs as certainty courses through me. "We have our first lead to follow!" His side smile is not only endearing…it's grateful as he watches me. I clap my hands together, exclaiming, "We're going to vet the coworker and the ex. And I think I know just where to start."

CHAPTER 15

Novalie

Against Ren's wishes, I'm going this alone. He was adamant that he join, but we can't chance that. Not with everyone looking for his face. After our lengthy conversation this morning, he told me the coworker's name was Dean Porter. He was also a nurse at the hospital. With a little Googling and sleuthing, it wasn't hard to find the man. I was able to discern that he still lives around here and also still works the same second shift at the hospital.

So, here I am. Checking into the lobby, pretending to be having an anxiety attack. In this moment, I wish Mel was around. She would be doubled over dying of laughter at my newfound boldness.

But once I check in, my nerves get the better of me. The bland pewter triage room seems to be closing in, suffocating. What the hell was I thinking? This is asinine.

"What symptoms are you experiencing today, ma'am?" the round-faced nurse asks me. Her bobbed brown hair swishes as she listens to my heart, checks my oxygen level, and blood pressure.

Making my voice shaky and hopefully convincing, I say, "My chest feels like someone is squeezing it."

Her brown eyes turn down in sympathy. "Oh dear, I'm so sorry to hear that. Do you have any prior conditions? Are you short of breath?"

"I have a history of anxiety…since my husband's death." *Not exactly a lie*, I think.

Her empathy is evident in her tone. "I'm so sorry for your loss. Let's get you to a room." She smiles solemnly.

I follow her to room seven. This is a small hospital but doubt swarms me like wasps. What if I don't get him as my nurse…what if he's assigned to a different room? I'm suddenly wishing I'd thought this through more thoroughly. His social media couldn't be accessed without being his friend, and so I'm going on what little I could find from other sites. My hands are clammy as the triage nurse leaves me in the bed to await the nurse assigned to me.

Clenching my fists, I close my eyes and take a deep breath. Holy hell, this is insane.

The door opens, startling me. A tall, handsome man walks in. In his late thirties perhaps. His short, light brown hair is spiked haphazardly, and he has a cleanly trimmed beard that's short and cut to match his jawline. His hazel eyes assess me, and a soft smile reveals straight, perfect teeth that can only be veneers. There's no way he was blessed with those, right? None of that really matters though; what matters is that it's *him*…the coworker Dean Porter. I'm baffled at my luck.

"Hello there, can I have your name and date of birth, please?" he asks, and I rattle it off for him, noticing how scared I sound.

I watch the way he moves, his mannerisms as he asks me all the same questions as the triage nurse. Even though we're in a full, engaged conversation, my mind is not in the least here. I'm trying to picture him with Victoria—trying to see through his façade, but I come up lacking. I decide on the best method I can think of to draw him into a more personal conversation.

"I lost my husband," I say and let my voice hitch a little. "That's when the chest pressure began. Anxiety they tell me, but it feels like I'm having a heart attack."

He takes a soft breath in and clutches my hand in his. "When did you lose him?"

"Last December," I say in a whisper.

"I know you probably hear this a lot…but it does get easier over time. The hurt and pain of losing them will always be there, but somehow it lessens enough to live life fully again. I promise." He tilts his head, rolling his lips inward sadly.

I raise one solitary eyebrow at that. He knows how it feels *because* he's lost someone too. "When did you lose a loved one?" I ask, trying to remain calm and not sound interrogating.

He blows a short breath from his nose, shaking his head. "It's hard to believe, but it's been like five years."

The blood drains from my face as I release his hand and pick randomly at the hem of my tank top. Looking down, I can't meet his eyes now as I mutter, "I'm sorry. Was it a spouse…if you don't mind me asking?" My breath halts as I await that response.

Dean stands, slips on my blood pressure cuff and oxygen monitor as he talks. "No, I've never been married, actually."

"Oh," I say quietly, eyeing the back of his head as if I could rip it open and read his thoughts. "So…who was it?"

"A dear friend of mine." He turns back to me and smiles sadly. "I don't tell this story to many people, but I guess a stranger's ear couldn't hurt, right?" He begins hooking up lines for my EKG, lifting my shirt and making me tense up uncomfortably. If he notices, he doesn't acknowledge my behavior. He just continues talking. "More than friends really, but we were secret in our love for each other."

My heart hammers away in my chest, and the rhythm is just as chaotic on the monitor beside me. He eyes it and presses a few buttons. "What was she like?" I ask timidly, my throat feeling as if it's closing up from all the nervous energy radiating through me. Five years ago he lost someone…*five*! And it was a *secret* love.

He smirks, and that throws me off kilter. "*He* was everything. He was fun, ambitious…" his voice takes on a lilt of humor, "and sexy as hell."

"Oh," I say simply and dumbfoundedly, feeling a quick rise of embarrassment flush my cheeks.

He smiles knowingly. "Back then we were still in the proverbial closet, my dear, but I wish we would've had the courage not to be. After he passed, I decided to live my life fully…no more hiding from anything I wanted or desired."

The once fast-beating heart in my chest seems to stand still. *He*, he said he. Then it definitely wasn't Vicky. Dean's last statement warms something inside me like a spring day—like a new sprig reaching from the earth to catch the sunlight. "Did you…I mean, do you find that you can live your life how you choose now…are you happy?"

Dean walks toward the door. He pauses there and turns to look me over one last time. "Yes, I've found happiness and so much more."

A lone tear rolls slowly down my cheek as I nod to him. Dean walks out, and I deflate completely. His words clawing at my insides. I'm embarrassed for even being here now…accusing him in my head. Not only was that absolutely nerve-racking to play investigator, but now we're back to the drawing board. Dean Porter is eliminated. There's no way that man had anything to do with this.

A message on my phone has me scrambling to pull it free from my tight jean pocket. No sooner than I do, my breath hitches and clogs in me, threatening to suffocate. I read it twice to make sure I'm not seeing things.

Uncle J: Nova coming by, See you soon.

CHAPTER 16

Novalie

I left the hospital so fast, yanking off lead lines, nurses scrambling after me, but I made it to the parking lot and almost slid my car sideways leaving. The message I'd sent my uncle, responding to his, sitting there…unread on my phone like a stab to the chest. I tried to convey that I wasn't home—I'd be there shortly, but he hadn't seen it. I didn't even think he texted, or at least, he didn't use to.

Thanks to this ridiculous plan, I'll have a gigantic bill, but that's not even the worst of it. My retired detective uncle is on his way to my apartment. I burn the tires off my car, breaking several laws as I push toward home. Not stopping momentum forty minutes later as I park, slam the door and bolt for my shop. Heart thrumming, breath panting, I race through the back entrance and up the stairs two at a time.

Just as I reach the landing, I hear a faint knocking on the door and suck in a breath.

Uncle Jim stands there, casual as ever in his slacks and crisp button-down striped shirt. His short gray hair is styled forward and freshly trimmed, by the looks of it. I choke as I hear what sounds like footsteps in my apartment heading for the door.

"Uncle Jim!" I blurt out remarkably loud. Shaking uncontrollably, I listen as the footsteps inside my house falter and my uncle turns, confused to see me coming up behind him.

"Nova. Hello honey." He smiles in his sweet way but looks back to the door again…as if he *too* heard those steps. Then he drags his gaze back to me, cocking his head. "I got your missed calls and decided it's been too long since I laid eyes on my favorite niece."

I take a ridiculously long calming breath, still talking louder than normal, praying Soren hears us. "It *has* been too long…how've you been!"

His eyes take me in, my obvious nervousness that I'm failing to hide. "Is everything okay? And do you have company? I could come back another time."

My mouth opens and closes, but words take far too long to form. Finally, I manage a rational thought. I *need* him. I need his help with this. "No…no. Stay, please. I don't have company. I did need to see you," I say, as I give him a quick hug, inhaling the scent of Old Spice and mint.

"Oh, what about?" he asks, giving me a squeeze and seeming to forget the footsteps inside.

My nerves drop down a notch, and I move to the door, purposefully rattling the key and still speaking loud enough for Soren to get the point…*I hope.* "It's going to sound strange maybe, but I need help with a case." Opening the door, I peer inside quick, not seeing Ren anywhere, I open it for Uncle Jim to follow me in.

"A case? That *is* strange. Why are you looking into a case?" he asks, following me in.

Walking over to the couches, I wave my hand toward the one facing away from my bedroom, where I'm certain my ex-con is. "Have a seat, let me get you a drink."

"I'm good, thanks. What's this about Nova?" he asks, his voice now dripping with concern.

Plopping down across from him, I roll my tense shoulders. "I'm writing a book, like I always wanted to do."

"Oh, that's fantastic, sweetie…so it's on a case then?" He sits back, more comfortable now. He crosses an ankle over his opposite knee, his loafers shining as if freshly polished.

"That's right. So, you know the guy who recently escaped prison? Soren Marshall?" His face hardens, but he nods. "Well, I thought…what a perfect opportunity this would be. I want to write a story on his case…bring about new information if I can."

Jim looks skeptical. "I thought you were into romance and fantasy books. You want to write a nonfiction?"

I bring my hand to my neck, covering the redness I'm sure is blooming there as I lie to my sweet elderly uncle. "Yes. I find the case to be very interesting."

He nods, lips pursing in thought. "How can *I* help?"

My breath seems to come easier now as he settles into this plot of mine. "Well, I know you have a ton of pull in the police department. I also heard you volunteer on cases from time to time, helping rookie detectives." He grins as I continue. "The thing is, I'm not certain the man is guilty."

His head jerks back, brows wrinkling his forehead. "What makes you think that? He's convicted of killing his wife."

Now I smirk. "I seem to remember a case of yours where an innocent girl was taken from her parents after a car wreck. A wreck that was faked to kidnap her." He sighs but smiles as I continue. "She was rescued and hidden by Callon Wolfe, who…if I remember correctly was wanted for the murder of her parents and possible murder or kidnapping of her…but *you* helped solve that case. You cleared Callon's name. How are Maisy and Callon, by the way?" I ask, knowing I have him snared now.

"They're fine. Coming here soon actually for a visit. And Callon was the hero there, not me."

I wave a hand at his humble response. "If it wasn't for you, they would've had to live in exile. You cleared his name," I say again. "So, now I'm asking you to help me clear another's."

"What if you're wrong? What if I help you and he's guilty?" He readjusts himself, uncrossing his leg and leaning forward to pin me with those questioning eyes.

"If I'm wrong, I'll still write the book. It just won't have the preferred ending."

"Preferred?" His eyes flick up and down me curiously. "You'd prefer his innocence. Why?"

"It'd make a better story," I say steadily. He leans back into the cushions, inhaling deeply through his nose. I can feel that he's on the edge of submission, so I push with, "You know you can't sit idle and love a good mystery. Help me. *Please*?" I pout.

His soft chuckle makes me smile in return. "You're so much like your lawyer father…you know that? Never backing down…but yes, sure, I'll help you."

Leaping from the couch, I throw my arms around him and squeeze. "Thank you. You won't regret this! Love you, Uncle Jim!"

He exhales against my shoulder and finally pulls away to hold me at arm's length. "Tell me what you have so far and let's make a plan."

Dimples sink into my cheeks as I grin. "Okay…it's not much, but here it goes."

CHAPTER 17

Soren

I was almost to the front door after hearing the knock when I heard Nova's frantic voice speaking to someone. I'd paused and listened. It only took a few seconds to realize who she was talking to. I moved as quietly as possible to the bedroom, almost staying behind the door like when her friend Mel had shown up, but then remembering this is a detective coming into the house. What if he decides to scan the place or just use her restroom for that matter?

So here I sit, cramped up in her closet, praying Nova keeps him occupied.

I can still hear most of the conversation taking place, although some of it is muffled. She's not only convinced him to help her research the case, but by the sound of it, is laying out all her thoughts and knowledge of it to him. Pride swells inside me and an overwhelming feeling of gratitude for this woman. After the way I barged into her life, she should be turning me in, but no. Here she is, playing spy at a hospital and enlisting her detective uncle to help clear my name.

But that was the plan all along, wasn't it? I knew from the moment I saw her picture in the paper that she was the one—a good target, a good place to hide. A woman who just happens to have a famed bulldog detective for an uncle. Guilt is a fickle thing. It comes and goes in waves for me, but right now seems to be crashing into my chest like a raging sea against the side of a cliff. I've played them like chess pieces, never worried about the aftermath, never concerned with who's taken out along the way. Right now though, I let myself feel the acrid burn of guilt.

Their voices carry, and I can just make out parts of the conversation again. It pulls me back to the present…to the reason I'm here.

Nova's voice is firm and to the point as she says, "Here's what I need first…and don't get angry." Before Jim can say anything, she surges on. "I managed to get into Victoria Marshall's storage unit and found this."

A paper rattles, and Jim says, "Do I even want to know how?"

She laughs. "Same way I talked you into helping me. I told him about the book I'm writing."

I have to admit, she's a good liar.

Jim chuckles. "Go on."

"I need you to figure out who this number belonged to and when it was in use…or if it still is. And this key…it was with a…bank statement. It's a safe-deposit box key. If it was hidden, then maybe there's something to it. And I need you to see if you can get copies of the actual case files."

There's silence between them briefly, then he replies, "To do this, I'm going to have to pull some strings. This isn't a cold case, so it's not like I can volunteer to help solve it. It's a *closed* case, but I do have connections. I'll get you the information. And I know exactly who to ask about tracing this number. You remember Bowen, right?"

"Of course I remember Bo," Nova says. "I haven't seen him since I was younger, but I hear he and Callon are still best friends and he runs a techy company in Mexico, right?"

"Right, but he runs one here now too. It's discrete and paid to be that way. Everything he does for people is not always on the up and up…if you know what I mean."

She laughs. "Sounds like Bo. Okay, so have Bo trace the number, you get me some files, and in the meantime…I'll continue my own sleuthing."

"Listen, Nova." His tone now carries weight to it. "Cases can be dangerous. Even ones that you think are cut and dry. If this guy happens to actually be innocent. That means someone out there isn't, and that means someone out there is *very* lethal."

I suppress the guilt that floods me again; her silence speaks volumes. I imagine she's nodding her head in understanding, but also seriously contemplating what I've gotten her into.

"I understand, and I'll be careful. Promise," she replies.

They spend another half-hour discussing possibilities while my legs threaten to go numb in my balled-up position inside this damn closet. Then they catch up on life. At some point, I finally hear their quiet goodbyes and the click of the front door shutting. I don't move just yet though. I shift my legs underneath me and stand, feeling the thousands of pricks sting my limbs.

Just as I exit the closet, she's there, so close I almost bump into her. I'm not sure what I see in her gaze, but it has me cemented to the floor, unable to move an inch. Her hazel eyes travel over me slowly as she says, "I was so scared that you'd open that door thinking it was me."

Fear. That's what's in her eyes. She was worried about *me*.

Her head tilts, and she moves even closer, head now leaning back to look into my own eyes. "Did you catch most of that exchange?" I know I'm supposed to be answering her, but my eyes are locked onto her plump pink lips as she licks them nervously. "Did you hear anything that was said?" she asks again.

My stare moves to her imploring gaze, and I nod. "I heard enough. He's going to help you."

She smiles sweetly, and it threatens to make me drop to my knees. "No, he's going to help *us*," she emphasizes.

"Us. I like the sound of that." The huskily said words are out of my mouth before I realize the intent. I shake my head, mouth opening to rephrase that statement, but she grabs my hand and gives it a squeeze.

"I do too," she says softly.

I suck in a breath, heat rushing to places it has no business traveling. I lean my head to the side, cracking my neck nervously. Nova moves closer. My body stiffens, and it takes everything in me not to close that distance. I eye her, confused, but then she reaches up her hand, her finger gently touching the bridge of my nose. "It's almost healed." Her voice is jagged.

"Uh huh," is all I can manage. Pieces of her silken hair are falling loose from the ponytail to hang around her face. Unable to stop the urge to touch her skin, I reach up and smooth a lock of hair until it rests behind her ear, but my thumb drags lazily there, leaving a trail across her lovely cheek. Her face goes pink as she drops her own hand from her assessment of my nose, but she doesn't push away. I watch with amusement as goosebumps litter her arms. This magnetic pull between us is all-consuming. I can't deny that, or the fact that I can see it in her eyes, but it's wrong. The wrong circumstances, the wrong timing. It should've been all those years ago when she hustled me for a car, when things could've been normal. Back before my life was destroyed.

She brazenly leans closer, head tilted back, lips inviting as she smiles. All I have to do is lean down, and I could taste her for the first time. I reach up slowly, cupping her face with both of my hands, thumbs caressing her cheeks. She closes her eyes, bliss and nervous energy written all over her. Leaning in, I press my lips to her forehead. I sink my fingers into her hair, just to feel the silky texture this once. I hold her there, lips pressed against her head, everything in me screaming to take her…*take* this woman. Her chest is rising and falling in tandem with mine. The room seems to vanish, and it's just us there, holding on by a thread in this crazy life.

Gathering my wits, I swallow hard and release her. Cold seems to envelop me with the loss of her warm skin. I shake my head as I take a step back. "I'm sorry."

Indecision mixed with loss blankets her features. I'm scared I've gravely offended her, but her words rip me apart in a different, unexpected way when she says, "I know…me too." There's a tint of *regret* in them.

There's so much I want to say to her, but I settle on, "Thank you for everything you're doing…everything that you *shouldn't* be doing. Everything you don't have to do but are choosing to anyways."

Her eyes water, and a tear breaks free and slides down her cheek, shattering me completely. "I'm pretty stubborn, so you couldn't stop me now if you tried," she jests, but her smile falls flat. Her eyes rove over mine, looking, searching for something, then she pleads, "Tell me what you're thinking, Ren."

I'm surprised at my candor as the words fall from my mouth easily. "You know nothing about me, and I barged into your life by force. I…" Suddenly, I feel sick at the thought of how scared she must've been, of what a monster I probably looked like. "I'm thinking that I don't deserve your kindness."

Nova moves forward again, but I take a step back and she pauses, brows pinching together, as she says softly, "You were desperate. Desperate people do desperate things. I get why you had to do it this way. I'm on your side…until the very end. It's what *I'm* choosing."

I run a hand over my stubbled chin. "In any case, you've been through so much. You were lonely and stuck in the same everyday cycle—"

Her eyes darken as she cuts me off. "You think I'm *bored* with my life and *depressed* and that's why…" She doesn't finish, but I get her meaning. That's why we almost kissed just now. I know she would've melted into me had I closed the distance between our lips. Her eyes slice me up and down as she says quietly with venom and clarity. "I may have been devastated by what happened to me and living this day to day quaint life, Soren Marshall, but I'm not a simpering fool. I'm a grown woman who can make rational decisions or spontaneous ones if I choose. I know everything we're doing is uncertain. What I want *you* to know, Soren, is that I make my own decisions. Don't treat me like an invalid because of my circumstances."

She moves even closer, and I'm forced to stop as the bed hits the back of my legs. She leans in to me, close enough that I could spare myself this torment and take her mouth right now. Her eyes dip there, and it's clear how much she wants exactly that.

Nova takes in my firm jaw and tense stance before she adds, "I can't help you if you don't believe in yourself, and this won't work without some lines being crossed. I've already stepped over those lines and so have you. There's no going back. I am choosing this." She closes the last of the distance between us very slowly, with heated eyes and parted lips.

Before we can do something unfixable. I place my hands on her shoulders, halting her. It takes every bit of patience and restraint I have to stop myself. "Nova," I say in a low but warning tone.

Her eyes grow stoic. She turns without another word and walks out of the bedroom. I hear her footsteps in the kitchen before I breathe again. She is such a fierce little creature, and her absolute loyalty to my cause is unmatched. But the feeling I have when she's close to me…that has to stop. It's getting worse by the second. I'm on the edge, looking over at paradise, and preparing to jump. Does she realize how close I am to that fall? Does she even realize what she's doing to me by just *existing?*

I can only imagine how uncomfortable life with her is about to become. A *supernova*…I heard her friend call her that. What a fitting fucking title.

CHAPTER 18

Novalie

I stand in the kitchen, fingertips grazing my lips. That was bold, reckless, and I'm not sure what came over me. I can't deny that I was pushing him—closing that distance, in hopes of…I'm not sure what. Okay, maybe I am sure, but refuse to admit it aloud. I wanted him to kiss me. I was scared and worried for his safety the moment I got my uncle's text. It was ripping me to shreds and then seeing him…I don't know what happened. When his fingers had sifted through my hair to wrap around my head…it was like being lit by a match, but then his mouth pressed against my forehead, and while that act of gentleness caused my heart to somersault…I wanted *more*. But he stopped me. The thought is sobering and leaves me feeling wobbly, like a boat adrift in an endless ocean.

Maybe I was trying to prove my point in there, but did I? Or the more sordid question is, is he right? Do I feel a pull to this man because of loneliness and boredom? I place two pizzas in the oven as I ponder our short but strangely intimate interaction.

Several minutes later, his voice startles me from behind, making me jerk around. "What's wrong, princess? You seem out of sorts." His tone is cocky once again.

"Quit doing that," I snarl.

"Doing what?" He eyes me up and down.

"Sneaking up on me." I roll my eyes and turn away, walking to the fridge. I pull out a bottle of wine and proceed to find my wine opener and begin twisting.

"Need any help?" he asks, sounding amused at my struggle.

"Not from you," I bite out and then finally pop the cork. "There, see…all good, no man needed." His head cocks to the side, eyes taking in my now agitated state. Which I have no business being. Can he see right through me? See what's lying underneath my frustration. My face heats up.

"We're useful for some things," he says, baiting me, letting his voice drop low.

I stand a little straighter. How dare he bait me with filthy words after quite literally stopping my embarrassing come-on in there? Scowling his way, I release my hair from the tie. It was coming loose anyway after his hands had…ugh. I flip my hair over my shoulder, grinding my teeth. I smirk at him and say, "True, men make useful targets on a gun range."

He chuckles as I pour two glasses of wine without asking if he wants one, then set his down harder than necessary, sloshing a little over the edge. Smiling, I take a large gulp.

He seems to be suppressing a laugh as he says, "Feisty. I like it. But I was thinking more like useful in the bedroom." He leans forward, dips his finger in the wine and then drags it slowly over the rim before bringing it to his lips and licking the tangy liquid off. My mouth opens, eyes blazing, but I ignore him, taking another sip just as he says, "Did you know that immense clarity and peace flood the body after an orgasm?"

I choke on my drink and then bat my mouth with a napkin. Turning away from him to grab the pizzas, I pray he can't see the redness flooding my neck and creeping onto my face. I walked away in that bedroom, tail tucked between my legs, because he stopped that kiss from happening…and now he wants to get a rise out of me.

His mood changes are *pissing* me off.

Setting the spinach and feta pizzas on the cutting boards, I slice each one and purposefully lean into each stroke, knowing the view of my ass is torment. Then I smile as I say, "Oh, I do know. That's what my little pink friend is for." I'm rewarded when I hear *him* choke this time. Rolling my lips inward, I hold back the laugh scratching to come out.

Absolute silence greets me from behind, and when I turn to look at him…he's utterly still, eyes distant as if he's imagining my little pink…he clears his throat, Adam's apple bobbing. "What's wrong, Soren? You look out of sorts," I throw at him, glad that I'm not the only one feeling this immense frustration.

He licks his upper teeth, and a guttural sound emanates from him. "We need to call this a tie…whatever this is we're doing here, or else I'm taking you right here, right now on this counter and the hell with the consequences. Don't take my gentlemanly behavior in that room for my true desires."

My face falls, mouth hangs open in shock, and I fear I've lost all color. This little battle of wills we are waging…I've just lost it too. I want to scoff at his reference to gentlemanly behavior, but I can't even do that. My hand comes to rest at my throat, and I don't miss his eyes following it there. Pressing my shoulders back to feign strength, I nod. My voice is barely a whisper as I say, "Deal."

"Deal," he says back to me, but I can't help noticing the disappointment in the way he says it.

He clearly wanted me to buck him one more time. And I'd be lying if the thought didn't cross my mind. Picturing him grabbing me and taking me right here…shit, I need *more* than one bottle of wine. I snatch another from the fridge and begin twisting with gritted teeth.

Soren helps himself to pizza and more wine as I try to gain some composure after that. His voice snags my attention, bringing me back from the unlady-like thoughts swarming my senses. "What did you find out about Dean Porter?"

Dean…the nurse. I was so caught up in fear of Soren being seen by Uncle Jim, and then our heated interaction, that I forgot to mention that tidbit of my day. Releasing a breath, I say, "Good news and bad news." I continue as his brows rise with interest. "The good news is that your wife most definitely didn't have an affair with him. The bad news…he's a dead end."

"Are you sure?" he asks after another sip of wine.

"One hundred percent. He's gay…had a lover around the time Victoria died who he also lost tragically. He was very kind, and I can't see any reason he would've had for murdering her. Not that I know him personally, after a brief conversation, but he wasn't her lover. So, if you think she was unfaithful…it wasn't him."

I pause, watching his face change with the thoughts running around in his head, then ask, "Didn't you know her friends? Wouldn't she have mentioned details about Dean to you?"

Ren clenches his fists, popping the knuckles of his right hand, not meeting my eyes. "She never mentioned much about him, just that they were friends. By the time she was working with him, we were already having…communication issues."

"Mm," I hum in understanding. "Well, back to the drawing board. We need to look into her ex next. The abusive one. Or anyone else you can think of that might have wanted her gone." My mouth twists as an off-subject thought comes to me. "By the way, on Monday, I have to open my bookstore up like normal or my family is going to know something is up with me. Not to mention, if my uncle talks to my mom or dad, they will *know* I'm not sick."

He nods in agreement. "Tomorrow we can figure out a way to delve into the ex. His name is Jace Farrow, and sure Monday, I'll lie low while you work and we can…take it day by day."

I don't like the way his demeanor has shifted, as if we're failing horribly at this investigation, and worry tinges his face. "Ren," I say, making his eyes meet mine, "we *will* figure this out. We've only just begun." He nods and absentmindedly touches the bridge of his nose. My head tilts, and I shake my head as I ask, "I can't believe I haven't thought to ask this, but how did you escape?"

The smile that pulls up his strong jawline surprises me. "You really *never* watch the news, do you?"

Snorting, I shake my head.

"They were transporting me to the hospital." His grin widens. "I may have faked several episodes of seizures over the period of a few months…each time they took me to the hospital, I paid attention to how many guards were with me, the driver, everything." He takes a sip and then sets the glass back on the counter. "One of the times before, when they took me, I managed to steal a key to the cuffs. The idiot they had with me that day had scuffled with another inmate and broken the clip holding them on. Before anyone realized…those keys were gone. I stuck them under a seat in the transport van. They did a search of all the inmates who'd ridden in that van and the van itself but came up empty." He laughs. "There was a rip under one of the seats…perfect for a stash. I waited so long for the right day. One time, when I faked a seizure, they sat me in a whole different seat…so I couldn't even attempt it. And one of the times before that, an ambulance transported me."

Now I'm laughing as I ask, "How many times did you have 'seizures'?"

"Several." He swipes a hand through his hair. "Finally though, the day came. Instead of a full-blown seizure, I told them I felt faint, like it was going to happen again to make sure they didn't call an ambulance. They stuck me in the van…in the *exact* seat I'd been waiting for. They latched my chains, and we were off. As soon as we were far enough away from the prison, I began shaking and fell over. It wrenched my hands into an awkward position, but I managed to pull off the ruse long enough for the guard to bolt to the front and stop the driver. I had a few measly seconds to get that lock undone."

Leaning forward, imagining it in my mind, I ask, "What happened next?"

He shrugs, looking proud. "I got them off, managed to take my guard by surprise and wrap the chain around his neck, his back to my front." He pauses, eyeing my shocked face, and his features soften. "I didn't hurt him…too bad." My mouth flounders, but he keeps going. "I had his gun just as fast, and when we spun around, the second guard released the taser."

"Oh my God, so he was about to tase you and it hit the man you were holding?" I ask, pizza perched halfway to my mouth in my hand that's frozen.

"Yeah. I ran forward toward the front of the transport van and smashed the shaking guard that I had in a chokehold into the other, toppling us all to the aisle floor. The driver was already outside the van and had stepped away to call for an ambulance…not knowing what was happening inside."

"And you what? Just ran? How did they not catch you?" I ask.

He laughs low. "The tased cop was out cold from hitting his head on the way down, the cop under him was held up long enough for me to climb over them and run." He shakes his head at the memory. "I didn't account for the driver, who by this point was headed for the van door as I ran out. I was too close for him to pull a weapon. We almost collided. He swung on me with a hell-of-a punch." He gestures to his nose, and I grin, amused. "I caught him with the butt of the pistol I was still holding and he dropped, but the guard behind me was up and coming through the van fast."

I bite my lip nervously, as if this is all happening right before my eyes.

He takes a deep inhale and leans back in the chair. "I ran for the road, for the traffic, hoping that the guard wouldn't shoot toward innocent people driving past. There was a forest on the opposite side of the highway, and I didn't stop moving, not when cars almost clipped me, not when I heard shouts, not even when I heard gunfire."

He watches me carefully. Maybe to see if I'll have a more feminine-feared reaction to this, but he finds me enamored with his story and continues. "I made it through the woods that led to another road. I'm not sure how long that took, but it felt like forever. I could hear sirens in the distance and knew they would be all over me in an instant. I knew they'd also have roadblocks." He shakes his head in awe. "I hid behind an old oak tree on this snaking back road. As luck would have it, along came a truck hauling a horse trailer."

"You didn't," I say, smiling. "You snuck in with the horses!"

He winks at me, making my damned toes curl as he says, "Slipped right inside when he was stopped to make a left turn. Me and that damn horse became very acquainted for about thirty minutes. I decided to call him lucky…it fit the situation."

With my mouth full of pizza, I have to cover it to hide my laugh and not choke. After I swallow it down thickly, I ask, "Where did you end up?"

"A farm not too far from the city. I could hear a man get out, talking on his phone. I waited until his voice trailed off before I snuck out…after loving on Lucky, of course." Ren takes a sip.

I suck on my front teeth and then make a tsking sound. "The clothes that didn't fit you. The boots that looked too small the day you…*found* me." I see him grimace at the way I say, 'found me.' "You stole that man's clothes, didn't you?"

He shrugs. "From a clothesline…I took those and some veggies from his garden…and horse blankets. Anything I could find to get me by a few days."

I look at him knowingly now. "You needed time to find me." It's not a question.

Ren nods. "That's that. I hid out in the woods for two nights and in the abandoned building across from you for…a couple days, before deciding it was time to make my move." He downs the wine and blows a tired breath through his nostrils as he says, "It was like fate was finally riding shotgun with me that day I escaped, because *everything* that happened…had to happen the way it did. Or I would be back in prison or…*dead*."

"Bob Ross happy accidents," I whisper through a soft smile.

His forehead creases. "What?"

Downing the last of my wine as well, I lick my lips but can't bring my eyes to his as I reply. "It's something I've always said—always *believed* in. I used to watch Bob Ross's painting shows for relaxation. Bob always said that there were no mistakes, only happy accidents. I thought, and still think, that's the best way to look at life. Levi…" I clear my throat before continuing. "He said that we make our path…that there are no accidents, but it still made him laugh when I'd say it."

Soren's face has gone slack. His breathing is slow and calculated when I look at him, and his eyes are intense. The blue-gray of them glow under the kitchen light. "I love that Nova. It's a beautiful way to think about life."

All of a sudden, my throat feels clogged, but I hold back the water threatening to leave my eyes. "Thanks Ren. You being here…it's a happy accident."

"As long as it's happy…that's all that matters," he says softly.

"And I meant what I said earlier," I add. "We've both crossed a line that we can't retract from. I'm in this till the end with you. If…and I mean *if* we cannot clear your name. I'll help you get passage to another country of your choosing." The thought brings an unexpected pang to my chest. "I promise."

Inhaling, Soren leans onto the counter. His stare penetrates every part of me as he gives me that breath-taking side smile. "*You* are the real happy accident, Novalie."

CHAPTER 19

Soren

It's the last day before Novalie has to spend most of her time working. We've searched the internet for hours since we woke this morning and ascertained several things about the elusive Jace Farrow. For one, he's not a fan of social media. We couldn't find any accounts with that name that matched anyone resembling him. I could still vaguely recall what he looked like from past pictures of the two of them together that I found in an old box of hers. And none of the guys we've found on Facebook or Instagram have looked anything like him. We also scrolled through the jail logs for our county and the surrounding ones and found nothing.

"Damn." I huff out a breath and stand from the couch, stretching my back. "I thought for sure that guy would have mug shots somewhere on the internet considering he abused women."

Nova hums to herself, but keeps looking, then adds, "Well, he could be dead by now, right? Let me check obituaries."

"Good thinking," I tell her. Walking to the kitchen, I pour us a couple glasses of orange juice and pull the chocolate chip muffins from the oven. Taking a plate with four on it, I bring it back to where she sits, hunched over her laptop. "Here, stop and eat something."

Nova reaches for the muffin without looking up and continues her search. It brings a smile to my face watching her concentrate. She's sunk into the couch cushions, legs crossed with a pillow over them to prop the laptop on. Her messy bun is…messy, but also cute.

When we parted ways last night, I was fairly certain I'd never get sleep again. Everything that we said to each other, along with how close we came to doing something she might regret, played through my head like a broken record. Somehow, I did sleep. I woke up refreshed, invigorated, ready to take on the day…and then she walked out of her room in her silken sleep shorts and tank with bare legs, and I'm pretty sure there's no bra under that top.

It's been…*difficult* to concentrate, to say the least. Even just sitting beside her, I can smell the shampoo in her hair from her shower last night, and the scent mixes with the mint of her breath. But here I am…trying my best to concentrate on the task at hand.

"There's no one in the obituary logs by that name…from around here anyways. He could've moved or something. Ooo, I could check county tax records. Those are up-to-date and readily available." She says her thoughts aloud through a bite of muffin, mumbling her words.

I snicker and throw her words back at her. "You're a real slob, you know that?"

She raises her glare to me, swallowing hard. "Maybe your disgusting behavior is rubbing off on me."

I purposefully take a bite and mumble back, "Good. You needed to lighten up, nerd."

"Ugh," she groans, turning back to the screen, mumbling to herself, "*barbaric ass.*"

Plopping down roughly beside her, I scoot close enough that my gray jogging pants are grazing her bare leg and see her tense slightly. "You like the caveman type, huh?" I ask playfully.

"I like the strong, silent type," she retorts, not looking at me.

I repeat her words mockingly under my breath. "*I like the strong, silent type.*" She doesn't fight back with me, and that makes me turn to her. Her eyes have blown wide, and her mouth slack—lips parted. "What?" I ask, leaning over her shoulder.

She turns, tilting up her head to meet my eyes, putting our faces far too close together when she says, "I found him."

Gingerly, I take the computer from her, looking over the unpaid taxes listed in the county log. There's only one Jace Farrow, and he has an unpaid tax on land. It's only about a month behind, but it's there and it's not very far from the city limits of Asheville. "This could be him," I agree. "Can't be many people with the name Jace, right?"

"Surely not," Nova agrees. "Plus, even if it's like his dad or something, we can use this to find him. It's a start…at least until we get those case files and find out about that odd phone number."

Nodding. I take her notebook and pen, writing down the address. Then we spend a little time mapping out the property on Google Maps. We split up after that, both taking turns in the bathroom getting dressed, and then we meet back up in the kitchen. Nova is in a breathtaking white sundress and heels, her hair down and sleek. It makes me do a double take and wish that I had something better to wear than Walmart jeans and a black tee and hoodie.

I'm just about to ask her why she looks like that when, just then, Nova's phone goes off. She grabs it and gasps as her eyes rove over the screen.

"What is it?" I say, rushing to her side.

"It's my uncle." Her face changes to a grimace as she turns the phone to me.

Uncle J: I didn't want to mention this yesterday but I just want you to know that it's okay if you've moved on. You don't need to hide that from family. I saw the manly toiletries on your table. Really, it's okay, honey. We love you and want nothing more than your happiness.

"Wow," I say, holding back a smile. "That man doesn't miss anything."

Nova covers her face with a hand. "I even remembered to toss out the old, stolen boots of yours and keep everything else put away. Ugh, I guess I forgot that I bought more for the bathroom."

I move to stand in front of her and pull her hand from her face and take the phone to place on the counter. Then, I tip her chin up and flick her nose, making her scowl. "At least they think you're just shacking up with someone and have no idea he's a hardened criminal."

She shoves me lightly. "Church it up all you want, he's going to demand to know more, and I'm sure he's had a talk with my father by now."

"Let's deal with one tragedy at a time…okay? Let's save that for another day." She nods, and I add, with a look down her body, "Why are you dressed like that?"

She gives me a coy look and saunters past me to her purse on the counter, sifting through it, and says over her shoulder, "I find that this look creates loose tongues far better than jeans and shirts."

Leaning against the counter beside her, I watch as she pulls out a tube of pale pink lipstick and applies it slowly. I ignore the blast of heat that soars through me at the sight. "What do you think you're doing? What's the plan here because I don't remember agreeing to one."

"That's because we didn't discuss one," she chirps, flitting her hair over a shoulder. "*I* am going to find out who this Jace Farrow is."

I'm off the counter in an instant, taking her arm and spinning her to face me. "There's no way in hell you're doing this alone. We have no idea what that guy is capable of, and you're not traipsing around town…" my eyes trail her body again, "looking like that around a guy who puts his hands on women."

She doesn't jerk away from my touch but also refrains from backing down. "I have to do this alone, Ren. You know that. You can't be seen. It's too risky."

I back away from her and move to the bedroom, grab my boots, and shuck them on quickly. She eyes me from the open doorway as I find her college hat and aviators. Walking back to her, I smile and wave a hand at the door. "I'm going with you. Just try and stop me, princess."

Indecision laced with fear has her fidgeting, but she groans angrily after a few seconds and snatches her purse off the counter. "Fine, but if you're caught...I'm going to say you *forced* me to do this, and...that you're a pervert."

I can't help the smile that cracks my face. "Good. That's what I want you to say, and I'll make sure I tell the police that you liked it."

She stomps pettily to the door, ranting the whole way. "This...ugh, *you*...are such an idiot."

"An idiot, maybe, but I'm also not a piece of shit who'd let you do this alone."

My words hit her, and she sighs, turning to me. "For real. No jokes this time. If you're seen. You run, Soren...don't look back. I can handle the aftermath of questions. Stay low in the car and..." Her expression grows weary. "Just don't be seen, okay?"

I know she said no jokes, but right now, I want to see her smile. This look of fear on her tears at my heartstrings. So I say, "I know your life would go back to being boring without me, princess, so I'll be careful."

Her head tilts animalistically, eyes narrowing. Her mouth opens to scold me, but I interrupt her with a hand to her jaw. I lean in fast and place a chaste kiss to her cheek, effectively shutting down her thought process like I planned. I relish in her stunned silence as I open the door for her and say, "By the way, you look ravishing, my little supernova."

CHAPTER 20

Novalie

Soren makes me want to murder him. His playful, chipper attitude as we walk into the unknown, grinds on my nerves…or at least until he saunters into the parking garage and lays eyes on my antique car. His pace slows as if he's walking through a thick barrier. I stop completely to watch, simultaneously eyeing our surroundings to make sure we're alone. His muscular back in the black hoodie he's wearing seems to tense, shoulders rolling once. The black boots I bought him scuff the concrete floor when he comes to a stop beside it. Ren's hand reaches out tentatively, stroking the deep blue paint along the hood as he shifts around it *very* slowly. His jaw flexes beneath the hood pulled over his hat and head.

I can only imagine the memories surfacing for him. My chest aches at the sight. Walking over to him, he startles slightly when I rest a hand on his shoulder and turn him to face me. "Are you okay?" I ask.

A curt nod is all I get before he swallows hard and moves from my touch. My hand falls to my side as I watch his face change to nothing. Without a word, he opens the passenger-side door and slides in. I falter for a moment, feeling too much for this man I barely know. Sorrow, fear…it collides within me, almost making me second guess everything we're doing. But I shake it off, move to the driver's side, and slip in.

He's leaned way back in the seat with a hand stroking his lower jaw when I turn to him. "Are you good? Want to talk about it?"

A worn exhale leaves his nose. "I'm fine. It's just…it's been a long time since I laid hands on my work. Remodeling cars was something I loved—something I was proud of. And it was stripped from my life along with every fucking thing else."

"I'm sorry, Ren," I say sincerely. "I can't imagine what you're going through…what you've lost."

Surprisingly, his cheek pulls into a sad smile as he whispers, "Yeah…you can."

I have to choke back the emotion coiling in me with his words. He *is* right, though. I don't just imagine it; I know what losing an entire life feels like. In a way, my world was also stripped from me the day Levi died.

Cranking the car, I let it idle for a bit. She's old and doesn't like quick starts. Keeping my eyes forward, I ask, "You sure you want to go with me? You could always hang back here. It'd be safer."

"I'm coming with you." His voice is flat and firm.

I nod once and shift into reverse. I don't miss the way he fingers the dash. It's like he's marveling at every detail. When we pull out of the garage, he drops his hand, leans back again and tucks his hood lower, then slips on the aviators. We ride in silence for a few minutes, both of us hardly breathing. Once we hit the freeway, I exhale forcefully.

Breaking the silence, I glance at Ren and ask, "Tell me about yourself."

His eyes dart to me, both brows raised in question. "What do you want to know, princess?"

A groan pulls from my chest. "Stop calling me that…and I don't know, tell me about your past, or your family. Just tell me about *you*. What makes you who you are today?" I don't look at him but can feel his stare.

"Okay. I was fostered growing up," he says first. My head snaps to him and back to the road, but he keeps going. "It's not what you think. They were great parents…not those shitty ones you hear about on the news. My birth mother put me up for adoption when I was born because she was apparently very young and irresponsible. She didn't know or say who the father was either. My foster parents, Jolene and Tom, were great. They gave me a good life—made sure I went to college. I ended up in auto mechanics. It's all I ever cared about doing, anyway. I used to help Dad fix up his old El Camino when I was a kid. He nurtured my love for old cars and…I ran with it as soon as I could grow my credit enough to get a loan."

I smile at the idea of a young and ambitious Soren Marshall, but then I remember something Soren said once.

"I thought you grew up around a lot of women…the ones that had you watching old Julia Roberts movies?"

Soren's mouth tips upward in a wry grin. "Ah, that would be my mother's clucking hen group of book enthusiasts who were really just *wine* enthusiasts. They took breaks from book club nights to have movie nights."

My mouth cracks open with a laugh. "So your mom was a book nerd too, huh?" He shrugs when I look his way, and I notice the softened features of his face—the memories filling him with light. "Your parents…they sound wonderful," I say, trying to hide the emotion crackling in my voice.

"They were," he says back with sadness tinging the statement.

"Were?" I ask, even though I know I shouldn't press him.

"Yeah. They were older when they became foster parents…old enough to be grandparents. They were in their fifties at the time. They'd never had kids of their own and, late in life, decided that's what they wanted. So, they fostered me for a few years and then finalized the adoption when I was still really young. They passed away a year apart. Dad died of colon cancer, but he'd lived a good long life, and we were by his side at the end. I'm sure it was a broken heart that took my mother away. She used to sit by his grave every night of the week…just talking to him, even when she could barely walk."

An embarrassing sniffle comes from me, and I quickly wipe the tears stitching their way down my cheeks. I flinch when Ren's calloused hand is on my face, thumbing away the moisture there. "You crying for me, princess?" he asks softly.

Composing myself, I take in a shaky breath. "I cry easily," I say matter-of-factly. His hand moves from my face, but I feel his gaze penetrating from the side.

"I think you just feel everything more deeply than others. It's nice…honest even," he says.

My brows pinch together as I steal a glance his way. "What do you mean…honest?"

"I mean, you aren't shy about showing your emotions. You don't hide it. That's honest," he says.

A small laugh bubbles up. "I thought I was a soppy mess and a weakling for breaking down so easy. I like your take on it better."

He smiles at that. "You're most definitely not a weak woman, Nova. Do you think anyone else would be doing what you are doing right now…for me?"

I shrug. "I haven't felt very strong in some time."

He studies me for a beat, almost uncomfortably so, before he asks, "What happened to your husband? You never told me."

"You never asked," I toss back at him. "*And* I would've thought you already knew based on the fact that you stalked me out specifically."

He chuckles. "I stalked you out because of who your uncle was and…"

My head shifts to catch a glance of him, brows raised in question. "And?" I ask.

He shakes his head, clearing his throat. "I'll admit that your uncle was the help I needed to find, but…it was you. Your face kept me going. Sorry if that sounds creepy, but I knew if my plan ever came to fruition, more than anything, I needed to see you in person. The woman with the sad eyes on the front of that paper."

I feel like I can't breathe; air catches, suspended for a moment in my lungs, and I can't face him. I'm not sure how to feel about that. A picture forms in my head of Soren in a dark cell, my article on the wall. Eventually, I breathe and give him a small smile before bringing the subject away from his words and back to his original question. Gripping the steering wheel hard, I say, "Levi was killed in a car wreck." I still don't look his way, but he's watching me. I see him in my peripheral vision. When he doesn't respond or ask anything else regarding that day…I feel an overwhelming urge to speak up—to release what I've been holding back for so long. So I do. "Levi wasn't the only one who died that day."

"What?" Ren asks, confused. "Who was with him?"

A humorless laugh leaves my mouth, and then a frustrated sigh. "I've yet to talk with anyone other than Mel about this. I blatantly refused to discuss it with my parents…or with his parents." I pause and glance his way, and he's waiting patiently. Turning back to the road, I curse under my breath. "There was a woman named Alina who was in the car with him." I can hear Ren shift in the seat uncomfortably. I keep going because I want to get it out of me—rip it off like a Band-Aid. "I'll never know the full story, but the gist of it was found on their phones. He was having a relationship with her…she was one of his patients actually—went to the same gym too."

"He was a psych doctor…right?" Ren asks carefully.

"Yes…he was a psychiatrist," she corrects me. "Her family and her husband blamed Levi for her death, and for seducing her. Levi's family blamed Alina in the same way."

Ren's voice is smooth, soft and gentle when he asks, "Who did *you* blame?"

I square my shoulders and put on the turn signal to take a right off the freeway. A blank smile tugs at my cheek. When I come to a stop sign, I look at him. "Me," I say. "I blame myself."

"Why would you blame yourself?"

Pulling onto the next road, I shift gears, taking off faster than I should—anger swelling in me…threatening to combust. "Because Soren. I *am* to blame. I was an idiot who tried to do everything perfect…everything to his liking. I loved him without question. Doted on his every need. Gave him what he wanted and shoved back everything that *I* wanted." I slap the steering wheel with my palm. "I should've known, right? Aren't women supposed to know that their man isn't being loyal? And the worst part is that everyone still referred to him as being perfect. You should've heard them at the wake…it was *fucking* absurd."

"Don't get pissed at me over what I'm about to say." I glance at him—at his curious demand—but he keeps going. "You did the same thing when you spoke about him to me. You put him on a pedestal…one he never earned."

My mouth flounders, but nothing comes out because he's right. Finally, after a few seconds, I nod. "You're right. Deep down, I've been trying to find the good in what we had. My soul couldn't take the rejection I've been harboring. Because that's what it was—pure rejection. To have the person you love the most in the world…choose another, it's debilitating. And I can understand your loss of everything since you've been locked away, because I *too* felt like I was locked away."

Ren's hand moves to my cheek to clear away more frustrating tears. His voice is ragged enough to bring me to my knees when he says, "You're free now, princess. There's nothing holding you back from doing the things you want. You were caged for your married years, not cherished the way you should've been. Any man would be lucky to have the chance to be in your presence…sorry to be straight with you, but Levi was a fucking fool. You were broken after his death in more ways than just from loss. *But* you're free now. You see that, right?" His hand drops, and his voice softens. "You shouldn't let him hold you back from the grave."

Nodding and releasing a breath, I let my shoulders sag, the relief hitting me like a freight train. It's like being untangled from barbed wire, one jagged, sharp slice at a time. "Thank you for that. I needed to hear it," I tell him as we make the last turn toward the land we found listed on the county tax website.

"Anytime," is all he says.

Just then, the address comes into view, and it is *far* from what I expected.

CHAPTER 21

Novalie

A sprawling farm that could rival a Better Homes and Garden cover unfolds before us on the right side of the road as we drive slowly past. An old, remodeled, two-story farmhouse sits far back off the road with a porch that wraps all the way around it, ferns hanging in the center of each break in the balusters. A yellow labrador retriever bounds through the neatly cut lawn with two little boys chasing it—faces lit up with laughter.

Beside the home is a four-car garage with one door open, a new Chevy diesel truck parked inside. On the left are rows and rows of grapevines, and past that there's a massive barn that could house twenty horses easily. As we continue, we see a garden and greenhouses manicured to perfection, and just as we're nearing the end of the property, there's a farm stand that sits close to the road. A sign that reads *Farm Fresh Eggs and Produce* hangs atop the beautifully crafted wooden stand, and ivy vines grow in unison along either side.

"This place is gorgeous," I murmur as I slow my car to a near stop. At the last second, I see a man walking toward the stand from one of the rows of corn. Hitting the clutch, I downshift and pull us over onto the side of the road.

Soren slinks down into the seat when the car stops. "What are you doing?"

"Look over there." I point to the man in the distance. "Is that him?"

Ren peeks out. "Shit…yeah, that's the guy."

"Are you sure?" My brows snap together.

Ren looks again, waiting for the man to close some of the distance, then he nods once. "That's him. I remember his face."

"Okay then," I say confidently. "You lie low. I'm going to…*buy some fruit*."

"Nova—"

I interrupt him. "It's going to be fine. I've got this."

Before he can stop me, I'm out of the car. Shutting the door quickly, I smooth my dress and head for the stand. Giving Ren a quick glance, I find his intense stare already on me. Looking away, I sashay over. I parked just far enough past the stand so that, even if he sees a passenger, they'd be no way of seeing who it is.

Stopping amongst a pallet full of watermelons, I feign interest—tapping on a few and inspecting the yellow sides. Before long, a voice comes from behind me.

"Can I help you with anything?" the man says.

I spin, giving him a beaming smile when I meet his gaze. Jace Farrow is quite handsome. His blondish-brown hair is trimmed short, a little haphazard on top as if he's raked a hand through the sweaty strands several times today. His brown eyes are lined with lighter lashes, and he has a short beard that is a mix of brown, blond, and even red. He leans against the frame of the stand, his white shirt clinging to him from the heat of the day, and his dark jeans showing years of wear.

"I'm not sure yet. I saw your stand as I was passing by and…well, it's just lovely," I say.

"Thanks. Have a look around. If you have any questions, let me know." He stands fully and walks over to a pile of egg cartons and begins stacking them neatly. His eyes keep trailing over to my car. "Is that a seventy Nova?" He pauses his work as he asks.

Purposefully, I walk to the other side of the produce, blocking part of his view. "It is. You know your years. My name's No…Nola, by the way," I stutter out, almost saying my real name and not even sure why it would matter if I did, but suddenly I feel like a spy in a movie in need of a false alias.

He keeps working but replies, "I'm a big fan of the sixty-nine and seventy model muscle cars. And I'm Jace. Jace Farrow."

"Nice to meet you, Jace. Your place is incredible. Are those your kids in the yard over there?" I ask, making polite conversation.

"Yeah, those are my twins. They're almost four now. I have a baby girl too, six months old." He chuckles. "Time flies."

I look around for any way to feel this guy out, and my eyes snag on the rows of flowers for sale. "That it does," I reply. "These begonias are nice." I finger the delicate blooms. "Did your wife grow these in the greenhouses? I've always wanted a greenhouse of my own."

He looks over a shoulder at me as he moves some crates around. "Yeah, she handles all of the greenhouse work, and I typically handle the gardens."

"Mm. Have you guys lived here long? I never knew this was out here. Your farm's beautiful."

"We've been here about four years now. It was my father's. He passed and left it to me. We added the greenhouses and the grapevines, but he already had the barn and gardens going."

"Oh, I'm sorry for your loss."

He shrugs nonchalantly. "It's okay. He was older, had health issues. We love it here, though. I was tired of city life."

"You lived in the city?" I ask, taking a basket and putting some peaches inside.

"For several years, but it wasn't for me. I met Marley, and that was that. We decided to try and find a place in the country, but then everything happened with my dad, and well, I guess things just happen how they're supposed to."

"Happy accidents," I mutter too low for him to hear me. In his case, a sad but happy accident. He lost his father but gained a home for his children. I have to mentally shake my head. I'm here to find out if this man is *homicidal,* and I'm already gaining empathy. My damned heart can't be trusted. How am I supposed to figure out if he is in fact a killer within this casual conversation?

Placing several things on the counter, I shift my attention to the house where I see, what I assume to be his wife, holding a baby in her arms and smiling at her chaotic sons in the yard. Seeing his beautiful family, I feel the twinge of guilt rising, but then I remember the man in my car and how much he needs my help. It hits me then…a way to get some feel for Jace's character.

"Jace," I say, walking toward him, squinting my eyes as if in recognition. "I thought you looked familiar…but then shook it off, but now I remember your name. Jace Farrow…didn't you date Victoria Styles?" I ask in wonder.

His body goes rigid, face falling. I watch his throat work as he gives me a once-over. Chills break out over my skin, but I manage to keep my face kind—inquisitive. Jace sets down the crate he's holding and drags his eyes away from me. His voice changes to one of suspicion. "How did you know Vicky?"

My heart leaps into my throat. He's not denying dating her. Rolling my lips inward and squinting as if in deep thought, I say, "I can't remember the year, but it was a long time ago now when I worked with her at the hospital. I was a CNA at the time; we became work friends. I recall a picture she showed me of you."

He eyes me warily now with an obvious amount of distrust in his mannerisms. "Really? Cause I seem to remember almost all of Vicky's 'friends' and I don't remember anyone named Nola."

I'm taken aback by that, my cheeks reddening, heart racing a bit now. He definitely has animosity buried inside him about Victoria. "Well, you know how work friends are. We laugh and gossip, but don't actually hang out after work." Nervously, I begin a slow walk past him, gathering fruits and vegetables along the way. "I didn't know her personal life that well, just remembered a picture of you…her boyfriend." Carefully, I tiptoe into this part of the conversation, hoping it doesn't anger him further. "We were all heartbroken after what happened to her."

He watches me, eyes narrowing. "Are you a reporter?"

Mouth agape, I inhale as if offended, keeping my hands busy, so he doesn't see the trembling there. Brows drawn together, I turn to him fully. "Why would you ask that?"

He steps closer to me, and I take one back, beginning to regret this entire plan. From this new position we're in, Jace's back is to my car…he can't see, but I can. Ren has opened the door, stepped out, shoulders tensing for a fight. He takes one step toward us right when Jace glances toward his house, looking at his wife as if to make sure she's far away. In that second that he's not looking at me, I very subtly shake my head at Ren. *Please stay there*, I mentally beg.

Jace turns those untrusting eyes back on me. "Because you aren't the first. Ever since her husband escaped prison, people have been hounding my family, wanting past stories of us, wanting any *fucking* thing they can print and make a dollar off of." He looks me up and down. "And I'm not buying what you're selling, lady. I knew Vicky's friends, however few there were, and you weren't one of them. Now, if you're finished here, you can leave the cash in the box by the table."

He storms away, never seeing how close Ren was getting, never realizing the danger lurking in those stormy eyes. But I see it. Soren would've ripped this man apart right here if he'd taken one more step too close to me. I nod my thanks to Ren and watch him back toward the car, never taking his eyes off of Jace's back as he heads for the garden. With shaky limbs, I reach into my dress pocket, pulling out more money than the produce in my basket is worth, and dropping it in the slitted box. My heels sink through the grass and back to the road at a rapid pace. Ren is already back in the car when I shove the basket onto the back seat and smooth my skirt, sliding in quickly.

"What the *hell* was that?" Ren growls out. "What was that son of a bitch saying?"

"It's okay, Ren. He thought I was a reporter, that's all." Ren's brows pinch together, but the anger doesn't reside.

I feel him in on what was said as we take off toward home. He lets it sit inside him for several minutes before saying, "His anger doesn't bode well for me. Something's there…under the surface of that kind of hatred."

Nodding repeatedly, I add, "I agree. Something happened with him and Victoria for it to fester."

"She swore he was abusive. Said she filed a restraining order against him more than once before she left him for good and met me."

Pursing my lips, I ponder that for a minute. "I'll get Uncle Jim on that too then. He can get records for me, and we can find out the details of those restraining orders. Plus, he should have copies of the case files this week, and Bowen's supposed to be finding out anything he can on the phone number."

My eyes drift to Ren and then back to the road. "Thank you."

I feel his eyes on me as I drive when he asks, "For what?"

"For coming to my rescue. I'm just glad nothing happened back there. But thanks." I chance a glance at him quickly, finding his stunning eyes dancing with promise.

"He wouldn't have gotten one hand on you, love."

The way he says that one word has fire spreading through me. My mouth goes dry, but I somehow manage to respond. "I have no doubt of that."

Ren nibbles his lower lip, leans back in the seat and pulls back on the aviators that he must've discarded earlier. His voice is low and dark as he says, "I'd never let anyone hurt you, princess."

In that moment, I more than just believe him…I feel the certainty of it like a sealed fate.

CHAPTER 22

Soren

Back at the bookshop, we make sure that no one's around before I take the produce from Novalie and follow her inside. My mind's been a raging beast ever since we left that prick's farm. I've tried to keep it to myself, to not let her see how much it scared me…her putting herself in danger like that. True, she was likely in no danger in the broad daylight with his family nearby, but still, she did that for me, and I didn't like the way he was acting.

My knuckles go white from gripping the basket handle so hard as I watch her walking in front of me. The sun catches her hair, creating an auburn fire. It shines and cascades down her spine, flowing with her every step, the white dress flowing with it in a dance. Her smooth legs, calves taut in her heels, have me biting my lip. *Damn*...she's like a force of nature.

Taking the stairs, her heels and my boots create an echo as we ascend. She giggles and looks over her shoulder. "I called myself Nola back there...you'd think I could've come up with something...not so close to my actual name. I'm a terrible undercover agent." She laughs again, but her footsteps slam to a stop on the landing, and I bump into her, steading her with a hand. My own laughter fizzles out.

"Wha—" I start but the word falls flat as I look over her head toward her apartment door.

"*So*, this is the slob...right? The reason you're still ignoring me and your family? I think I deserve an introduction considering I *am* your best friend," Melina says with a thick amount of sass.

My hood is down, sunglasses off. I don't breathe or move. The air is thick with tension, and most of it seems to be pouring off Nova. Melina's long brown curls spring as she shakes her head, then adjusts her fringe purse and crosses her arms. Her large golden brown eyes hover over Novalie, taking her appearance in before those demanding eyes sight in on me. Her forehead pinches, then goes flat, eyes widening with dread and...*recognition*.

She fucking knows who I am.

Nova sees her face change too and opens her mouth to say something when Melina loses it. Her manicured finger jabs the air in my direction. "*You*! I *know* who you are. You're the murderer that escaped prison! *Holy fucking hell*!" Her blazing eyes dart to Nova. "*Please* tell me I'm wrong. For the love of everything holy...TELL ME I'M WRONG, NOVA!" Melina's voice rises to a screeching pitch that has Nova flinching.

I take a step, moving to Nova's side. Her fear is a palpable thing—dense like fog on this stuffy landing. I nudge her gently, bringing her out of her frozen state of mind, and say, "I see your friend *does* watch the news, unlike you."

Mel looks at me scathingly, clear fury on her face at my comfortable inside joke with Nova.

Nova breathes *finally* and speaks to Melina as if calming a wild animal. "You don't understand Mel. And we," she gestures between herself and I, "can explain. It's a crazy story." She smiles flatly.

It's not failed my notice that Melina had shifted a little every few seconds, her hand now resting precariously on her purse, fingers out of view. Just as I realize what's likely inside that purse, she says calmly, "You need to step away from him, Nova…*now*."

"Mel…" Nova moves a step closer to her. "Don't you dare! You need to hear us out."

Her furious eyes meet mine and stay there, but she speaks only to Nova. "Do you understand what he did? He killed his wife. Slaughtered her and chopped up her body somewhere. He's the *worst* kind of monster…so whatever bullshit you're trying to spin won't work." She looks back to her friend, tears now brimming her eyes. "However…or whatever he did to get to you is only because he's taking advantage of a woman living alone…manipulating you. Can't you see that? Not to mention, you're now an accomplice."

Slowly, I've taken a few steps forward each time Nova has. Only a couple feet separate us from Mel. Her hand has slipped deeper inside her purse, and cold dread coats my stomach. Nova speaks to her, but I can't hear anything else as I see the glint of metal peek over the rim of her purse. Her arm lifts at the same moment that I strike. The basket of produce drops to the ground, food flying everywhere as my hand lashes out. I snatch the end of her gun simultaneously slamming her wrist with my other hand. She releases her hold instantly, eyes wide, stumbling backward. I'm behind her fast, hand over her mouth stifling the scream before it has the chance to rip through this stairwell. She tries to bite and fight me as I tighten my grip.

"*Ren*!" Nova yells, hand clasped over her mouth. Her eyes pinned on the gun I'm still holding.

A guttural sound leaves me as I growl at her. "Open the door, Nova…NOW!"

She moves, flushed face panicked as she shakily unlocks the door and follows me in. I drag an unexpectedly strong, raging Melina in with me. She attempts to bite my hand again, but I press harder. "Get me a bandana…or something to put in her mouth," I say through panting breaths.

"I'm not helping to restrain my best friend Soren! Are you out of your mind?"

"Novalie…does it look like we are going to have a calm conversation with her? Huh…does it?"

Nova really looks at her friend then, taking in her rage. Mel's eyes widen in shock, and her fight pauses when Nova nods and says, "Okay, but don't hurt her, just restrain her long enough to hear us out." She meets Mel's fury with determination. "Mel, he won't hurt you, but you need to listen, and if you won't cooperate…this is the only way."

Mel watches her leave the room and come back with a string and bandana. She shakes her head and mumbles through my palm. Leaning in to her ear, I say through gritted teeth, "I'll let you speak, but only if you promise not to scream. Nod if you understand."

She nods, and I tentatively release my hand from her mouth. She takes in a large gulp of air—panting, she says, "I won't scream…just don't tie me up, please." Her eyes plead with Nova's.

Nova pauses, restraints in hand. "Mel, don't make me regret this." Then she looks to me in a silent request.

"I'm sorry if I don't trust the woman who just tried to shoot me," I grind out between bared teeth.

Mel snaps her head to the side, seething, "I'm sorry if I don't trust the convicted murderer that's squatting in my best friend's house!"

Arms tightening around her ever so slightly, I growl into her ear. "While I can appreciate your fierce protective nature for Nova, I'd *never* hurt her…in fact, I'd lay down my fucking life for her." Nova's eyes snap to me at the same time as Mel's, but I ignore them both. "I'm releasing you…don't fucking test me." My grip lessens, and I slowly release Mel and then take a step back, sticking the gun into the waistband of my jeans.

She turns on me, watching my every move, as I retreat to the couch and sit. Leaning back, I raise the hem of my hoodie and tap the gun at my waist. "Nice piece, by the way. I'm a huge fan of Sig Sauer's."

Nova huffs out a loud breath and takes Mel by the arm, pulling her to the couch opposite me, practically dragging her rigid form. Once they're both seated, Mel's angry eyes still drilling into me, Nova says, "Look at me, Mel." With reluctance, she does so slowly, prompting Nova to continue. "I'm going to be honest with you, but you have to promise me that you'll keep this secret."

Mel scoffs. "There's no *fucking* way I'm agreeing to that without hearing it first."

Nova glances to me, and I give her a nod. Because why the hell not add another complication into my life. It's not like I can silence her friend. Might as well attempt to lure her to our side.

This is the day that just keeps on fucking giving.

Nova starts at the beginning. I listen intently, noticing *everything* she leaves out. Like the way I took her by force. She plays it down to mere convincing conversations and not the actual kidnapping that it was. She makes me look like a complete gentleman and not the villain. It's a more pleasing story to the ears—a story Mel might actually take into consideration—but a far cry from the real version.

When she's finished, Mel's shoulders have somewhat relaxed, but her eyes seem to tell a different story…one of indecision and fear.

Mel leans back on the couch, crossing her jean-clad legs, and then her arms. Her eyes pin me in place like a dart hitting the bullseye. "*You* are endangering her life. You know that, right?" I open my mouth, but she stops me with her next words. "*If* you are innocent, then you're putting her in the position to unveil a killer. If you do *not* find this killer, then you are chancing going back to prison, and she could be charged for aiding and abetting you. And *IF* you are the killer…" She lets that linger in the room before adding, "You see…either way, you're endangering my friend."

An argumentative train of thought slams to the forefront of my mind…but I file it away. She's not wrong. In fact, it's why I carry so much guilt inside, because Nova is a genuinely good person and I've brought her into this mess.

Nova chimes in, breaking the stare-off we're having. "I'm choosing to help now. It's my choice. Yes, in the beginning..." her eyes flit to mine and then back to Mel, "it took some convincing, but I *am* choosing this now. I want it."

Mel visibly swallows hard and looks between us. Her now solemn eyes meet Nova's. She tilts her head and says, "If I keep this secret, and I'm *not* saying I will just yet...you two have to stay in contact with me *every* day. I need to always know what's going on and that you're okay."

"We can do that," Nova says.

"No problem," I add.

Melina cocks her head at me. "And you need to give me back my pistol."

"I will," a smile pulls at my cheek, "when you leave. I'd like to remain amongst the living."

To my shock, she grins, saying, "That makes one of us," then analyzes me slowly. "So, at least it's good to know he's not really your boyfriend."

My head jerks back, and Nova's mouth hangs open. "Why is that? Am I not her type?" I ask Mel with my hand to my chest, feigning shock at her words.

"Not at all," Mel says casually. I don't miss the warning pooled in her dark eyes. She's saying, don't cross that line...*stay away*, without actually saying *stay away*.

Nova smacks her arm. "Don't be an ass, Mel." I smile faintly and watch the heat creep into her cheeks, because she knows and I know just how close we've come to crossing an entirely different line.

"What? I'm just being honest," Mel replies as she recrosses her legs and relaxes back into the couch again. "Well...I'm not leaving here until I feel safe leaving my best friend alone with *you.*" She glares at me some more before saying, "I say we have tacos and watch a movie…or better yet, let's watch a crime documentary…that'll help get the neurons firing off in our heads, right? Maybe the Scott Peterson documentary."

Nova slaps her arm again. "That's not funny, Mel."

I snort and do my best to ignore the jab. I remember the Scott Peterson case well. He murdered his wife. Mel's a *clever* one with a biting tongue. Shaking my head, I say, "You ladies seem like you need a moment…I think I've had my fill of excitement for today." I leave the couch and head out the front door, quickly cleaning up the mess left by the dropped basket of produce, then put it away. The girls talk softly while I get a beer from the fridge and head to the patio. I purposely leave the glass door slightly ajar…just in case Melina decides to call the cops or come at me with a hidden knife. I hear their hushed words muffled behind me, but I can only make out certain parts of their conversation.

Cursing under my breath, I sit, spine stiff. Several things are bothering me, and I'm afraid that at any second I'll lose my shit. Nova confronting Jace today, having a gun almost pulled on me, having another person liable for my secrets and depending on them keeping those secrets. Then there's the words Mel said. I'm responsible for anything that happens to these women now because I've roped them into this. I *am* endangering Nova, and it's eating at my very soul. And the last, and most insignificant thing on my mind is Mel saying that I'm not Nova's type…*not at all.* It shouldn't have made such an impact on me and is by far the least of my worries…but it snakes down into me and bites hard with razor-sharp teeth. Because it's clear to see…she's right about that too. Novalie shines like that moon she stares at nightly. I'm merely a dark cloud rolling by.

It's hot as hell outside, but I keep the hood up, not chancing being seen, and tip back the beer. I let it wash down my parched throat and then narrow my darting thoughts down to one. This thing between Nova and me. It can't go any further. We barely know each other, but I can't deny the strange chemistry that fires off between us. Every time I'm near her, I feel those pinpricks of awareness dotting my skin. When this all ends, no matter what the conclusion is, I'm not what she really wants or needs. I'm just the man who shoved his way into her life by force. She'd never willingly have chosen me had the circumstances not been what they are.

But then I remember the boho-looking frozen girl who burst into my shop all those years ago. I was covered in grease, coveralls filthy…and she had *flirted* with me.

Raking a hand over my face, I groan aloud. What is she doing to me? I'm beginning to question whether or not I should give up the investigation and just run—disappear and never be seen again.

CHAPTER 23

Novalie

I've spent the last half-hour trying to convince Mel to trust me, thankful for Soren's exit earlier. It gave me the alone time I needed with her…not that she's on the 'Soren's innocent train', but she's reluctantly agreed to zip her lips for now and at least sit on the train seat for a moment.

I watch Soren's back as he sits on the balcony. Even from here, I can tell he's faking calm. And why shouldn't he be upset? The rest of his life rides on every single decision we make…and any unintentional mistakes. So, there can be *no* mistakes. We have to be careful, and that includes Mel now.

Mel takes my hand in hers, giving it a light squeeze and snagging my attention back to her. "Are you absolutely sure you want to go through this?"

Nodding, I say, "One hundred percent."

"Alrighty then, we're officially criminals now…*great.*" Her sarcastic tone has a lilt of humor to it. "Just so you know, I'll look amazing in orange, but it's really not your color." Her finger twirls a strand of my dark auburn locks.

I nudge her with my shoulder. "We're not criminals." I sound less confident than I intended with that. Clearing my throat, I ask, "Do you want to get to know him? Have a beer on the balcony with us?"

Her groan has me rolling my eyes, but she quickly reins it in and stands. "Sure, I'll grab two." She pauses, looking back at me. "He's far hotter than you let on the other day when I saw those dirty old boots by the door. And is he really a slob?" she asks as she walks over to the fridge, opening it.

Shaking my head with amusement, I say, "He's not *really* a slob…it's been an…inside joke of sorts between us." I refrain from telling her about all the pervert comments. "And he's alright looking, I guess," I concede. She's staring into my fridge, unmoving, and then giggles. "What?" I ask curiously.

"You're kidding, right? He's got that dark, tattooed, mysterious thing going…he's hot and you know it, but that's not why I'm tickled." She waggles her finger at the contents of my refrigerator. "Where did my neat-freak friend go? Your fridge looks almost…*normal.*"

Fucking Ren. "That neat freak is still inside me…agitatedly sitting dormant," I say.

I ignore her arched eyebrow as she smirks at me and grabs the beers. My eyes flit to the door as I chance a glance in Ren's direction and find that he's shifted in his chair, his head is turned as if he's *listening*…then I notice the door is cracked open. Oh, for *fuck's* sake. He probably heard what we just said. They'll be no living with him now. My cheeks flame red, but before I can join Mel, who's heading for the door, my phone rings.

Grabbing it, I wave to Mel, gesturing that I'll be out shortly. Excitement shoots through me, and I dash to the bedroom for privacy, shutting the door before answering the call from my uncle.

"Uncle Jim," I say too loudly.

"Nova, how are you, honey?" His voice rattles out, sounding entirely too worn today.

"I'm fine…but are *you*? You sound off."

"I'm good…just tired. I was calling about the case. You got a minute?"

"Absolutely!"

He must hear the enthusiasm in my tone because he chuckles lightly. "I was able to use my pull and gain copies of the case files."

"Already?" I question.

I hear his haggard laugh. "I might've gotten a little excited about having another case and went straight to the station after our visit. Also, Bowen says he's going to call you in a week or less with anything he can find on that phone number…he's not been able to start on it due to being out of town."

Sitting on my bed, I stare at the wall, smiling. "This means a lot. Thank you so much."

"No problem. I just hope it helps with your book. I can't wait to read it one day." His words brim with pride.

"Yeah, I…can't wait either." My words fester and die. I've never lied to him, and it's a hard pill to swallow. Biting my lip, I fall back onto the bed with a flop.

"I want you to be careful," he says. "Cases…even closed ones, can be dangerous and hold secrets. And secrets get people killed. You might just be writing a book, but if this convict is actually innocent…then there could be someone out there that wouldn't think this book is such a good idea, if you know what I mean."

"I'll be careful, Uncle Jim." My reply is so soft and unsure that I feel like a child again when answering him.

"I'll get the files to you soon."

"Thanks." He's silent for a moment, so I ask, "What is it?"

"I looked through the folders briefly. I haven't finished yet, but the case against him doesn't look good. From what I gathered, there was an extensive amount of blood on him and in the house. No visible signs of anyone else being there…not even a footprint in the blood other than Victoria's and Soren Marshall's. Not to mention the burned belongings of hers not far away and that body part…the finger."

A shudder works its way through me as I replay everything Ren told me. "It does look bad," I admit quietly. My lips roll inward, and then I'm nervously nibbling the lower one.

"It does," he replies, "but that's the beauty of the search."

"Oh?" I say, interest piqued.

"How boring would it be if everything was cut and dried and given to you on a silver platter? No matter where your research takes you, honey, there's beauty in the discovery of truth. And I've never looked in only one direction on a case with tunnel vision…a good detective see's in *all* directions."

His words tug at my heart and bolster the confidence I didn't know I was lacking.

About that time, Ren walks into the room with a look of concern, his sharp jawline pulled tight. Still lying on the bed, I raise a finger to my lips for him to be quiet. He nods once. "Thanks for that, Uncle Jim…I needed to hear it. And thanks again for all your help."

His breath rattles on the other end. "I should be thanking you. This is the most fun I've had in years." He chuckles lightly. "I'll see what else I can find."

Ren has moved to the bed, hovering over my supine body as I tell my uncle, "Thank you again…I love you…you know that right?"

"Always sweetheart. Love you too."

Hanging up, I toss the phone beside me as Ren asks, "Everything good?"

"I think so. He has copies of the files and has Bowen working on that number."

"So why are you so deflated on this bed?" he asks carefully.

Inhaling through my nose, I close my eyes. "From his little scan of the case, he doesn't think it looks good." Seeing Ren tense and shift from foot-to-foot, I hurriedly add, "*But* he doesn't see everything as cut and dry…he said that there's beauty in the discovery of truth."

Ren seems to contemplate those words. "I like that." Ren's voice is low and gravelly when he replies. I open my eyes to see him scanning me intently. He leans over me, taking my hands in his and pulling me up to stand before him. His eyes drop to our hands still laced together. He keeps his eyes locked onto them for a while before bringing those stormy orbs back to mine. "It's Sunday…" he whispers, making my brow furrow in confusion. Clearing his throat, he explains, "You said I had until Sunday to convince you of my innocence…so are you convinced?"

I open my mouth to say something smart-assed, but instead I tuck away the snarky comment. "Yes, I am," I say with absolute certainty.

The smile that tips his lips up in that all-too hot way has butterflies flittering in my stomach. He releases my hands, then a shit-eating grin takes over the enticing one from a second ago.

"What?" I tilt my head and ask.

"You think I'm alright looking, huh?" He bites back a laugh at my shocked face.

"You're a dirty, eavesdropping snoop," I say, jutting out my chin in defiance.

He turns, walking out of the room and toward the balcony, saying over a shoulder, "It's okay if you find me attractive, princess…irresistible even." I plant my feet on the hardwood, my eyes burning a hole in his back. "You coming?" He asks.

Smoothing down my white dress and tucking in my pride, I raise my chin and follow him.

"What's the next step in this rogue investigation?" Mel asks the moment I step outside with Ren, effectively drowning out my embarrassment over what he heard. Her dark curls bounce and sway in the light breeze that's settled over us. She has a resolute calm about her now, as if she's feeling us out in order to determine just how crazy we are.

Popping the top on the Corona, I take a long pull and sit across from her, Ren to my right. "We have to find out why Jace Farrow was acting so strange…angry even. When I mentioned Victoria, he just snapped at me." Mel's lip juts out in thought. I told her about today's adventure too. So now she is one hundred percent caught in this web with me.

"And we'll have the case files soon." Ren adds, "Then we can see if anything was left out of my trial."

Mel leans forward in her chair and focuses on Soren. "Tell me about Victoria. It might trigger something you'd forgotten."

I incline my head to her good idea but see Ren grimace. "You don't have to if you don't want to," I say, realizing how hard this must be for him. He's had to live in this hell for so long. He's probably sick of rehashing it.

"Nah, it's fine." Ren shifts uncomfortably in the chair before leaning back and taking a drink. "Vicky was…for lack of a better word, uppity." His gaze flits between us as he speaks. "She was pampered growing up, put on a proverbial pedestal. She was babied…an only child with the sole beneficiary of all her parents' love." His eyes drift away from us, staring at nothing but the memory he's describing. "When I met her, I was certain she came from some socially elite family, by the way she walked and talked. She had an air about her. People noticed when she walked into a room. You'd never know that she was born to a middle-class family, because they made sure she never seemed middle class. She always had top-of-the-line clothing—those name-brand heels that have the red bottoms—went to the best college, had purses that cost more than some people's cars. When we got together, she was already finished with nursing school, starting her path to becoming a PA, and had been working for a while."

"What was she like to be around?" Mel asks.

"She was fun in the beginning. High maintenance, but fun. She loved to be doted on, but she gave back equal affection. She was *obsessed* with holidays and birthdays—made a huge to-do about them. Especially her birthday. It was like a week-long ritual of shopping, pampering, and places to go."

He rakes a hand over the hood, letting it fall from his head as dusk has settled and with it, less chance of being recognized from people walking on the streets below. His face dulls as he adds, "Her birthday is coming up soon. June fourth."

"You said she was fun in the beginning. What happened?" Mel ignores the heavy look in Ren's eyes, and I cut her a glance of warning, but she ignores me. "What changed?"

Soren takes her questions in stride and doesn't seem to mind her forwardness as he replies. "I'm not sure when exactly it started going south, but it wasn't a slow progression; it was like a landslide. After we married, she began to distance herself. We were arguing more, usually over work and bills, like most couples. I thought we just needed time to adjust to living together, but over time it wasn't improving. The fights got worse but were *never* physical." His eyes sharpen when he emphasizes that point. "I *never once* laid a hand on her to inflict pain. I *did* have to hold her off me several times. She was scrappy."

"Did she have childhood trauma? Mental issues?" Mel continues hounding him while I remain silent and contemplate everything he's saying.

He shakes his head. "Her childhood was good. She was never diagnosed with anything, though she took Adderall against my wishes. Pretty sure that was just to stay skinny."

Sip after sip, I listened to Ren and Mel discuss his wife. Everything ebbs and flows through a stream of ideas, but nothing snags. She sounds like a typical spoiled woman who married young and couldn't deal with a workingman's life. That alone couldn't provoke a murder. Although I'll have to admit I can see why the police focused on Ren…he's the poster child for crime dramas where the husband kills the unaffectionate, heinous wife and moves onto a mistress. But that's not him. After spending these few days living with him, there's no way he's a killer.

Or maybe I'm delusional.

Ren's voice interrupts my thoughts as he exclaims, "There's no flushing out this killer. He's likely long gone by now, so we're going to be relying on mistakes in the initial investigation. We need evidence. Even if it's only a little. We just need to cause enough doubt to get my case reopened."

There's no flushing out this killer. My mind focuses on that and then doubles back to something Ren said earlier. Mel and Ren are slinging around more facts when I blurt out, "I have an idea! What if we *can* actually flush out the killer?" Brows notched together, Ren turns to me, and so does Mel. Setting down the beer, I steeple my hands together with my elbows resting on my knees. I keep my eyes on Ren. "You said that Vicky's birthday is coming up soon…and with you being an escapee, this case will be on every news station across the country." Ren nods, cocking his head, unsure of where this is going. "This is good. All this media coverage is *very good*."

"I'm not following," Ren says.

My smile is wide and conspicuous. "I watched a documentary on a case one time, and they tracked down a killer by pinging IP addresses that did searches on the case repeatedly and especially on the anniversary of the case or the person's birthday who passed." I wait for them to start catching up with me. I can see it on Ren's face when he realizes what I'm saying, so I continue. "Don't you think the killer might be invested in whether or not Soren Marshall is captured? There's no way that our killer isn't out there keeping track of everything that goes down in this case. I can have Bowen Littlejohn search for hits in the news reports related to your case and Victoria. I can put in a word with my uncle to see if he can get the local news to run a whole recap of the case on her birthday. If we are lucky, the killer will be obsessively searching for the case details enough to leave an IP trail."

"Oh, my little supernova!" Mel squeals. "This might actually work."

I smirk at her. "You've saddled yourself with the dark side awfully fast."

She shrugs. "I'm bored."

"Bored, huh?" Laughing, I pick up my bottle, tap my beer with Mel's and then Ren's. "What do you think?" I turn to ask him. "Do you think it could work?"

"It might, even if we can get a ping on some new suspects, it's worth a shot," he acknowledges. "I think you've just given this case another happy accident."

Mel tilts her head, mouth open, as she looks between the two of us. She knows my favorite quote well. "Cheers," she raises her beer, meeting ours in the middle, "to happy accidents."

CHAPTER 24

Soren

I'm about to do something very foolish—borderline insane, really—but my patience is running thin. I hide it well in front of Novalie, but it's festering under the surface. It's been almost a week since Nova spoke with her uncle, and Mel made her grand appearance into the mix. It's been a week of living in Nova's world—basking in her grace and beauty. I've made sure to keep my distance…trying to avoid any more of our heated encounters. I have no intention of sullying her life any more than I already have. The closer we get…shit…nothing good could ever come from it. So, I've been on my best behavior…patiently waiting. My reservoir of patience has run dry, though.

Every time Nova's called Jim, he's been busy. He's yet to get us those files, and Bowen is also elusive. Nova's kept to her word and opened the shop. She's played the part well, selling plants and books, smiling at customers, and no one is the wiser of the criminal squatting above them.

But...I need a backup plan. If this fails...I need another option. Her uncle's words have stuck into me like a sword—a sword that's been twisting ever since. *'It doesn't look good,'* he'd said about the case. He's right...it fucking doesn't.

So, here I am, watching Nova from the shadows of the rear exit doorway. Her hair moves like a waterfall over one shoulder as she leans down to pull a book free from a lower shelf for an elderly man. Her lacy skirt is pooled on the floor. Her smile brightens the whole damn room, and from here I can see the old man's face crinkle all over when she places the book in his withered hands. Something pulls and tugs inside my chest—a longing that I'll likely carry with me forever.

Backing away, I slip through the rear door quiet as a mouse. Hat tucked low on my face and glasses on, I head for the parking garage with her car key squeezed so tightly in my fist that I'm sure the imprint of the cold metal will be there long after I release it. She'll flip her shit if she finds out, but I'm praying she's busy enough that she won't come to check on me.

She'd ask me in the beginning of discussing my case if I could contact my old business partner and best friend, Micah Talon. I'd said no, and for good reason. I didn't want to involve him, and it's a good bet that his phone's being tapped. Who else would I have to go to other than him? The cops are surely all over him, probably questioned him several times by now. But, circumstances being what they are, I'm taking a big risk here. I'm going to get a message to

Micah, and if luck is with me…he'll meet me at our old fishing spot.

Cranking the car…I don't give myself a moment to enjoy the rumble of the engine as it skitters through me, lighting my veins with adrenaline…don't give myself a moment to change my mind. I'm out of the garage, heading away from the city.

Half an hour later, a veritable sea of pine trees rushes by as I maneuver through the winding mountain roads. My mind, just as winding, drifts back to Micah, to all the good times we had. Fishing, hunting, boxing at our old gym…we did everything together. He's the brother I never had. I just hope his view of me isn't tainted.

I veer the car onto a hidden dirt road and stop long enough to send a text message. One that simply says, *Valhalla.* Smiling, I turn off the phone, remove the battery, and double back in a completely different direction through the mountains. If Micah gets it…he'll know where to go.

It takes another long while to get to the actual location. I'm no fool and couldn't chance the phone being tracked. My only fear now is that he could be followed. If they're tapping his phone and find that message…it could be odd enough to cause concern. I hide Nova's car a mile away near a walking trail and hike toward a hidden spot Micah and I used to frequent. The dense forest comes alive around me with the skittering of animals and bird calls as I disturb their peace with my presence. Sweat gathers on my brow and begins dampening my black shirt. Limbs crunch under my boots no matter how careful I am. The forest is dense and natural, no trails in this area—completely untouched. Before long, a familiar sound dances through the oak trees' leaves, creating a welcome feeling of home. I can always hear it before I see it…the rush of the river over rock and the crash of the hidden waterfall.

Micah and I found it when we were around nineteen years old while on a hunting trip. Imagine our surprise to find an untouched raging river, wide enough to hold several boats side by side. While the river was a sight and the fishing here was unmatched, it was always the waterfall that stole our breaths. Banked by pitching pines and massive oaks, with one lone patch of bamboo creating a border on the right side, and wildflowers blooming along the bank's edge. It was perfect. Slowly, I spin in a circle, taking in *every* inch of this paradise…our Valhalla. We spent several hours smoking pot the day we found it…getting high as a kite, snacking, and didn't kill a damn thing except Twinkies he'd had stashed in his backpack. We'd cleared a spot for a fire near here, not enough to taint the forest, but enough to where we could claim this spot as our own. A grin breaks free on my face as I remove my shirt, tossing it on the ground, and let the sun bake into me. My smile falters only for a second as I imagine bringing Novalie here. She'd love this.

Walking near the falls edge, I creep as close as I can safely, leaning over to see the sheer drop off. The river so far below is littered with boulders and broken trees from the recent hurricanes, all except one pooled area that looks deeper than it should be.

We had a rather fitting name for this drop-off back in the day. The *Widowmaker.*

A branch breaks nearby, which has me spinning, knife already flicked out and waiting. A gun would be nice, but sadly…I discarded the guards I stole when I escaped, Nova doesn't own one, and Mel took hers back from me. Muscles flex in my body as I step lightly, moving toward the sound, rather than away. Heart pounding, breath quiet, I inch closer. I hear the faint rustle of leaves as if someone parted branches to pass through. Ducking behind a fallen tree, I crouch and wait. The wind picks up, creating a blend of noises, but I can hear clear footsteps through the wild serenade…heading straight for me, slow and steady.

Knuckles white with the grip I have on the knife, I turn my body, ready to pounce, but still hidden. Booted feet are the first thing I see, and without hesitation I leap up behind the man and pull his large form back against me, knife now to his jugular. The rifle on his back digs into my chest. His holler echoes through the open space before I can slap a hand over his mouth and muffle it. Through gritted teeth, I growl into his ear, "*Are you alone?*" Micah cuts his eyes to the side, frantically shifting them over my face before he nods, head bobbing. "You better be telling the truth," I whisper with deadly calm, as I release his mouth and shove him forward.

Micah's strained face spins to glare at me. Head to toe he's wearing camouflage, his rifle slung across his back. He hasn't changed much in five years, still a powerhouse of muscle from lifting weights. He's a few inches shorter than me with a head full of sandy brown hair curling slightly under his camo trucker hat. His large brown eyes are made even wider with the pure rage he's exuding…his face furious…but also *shocked* as he takes me in. His mouth hangs open, eyes moving over my bare chest littered with a few battle scars from prison and then to my beard that's grown in some now and finally to the knife in my hand. His face somehow hardens more, mouth thinning, jaw tightening. "You pulled a knife on me, you fucking bastard!"

I shrug off his anger. "I had to make sure you were alone."

He smirks. "And you're so sure now?"

"I am," I say matter-of-factly.

"You're a fucking moron. What were you thinking contacting me?" he spits back.

My hackles rise, and I cock my head at him predatorily. "*Do* I have something to worry about with you…or are you on my side?"

"Of course, I'm on your side, but I've had cops all over my ass and watching my every move since you escaped." Micah shakes his head as he looks me over again.

"I figured as much," I concede with a sigh. "I'm glad you got my message."

"How could I not?" He gives a minuscule smile. "No one knows about Valhalla but us…I knew it was you." He shuffles from side to side on his feet.

"Did you get rid of the message?" I ask, swiping sweat from my forehead with the back of my hand.

"I deleted it and reported it to junk…but if they want, the cops can look into any messages. They might find that one suspicious."

I step forward, eyes locked on his. "Are you certain you weren't followed?"

"Positive. There wasn't a single car behind me for miles on the road. I parked where we used to come into the woods to hunt."

I nod and exhale deeply. "Okay. Thanks for coming but seeing you wasn't my top priority…I need your help with something."

He eyes me warily. "Soren, you know I'd do anything for you, but if I get caught—"

I cut off his words with my own. "*If* you get caught in *any* way, you tell them I forced you. You tell them I threatened you. You understand that?"

His lips pinch together in thought, eyes down-turned before he finally nods. "What is it you need?"

"I need my money. My half of the shop's selling price…and I need you to empty my safe-deposit box too, and I need all of it brought back here in one week—same time, same place."

Micah crosses his arms over his chest, feet planted firmly, and he assesses me like a father would a son. "You're running…where to?"

"I'm not sure yet, and I…" I hesitate for a moment, Novalie's face in my mind giving me pause. "If everything doesn't pan out, I'm leaving. I won't go back to prison…I *can't*."

Micah walks past me to the fallen tree and sits down, flipping his hat backward. He drops his elbows to his knees. His voice and expression change as he looks at the ground. "Where have you been? I hoped and prayed you were already gone…out of the country on some island somewhere." He looks up to me. "It hurt to know I'd never see your ugly mug again, but damn, I thought at least you'd be living your life outside a cell, but no…here you are, not even an hour away from the prison you escaped. *Fucking idiot*," he mutters.

My chuckle surprises him, making his forehead scrunch. "It's been an interesting ride…one I won't be sharing with you. The less you know, the better." His mouth turns at that, but I add, "I *will* tell you that I'm in a safe place for now."

He considers that before stating, "You're trying to prove your innocence, aren't you?"

I tip my head to him and move to sit beside him. "It was a long-shot idea, but I'm going to stick it out…until I can't." He seems to get my meaning…until I can't chance being here any longer. "So, can you get my money to me in a week?"

He rubs a hand over his mustache and down his shaved jaw. "What if they're watching and waiting for me to touch those assets? They know I have access and control over your account, but if I was to take it out…they'd know what for."

"You're right," I agree with a curse under my breath. "What about the safe-deposit box? It's not likely they know you're a lessee on that account."

"It's possible," he agrees, then adds, "If not, I can give you some out of my own account and you can owe me later." He nudges my arm.

I give him a thankful smile, but it doesn't reach my eyes. "I'll take whatever you can get, but don't put yourself in a bad situation."

"Oh, I'm good financially…mentally not so much." He laughs a little. "And let's make it two weeks. I need to make sure I'm not being watched and have time to take the money out slowly."

I give him a nod in agreement. "Two weeks," I say. Suddenly, I realize what a shitty friend I really am. I haven't asked him about his life in the last five years, his relationships, his family…nothing. He did visit me in prison once before I told him not to come back. It was too much for me to see him…for him to see me like that. I knew how much losing me and the business affected him back then, but I was too sullen and stuck in my own personal hell that I didn't stop to consider his.

Now I'm here asking for a favor.

Turning to Micah, I tell him the things I should've said a long time ago, and he tells me about his life, his failed relationships, his parents' new adventures since retiring. The wildlife seems to resume its scurrying and rhythmic musical noises only partially drowned out by the Widowmaker waterfall.

If I close my eyes…I'm nineteen again, and this is simply a hunting trip and nothing more.

CHAPTER 25

Novalie

Locking the door to my shop, I flip the open sign off and head toward my stairs in the back. It's a little after five on a Friday night and today was surprisingly busy. My heeled feet ache with each step. My mind is as exhausted as my feet due to my mother. She called at lunchtime, ranting about my absence and about my lack of communication. The guilt trip lasted a good fifteen minutes before she admitted talking to her brother-in-law…my Uncle Jim. She was furious that not only had he seen me but that we were working together and that I didn't care to include her in the fact that I'm writing a book. Just when I thought she was almost done raging at me…she mentions the mystery man that Jim says I'm seeing.

I smoothed that mess over with another sloppy lie about meeting a guy in the bookshop, but that it was new and nothing serious. I guess it's not technically a lie. I *did* meet Soren in the bookshop, and he is a *new* acquaintance. Regardless, it feels dirty to lie. But I could never put Soren in any danger of being caught…so, I'll lie as long as it takes.

This week with him, being in my home…right above me, has been taxing. It's like my nerve endings feel him up there, like they're hyperaware of the man waiting for me. Then there's the change in him. He's *comfortable*—relaxed and even seems excited to see me come through the door. Without me asking, Ren has made me dinner three times, and in the evenings, we usually spend the last hours of the day on that balcony—him asking me about my day. We've put off the case until the files get to us or any word from Bowen. We've grown accustomed to each other's living habits far too fast and acclimated ourselves to a routine.

If I'm being perfectly honest with myself, it's scaring the shit out of me.

When you lose someone close to your heart, reality sinks in, and time becomes the enemy. Suddenly you're scared to get close to more people because…in the end we lose everyone. It's a morbid thought, but one that I can't shake over the last week. I feel a sense of responsibility for this man that I've sworn to help, and I am absolutely terrified that I'll let him down. And if I'm continuing the honesty with myself…I really like having him here.

Muffled music greets my ears the moment I hit the landing entry to my apartment. Pausing, I place my ear to the door curiously. The guitar intro from Metallica's song *One* is hard to miss thrumming from inside my house. Quietly, I open the door and move in slow, then slip off my heels, dropping them by the mat. The music is coming from my bedroom's retro stereo. My mouth quirks upward as I pad softly through the house, toward my room. The smell of breakfast has me smiling and remembering the nights my gran would make breakfast for dinner. I peek inside my room but don't see him, so I turn the corner and notice the bathroom door open. I'm just about to spin to give him privacy but…not fast enough.

My face flushes profusely as Ren saunters from the bathroom, skin dewy from the steam, muscles rippled and gleaming down his torso and the barely hidden parts of him wrapped in a towel that looks far too small for his tall frame. My hand snaps to my mouth. "Oh…oh shit, I'm sorry," I flounder. "I didn't know you were…indecent!"

Soren's eyes flit to mine in shock—shock that quickly morphs to humor. "I'm never *decent,* princess." He laughs coarsely, and I feel that sound reverberate through me.

My hand falls from my mouth as I clear my throat, but my gaze is a wry thing, doing as it pleases. How could I not give him a once over…looking like that? Between the wet dark strands of hair sticking every which way, the glistening tattoos over taut muscles, and the veins in his lower abdomen stretching toward, and passing behind the sliver of towel around his waist.

He clears his own throat, making me lurch from my embarrassing survey of his body, then says, "Eyes up here, princess."

Fire. I must be on fire because every part of me is hot…in one way or another. I finally find my voice. "Oh, for fuck's sake, Soren," I say when I see his shit-eating grin. "If I was parading around the house in a towel—"

I don't get to finish that sentence before he's stepped closer and interrupts me. "For one, I'm not parading around the house, I just showered and was letting the steam out of the bathroom before dressing and for two…" he moves another step to me, invading my space, "if you were in a towel right now I'm not sure we would be speaking at all."

My throat dries out along with my senses. His manly scent caresses my nostrils like a beckoning touch. I move back a step, but my back bumps into the open bedroom door. His eyes are searching mine now, brows drawn tight. He's silent, contemplating…what, I'm not sure. He draws his lower lip into his mouth once, and moisture lingers there as he releases it. I'm standing there…quiet, transfixed on it. What the hell is wrong with me? I can't seem to function. My brain is screaming at me to say something smartassed or witty, but I can't.

He's moved closer, but I'm not sure when that happened. He's close enough that, if I so chose to, I could touch him…feel his strength. I don't recognize my own voice when I ask, "Why are you looking at me like that?"

Ren drags a hand through his wet, unruly hair, body tense and his eyes still not leaving mine. I can't help but notice his chest rising and falling in a fast rhythm that matches my fluttering pulse. He's been a perfect gentleman this week…steered clear of the flirting and our usual banter, but today…he looks as if something in him is about to crack wide open like a chasm.

His throat bobs with effort, head tilting animalistically. "I'm sorry," he says in a deep, guttural tone.

My forehead pinches in confusion, voice but a whisper when I ask, "For what?"

"This." He says simply. Before I can register what's happening, Ren's hands grasp my waist and lift me from the ground in one smooth fluid motion that has me gasping aloud and then babbling a protest. When my body is pulled against his, I automatically wrap my legs around him so as not to fall, and my hands grasp around his neck and shoulder. All the protests die from my open mouth. Our noses are so close they brush once as he's moving. My long skirt is bunched around us, pulling in places, but I've lost all sense of time and place because the intensity in his stormy eyes has me shellshocked.

In a blink, my ass is dropped onto something…my dresser, I think. Soren's hands move from my waist to glide up the expanse of my outer thighs, bunching my skirt even more, giving him ease to push into my space. My mouth flails open to say something…anything, but Ren shakes his head—a silent warning not to speak.

His eyes have turned a shade of gray that I've never seen on a person before as he looks down into mine. The hard lines of his muscles flex as he reaches up between us, cupping my jaw with his large hand, thumb caressing over my lower lip. A shutter racks my body, and a choppy breath leaves my mouth. He fingers a strand of my hair with the other hand and then slides his fingers over my neck, leaving goosebumps in their wake.

"I really am sorry," he whispers against my mouth.

I search his gaze, trying to understand, but when he leans down more to drag his tongue up my neck and onto my jaw, I make a ridiculous sound, eyes falling shut with the electricity that is now zinging through me. Ren keeps one hand locked on my jaw and neck, holding me in place, and the other finds the back of my neck as he fits his lips over mine.

Fire erupts inside me like I've never known. A gravelly groan seems to rumble from his chest as he takes this first chaste kiss and deepens it. My hands have somehow found purchase on his back, and I'm finally *touching* him. It's something that, if I'm being honest, I've been craving like a drug…human touch. One leg, then the other, wraps deftly around his torso, bringing our bodies flush, nothing but the towel and the fabric of my skirt separating us. I feel his hard length press against me with fervor. When his tongue delves into my mouth with the most erotic motion, I come apart, nails digging into the flesh of his back. I angle my head to take his mouth again and again. Nothing has ever tasted this fucking good.

Ren uses his thumb to force my head back, giving him access to my throat again, and I immediately moan when he nibbles at my jawline. My breasts heave against him, pulling him closer, as if that's even possible. "Ren," I say hoarsely. It comes out as a plea—one I'm not embarrassed to admit. I want this man, and I don't care about the white noise in my head that tells me how absolutely wrong this could all go. I *want* him.

His face moves to hover over mine again in an intimidating, dominating way, then his mouth is back on mine, short beard scratching against me in the most enticing way. I feel his hands grip my hips again, and then he's grinding against me with need. We kiss as if the world around doesn't exist, as if we're the only two beings left on this planet. My skirt is suddenly wrenched up higher, his calloused hands skim my thighs until they reach the sides of my panties, and then he somehow lifts me enough to yank them down. Ren backs away just a few inches as he slides them off my legs and over my bare feet, and then he's back against me…the towel suddenly not between us.

Just as his mouth claims me again, a knock sounds at the door. A sharp intake of breath is shared between the two of us as our lips part. Ren grinds his teeth, making his jaw clench before he lays his forehead against mine. Our mingled breaths are quick and ragged. When he finally looks at me, there's so much unbound heat there.

Placing a palm to his cheek, I say, "Whoever it is…they'll go away."

He shakes his head as the knocking repeats. "It could be important."

Licking my lips, I whisper, "*Nothing* is as important as this." His brows furrow, and for some reason, a touch of sadness tinges his face.

When the door sounds a third time, Ren backs away from me, albeit very reluctantly. I glimpse the hardened, impressive length of him before he snatches the towel off the floor and wraps it around his waist again. It was only a glimpse, but one I'm likely never to forget. He steps forward and I'm elated…thinking he's changed his mind but deflate in the same instance as he grips my hips and lifts me from the dresser.

"You need to see who that is," he says solemnly as he backs away and moves to my bathroom to hide.

Standing on wobbly legs, I walk out of the bedroom and to the front door.

CHAPTER 26

Novalie

Patting down my skirt and attempting to smooth my hair, I open the door, praying I don't look like I've just been thoroughly wrecked by the naked man hiding in my bathroom. The door swings open, and there stands a man I haven't seen in a *very* long time. A smile splits my face as I take in his long braids that lie down each shoulder…streaming with silver now but still retaining most of the black. His high cheek-bones are made even more prominent as his brown eyes crinkle around the edges with the smile he gives me in return.

"Bowen Littlejohn! How have you been?" I ask, waving him through the door. I notice the box he's carrying and cock my head.

"I've been good, can't complain. Nova…you are as stunning as ever. How's life these days running the bookstore?"

"Can't complain," I throw back at him with a smile. My brows rise when I see files sticking out of one corner of the box. "Is that what I think it is?"

He nods, setting the box down on an end table. He dusts off his band tee and takes a seat on the couch. "It is. Sawyer told me what you were doing. That's pretty awesome. How's the book coming along?"

I somehow manage to hide my grimace. "It's…moving right along." I shrug. "Why didn't Uncle Jim bring it?"

Bowen's shoulders lift. "Not sure. He asked me to since I was in town finally. Sorry it took so long to get back to you. I haven't started the search to ping any addresses yet or look up that phone number, but no worries, I'm back now and can get right on it."

"I'm sure you're a busy man, and I don't mean to drag you into something for free. I can pay you of course…for your research."

He waves a hand at me. "Are you kidding…no way. I live for this kind of stuff."

A small laugh bubbles up. "Yeah, I seem to remember that about you. You are proficient at digging into people's lives." I sit across from him and lean forward, elbows braced on my knees. "How's Callon and Maisy these days? And Laya, is she good?" I ask, thinking about the enigmatic duo and their harrowing story that lives rent-free in my head to this day. And their daughter, who's like a cousin to me.

Bo's smile widens, if that's at all possible. "They're the same lovesick, crazy fools they were years ago. Maisy told me to tell you to come visit sometime; she'd love to catch up. Laya is dying to see you."

My heart sings at the thought. I was around them all quite a bit as a child and some as a teenager, but it feels like ages. My uncle was extremely close to them, seeing as how he was a part in solving the human trafficking case that involved Maisy's kidnapping. "Tell her it's a plan." I reach over and tap the box. "Have you looked through this?"

"No, I came straight over with it after Sawyer called. He left it on his porch for me."

My brows furrow at that. It doesn't sit well with me. My uncle handles everything himself and never asks for help or favors. "Is he alright?"

"Like I said, I'm really not sure. He seemed fine over the phone." I nod, unconvinced. I'm making it a priority to show up at his house and *soon.* Bo leans forward, lacing his fingers together. "Now tell me about this case? Is there any reason to believe the guy is actually innocent?"

I rattle off facts about the case for a few minutes and then add, "That number I found was hidden in an old clock, and I just thought it was odd…that and the fact that the husband, Soren," I try to maintain no emotion when saying his name even though my entire being is still thrumming over our encounter just moments ago, "never had a blemish on his record before that. I also didn't like that the investigation moved quickly and in one direction…toward him. It was strange. It's like they didn't even consider any other possible suspects."

Bo's mouth twists in contemplation. "It's usually the husband in these cases, but I did watch the news reports and a few interviews. I will agree with you on this; the case *was* strange. Why kill your wife, sleep with the blood all over you, and then have her remains a short distance from the cabin?"

"My thoughts exactly." I nod.

"Was he tested to see if he was drugged?"

"Re…" I snap my mouth shut the instant his shortened name almost leaves my lips and clear my throat. "Really not sure, because it was never mentioned that I know of, but that's what I'm hoping to find in these files."

After discussing the case a while longer, we say our goodbyes, and I slump against the door after locking it. Ren peers around the edge of the bedroom door before walking out of it. He's completely dressed in dark jeans and a heather gray T-shirt…to my absolute dismay. He smiles, but it isn't much of one as he makes his way to the kitchen. Pushing myself to standing, I pad over quietly, watching him. He takes a bite of a cold piece of bacon.

"I completely forgot that you made breakfast for dinner," I say softly. "Thank you for that…I can reheat it for us…if you'd like."

He nods once, and I start working on the food. He doesn't say anything, and his silence is killing me. I start coffee, and once everything is ready and the plates are made, I stand across the island from him, pushing over the mug and plate. "What is it, Ren?" I break and ask.

He pauses with a bite close to those decadent lips that were against mine not very long ago. "I shouldn't have done that."

I rear my head back with a short quick movement. "Done what, Ren? Kiss me? Why?"

He drops the bacon back to the plate. "There's a far greater chance that I'll be on the run forever than finding who did this."

I scoff at him. "Wow, you're throwing in the towel awfully fast."

"It's true, and you know it. I was pumped up in the beginning...determined, but the more I drag you into this...the more I'm realizing how far-fetched it is."

"So, you wished you hadn't kissed me because of the unknown?"

"Because if I have to run one day...I can't have anything holding me back," he says quietly.

My face falls as if I've been slapped. The truth of his words aren't lost on me, but damn it feels like a dagger is sinking in my gut. "Anything...meaning me," I say, and he looks away. "Well, I'm in this because of *you*, but what just happened in that bedroom is because of *us*." His eyes snap back to mine, and the sadness and longing in them threaten to bring me to my knees. "Soren...no one knows what tomorrow brings, but that doesn't mean you need to live each day protecting yourself from it. I've been doing that for far too long. I have no regrets about what transpired in there...you shouldn't either."

His brows raise and a hint of a smile graces his lips. "Trust me, I have no regrets...just worries."

We both take a steadying breath and then silence falls as we eat our dinner and continues long after the kitchen is cleaned. I grab a throw blanket off the back of the couch and wrap it around my shoulders as I heft the box of files off the table. Ren watches me, and I stop to say, "Well, are you coming?" I continue into the bedroom. I plop the box in the center and settle myself onto the bed.

It's a few seconds later before Ren walks into the bedroom...looking me over. "You want to go through these tonight? In here?" He gestures to my bedroom.

"Do you have a problem with that?" I raise an eyebrow at him in challenge.

He smirks, shaking his head, his macho attitude finding its way back to him. "Not at all, princess. Ren climbs onto the bed beside me with the box between us.

We sift through it, separating it into two semi-equal piles, and start reading. Much of the documented information is what we already knew, but to read through it firsthand is gut-wrenching.

Suspect was covered in blood upon arrival, disheveled appearance. He was identified as Soren Marshall. He was erratic and combative. After several attempts to subdue him, police action was taken to contain the suspect. Scratches along his forearm were noted, and photos were taken. There appear to be some drag-style marks leading from the entry door toward the dirt drive. Blood spatter was noted along walls in the bedroom and living room and on the front porch.

I have to stop reading and swallow the bile that pushes at my throat, threatening to burn me alive. I can't shake the image of him like that. "You okay?" he asks carefully, eyeing my demeanor.

"I'm fine," I say, clearing my throat, and sift through the box.

"We can do this tomorrow if you want," he adds.

I shake my head. "I'm fine, Ren," I say, shutting down his worry.

After another hour of reading through, not only the case, but the trial notes, we've found nothing of use and only one strange detail. There was sulfur casting done of a boot print in the snow but apparently nothing came of it.

Frustrated, I toss the ones I've read into the box and drag the remaining ones to me. "There's no notations anywhere of your lab results." He turns to look at me, prompting me to continue. "They would've been required to take blood and urine samples, but I don't see any. And there's no way in hell you were drunk enough to have slept through whatever happened in that house."

He blows a sharp breath through his nose. "They said during the trial that I was inebriated, which I never denied, but they didn't mention anything else being in my system."

My eyes skim his face, and my lips form a thin line before I demand, "Tell me more about your last encounter with Vicky."

"Like I've said before, we argued. She was the jealous sort, and so was I. When she repeatedly excused herself to go to the restroom at the last bar, I was certain she was messaging another man…but when she was gone one time, I took her phone." He shrugs. "I know, jerk move, but I had to know. There weren't any messages to *anyone* that night. I couldn't shake the feeling, though. She was distant, more than usual. When I drilled her about her attitude, she unleashed on me. I thought we might get kicked out of the bar if we didn't leave right then. We Ubered back to the cabin, and at that point, I was fairly drunk but I *never* got blackout drunk. It was a typical night of her making me feel like everything was my fault. I remember having one more Jack and Coke, and after that, I crashed. She didn't even come to bed…that I know of."

I let the night play out in my head. "Whoever took your labs," I say, thinking out loud, "we need to speak with them. We need to further our research on Jace Farrow, and we also need footage of the last bar you were in that night. Maybe there's something they missed. The cops would've surely asked for the videos."

"We can try," Ren says softly.

I watch as he fumbles through more and more documents, but I can see the light dimming in his eyes…the hope waning. "Hey, look at me," I say. When his head raises, I give him a small smile. "We'll figure this out. What do you have to lose now?"

His eyes, deeper blue now in my low bedroom lighting, rove over me. "I have so much more to lose now," he says gruffly.

His words sink into me, latching onto every cell inside, transforming and changing. Once his words are out…I know I can never go back to who I was before them.

CHAPTER 27

Soren

The smell of vanilla and honey surrounds me and envelops my senses. Morning rays of sunshine stream in through a crack in the curtain, making me stretch and come alive. I stop abruptly when I feel the small form tucked into the front of my body. My arms have Nova caged into me protectively, her head against my chest. Slowly, I lift my head to survey the room, finding the box of files pushed to the end of the bed with papers sticking out haphazardly.

I should move, but my body refuses to do so. Last night, after hours of reading documents, she had lain on her side, head on the pillow as she read through one more. I'd watched as exhaustion got the better of her and she'd fallen asleep. The right thing to do would've been to move to the couch…but I didn't. I laid awake for the better part of an hour watching her sleep, watching her face change as she dreamed…of what, I don't know.

Does she realize what's at stake here?

I meant what I said last night; I do have so much more to lose now…because of knowing *her.* She's given me a glimpse of what normal would look like. It wouldn't be the turmoil Vicky and I had. No. Nova is patient, kind, understanding, and passionate. It's stupid to wish for something so far out of my reach, but damn, I can't help but picture it. I wish I didn't want her…this would be so much easier. *It was so much easier* when I had nothing to lose. But I'm afraid that now…she's ruined me. I could never leave her and not think of her daily, not get a whiff of a certain scent and think it was her, not dream of her every night, not see her face every waking moment.

So I should've moved to the couch. Especially now with the realization hitting me that her panties are still on the floor from yesterday and she's in that skirt with *nothing* underneath. Pressing my face down and into her hair, I inhale deeply, suppressing a groan.

Nova moves against me in her sleep, and my reserve returns. Easing my arm away from her, I start to move away, but she grabs my arm and pulls it back around her. My breath catches, body tense as she whispers sleepily, "Just a few more minutes."

Looking over her head to the alarm clock, I see that it's almost seven in the morning. I tuck my arm around her once more and try to release some of the stiffness in my body as I say, "You have work in one hour."

Her head shakes subtly. "I changed my hours to weekdays only. I'm not working weekends for a while."

I lay my cheek against her silken hair. "You didn't have to do that."

"Yes…I did," she says matter-of-factly. "I needed the time to help you."

I don't want to think about what her words and actions are doing to my heart. "Thank you," I manage to say. We stay like that, holding onto each other for a long time before parting ways and starting showers and such.

Two hours later, I'm pulling muffins from the oven when Nova emerges from getting dressed. Her hair is swept up in a high ponytail, still damp from her shower. Her light jeans are skintight and barely meet her blue crop top. She has on baby-blue Converse to match and a distinct pep in her step as she enters the living room and heads for the door.

"Mel messaged me; she's heading up," she says over her shoulder.

I flip on the TV as I plop down on the couch, taking a bite of muffin. Nova opens the door just as Mel breezes past, eyeing me. "Hey convict." She glowers.

I tip my muffin to her. "Hey…Mel," I say back, barely stopping myself from saying something asshole-ish.

She walks over, sits beside me and snatches the second muffin I had on the plate. Ignoring my glare, she asks, "So guys, what's on the agenda this weekend? Breaking and entering, espionage, something of that reckless nature?"

Nova rolls her eyes at her friend and sits across from us. "We haven't made it through deliberations yet." She looks to me briefly before jerking her eyes away. *Interesting*. Is she afraid her friend will see into her mind that we made out yesterday?

Mel huffs and starts a long list of how fucked up this is when a name on the TV snags my attention. I swallow the last bite of muffin, dust off my hands quickly, and fumble for the remote. Turning up the volume, I wave a hand at the girls to stop talking. Holy fucking shit. Jace Farrow's face is on the screen, laughing with his wife.

"You two are such a lovely couple," the reporter says fondly. *"And this farm is absolutely stunning."*

"Thank you so much." Jace grins and holds his wife tight to his side. *"It's a lot of hard work, but we manage. And we're excited to see this weekend's turnout. It's been a two-year dream in the making to have a craft fair and market someday...and today it's happening."*

The reporter looks to the camera. *"The Farrow Craft and Market Fair opens at eleven, folks. Over sixty vendors are expected to be here and fifteen other farms bringing in everything from jarred jellies to fresh veggies..."*

The reporter is still talking, but Nova is now standing, looking over to the clock on the wall. "It opens in an hour. We're going." She looks pointedly at Mel.

I stand facing her. "The *hell* you're going without me."

Her hands press into her hips in defiance. "There's far too many people there, Soren. You can *NOT* go."

Mel jumps in between us but looks only at me. "She's right." My gaze burns into hers, but she pushes on. "Soren...with that many vendors, this place will be crawling thick with people, and while I'd pay to see you tackled and handcuffed...Nova wouldn't enjoy it as much."

I glare at her. Cursing under my breath, I walk away from them into the kitchen and down the last of my coffee. Nova drops her arms and follows me, leaning against the counter with one hip. "We'll be safe, besides...there will be a huge crowd."

"And what do you expect to gain from this? Do you think he's going to magically open up to you about his past with Vicky?" I ask without looking at her. "He didn't the first time."

She bites her lip. "I'm not sure yet, but we have to eliminate all suspects, right? He's top priority right now. Maybe we can gain a better understanding of who he is." When I raise an eyebrow at her, she adds, "Okay, so I have no plan! But we're going and in the meantime, you are staying here where it's safe."

I'm taken aback by her words and scoff. "I should be protecting you, princess, not the other way around."

"*Princess*, huh?" Mel mocks from the living room but immediately feigns disinterest as I glare at her again.

"Let me do this for you," she pleads. "And by tomorrow, maybe we will be on a new lead. And Mel and I can use this opportunity to check out that bar you went to with Vicky…maybe they kept copies of those recordings for nostalgic purposes…your case was national news."

"I just wish I could be there with you," I admit, making her blush.

Mel grabs the keys to the car. "I'm going to give you guys a minute…be in the car waiting for you, Nova." She waggles her eyebrows before leaving.

"She's annoying," I growl.

Nova smacks my arm. "She's my best friend. You be nice."

"Yeah, yeah. Go then. Leave me here to worry about you." I flick my hand toward the door in dismissal.

Nova takes my shoulder and ushers me to turn and face her, then she reaches up on her tiptoes and kisses the side of my mouth…barely grazing the latter edge of my lips before saying, "We will be okay…don't worry." I watch her leave and finally exhale the breath I was holding.

Frustrated, I rage-clean the house just to burn time. When that's not helping, I fix the slight drip she had in her kitchen sink. When that fails too, I decide to use some of the space in her closet to put away my things that are stacked in places.

Inside her walk-in closet, she has organized rows of clothing that are damn near perfectly arranged by color and by what weather they're for. I make quick work of screwing with her by rearranging those, then I make space in the corner to hang the few items I have that came from Walmart. I happen to look up and notice the box containing her husband's things. Curiosity gets the better of me, and I tug the box down, intending to rifle through it.

"What the fuck am I doing?" I whisper. I shouldn't be nosing through her things, well not *anymore*. I lean down to pick it up, intending to put it back on the shelf when I see a leather strap sticking out from the corner. Opening the box a touch to tuck it back in, I see handwriting and pause. Cocking my head to the side, I pull the side flap on the box, giving me a view of what's inside. A tan leather-bound journal lies flopped open, Novalie's clear and precise handwriting in ink swirling on the page. I know her handwriting well now. I watched her make lists for groceries and notes on the case this week. I recall her telling me how she used to write.

"Fucking hell…she's going to kill me," I say aloud as I snatch up the journal and move to sit on her bed. This is wrong on so many levels, but I did kidnap her, so on a scale of bad deeds, I guess I've done worse. I turn to the last entry in the journal, dated 12/05/2024. My brows furrow. That was just a few days after her husband's death. I let my eyes fall over the page with a tinge of guilt, but not enough to stop me from reading.

What is the point of all this…a fucking wake. I give you kudos for control Levi. You were young and virile but somehow still managed to have a living will with all your elaborate expectations. Let's see, there was the obvious demand of no funeral and no burial. Cremation and a wake was what you wanted—a party on your behalf. A plaque was to be completed and placed in your college and in your practice. Then there was the bolded section where your ideas were drawn up for a memorial in the park where you jogged. Let's not forget the money dispersion…where most of your funds magically disappeared into an account not to be discussed with me. Karma is a bitch though…isn't it? Because the woman you left half of our married savings to is dead…frolicking with you no doubt in whatever afterlife would take you. And why are there so many white lilies here? I'm not sure if that was you're doing or your mothers but they're a hideous, atrocious flower of death.

Here I am…chastising a dead man again. I did love you…and you knew that. I wish we'd had more time, but not for any fanciful reasons. I wish I'd had more time to catch you…to see through the lies you so artfully twisted. The nights you'd come home and worshipped my body, making me feel alive…was that only the nights you couldn't be with her? All the questions and no answers. That's what I'm left with. I shouldn't feel guilty…why do I feel so fucking guilty? Is it because I'm mad at you or is it something more ludicrous? I could never say these things aloud. Can you imagine the shock and awe if people heard my true feelings? But here…here I can say what eats at my soul every damn night.

Love is bullshit. Love is a trap that snares your soul like a frantic hare and cages it for its own guilty pleasures. It leaves you blind and blissfully unaware of your own fleeting, inconsequential existence. You bask in its glorious radiant light, unaware that it's really just a magnifying glass, burning a hole through you.

Would I burn for it all over again if I could turn back time? That's the real question. Would I choose to have known love in that way…just once, knowing what I know now? Was it worth it?

I rub my finger along the wrinkled dots on the paper, knowing right away that they're tear stains. Suddenly, a whole other side of Novalie emerges in my mind's eye. Far from the angel that has wrecked my metal shields and broken through my defenses. I see now where her fire comes from. She gave her heart to this man, and from the hurtful words she spewed…she must've loved him deeply once upon a time. He controlled and manipulated her life, taking away her career potential, her freedom, her spirit. No wonder she was so lonely and hidden from the world after. She had her freedom for the first time in years but was scared to fully embrace it. Then I barged in and turned her life upside down once more. Once again…a different man, but the same manipulation.

Feeling as if I may be sick to my stomach, I reach for a pen on her end table and settle back against the headboard of the bed. One day…I'll make sure she has the life she deserves, even though that life won't include me.

CHAPTER 28

Novalie

Mel eyes me from the passenger seat as I half-jog to the car. Swinging the door open, I freeze, gaze locked on the seat. "What?" she asks, confused. My mouth opens to answer, but nothing comes out. My driver's seat is as far back as it can go.

What the hell?

"*Nova*, are you okay?" Her voice drags me from the trance I'm in.

"Yeah…fine, just thought I forgot something." The lie slides easily from my lips. She doesn't look to buy what I'm selling but doesn't push me further as I hop in and crank the car.

Mel is making idle small talk, and I'm somehow answering her, but my mind is far from this conversation.

Soren's been in my car…he's gone somewhere while I was working. What is he hiding from me? Why would he keep *anything* from me after everything I'm doing to help him?

"So, what's the plan here?" Mel asks. "Cause I know you have one."

I store away the knowledge of Soren's untimely betrayal and smile at Mel. Her deep brown curls are framing her face today with the back half up, half down. She has on a retro paisley top that looks authentic with her signature flare jeans. "I may have an idea of how to find out if Jace is a good guy or a piece of shit."

Her cheek dimples. "Okay, how then?"

Changing gears and launching us onto the freeway, I talk a little louder over the noisy engine. "I think the best way to find out is through the wife. If we can get her to spill the tea, that is."

"How do we do that?" Mel asks.

"We lie, of course." Mel's brows rise. "I continue with the lie that I'm writing the novel about Victoria's murder. We corner the new wife and tell her that we have insiders willing to go on record that he was abusive. If she values her privacy and wants this omitted from the text, she'll either vouch for his innocence or stumble, and we can gauge her reactions. It's not foolproof; some women abused hide it really well, but I imagine we can gather enough from her to decide for ourselves."

Mel frowns when I glance her way. "What?" I ask.

"This will only give us a little insight into her relationship, but I don't think this is going to be enough to mark him off the suspect list or raise him to the top."

"True, that's why I'm also meeting my brother here today." Mel makes a face. "I might have sent him a message on my way to the car. I'm tired of waiting around on pins and needles for a smoking gun, so I asked him to get me a background check ASAP. Uncle Jim is being unusually elusive, and although he's helped immensely with the case files, he's not answering my texts and getting back to me with anything else."

"So between Jace's wife's answers and the background check, we could potentially ramp this up," she says to herself.

"I sure hope so," I mutter.

An hour later, we pull into the craft fair. The enormous field is made into a makeshift parking lot and is completely filled to the brim. People are thickly packed, walking toward the entrance, and the smell of grilling meats fills the air. We walk side by side through the gate and stare out at the lines and lines of vendors. Everything from handmade wooden signs, resin art, jewelry, and baked goods clutter the tables along the way. Children rush past in a flurry of dresses and swinging braids.

"I have to give it to Jace…he's created something amazing here," Mel says in awe.

My eyes cut to her. "Seriously, Mel? He's a potential murderer…let's not give him any credit just yet."

She smiles and shrugs. "I'm just saying."

Scanning the crowd, it doesn't take long to find Jace Farrow in a group of men leaning against an antique tractor.

We keep our distance as we move past, looking for any sign of his wife. The two little boys that are fighting over the tractor seat, I recognize instantly as his sons.

After a while, I finally catch a glimpse of his wife seated at a picnic table, her baby clutched in her arms as she laughs with an elderly woman. "There she is." I point.

"What do you need me to do?" Mel asks with clear excitement.

"Convince her that you have some handmade baby items that you're interested in selling here next year and that you want her to take a look to see if she thinks they'd be a hit."

"Where do I have her follow me to…this place is crowded."

Looking around again, I spot a tent on the far left side of the selling area. It's vacant, as if a vendor didn't make it here today. "See that tent over there?" I gesture. "I'll be waiting behind the curtain."

"Like the Wizard of Oz." Mel snickers.

"Ugh, just go." I push her playfully.

"Okay, okay." She curls her lip at me before walking away.

Once inside, I drop the side curtains that are tied back, hiding me from view of the people passing by. I pull a chair over to the corner and wait. It's not long before I hear Mel's voice nearby.

"You'll love the onesies…they give that seventies vibe, but for little ones," Mel gushes, and I bite back a laugh.

"Ooo, can't wait to see them. I love anything retro," the woman says sweetly.

The curtain pulls back and in walks the wife, no longer holding the child, followed by Melina…child in *her* arms. I cock a brow at her but smile at the woman in greeting. "Have a seat." I wave a hand to the chair in front of me and watch as Mel coos over the baby girl grasping at her fingers.

Two lines form on Jace's wife's forehead as she glances around, seeing no merchandise. She's a stunning brunette who is one of those women who look like they've never given birth, with her slim, toned body fitted into a yellow sundress. Her hazel eyes search mine, but she sits anyway before asking, "You have something to show me?" She looks around again, puzzled.

"What's your name?" I ask, leaning forward in my seat to make eye contact.

"Marley…but I assumed you'd know that if you wanted to sell here," she says blatantly.

"Marley, my name is…Nola." I give her the false name I'd given her husband that day at the farm stand. "And I'm sorry to have lied to you about our intentions."

Marley glances at Mel and then snaps her eyes back to mine. "What's this about? And Nola…you say? I remember your name. Jace said you might have been a reporter the day you stopped by…is that what this is?" she demands and starts to stand, but I place a calming hand on her leg.

"I promise you, we're not reporters." It's one truth I can give her at least. "We're actually here on your behalf…to help you."

She drags her eyes over me scathingly. "How *exactly* are you here to help me?"

Let the lies begin. I mentally groan. "I'm actually writing a book about the murder of Victoria and the arrest and escape of Soren Marshall."

"*And*? How is that different than a reporter? You're here to suck any information from me you can get for your benefit…same as a reporter." She eyes Mel with her child.

"This *is* different. If you don't want your husband's name drug through the dirt, that is," I say, snagging her attention back to me.

"How so?" she asks, face curious now.

"I have insiders telling me they're willing to go on record stating that Jace Farrow was abusive." I stop there, Mel and I both watching for shock, or fear on Marley's face but find humor instead.

My forehead creases when she actually smirks at us and flips her hair over a shoulder. "You're kidding me, right?"

I shake my head. "No…not in the least. There's been others claiming he abused Victoria, which in turn could affect Soren…if a new trial is ever granted."

She chuckles, further baffling the two of us. Mel has stopped rocking the child and just stares at her. "You two should fact-check these informants more thoroughly. Jace Farrow would never and has never raised a hand to a woman *in his life*. My husband is a giver, a gentleman, and a wonderful father." Anger begins to rise in her. "How dare you come to our land, our home and accuse him of such a thing!" She stands abruptly, reaching for her daughter, and Mel gladly hands her over.

"Wait, please," I beg, standing too. "I'm not accusing him. I'm trying to decipher the truth so that I can save your family from being hounded further."

She pauses with her back to me and slowly turns to face me. "How am I to convince you that he is a good man? Huh? Convince you to disregard whoever's spewing that nonsense?" She bends to kiss her baby, who's becoming restless in her arms, then she glares at me in a way I'd wish on no one. "Here's a tidbit of information for you...*Nola.* Jace was a wreck when I met him, and not because he was missing Vicky...he was wrecked because she left him desolate." My head snaps back, but she keeps going. "That's right. She maxed out every card he had and started more and maxed those out too. She sold off items of his behind his back, and before he finally caught onto everything and left her...*he* filed a restraining order against *her.*"

Mel takes a gulp of air at the same time I do. "For what?" I ask.

Marley smiles, knowing she's thoroughly kinked our idea of Jace. "He filed it to keep her away and because of the last argument they got into...she hit *him.* He held her off, of course, but she was the one arrested that night." She gives me one more glowering look before turning to exit the tent, saying over her shoulder, "Hope that helps your view of my husband...now leave my property...NOW!"

CHAPTER 29

Novalie

"What about Ian? When's he coming?" Mel asks, sitting beside me to the right of a long oak bar.

"Oh, you know my brother. He's fashionably late for everything," I mumble and then take a long drink from the margarita. We promptly left the craft fair and headed toward the city, but not before Jace himself saw us. He looked murderous, yelling as we ran, but we fled before he could confront me. I had Mel message Ian, filling him in on the change of plans as I drove.

"He says he's about an hour away now," I tell her.

Before we got to the bar called The Watering Hole…the *last* bar Ren ever ventured into with Vicky, Mel made me stop by Palmetto State Armory, and now I'm the proud owner of a Sig Sauer P320. It matches the one she carries.

She insisted that I go no further with this civilian investigation without some sort of protection.

Now here we are. Drowning our sorrows with beer and sad country songs. I laugh out loud, making Mel blanch. "What's so damn funny?" she asks.

"Well…everything. I can't believe we cornered that poor woman and failed miserably. Now, I'm back at square one. The nurse was a bust, Jace was a bust, and Vicky has turned out to be a complete *bitch,* so she could have countless enemies."

"Like her husband," Mel throws at me.

My glare has her looking away. "He's innocent, Mel, I know it."

"Maybe you're giving him the benefit of the doubt because you like him," she says carefully.

"I don't *like* him. You're ridiculous. I…I just…" Words fail me.

She pats my arm before taking a drink. "Okay, tell yourself whatever, but I see the way he looks at you and you him. He's been alone for a long time and so have you…just be careful."

I clench my teeth to keep from saying anything damning. I'm sure she can see right through me. Hell, I can't deny what transpired in that bedroom. It was intense, powerful.

"If…and I'm saying *if* you like him, or if something has happened between you, it could rip your heart out again, Nova, and I don't want to watch you go through that a second time."

I contemplate her words. "You're right, and I know that, but—"

"But what?" she asks. "I'm your best friend. You're my supernova. You can tell me anything. I can't say I won't judge you, because I'm one thousand percent going to judge you, but you can tell me anything." She waves her hand around the bar. "I'm here, aren't I, helping you do something that seems impossible, but I'm *here*."

Taking a deep breath and then a very long drink, I sit the glass down and face her. "We made out."

Dimples deepen in her tanned cheeks, and I swear she looks sixteen again. "I knew it."

"You didn't know shit." I giggle.

"*I did too.* That man called you princess, and you should've seen your face." She watches as a blush creeps over my neck. "See, that right there. You're blushing just thinking about it. Was it a good tongue-lashing then?" She waggles her eyebrows.

My lips purse as a breath rolls out slowly. "Better than anything I've ever felt."

"Damn," she says, impressed. "Sign me up for the next con man."

We laugh together as a new bartender comes around to take orders from a couple near us. Mel stops laughing instantly and points at him. "Hey…that's Ben…the guy that used to have a major crush on me in college, remember."

I squint his way. "Holy shit, it is him."

Mel's face perks up, and she grabs me to whisper, "This is *perfect.* I bet I can flirt with him and see about gaining access to those old tapes…if they have them."

A grin splits my face. "Not perfect, Mel…a happy accident."

She bites her tongue between her teeth, smiles, and then goes to work over the bartender. I watch as she tugs her top a little lower, showing her perky cleavage, and then sashays to him, a thumb hooked into her belt loop. His cherub face lights up at the sight of her. Ben rakes a hand through his blond hair and leans over the bar, smiling and chatting it up with her like old friends. After a few minutes, I feel as if this might be another fail today because she's yet to come back to me.

I startle at a voice behind me. "Just how are you two getting home?"

Spinning on the bar stool, I find my brother looking down on me…with his police uniform on. He glances between the mixed drink and me as I snidely say, "Couldn't you have changed before coming here? Damn…no one wants a cop in a bar."

"Actually," he moves to take Mel's seat beside me, "I'm heading in for duty. I have a little time to spare."

"Oh." I glance around the bar, seeing other patrons uncomfortable at his sudden appearance. "Well, did you get anything on Jace Farrow?" I ask, lacking my enthusiasm from earlier now that I was thoroughly chastised by Jace's wife.

"I did. And why did it take you so long to tell me about this book you're writing?" He tilts his head, looking wounded.

"I'm sorry. It…all kind of happened fast." *That's an understatement*, I think to myself.

"It's okay, just keep me included next time. I *am* an officer…I can help you, you know…with fact checking."

"Thanks, Ian, I appreciate it," I say as he hands me a folded paper from his pocket. I snatch it from his hands and flip it open quickly, scanning the document. My shoulders droop.

"What's that look for?" Ian asks, brows notched together. "I would assume you needed factual stuff for this book?"

"I don't know, Ian. I'm getting conflicting information about this case. Jace Farrow was supposedly an abuser. He was a person of interest, but not now." I fold the paper and put it in my purse. "According to this," I tap my purse, "he actually filed a restraining order against Vicky. I *was* leaning toward Soren Marshall being innocent."

He jerks back and smiles sarcastically. "What would make you think he's innocent? This was an open and shut case, Nova."

"Yeah, well, Uncle Jim never looks in one direction; he looks in every direction. I'm just trying to cross all T's and dot all I's."

"Fair enough." He huffs a sigh.

Mel skips over to us, eyes wide. She sees Ian and gives a small smile and half-wave but grabs me by the shoulders. "They kept them! They kept copies of the footage that night, like you thought they would. ANDDDD Ben can sneak us back to view them. The manager is out for the day!"

"View what tapes?" Ian asks, making Mel straighten up and shoot a look between us.

I ease her worry that my brother may be a hiccup in this plan by saying, "We have access to the tapes from the last night Soren was here in the bar with Vicky."

"You guys probably shouldn't be doing this." He gives me a stern, brotherly look.

"What?" I ask. "It's part of the research for my book. And besides…I know this stuff intrigues you too. Don't pretend otherwise…come back with us."

Ian looks at his watch and then back to me. He drags a hand over his clean-shaven face. "I have fifteen minutes, then I'm out, but…okay, I'll have a look." His high cheekbones rise with a smirk. "I'll admit, you have piqued my curiosity."

In the dark office, lit only by a flickering fluorescent light, we sit on three rickety old rolling chairs watching the small screen before us. Ben hovers over the fast-forward button, speeding through the night until he gets to the time marked on the tape.

Mel's shifting in her chair to eye the room and wrinkles her nose in distaste. "Is everything in here from the dawn of time? She leans forward and touches a Budweiser poster of a bikini-clad woman, dragging a line of dust away.

"Stop that." I nudge her. She bites back a smile.

Ben ignores us and stops the tape once he hits the mark. "Here's the footage you're looking for. You guys can't tell anyone I showed you this…I'd be fired for sure. They weren't supposed to have copies."

Mel winks at him, causing a blush to form on his neck. "I'll keep your secret, Benny Boo."

"*Benny Boo*?" I whisper to her. "You're laying it on a bit thick, aren't you?" She shrugs.

We all three watch the night unfurl before us on a shitty screen with even shittier video quality—fuzzy, scratchy lines hiding parts of the scene, but finally dissipating. My breath catches in my throat when Soren comes into view—choking my senses. His tall frame is imposing as he parts the crowd and heads for the bar. Noticing my body language, Ian leans in closer to look at the man, and so does Mel. The first several minutes are casual, but you can sense something's not right.

Victoria sits beside him, with some sort of black dress on and a shimmery purse. They're seated at the bar…not too far from where Mel and I were just perched. There's no playful laughter, just heated conversations that look as if they're gaining in volume. From this angle, you can see Victoria when she gets up and goes to the restroom each time…like Soren had said. More time passes and they have several drinks between them. It's hard to tell what Soren is wearing. All I can see is a black jacket that could be leather and dark jeans. He doesn't have a beard either.

I glance at Ian when he looks at his watch again, but he makes no move to leave. The last time Vicky excuses herself, we watch as Soren takes her forgotten phone and flips through it. I recall him telling me about that and how she didn't have *any* sent messages. He'd thought she was having an affair, but there was nothing incriminating on her phone.

"What was he looking at there…her phone?" Ian asks. "It looked like her phone. Maybe a jealous husband move," he notes.

"Maybe," I say derisively.

Victoria comes back from the restroom and proceeds to have another heated conversation based on her facial features and arm movements. She drags a hand through her blonde hair, sitting up taller. Even from this crappy footage, you can see she's furious, but also nervous. I haven't missed the way she looks around the bar every few minutes. Her gaze travels to the same corner repeatedly. It's one that's barely in view. A man is seated there, but he's unrecognizable in this footage…all except for his boots. The tips catch the light occasionally. Like they're tipped with silver at the end. Old cowboy boots, maybe?

Soren's shoulders roll forward as they lean into each other, saying what…who knows.

"There's not much that happens here, just more of the same," Ben says. "They leave the bar shortly after this part."

Ian stands and turns toward the door, and Mel follows suit. Ben is just about to turn off the monitor when I see something. "*Stop*!" I throw a hand over his and lean closer, causing Ian and Mel to freeze and spin toward us. Ben moves back a step, giving me a clearer view. Ren has gotten up from the barstool and is almost at the restroom. To anyone else, it would look like Vicky had already stepped out of the camera's range, but I notice the shiny metallic bag that she walked in with barely in the cameras view—just a corner of it showing, but that is definitely it. A man stands, facing her direction in a short sleeve button down navy blue shirt…mechanics style. He's in the direct line of sight from this angle, and based on their proximity, he *has* to be face to face with her.

I point to the purse barely in the frame. "That's her purse. I used to have the exact sequin one that Victoria's Secret came out with some years back."

"Oh my God, yeah, that was a nice bag," Mel says dreamily.

Shaking my head, I ask, "Who's this guy she's talking to while Soren's in the bathroom?" I ask aloud, not expecting an answer, simply voicing my thoughts.

"Are you sure that's her?" Mel asks.

Before she can get an answer from me, Ian says, "That's her alright."

"Yep," I concur. Eyeing the man closer, I'm rewarded with a shift in his position. I get full-body chills as his features become clearer. He looks…familiar. Why does he look so damn familiar?

"Could be someone random she knew," Mel says, and Ian nods.

Ben looks at the screen and then at all of us. "I've never noticed that before, but…I know who that is." Our heads turn creepily in unison to glare at him. Ben looks between us and shrugs. "What, it's a bar. We see and know everyone that comes in or out, and I've been here a long time."

"*Who is it?*" I ask impatiently.

"That's Micah Talon. He helped rebuild my dad's square-body Chevy years ago. He comes in all the time."

Ben is talking, but I am *combusting* inside. It's like a bomb has been dropped and shrapnel is tearing me to shreds.

"Are you okay, Nova?" Mel asks. I look vacantly at her and Ian…Ian, who is no fool and likely knows the case. He must be putting two and two together right now. *Micah*…Soren's best friend, Soren's *partner*, Soren's *co-business owner*. The man who had access to Soren's financial accounts.

Ian speaks up. "Well, Nova…this just made your book all the more interesting."

CHAPTER 30

Soren

The night sky is flecked with stars barely noticeable over the lights of the city. Nova has absolutely wrecked my nerves, and all I can do is sit and look at that moon…the way she used to when I watched her—when I hid out across the street. Wow, that sounds worse and worse in my head when I think it.

Sipping my coffee, I check my burner phone again. Nothing, no message, no missed calls. *Fuck*. It's almost eleven o'clock. She's been gone all day without a single word to let me know she's fine.

The night air is still warm from the heat of the day. Ripping my shirt over my head, I let the breeze run over my skin and stand to lean over the railing. Several times today, I almost called her. The only thing stopping me was the fact that I didn't know who she was around. I didn't want to chance someone being curious and picking up her phone. My worst fears have started to sink in and grab hold of my chest in a vice-like grip. What if Jace did something? What if the police somehow caught wind of her involvement and she's being interrogated? What if—

The questions wither and die away when a familiar laugh echoes on the street below. Launching to the right side of the balcony to get a better view, I lean over and search. It only takes a millisecond to find her. Nova quite literally stumbles out of a black Sedan, Mel laughing maniacally behind her as she *too* staggers out. Squinting, I can see the large sicker on the rear window of the car displaying the license number and driver name below an Uber sign.

Are they drunk? Frowning, I watch them stagger again. Where's her car?

Their laughter continues, and I hear Mel say, "Benny Boo was rather accommodating though, right?" Nova stumbles again, but Mel catches her around the waist.

"I think he would…of given you the…the keys to his house if you asssked," Nova slurs.

"So would that hunky hunk of a slice of meat hitting on you tonight," Mel croons, and Nova slaps a hand over her mouth to stifle a giggle.

My. Blood. Boils. Just the thought of her drunk in a bar…looking like that and other men scrapping for her attention has me wanting to do *very* bad things.

"He…was insistent," Nova says, still clutching onto Mel as they pass below me, not seeing me at all.

"That's an understatement, honey." Mel's voice grows distant and muted as they pass out of range.

Inhaling a calming breath, I unlock the front door for them, but retreat to the balcony to sit, afraid of saying the wrong things when she walks through that door. It's not long before I hear the trampling of uneven footsteps and fits of more giggles. Then silence, as if they're realizing just how loud they are. Another muted snicker and then whispers find my ears. The clunking sound of what I assume are shoes is next. Several minutes pass with quieted words, but then the sounds stop.

Finally, I can't take the curiosity eating at me anymore. I throw back the remainder of the coffee and set down the mug, albeit too hard, then walk into the living room expecting drunken shenanigans from these two, *only*, I find Mel leaning over Nova on the couch. She positions a pillow under her head—Nova's bare feet and legs dangling over the edge.

Tsking, I move to help her. "I got her legs," I say, lifting them onto the couch. Mel stands wobbly, watching me cover her with the blanket that I've been using every night. Once she's covered, I reach behind her head and easily remove the hair tie, letting her hair rest comfortably behind her. Then I'm standing full height, looking down on a smirking Mel. "Where *the hell* have you two been?"

Her brows raise, and she cocks her head back sassily, making her curls fly over a shoulder. "Interesting? Were you *worried* about her?" She glances at her friend, who's out cold.

I give her a withering look but relax my tone. "Where were you?"

She wobbles again, and I take her arm and lead her to the opposite couch. She starts to protest but then thinks better of it when I lay a stern look on her. Mel bends her legs to rest underneath her and hugs a pillow as she falls against the armrest but watches me curiously. She finally deigns to give me an answer. "We did what we set out to do. We went to the craft fair and The Watering Hole."

Just picturing them there…where I spent my last night gives me a sick feeling. Even though that place had nothing to do with what transpired later…it still makes me ill. "And was it fruitful?" I ask, trying to contain my agitation.

Mel grins, making a dimple dip in her cheek. "It was and wasn't—some fruits, some rotted." She laughs.

My face lets her know how unamused I am. "Don't play games, Melina. What happened today?"

She bobs her head side to side, gives me a mocking mumble, then says, "Okay, okay. Jeez. Jace Farrow isn't our guy."

Sitting on the couch arm and looking down on her, I ask, "Why not?"

"Turns out his wife is a huge supporter of her husband and was willing to go to bat for him. She told us that back when he was with Victoria, he filed a restraining order against *her* for attacking *him*…and that's not all…she took him for a lot of money and left him in major debt."

Standing, I pace the room, cursing. Mel's words from earlier stop me. "What was fruitful about today then?" I ask.

"We saw the video of the night you were with Vicky…a guy I used to know let us see the tape."

I spin to face her, walking closer. "And?"

"And," Mel yawns, "you need to have that conversation with Nova…tomorrow."

My brows drag together. "Why? Tell me what you saw," I demand.

Mel's eyes drift closed, but she replies sleepily, "No, Soren. Talk to her tomorrow." Frustrated, I clench my fists, about to demand again that she tell me something, but her next words stop me. "She's mad at you, by the way." She opens her eyes just a sliver to look at me.

"Why would Nova be mad at me?" My question is quiet…and contemplative.

"She wouldn't say why, but the drunker she got, the more she tensed up when I talked about you. I know my friend better than anyone else. She's mad about something…question is…*what?*" I stare at her dumbfounded before she says one last thing. "Don't fucking hurt my friend Soren…*ever.* Make it right…whatever it is you've done."

Mel watches me fidget and rake a hand through my hair. This time when she talks, her voice has softened and loses its normal edge of sarcasm. "You know why I call her supernova?" she asks but doesn't wait for a reply when she sees my wrinkled brow. "We were in middle school…like seventh grade. I had this teacher who was a…bit of a creep." Her eyes have that far-off daze that people get reminiscing but turn haunted fast. "He kept me after class one day. Said he needed to see me about an assignment. When everyone left, he…" Her cheeks pinken ever so slightly. "He touched me inappropriately." Anger replaces her embarrassment. "I was always the one to stand up for myself. But he was so strong, he held me there and I was frozen, couldn't scream, didn't know what to do."

Nausea roils through me at the image she's describing. "I'm so sorry that happened to you."

"Oh, it didn't last long." Mel smiles.

"The other kids had left for the day. The halls were empty, parking lot clearing out. What he didn't know was that Ian, Nova's brother, was picking us up that day. When

I didn't come out behind her, Nova doubled back. She cracked open the door, peeped into the classroom, and saw his hands on me. Her eyes met mine, and that was it." Mel releases a breath through her nose and then snorts. "You should've seen her. She became a wild animal…a totally different person. She raced toward us, swinging her bookbag full of thick texts, and he didn't have time to flinch as she clocked him with it."

I can't hold back my grin. "She hit him with her bookbag?"

"Knocked him on his ass…but it gets better. She was lost to rage, like I said…not really herself. She picked up the nearest thing she could reach, which happened to be a beaker, and smashed it into his face."

I gape at her and then smile at the image. "Why the name supernova though?"

"We'd just studied supernovas that day. The chalked writing was still on the board that read, A supernova is a massive explosion that happens at the end of a star's life cycle, resulting in a dramatic increase in brightness that can outshine entire galaxies. I memorized that description after that day. Because *she* did that for me. Outshined everything. The brightness I needed in the dark." A sort of calm comes over Mel. "I told her that day…shine bright and give 'em hell."

"What happened next?" I ask.

"You know the justice system isn't all it's cracked up to be. No one at school believed us. We were suspended. He covered up what he'd done…for a time. Eventually, Nova spilled it all to her brother, and we finally got our justice in the end. It just took some time, but…he was arrested and carries a hell of a nasty scar to this day."

I nod and watch as Melina yawns, jaw gaping open and eyes closing. "Goodnight, convict," she says, making me smile and shake my head.

I watch them for another half hour, making sure they're both good and asleep. When I'm certain they're out cold, I carry each of them to Nova's bed and tuck them in, leaving water and headache meds on each nightstand. Standing over Nova, I finger a stray lock of hair away from her cheek and gently caress the soft skin with the pad of my thumb.

A worried crease forms between her brows, and to my shock, she murmurs, "*Soren.*" It's so low and whispered that I almost miss it.

Backing away, I exit the bedroom, shutting the door behind me, and end up back on the balcony—Mel's story playing out like a movie in my head.

CHAPTER 31

Novalie

Searing bright light has me cringing and sinking into my fluffy blanket, a croaky groan of protest leaving my lips. I hear a thunk, and someone curses and sucks in a breath. Flipping the blanket off, my eyes dart to the right to find Mel hopping on one foot and holding her toe before sitting on the bed to rub it.

What the hell? My foggy brain tries to analyze the room quickly.

How did we get in here?

Mel's head snaps my way when she catches my movement. "Morning, sunshine," she says brightly.

"What time is it?" I manage to ask.

"Seven-thirty. How're you feeling?" She smirks knowingly.

"Like I've been hit by a truck, then they backed over me to make sure the job was done correctly." She snickers. "How did we get in here?" I sit up and look around the room again, noticing the water and meds beside me. "Ooo, thanks for these." Snatching them up, I down the two pills and gulp water, coughing when I go too fast.

"That wasn't me." Setting down the water, I clear my throat as she adds, "Soren must've carried us in here and left this stuff."

My head swivels toward the closed bedroom door as if I can see through to him. Embarrassment floods my system with raging fire. "Oh my God." Covering my face with my hands, I moan. "I barely remember getting in that Uber."

Hearing her laugh has me peeling my hands away to glare at her. She stands and puts a hand on her hip to eye me. "Don't be embarrassed; you were quite the life of the party last night…but well behaved. I think it's sweet that he put us to bed," she says just as the door knocks lightly and cracks open.

"Everyone decent?" Soren's voice reverberates into the room. Mel walks over, opening it for him just as he says, "*Sweet*…was that a compliment from you, Melina?" He strides into the room, smiling at her arrogantly. I tug the blanket higher and run a hand through my hair as if that will help my disheveled appearance.

"Don't let it go to your head, convict." Mel side-eyes him.

Soren's eyes slip over to me, tracing my face in a gentle caress. "How're you feeling?" he asks, voice low and concerned, not condemning in the least.

"In her words, like she was hit by a truck and then backed over again," Mel says flippantly. I glare daggers at her, but she ignores my venom and skirts around Soren, saying, "Nova…call me later and keep me updated on everything. I need to go. I have two clients to meet with this morning."

"Uhhum, okay," I mumble, watching her leave. Soren and I stare at each other awkwardly until we hear the click of the front door.

"What?" I ask when it's obvious he has no intentions of speaking first.

"I was worried yesterday," he admits, his jaw set in a firm line.

I notice his ragged appearance for the first time. It could rival mine. His hair is spiked in all directions as if he ran frustrated hands through it. He's wearing a wrinkly tee and gray jogging pants. Dark areas smudge the undersides of his eyes.

"You don't look like you slept too well," I say, avoiding the conversation we're bound to have.

"I'm fine," he says unconvincingly. "What happened yesterday?"

Moving to sit on the edge of the bed and sipping the water this time, I give myself a moment to consider what and how I should broach this subject. I start by retelling everything that happened at the craft fair and the confrontation with Marley. Next, I tell him about my brother and the document confirming that Jace wasn't the bad guy we thought he was.

I hesitate on the rest. It's on the tip of my tongue, but *something* holds me back. Maybe it's because I don't know how to tell him that his friend could be involved. How do I break this man's heart all over again? He's been through so damn much.

I need a moment to think.

"Can we finish this after showers and coffee?" I groan and hold my head in my hands.

"Sure." He nods. "You go first."

I drag out the shower for far too long, shaving, washing twice, then standing at the mirror brushing my teeth forcefully…but eventually I can't hide any longer, so I make quick work of dressing in cut-off shorts and a white tank top, braiding my damp hair over one shoulder.

In the kitchen, I watch Soren disappear into the bedroom to get himself cleaned up. I make two mugs of steaming coffee with peppermint mocha creamer and a pan of chocolate chip muffins as I wait. It's not just the admission of what we saw on that tape that's concerning me, but the fact that Soren was in my car at some point. I want to outright ask him, but in another way…I want his honesty—for him to be forthright with me. What is he hiding? What was so important that he would chance sneaking off when I was at work…when the whole damn world is searching for his face? He could've been caught, and everything we're doing would've gone to shit.

Soren breezes through the bedroom doorway sometime later, and all the cacophony of noises in my head shrivels away to nothing. Holy fucking hell. He's…*beautiful.* His light wash boot-cut jeans are hung sinfully low on his waist. He's bare-chested, abs rippling with his movement, tattoos made even darker over his body by the steam-soaked skin. Ren drags the towel over his head one last time, wringing the last of the water droplets from the thick black strands. His bare feet move toward me as I brazenly slide my gaze from foot to head. Thankfully, he doesn't notice until I'm level with his eyes. Sliding the coffee to him, I clear my throat and try to stop ogling.

"Thanks." He smiles, and I literally curl my toes at the sight, noticing how his own eyes are now traipsing over me, appraisingly.

Giving his face a once-over, I point to his nose where the cut used to be. "You only have a tiny line there now. It's almost gone."

"Everything heals in time," he says gruffly.

I don't respond to that loaded statement. Instead, I pass him a muffin. We eat in silence for a few minutes. Anyone on the outside looking in would think it was *absolutely* normal. Two people having breakfast—starting their day. But you could cut the tension in this room with a knife. It's suffocating.

He's waiting for me to fill him in on my drunken night, and I'm waiting for him to tell me what he's done when I wasn't around. But that's not the only thing palpable in this house. We haven't been alone since the make-out session that rocked my world.

His eyes dip to my low-cut tank top, coffee paused at the entrance to his mouth. Looking up slowly, he finds my gaze on him. His dark lashes fan over his stormy eyes that are *burning* from within. Even with all the doubt spiraling out of control around us—all the questions we have yet to answer…that heated look swipes it all away.

"What are you thinking, Soren?" I break the silence, setting down my coffee.

He follows suit, sitting down his mug too, and moves slowly…like a predator, head tilting as he stands and walks around the island. Angling my head at him questioningly, I retreat a few steps as he rounds the corner, keeping my eyes locked on his. "What are you doing?" I ask, the whispered words shaking loose from my lips.

"What I should've done yesterday," he growls in a voice that could drop the panties off a nun.

Shaking my head and backing up again, I hold up a trembling hand. "Soren…we need to discuss—" He's on me in an instant. My shriek echoes through the house as he lifts me in the air, forcing my legs to wrap around him.

One of his large hands holds me against him while the other cups the back of my neck as we move. "Stop speaking Nova," he grounds out. "Anything we have to say can wait. *This. Can't.*"

"*But*—" No sooner than the solitary word is out, my back hits the wall. I gasp, looking up to him as his mouth crashes into mine with a frantic need I've never experienced before. My lips part on impact, letting him in, letting him breathe life into me with every caress of his talented tongue against mine. Soft, full lips and the scrap of his short beard send a force of need skittering through me.

He settles me against the wall, pressing into me, holding me captive with the hand behind my neck, ripping loose any control I thought I had over the situation. Not that I want any control here. On the contrary, I'd let him take everything from me right now and leave me with nothing but a void. That's how much I crave this man—crave his touch.

When his mouth and tongue tease their way down my chin and onto my neck, my fingers tighten their hold on him, sinking nails into his bare back. He hisses and bites the side of my neck, eliciting a moan from me, then drags his wicked tongue over the bitten area and whispers into my ear, "My princess has claws."

My fingers curl instinctively into his back again, but not enough to hurt. Then his words hit me, striking a killing blow to my chest…*my princess*…*my*. It's a foolish feeling, a *stupid, foolish* girly feeling. It's such a simple word but loaded like a gun.

Soren pauses his torment to look into my eyes. Before he can question what he's seeing there, I smash my mouth back to his, delving my tongue in and swirling it with his own. His body goes rigged with need, his pelvis pressing into me, letting me feel just how badly he wants me. The obliterating heat at my core has me wiggling and pushing into him, but it's as if we could share skin and it still wouldn't be close enough.

"Take. Me. *Now*, Soren," I demand against his parted lips, our breath mingling in a dance of desire.

A rugged groan rumbles from his chest a second before I'm being carried and tossed onto the bed with ease. Biting my lower lip, dragging my teeth there, I look him over and whisper, "My brutish caveman." Something flickers in his eyes, and it makes me wonder if my purposeful use of the word 'my' is just as devastating to his senses.

Ren looks barely contained with unleashed fire as he demands, "Remove your clothes, Novalie…now."

Heat blazes my neck and cheeks, but nervous or not, I sit up and drag my tank top over my head swiftly and then watch Ren's eyes grow hooded when I unclasp my bra slowly and toss it aside. My breasts move with every inhale, and I revel in the slight part of his hungry lips. Then, he leans over me halfway, hands on the buttons of my jean shorts. Leaning backward, purposefully arcing my breast forward, I lift my hips off the bed just enough for him to yank them away, panties and all.

Swallowing hard as he backs away, eyes take every inch of me in with exaggerated slowness. They linger exotically at the apex of my thighs. He resembles a wild animal stilled for the pounce. I finally *breathe.* The nervous energy dissipates into appreciation for the desire I've created in this man. It's powerful and glorious.

"Fair is fair." I wave toward his jeans.

Ren slides his pants and boxers away with ease, keeping his eyes on mine as if he's memorizing this very moment. My mouth goes dry at the sight of him, thick and hard for me. He's perfect. His strong body leans over me, corded muscles straining in his arms that are braced on either side of my head, chest rising and falling in a staccato rhythm matching my own. Striking hot desire flames like molten metal in his eyes that have become more gray than blue. He's absolutely feral with need and something *more* that I can't place. But then he voices the words, causing the strange possessive look in his eyes to make sense. And they hit me like a bolt of lightning, striking true.

"You're *mine* now, princess. No matter what happens. You're *mine* now. Understood?" His hot breath fans my lips as he dips closer to me. "*Say it,*" he demands.

There're moments in life where everything can change for the better or worse in a split second. Moments like seeing a deer in the road and you don't know whether to cut left, right, or stay straight and take the brunt of the impact head on. One way could have you careening into another car; another could have you flipping into the ditch—but facing the danger head-on can also lead to either. I take one more look into Soren Marshall's eyes and choose to smash the fucking deer.

"I'm yours, Soren." My words coat his lips and cling to everything as if we are now sutured together—as if the words were literal needles weaving two souls. Moisture threatens to prick the corners of my eyes as emotions bombard me.

Soren seems to notice the wetness gathering there. He lowers his mouth to brush the edges of one eye with a kiss, stealing its possibility of falling. This time when he hovers over me, there's an understanding between us. Without words, it's as if I can feel it taut between us…this strange connection. He licks his lips before dropping them back to my mouth, slowly, to claim me just as that hard length of him is pressed at my aching core, sliding against me. My legs move of their own accord to snake around his waist and draw him closer as our mouths fit together like lost puzzle pieces.

I let my fingers trail over his spine and shoulders and up into his soft, thick hair as we kiss. Nothing exists but the two of us. I feel one of his hands tug at my hair, dragging to the end of the braid before my hair tie is discarded. Fingers deftly move to unravel the long tresses, and then his hand is wrapped in them, holding me captive as he takes my mouth, deepening the kiss.

My moan is the catalyst for him. He dips his hips backward suddenly, coating himself in my wetness, and sinks into me, not slow, not being gentle, he pushes into me fast and with force until he's seated inside me completely. I gasp, mouth open, panting little bursts of air at the blissful feeling of him stretching me, filling me. "*Ohhh, Soren,*" I moan aloud.

My eyes open to find him breathing erratically as he watches, *gauging* my reaction. To my surprise, his body trembles with the restraint he's hardly able to contain. I press my hand to his face, cupping his bearded cheek, thumb grazing the edge of his mouth. "Don't hold back," I whisper, pulling his mouth down to mine again.

My words unleash that restraint as he grips my hips punishingly, moves back and then drives himself into me hard. Our mutual pleading moans drown out all logic. His tongue wreaks havoc on my rapidly dwindling senses as he thrusts into me in a perfect rough rhythm. The sounds in this room become an all-consuming erotic symphony. Lifting my hips, I meet him thrust for thrust. I'm awestruck when he leans back, muscles flexing as he goes harder. His hand rakes down my abdomen until he is there, pressing his thumb against my clit and then moving in circles that have me arcing off the bed, yelling his name unabashedly.

It's too soon, but I can't hold back as heat and pleasure flood my core, and with one more thrust I'm coming undone in his hands. My pleasured cries flood the room as the orgasm threatens to blacken my vision. Head thrown back, I ride the wave of bliss made more and more intense by his force as he pounds into me. Just as I'm about to come down from the peak of that wave, I feel Soren lift me up, our bodies never separating as he seats me on him, my hair coming around us like a curtain of deep burgundy flames. I cry out again at the feel of how deep he is inside me in this position.

Soren lifts me, and I move with him, matching the motion as he guides my body. My eyes roll back and close when I sink onto him, but they open when he pulls me flush to him and I feel his hand grip my chin. "You're perfect," he says against my swollen lips, his voice so sinful and wicked. He dips his thumb into my mouth, and I willingly coat it with a swipe of my tongue that has him growling. He then drags the pad of his thumb over my lips before leaning forward and biting my lower one just enough to sting.

I suck in a breath and then another as he lifts me up and thrusts into me again. I lean back and move with his body. The sensations have my pulse ricocheting. One of his hands moves between us to cup my aching breast. The electric current that shoots through my body only heightens with the flick of my hardened nipple as his thumb grazes the sensitive peak.

Just as quickly as he'd lifted me onto him, my back is flattened against the mattress once more. I squeal in shock and delight. Ren grips my hips and drives himself into me with enough force to cut off the sound I was making. The pleasure and heat building at my core are spiking once more. Ren takes me with complete abandon. There's no overthinking, no second guessing, he simply takes me like a man possessed, and I'm completely at his mercy.

"Put your hands above your head," he commands.

I swallow any protest I might have and stretch my arms above me. Soren catches them in one of his hands, holding me in place as he bends, taking one of my breasts into his mouth. A plea for more comes from me desperately. He leaves a blazing trail from one to the other, stopping only to blow a cooling breath over my wet nipple.

Pleasure gathers again, ready to make me combust. Soren's body seems to sense it too as he unravels and drives into me harder. The moment the heat floods my core, I scream out his name, coming around him, becoming *one* with him. Stars fleck my eyes and cause a haze of euphoria. I'm vaguely aware of his rhythm stuttering, becoming uneven, before he pulls out of me, making the sexiest guttural sound I've ever heard as he finds his release.

Soren lies beside me after cleaning us up. Our naked bodies intertwined, with my head on his shoulder. Sweat coats both of us—our breathing still labored. *Oh*, but nothing has ever felt this good. My body aches in a few choice places, and I relish it. It's like I can still feel him inside me.

"Are you okay?" His voice vibrates through me.

I let my fingers rake over his abs as I sigh contentedly. "Perfectly okay." I peek up to catch his mouth rising at the corner. "What about you? Are you good with," I wave a hand around the room in a gesture of what just transpired, "all this?"

"Perfectly good," he replies.

Just then, my cell rings from somewhere in the living room. I bury my head in his shoulder, cursing. "I probably need to get that." My words are muffled against him.

He chuckles but then sighs roughly. "Probably so…be quick. I'm not done with you."

I raise my head, cocking a brow at him. "You're insatiable," I say, as I slither out of his grasp and slip off the bed to stand.

His mouth parts when I turn, giving him a full view of my ass as I saunter toward the living room. I hear him say behind me, "I'm insatiable because you're a fucking temptress." Rolling my lips together to hide the smile, I grab a throw blanket, wrapping it around myself.

After the fifth ring, I find my phone on the counter hidden under a napkin. Seeing that it's Bowen, I hurriedly answer. "Bo, what's up?"

"Nova, hey…I didn't catch you at a bad time, did I? You have a minute?" he asks timidly.

I grin as I catch a glimpse of Soren's naked ass heading for the bathroom. "Sure. What's up?"

"I have something for you. It's from Sawyer," Bo says, voice strange.

"From Uncle Jim? What did he give you that he couldn't give me himself?" I ask, bewildered.

I glance to see Soren, now in boxers, heading my way. I smile, but falter when Bo says gravely, "Nova…I don't know how to tell you this, and I'm so sorry."

"What is it Bo?" Dark fear dampens my voice as I begin to panic.

"He…Sawyer…he's dead…your uncle has passed away." My hand juts out to catch myself on the counter as the room seems to sway on a phantom wind. "Nova…I'm sorry…I didn't want to do this over the phone…but I just didn't know what to do." His voice breaks during the silence. "Are you still there? I can come over."

I open my mouth to answer but snap it shut when I feel Soren behind me, thick arms snaking around my waist. A tear streams down my cheek as I choke out, "Now is not a good time." My throat feels clogged as emotions swell inside me. "Can you come by later? I probably need to call Dad…" My words somehow make it out in my shocked state.

Soren moves around me to look at my face, finally seeing the horror there. He lifts my chin as a tear rolls down my cheek. His brows furrow, creating two deep lines in the center of his eyes.

"I'm so sorry to have been the one to tell you, Nova," Bowen says, reminding me that he's still on the phone. "He was more than a friend to me. He was family."

I clear my throat as Soren pulls me against his chest. "What happened to him, Bo?" I ask through the choked tears.

Bowen breathes hard into the phone, and it's a clear sound of frustration. "That's what I need to talk to you about…I think it's got something to do with this case you're researching."

"*What?* No…that can't be…" My incoherent babbles are drowned out by another cry that releases from my throat.

Bowen's voice is insistent. "Nova, listen to me…something's not right here. It's *very* wrong. I need to see you face to face."

"*What happened to him, Bowen?*!" I yell this time.

He's silent for a few moments, enough for me to count the ragged breaths he takes before he finally answers. "He was shot, Nova…"

The phone slips from my hand and clangs against the counter along with my heart.

CHAPTER 32

Soren

My arms wrap around her knees and back as I swoop Nova into the air and against my chest. Bending, I manage to retrieve the phone. Cradling her trembling body against me, I carry her over to the couch and sit with her curled into a ball on top of me. Checking the phone, I see Bowen has hung up.

"What happened, Nova?" I ask gently.

Her sniffles grow more erratic, but she manages to answer through her tears. "Uncle Jim was shot, Soren. He's…gone." Her breath hitches as she buries her face in my collarbone.

Squeezing her tightly, my eyes focus on the front door, immediately checking to see that it's locked and dead bolted. Next, I scan the balcony door, just in case. Logic tells me that this couldn't be related to me. No one knows where I am; no one knows this family is involved, but my gut is saying otherwise. Coincidences are rare in my life.

Lacing my fingers in her hair, I kiss her head and breathe in her scent. Worry for her is a pit…no, more like a gaping ravine in my stomach. What if this has everything to do with me? Is this my fault? Selfishly, my mind latches onto the woman in my arms and the fact that we only just broke the surface—I just had my first taste of what she feels like to be mine and the threat that it could be taken away…it's too much.

"Does Bowen know anything? What else did he say?"

Nova leans her head back to look into my eyes, and they shatter me. "No, well…I'm not sure. He said, somethings wrong about all this, and that he wants to meet with me today." She wipes away tears with the back of her hand. "I can't face them."

My brows knit together. "Them? Face who?"

She chokes back a sob. "My parents…my dad. He just lost his brother Soren."

She begins shaking again, and I bring her head to rest under my chin and cling to her. "We'll get through this…maybe it's not what we think at all."

Nova pushes off me suddenly, and moves to sit beside me, legs curled under her. "What else could it be, Ren? This is my fault…I can feel it."

I shake my head and reach for her hand, but she pulls back. I take a calming breath, but my voice is hard when I say, "If anyone is to blame here, it's me, and you know it." We have a silent stare-down for a few seconds before I curse. "*Fuck* Nova…I never thought anyone would be in danger here. If I'm being honest, I didn't think we would solve the case. I figured I'd end up on some island somewhere and never know the truth." I snatch her hand up before she can pull away again. "You're what's important now…okay, not me. *Not* this case."

Her tiny fingers curl into mine as her watery eyes scan me. "What are you saying, Ren?"

"I'm saying…if this is my fault, and that's why he was killed, someone knows about us or at least that the case is being looked at. What I'm saying is…you could be in danger because of me…and I can't have that."

Her weeping slows, but her body is tense as if ready for a fight. "If you think for one second that you are going to run off and leave me…after *everything* we've been through…you're dead wrong, Soren. We *can't* back down now! My uncle would *never* quit searching."

Nothing shakes my normally hardened interior. I've been through enough to have built up a tolerance for what life can throw at you…but seeing this woman right now willing to go to hell and back for me, it's enough to bring any man to his knees.

"Why?" I ask. When her head tilts and her face shows signs of confusion, I add, "Why are you so willing to continue with this after what just happened? Do you have a fucking death wish? I could leave." Her head begins shaking back and forth, her deep red locks catching sun from the balcony door. It hits me then…she'd never be safe if I ran. She'd continue this research, consequences be damned.

"Just hear me out." I lift one hand to cup the back of her head, bringing her closer, and the other to caress her cheek. "There's another option. I can turn myself in."

She yanks away from my hold on her, shoving at my chest as she stands in a fiery, raging storm, barely keeping the blanket around her. "Soren Lee Marshall, if you turn yourself in, it *still* will not stop me! So *do not* play the martyr here and condemn yourself to suffer…because it will be for nothing!"

Her hair is hanging like a cape around her, determination and fury radiating from every pore. And now I see it. The supernova. The woman who protects those less fortunate, the woman who stands up for what she believes in, the woman who…even when she was being controlled by a narcissistic man, found ways to be herself…like when she bought a Chevy Nova for spite from a loser at a garage. Mel said that she would never stop, and she was right.

In this moment, I give her what she's asking for because who knows what tomorrow will bring. "Okay Nova. I hear you."

"You'll stay…you'll finish this with me? Side-by-side?" she asks, adjusting the blanket to cover her shoulders.

Leaning forward, I run both hands over my face and hair, unable to meet her eyes. "I'm here with you." My voice is barely audible in this room thick with tension.

"You're not just here with me…I'm *yours,* remember? You have me now, for good or bad. If you want me. We are in this together…we made a deal."

My head snaps up to find a fresh, solitary tear leaving a trail down her cheek and a rip in my chest. "We're in this together, Nova," I say with much less conviction than her speech gave.

There's a sudden, untimely knock on the door. Nova spins to face it, mouth agape. Her eyes find mine, but I'm already standing, silently creeping toward it. "Stop," she whispers. My jaw tics as I grind my teeth, my whole body on edge now with what's happened to Detective Sawyer.

"Who's there?" Nova calls out, and my eyes widen at her in warning.

Bowen's muted answer comes instantly. "It's me…Bo."

"Just a second," she calls back, then shoos me toward the bedroom.

Once inside, she drops the blanket on the bed and scrambles for sleep shorts and a tee. "Hide Soren. I'll be fine; it's just Bo."

Dragging my jeans over my waist, I scowl at her. "What if it's not *just* Bo?" I ground out, hopping on one leg to get the jeans on.

She's already walking away when she turns to me. "I'll be fine," she says forcefully but in a quieted tone, but then rushes back to her purse hanging by the bed and pulls out…*a gun*. "Take this." She lays the Sig in my hand, "and hide…*now*!" she ushers me.

Looking from the gun to her with raised brows, I open my mouth to ask where the hell she got it, but she's already leaving. I watch her walk out and slip behind her bedroom door, in order to hear the conversation better. I check the gun for ammo fast, then try to control my racing heart.

The door opens and closes as their voices carry to me moments later.

"Nova, I'm sorry to come by so unexpectedly, but I was nearby when I called, then the line went blank. Are you okay?" Bo asks.

"Hell no, I'm not okay. What's going on?" I can hear the rattle in her voice as if tears are still falling.

"The reports are starting to come in. It looks as if he was walking into his house when someone shot him…from a long distance."

There's a beat of silence before Nova asks, "Like a sniper?"

"Possibly, police are canvassing his land around the house for any casings or footprints. It was a clear assassination. Whoever this was…he was accurate," Bo exhales.

"But this could be anyone, right? Uncle Jim made lots of enemies over his career." Nova's voice has a panicked edge to it.

"Maybe, but…I don't think that's the case," Bo admits.

"Why? What makes you so certain it has to do with the research he's helped me with?"

"Because the day he left those files for me to bring to you, he also told me he thought he was being followed."

There's pacing footsteps reverberating in the living room and a gasp sound from Nova. "Why didn't you tell me that the day you brought them?" Her voice rises in frustration laced with tears.

"He asked me not to…until he was sure. I'm sorry, Nova. You know how Sawyer was—stubborn to a fault. He wanted to make sure he wasn't imagining it."

"Oh my God…oh my God…this really is all my fault, Bo! What have I done?" she wails, and the sound shreds another part of my soul completely in two.

"Listen to me, Nova. Your uncle was one of the best men I've ever known. He *lived* for justice. Don't for a second put blame on yourself. How could you have known where this would lead?"

Nova clears her throat, her voice scratchy as she asks, "What did he leave for me? You said he had something."

The rattling of paper has me shifting, listening closely. Nova takes whatever is handed to her as Bowen says, "He left this letter for me to pass along to you yesterday. It's sealed, I haven't read it, but whatever's in there…you need to let me in on. You're going to need help from here on out."

I hold my breath awaiting her response. A sigh that sounds so small finds my ears. "Give me a day or two. I need time to process everything. I need time," her voice breaks, "to talk to Dad. I'm sure he needs me with him right now."

"I understand that, but you shouldn't be alone here anymore…not right now. You need to come stay with me or your parents. I can get some of mine and Callon's former ranger buddies to form a detail around you. Whatever this is…it's serious, and that letter could hold damning accusations."

The paper crinkles. "I appreciate your help, but you shouldn't be involved anymore either," she says. "You need to back off the search. You and Molly have children to think about…friends and family. You can't do this anymore."

Bo snorts. "No way…not my style to quit. Besides, I've almost narrowed down the correlations from pinged addresses, and in a few days I'll have everything on that number. And Molly knew what she was getting into when she married me in Mexico."

Nova hums, and then her voice is unsure and tentative as she replies. "This was all for a stupid book, remember? It's not worth it, Bo, leave it alone."

"Like I said…not my style," he retorts.

"Fine," she huffs. "Just please be careful…I don't want a second call like the one today. Not *ever*."

"There won't be. I know how to skirt danger. But I'm not leaving you alone, so decide now how we're going to do this," he demands.

Closing my eyes and grinding my teeth, I wait for her answer. If she leaves, what do I do? Do I run? Do I find a new place to lie low…or should I end this and turn myself in and face the wrath of Nova? She deserves so much better than life has dealt her…than I've dealt her.

"I'll get my brother to stay with me," Nova says quickly. "Ian will understand once I explain everything." I shake my head at how quickly she came up with that.

Bo seems to breathe a sigh of relief. "That makes me feel better. Fill Ian in and give him my number in case he needs me at any time. And…I need to know what's in that letter if it could endanger you more."

There's once again a beat of silence before she says, "Understood."

CHAPTER 33

Novalie

Soren sits by my side an hour later, our arms brushing, our forgotten coffee's hardly touched on the table and the infamous envelope between the cups. It took an enormous amount of control not to rip it open the moment Bo left, but Soren pressured me to gain composure before reading it. But there's no composure to be had. The little tidbits of muffins we ate earlier, sit heavy on my stomach, growing rancid. Bile threatens to rise.

"You ready?" he asks, resting a hand on my thigh and bringing goosebumps to the surface with the mere touch of his calloused hand.

"Ready as I'll ever be," I reply through an exhale.

With a shaky hand, I pick up the wrinkled envelope that has my first name swirled in cursive along the front. Using a fingernail, I skim under the lip of the paper, cutting it enough to give me access to tear it the rest of the way open. I pull out a letter two pages long. Unfolding the parchment slowly, I read it aloud. Seeing the way my name is written has water immediately pooling in my eyes.

Novalie Annie Sawyer,

I hope this letter finds you safe and sound. I fear the same fate will not be my own. If I've seemed distant since your request to help with the case, it's not because I wasn't there for you...on the contrary, I've thrown myself into this wholeheartedly. I've been distant because I've discovered more than either of us bargained for. When you gave me the case details, I initially vowed that I would simply get copies of what you needed and pass along advice for your research, but that all changed when I began discovering the truth. Like I said to you before, the discovery of truth is a beautiful thing.

You said to me that first day that you believed this man, Soren Marshall, to be innocent. I will admit that after seeing the evidence, I was on the fence. While the case was odd, rushed, and sketchy, there were no definable leads to make me agree with you or disagree, that is...until I delved further.

I made some inquiries, and because of who I am, got access to a warrant to search the safe-deposit box. With the key you gave me and the warrant I had no issues with the bank staff. This was my first indication that something was wrong. The safe-deposit box was cleaned out, not a thing inside. Soren Marshall was incarcerated and his wife dead at the time. Therefore, I had to do some digging to find that there was a third lessee on the account, one Micah Talon.

My eyes flit to Soren, who's listening intently to every word out of my mouth. His face has gone rigid, jaw set, and mouth pinched. "Keep going," he says gruffly.

The records of who cleaned out the account had suspiciously been lost. I'd bet money on it that they had been tampered with. I always keep an open mind, and so should you. So, I ask myself, what else could be hiding in plain sight? Hopefully you've gone through the files and saw the boot casting done at the crime scene? Well, turns out that sulfur casting was never linked to anyone…not even Soren. Therefore, another person was involved, giving Soren the benefit of the doubt. After that discovery, I located the young lady who was part of the team that collected the evidence from the boot print and blood that was tested, including the lab work done on Soren Marshall. Her name was Serena Walter. The original blood collected from Soren took a few days before it was actually put through testing, while the blood coating his body and the house was tested immediately. In my opinion, there was time enough for Soren's blood to be tampered with. I was able to discern that some blood remains in the lab where they keep evidence.

Soren swallows hard, saying, "That's not my blood in that lab…is it?" Shaking my head slowly, I don't answer, I just keep reading.

None of this leads me to a suspect just yet, but it's a start. I hope I'm there at the end of this, to share in it with you…and with Soren. I know he's there…

My breath sucks into my lungs, and Soren moves, pacing the floor, hands flexing with nervous energy. Cursing under his breath, he stops and looks at me. I'm frozen, unable to continue reading, shock and fear zapping through me, threatening to fillet me from the inside out. His features match my own, and I can feel the fear and unease radiating from him. Soren takes the paper from my numb fingers.

"Let me," he pleads.

I let go of the letter and bring my knees to my chest as I listen.

Yes, I know. You underestimate this old man. The day you asked me to help, I was more than curious, but seeing the men's toiletries on the counter had me questioning…who's my favorite niece seeing that she cannot introduce to her family? I'm sure you're a thundering mess of emotion right now, so take a breath, Nova, and calm down.

Soren pauses his reading to watch me do just that. I nod for him to continue.

I came by again for a visit the day after you told me about the book you were writing, which I still think you should do, by the way. That Sunday, I'd just parked in the parking garage across the way, about to get out of the car, when I saw you exit the back entrance to the shop with a man, watched as you and the man left together. I found it odd that he wore a hoodie pulled over his head in this heat. I almost messaged you or followed but changed my mind. It felt wrong to question you. However, my curious nature got the better of me as usual. I rode by several times to watch your house. What can I say? I'm retired and bored. Tonight, I saw someone on your balcony alone. The same man as before. This time, I used the abandoned building across the street and a set of old binoculars, and low and behold what I found shook me to my core. Soren Marshall sitting on your balcony, scanning the streets. It's not long before you and your friend Melina show up…under the weather, so to speak.

I cringe when Soren glances my way and back to the letter.

In any normal circumstances, I would've barged in there, taken him into custody, but I needed to see something. I needed to see what was going on. I needed to trust you. I was fortunate that the curtain was thrown back, giving way to an unobstructed view of your living room. Keep that drawn from now on. Anyways, I watched as he carried you to bed. I watched as he cradled his head in his hands that night when he sat for a while longer on the balcony.

I knew right then that there was far more to his story and yours. I decided to give you this information I'd discovered as soon as possible, and I wanted to give you all my trust and aid you in any way I could. If it wasn't for the unmarked car that has been traipsing my neighborhood, I would've already done so. Either way, Bowen knows he needs to get this letter to you quickly.

I'm sure you noticed I started this letter with your birth name, Novalie Annie Sawyer, because that is who you are, dear. You are a Sawyer, and we do not yield to no one or nothing. You've made an old detective proud, looking in all directions instead of one. This is far from over, sweetie, but though the battle could turn into a war, you're a strong enough soldier to see it through.

I love you more than you can ever know. Take care of my brother for me, if I don't get to see this through with you…you know how he gets.

PS: Tick Tock Nova
Love,
Uncle Jim

Soren folds the letter carefully. He walks right over to the balcony and draws the curtains across, then double-checks the locks on both doors. I notice for the first time that my gun is stuck in the back of his jeans. The tears won't stop flowing as much as I sniffle and try to breathe through the pain.

Soren kneels on his knees and pulls me from my curled position until my legs fall to either side of him, and then I'm wrapped in his warmth, in his masculine scent that has somehow become my favorite thing. "I'm so sorry, Nova." His chest rises and falls at a far slower rhythm than mine. "I'm so fucking sorry for everything. For your uncle, for my part in all this. I'm sorry."

My tears fall onto his shirtless shoulder, and I tremble when he tightens his hold on me. Gathering myself enough to face him, I push back until I can rest my forehead against his. "We are in this together. I'm not sure a day will go by where guilt doesn't rear its ugly head, but we have to see this through. My uncle…he was doing what he loved to do, and though we both played a part in that, whoever killed him is responsible. Not you…and not me. Your life was taken the day this person framed you, and everything that's happened since is because of him."

Soren raises his head, using his thumbs to wipe away the tears, then kisses me softly on the lips. He doesn't reply to that, and I fear that it's doubt I'm seeing in his sorrowful eyes. "We *will* finish this," I whisper against his lips before I kiss him as if it's for the last time.

CHAPTER 34

Soren

Hours pass, and night creeps along the sky. Powdery clouds blanket most of the moon as I wait anxiously for Nova's return. She made several phone calls to family before leaving to meet with them at her family home to plan the funeral arrangements. Everything we had to discuss about that letter and its implications was put on hold along with all the unanswered questions I have about the night they went to the bar.

The last thing I should've done was watch the news, but I did. It was worse than I had imagined. Jim Sawyer was shot with a sniper rifle. No casings were found. A few partial boot prints were recovered in the ground where he had the rifle set up. They've been replaying old footage of the Maisy case and his involvement all day, not to mention when he received the Medal of Valor for saving a kidnapped little boy years before that. The man was a fucking legend and is…gone. Just *gone*.

His last act on this earth was to help his niece solve *my* case.

"*Fuck*," I shout, my hands fisting so hard my knuckles have gone white. I held in everything as best I could while she was here, but now I want to rip someone to shreds with my bare hands.

Female voices sound from the stairway outside along with the tap of heels. I dash to the bedroom, not immediately recognizing the second voice. Slipping behind the door, I hear the lock click and then, "Soren…it's just me and Mel," Novalie's voice carries to me.

Blowing out a breath, I walk back to the living room to find Melina carrying several plates of food and Nova barely holding onto four bags that are weighing down her arms, leaving red indentations where the plastic digs in. Rushing over, I take a casserole dish from Mel and two of Nova's bags. They follow me to the kitchen to unload.

"What's all this?" I ask.

Mel pulls her hair tie from the messy bun atop her head and shakes her curls loose. Nova is slipping off her black heels and dropping them by the balcony door as she says, "It's the south. When someone dies, everyone brings food…it's what they do."

Looking at the counter lying full, I scoff. "Who are they feeding, half of the city?"

Mel's cheek pulls into a grin. "This was only about ten percent of what was there…Nova's mom forced us to take some."

Nova pulls off her cardigan, leaving her in a fitted, lacy black dress that hugs every curve of her body. As soon as she's near me, I pull her into a hug. Her head rests immediately on my chest as she molds herself to me. I hear the snap of a picture and look over a shoulder to see Mel with my burner phone in hand. She just smiles, and I say nothing as I squeeze Nova tighter. "Are you okay?" I ask.

Mel's eyes are curious as she sets down my phone. I'm sure it's due to the sudden change between Nova and me that I didn't even consider hiding. Mel grabs her chest, unable to hide her smile as she interrupts my question to Nova. "Well, I guess we can add Stockholm syndrome to your list of red flags, Nova."

"Oh, shut up," Nova mumbles against my chest. "And yes," she peers up at me, "I'm okay…or at least, I will be."

I release her long enough to press a kiss to her head, then hold her at arm's length. "What happened today?"

She shrugs. "It was…rough. Dad is a mess—his anxiety hitting new levels. The family is in an upheaval. Tears were shed, plans were made. It was…awful."

Mel rolls her lips into her mouth, empathy written all over her face as she watches Nova closely. "Your girl here was strong though."

Her words warm my cold heart. *My girl.* If only everything were so simple and she could be my girl. Nova releases me and starts separating food and without asking, making me a plate for dinner.

"We have to talk, ladies," I say, watching them both pause over the containers.

Mel cocks her head. "Well, that doesn't sound pleasant at all."

I make a face, causing them to stop completely, giving me the floor. Looking to Nova first, I ask, "Where did the gun come from? And what happened that night at the bar?"

Mel and Nova give each other a look I recognize well from women. One that says…*do we tell him or not?* Mel smiles as she turns to me. "Are you jealous, Soren, about the guy that hit on Nova? It's unbecoming."

"I don't know who that douche was that hit on her, but I know who Nova wants in her bed, and it's not him," I say boldly, dragging my eyes over Novalie painfully slowly. I watch as her neck blooms pink, perfectly emphasizing my point.

Nova looks like she could rake her nails down my face for that or down my back. Darting my eyes between them, I ask again. "You two left out something about that night. What was it?"

Nova lays a hand on Mel, stopping her next words that would've undoubtedly been snarky, interjecting with her own. "Mel had me buy the gun for protection, and we didn't leave it out. I was interrupted and just haven't found the right moment to tell you."

"Tell me now." My eyes plead with her.

Her shoulders rise and fall with the deep breath she takes. "We saw the tapes at the bar. The ones from the night you were there with Victoria." She steals a glance at Mel, who looks nervous for once, then back to me. "She was seen, or it looks like she was seen, facing someone else that night…talking to them."

My brows furrow deep, mouth opening with a slow response. "Who was it? When was it?"

Nova frowns, her mouth twisting in thought of how to answer. "It was when you went to the bathroom…and it was Micah Talon," she finally says.

Dragging one hand over my mouth and chin, I scoff. Both women look at me hard. A chuckle comes out of me, further shocking their senses. "I'm sure there's a good explanation for that."

Nova's eyes widen. "Soren, he was there the night she was acting weird. And…my uncle said he was a lessee on that safe-deposit box. What if he had debts to pay? What if he was involved with her in something shady?"

I look to Mel, who isn't shocked in the least about the information from the letter, leading me to assume Nova has filled her in. My gaze shoots back to Nova. "He's my best friend. He'd never do anything to hurt me. And he and Victoria." I chuckle, but I'm sure it doesn't reach my eyes. "Micah hated her. Tried for years to get me to leave her."

Mel starts to walk away, and I shake my head. "Oh, no. You're in this too. You stay put." I point at her, making her glower. "Why are you just now telling me this?" I direct the question back to Nova.

Nova rears back. "I told you why! We got…*distracted*." I level her with a look, and she flares red. "I was about to tell you before we had sex!" Mel stifles a laugh while Nova glares at her before she continues. "After that, Bo called. It's been chaos since then." I'm nodding, feeling like an idiot for questioning her honor when she smacks the counter with her hand. "You want to talk about *holding back*? Why was my seat moved in my car last Monday? HUH? I've been waiting, *hoping* you'd tell me where you went because I *know* you went somewhere, Soren Marshall."

Mel's brows raise to the limit of her forehead as she takes a seat on the lone stool, watching as if she wished she had popcorn. Nova continues drilling me with those hazel eyes that dance with fire.

I have to pick my mouth up off the floor before sucking my teeth and cracking a knuckle. "Okay, you need to understand." Her back stiffens before I even get started. "I started to panic—to worry that we wouldn't find out the truth, and I needed a backup plan."

"What kind of plan, Ren?" she asks with venom.

"The kind that wouldn't involve you if I had to run."

"What did you do?" she demands through gritted teeth.

"I met with Micah." Mel's mouth falls open at the same time Nova's does. "Just hear me out. I sent him a discrete message, one nobody could understand but him. He met me at a place we used to call Valhalla in the mountains. It's where we used to fish and hunt when we were younger. I asked him to get my money for me in case there came a time for me to run. I wasn't about to ask you to do that with me or be a part of it…in case it went awry."

Nova shakes her head. "You told me once that you couldn't contact him because he's the *first* person the police would expect you to go to. What made you so sure that he wouldn't turn you in? What were you thinking?"

Squaring my shoulders, I eye her hard. "Because he is my Melina." Mel grins but drops it when Nova narrows her eyes at her. "He wouldn't have had anything to do with this. We can trust him."

"No, Soren, we can't," she says matter-of-factly. When I don't budge on the matter, she adds, "Don't you find it strange that he's in that video, speaking with Victoria the night she died, he had access to your money, and my uncle is dead not long after you made contact with him!"

Holding my head higher, eyes steely, I shake my head. "No. It's not him."

Nova leans on the counter with both hands bracing her, some of her fire dissipating with fatigue of the day, no doubt. "Okay, Soren, I admire your loyalty to your friend, but you need to stop any and all contact with him for our safety. And," she asks with a cocked brow, "what was in that safe-deposit box?"

Crossing my arms over my chest with a look of disgust on my face, I shake my head and look to the floor. "My collector pieces worth…a small fortune. It was something my dad passed down to me. He was serious about his collection of baseball cards and comics. We did it together for years."

Mel sits forward, her interest piqued. "Which ones did you have?"

"We had a lot that burned up in a fire when I was a kid, but luckily, my dad saved three things for me that he kept at the bank, a 1963 Pete Rose #537, a 1968 Nolan Ryan #177, and the 1963 Avengers comic…number one."

"Holy shit," Mel gasps. "Those are worth like," she thinks for a moment, "like 1.2 mil or more."

"You know your stuff." I nod to her. "Probably worth close to that or more by now. There were other, less valuable ones in there too."

Nova contemplates all this, face falling with a frown. "Ren, Micah had a key to that box. Did he know what was in it?"

"Of course he did," I say without hesitation. "If he took it out…it had to be for a good reason."

"So, you're agreeing that he could've taken it?" she prods.

A sinking, awful feeling settles around me. It's like falling into quicksand, slowly suffocating. Suddenly, I find it hard to continue this conversation. Without meeting their eyes, I just walk away.

CHAPTER 35

Novalie

Soren's in the bathroom by the time I catch up with him, laying a hand on his shoulder. Thick muscles harden under my palm, making me flinch. "I'm sorry that I was so blunt, but you need to understand that your friend can't be trusted right now."

"I'm showering, Nova. Get in with me or don't," he says flatly, grabbing the hem of his shirt, yanking it over his head.

"We need to talk about this," I say firmly.

"Talk then." He moves around me, shutting and locking the door. He turns on the shower and proceeds to drop his pants.

I have to relearn how to breathe as his tall naked form seems to rip the air from this small space. I watch as he steps into the spray. Water rivulets race down the slopes of his muscles in a flurry as steam begins to rise around me. The deep V muscles reaching low on his abdomen form an inviting trail pointing straight toward—

I snap my eyes away. "Okay then," I whisper, swallowing hard. Bending my arm awkwardly to reach the zipper of my mourning dress, I give it several tugs. Finally, it falls to the ground, pooling at my ankles. By the time I've freed my bra, Soren is watching me, gaze roving.

Slipping my thong down, I step into the shower. Ren moves back to allow me room. Facing him, I reach around his large chest, grabbing the body wash, then lather some on a washcloth. "Turn around," I command. He swallows hard, raking his eyes over my wet breast, but eventually turns for me. "I'll talk, you listen," I say, watching his back tense as I slowly drag the washcloth over his skin.

"All we have to go on is a woman named Serena Walter who collected your blood samples, an unknown boot print, Victoria's strange behavior, Micah being there and having access to your collectables, and now…an assassination of someone looking into the case."

Ren stays quiet, to my surprise, as I wash his back and arms. My stomach flutters with nerves as I trail my free hand down his side. The heat from the shower is nothing compared to the heat flooding my body at the sight of this man before me.

Gathering my words, I continue. "Based on what my uncle was alluding to, someone in the police department is sketchy. I'm not sure how to find them, but we can be sure that someone tampered with evidence—evidence that not many people have access to."

I motion for Ren to turn around, and he does. His hair is as black as night when wet, making him look devilish in a painfully sexy way. My blood thrums and burns in my veins, torching my cells, scorching my very being. I continue my exploration of his body as I wash him gingerly, taking my sweet time enjoying the feel of his body and reveling in the way I'm affecting him.

"Bowen will have the IP addresses analyzed soon and the phone number. We can see where that leads us. In the meantime, we stay hidden…stay safe. Other than the funeral, I'll close up the shop. We won't take any chances." Ren's eyes find mine through the steam. Try as I might, I can't tell what he's thinking.

"What about the last words your uncle wrote in that letter?" he asks, bracing one hand on the slick shower wall as he bows his head, relaxing his muscles under my strokes.

"Tick Tock," I whisper softly and then laugh even quieter. "I told him about my gran's grandfather clock story and about what I found in the storage unit clock." My hand pauses mid-stroke. "He has something hidden for me at his house…I'm certain of that. Today, everything with the family was held at my parents' house considering my aunt Katherine, Uncle Jim's wife, passed several years ago leaving the house they owned vacant."

"Does he have children?" Ren asks.

"Yeah, I have three cousins, all grown, and moved away. His two daughters fly in tomorrow and his son Donny in three days. The funeral is being put on hold until all family arrives and until the investigation has cleared enough to hold it. We have a family cemetery on his land. That's where he will be put to rest."

Ren straightens and turns toward me, eyes holding mine fiercely. "I don't want you going near that house alone. If someone sees you snooping, it might make you the next target."

"Okay, I can hold out until the funeral. That way everyone will be there and no one will suspect a thing if I take a walk down memory lane in his house."

Soren seems to breathe a bit easier. "I'm sorry if it seemed like I was being an ass in there, when you brought up the stuff about Micah," Ren says with a strained look on his face. "It's just that...he was the last person I could trust—the last person that I thought I could count on...before *you*."

My head bobs once in understanding. "I know."

Ren grabs my loofah that's hung over the bathtub spout and squirts a glob of my own body wash on it, raising a brow as he says, "Your turn."

I trace a mechanical tattoo on his chest of intricate gears with my fingernail. "I was just getting started."

He ignores me, sliding one hand to hold me at the waist, while the other starts agonizingly slow ministrations beginning at my neck and then slipping lower to my breasts. My lower lip fits between my teeth as I bite down on the moan crawling up my throat, begging to be released. My eyes fall shut as goosebumps prickle along my wet skin. It's amazing how my body comes alive for him so easily. He makes the world and all our problems disappear.

His gravelly voice has me opening my heavy eyes when he whispers, "Is Mel still here?"

I shake my head. "She left. Why?"

He licks his upper lip, leans down to place his face near mine. "I plan on making you scream my name again. Didn't want to scar her for life."

My mouth forms an O as a rushed breath leaves me. "Well then," I close the distance between our lips, flicking out my tongue to graze his mouth, "let's see if you can make me scream."

An animalistic growl reverberates from his chest as the loofah falls to the tub floor with a splat. Soren's hands are around my thighs and lifting me with a quickness that has me reeling. I gasp aloud as my back comes in contact with the wall—cold tiles bite into my skin in such contrast to the heat surrounding us.

His mouth crashes into mine, spiraling me into oblivion. His taste sinks into me, settling in my psyche to live forever as our tongues fight for dominance. Every time he kisses me, it feels *desperate*. It permeates the air, floods the system, encompasses everything in sight. The sparks flying from the collision of our bodies should be electrocuting us. His hard, slick body pressed into mine, fits like it was meant to be nowhere else in this godforsaken world.

I keep my arms wrapped around his neck, refusing to let go. Clenching his hair with my fingers, I moan into his kiss. He shifts my body, and I have no chance to prepare as he sinks me down onto him. My mouth opens, head flinging back to rest against the tile as he pushes in the last inch, filling me completely. The shock of the sudden blissful fullness has me clenching. "*Ohhh*," I whine, my body trembling, but he holds me there as he drags his teeth and tongue over my jaw and nips at my neck.

Just when I think I can't take the stillness any longer, he presses my back into the wall, pulls out, and drives into me hard.

"*Soren*," I cry out his name.

"Look at me, Nova," he says in that deep, commanding voice that has me soaking wet for him and has nothing to do with the shower. My eyes fly back to his. "Say it again," he growls.

It takes me a moment to understand what he's asking of me…but only a moment. "I'm yours, Soren," I whisper against his lips.

His sideways smile threatens to kill me dead as he leans into my mouth, parting my lips with his tongue. I open willingly as he starts a new rhythm of our bodies moving in time with each hardened kiss. A wave of pleasure so pure and so deep curls inside of me, building, and building in an unrelenting crescendo. As he thrusts into me, I fling my hand out for purchase, snagging the shower curtain rod.

Ren pulls me against him fast as the whole rod snaps loose from the wall, curtain and all crashing to the ground with a clang. His chest rumbles with his laugh just as mine does the same. "I'll replace that," he says, not releasing his hold of me.

"It was me, not you, who grabbed the damn thing." I say as he steps out of the shower, over the mess on the floor, without unlatching me from his waist. "What are yo—"

I'm cut off when he plops me onto the sink's edge, pressing my back into the contents of the counter and bathroom mirror. Water from our bodies drips to the floor. He shakes his head, making the sodden hair fling more droplets all over me and plastering his hair in a haphazard way that shouldn't be so fucking hot.

"Hush, woman." He grins. "I'll have you wherever I please," he says cockily and cuts off any kind of retort I could possibly come up with as his mouth takes mine again.

Something tips, smashes on the floor. Something else falls into the sink. My wet ass slides on the counter, destroying anything that was behind me. I'm pretty sure I hear water spray hitting the shower curtain on the floor but…I *don't* fucking care as he takes my pleasure and amplifies it a million times over. With every stroke, he drags large hands over my breasts, kneading them, squeezing. When he bends to suck my nipple into his mouth, I shudder, tightening and then I'm screaming his name again, exploding with an orgasm that rocks me to my core and keeps going. He doesn't stop his onslaught as wave after wave crashes through me.

Ren pulls his head back, watching me come apart beneath him, and then grits his teeth, jaw clenched as he slams into me one last time. I feel him harden more right before I feel his release. I watch in awe at the absolute raw perfection of it. Our eyes lock, everything could be on fire, and I wouldn't notice. His dark wet hair is spiking now, in cute disarray as he smiles with manly pride that makes me feral for him all over again, especially when his cheek tugs at the corner.

A clang snags our attention when my toothbrush hits the floor…right next to a shattered glass of cotton swabs and several other things. "Shit," I say through a grin. "That was intense."

Ren finally lifts me off the counter to stand. We survey the rest of the damage. "I think we can top it next time," he says with all seriousness. His head snaps to mine. "Are you on the pill?"

"Not that it matters after the fact there big guy, but yes, I am." I smack his ass, making him flinch.

"Sorry, I couldn't…*didn't* want to stop," he admits.

"I didn't want you to either," I say honestly.

He turns to me, holding my face between his long fingers. "I think you might be the most perfect creature I've ever encountered."

"I thought I was just, let me see, what was it you called me, oh yeah…an OCD, book nerd, and a priss."

He leans down, still holding me where he wants me, and kisses me so good that my body is fast becoming ready for round two. When he pulls away, he tips my nose with a finger like he did shortly after we met. "You're still all those things."

I swat at his hand, missing it when he jerks back. "And you're still a slob, a brute, and a pervert," I throw back at him.

He laughs and walks to the shower, grabbing the rod and attempting to fix it before my entire floor is left soaked. "True, we're all those things…the only difference is that you're mine now…and I'm yours."

I stand naked, frozen in place as I watch him work to clean up the mess. But I don't move. How can I? His words speared me to the ground the moment they left his mouth. This time when he said it, it was different. Not in the heat of the moment, but casually, factually, lovingly.

The closer I get to that feeling, the scarier this all becomes.

CHAPTER 36

Soren

It's been three days since the family gathering for Detective Sawyer. They've yet to have the funeral, and Nova is chomping at the bit to get inside his house. Bowen's been radio silent also—no word from him. It feels like I'm seated in a dark theater, watching a stage and the play is about to begin, but we don't know when or how it will begin…with a bang, slow and quiet?

Who knows?

Everything is still up in the air and the only thing on my frayed mind is Novalie's safety. I worry about her, even if she has to leave for a few minutes. Because I now feel the threat leaking into every crevice of this house. Someone is out there who holds the key to my freedom or my doom. And we *have* to be careful, because if that same person finds out that she's involved or where I'm hiding…I can't even think of it—can't consider the implications right now. Already, I've caused her so much chaos and pain.

But now I don't want to let her go—can't fathom letting her go. I've never had a connection like this before. I should've never touched her soft skin, tasted her pouty lips—should've never allowed her to get under my skin, but now she's everywhere.

I stand from the couch and shift in a slow circle, really analyzing her home. There's no sign of her in here; it's all below in her bookshop. It's as if she didn't know who she wanted to be after Levi died or as if she didn't know who she was anymore without him. The furniture is all plain and color coordinated, the walls bare other than landscape portraits that were probably placed here by the real estate agent. Another small one is on the bookshelf with the same bland scenery that doesn't even belong to the North Carolina mountains. No family photos adorn the tables, no trinkets that showcase her creative and quirky personality. The cabinets and fridge have remained disorganized only because I enjoy fucking with her. But after I learned the truth about her late husband, it all clicked into place. Little pits in my mind of her life before began filling with images.

Nova was pressed to be perfect in every way, all the while her shitbag of a husband was out fucking someone else. If he were alive…I'd kill him.

She left at almost four o'clock to meet with her mother and father to go over her uncle's final wishes. I made sure that she rode with Melina *and* made it very clear that she wasn't to be left alone. They have a dinner planned for after, so she'll be gone for a few hours. It's the longest we've been apart in days, and I can feel every agonizing second of it.

Sliding my burner phone from my pocket, I flip to the only photo I have. The one Mel took of me hugging Nova. You can't see my face by the way I'm turned, only a sliver of my profile. Nova's head is against my chest, eyes closed.

My eyes go back to the bookshelf and that solo picture frame there of the anonymous landscape. I smile. Going over to her computer, I plug in the phone and spend a good fifteen minutes trying to figure out her printer settings, but eventually…the photo prints. I made it into a 5x7. Slipping out the generic photo, and replacing it with ours, I gingerly set it on the shelf.

Now, she has something of *us* here.

Picking up the phone again, I hover over the keypad. Guilt gnaws at my insides just as it did the first time I did this. Today is *not* the day I'm supposed to meet with Micah. But it is *all* I've been able to think about. Novalie will likely lose her shit over what I'm about to do, but I have to. And I can't have her around…just in case. It's not spontaneous, no…this is an oozing malignant doubt inside me that needs to be cut out. I *need* to know where Micah stands in all this. The only way I can do that is to meet with him again…and to do it while she's not with me.

I've been biding my time, and now it's here. I have a scant few hours to meet with him and get back. Plus, I'm chancing this weather and the late hour. A storm is curling over the mountains outside, and hiking after dark can get tricky. The question is…will he even show? This could be a waste of time.

In my heart, I still trust him, and how could I not? We literally grew up together since we were in our teens. I've hunted and fished these mountains with Micah for years, listened to every sordid detail of his love life, shook his hand when we signed the papers naming us co-owners of M&T Restorations. He was there through my good times and my worst. How could I not trust him? But why was he at the bar that night? And why not tell me about it later, after Vicky was murdered?

My fingers move swiftly across the keypad and then hover over the words, *Valhalla now.* I don't press send. Not yet. Remembering our precarious situation, I think it's better to send it from a location far from her…just in case.

Pulling the hoodie over my head and then Nova's Appalachian State ball cap down low, I take her keys from beside the door and send up a little prayer.

There's a charge in the air from the brewing storm cresting the tallest peak on the mountain. The drizzle of rain has already soaked into the dark green T-shirt I'm wearing. I left the hoodie behind in the hidden car far from here. The message I sent earlier was from the city…*also* far from here. Without the phone on me, I'm not sure how long I have before Nova gets back. If I were to guess, I'd say I still have around two hours. I have no plans on keeping this from her; on the contrary, I plan to tell her all about it immediately. I just hope she's in a forgiving mood.

Sweat trickles down my neck from the heat, humidity, and rain. A thick band of fog has settled over everything, moving and writhing like a beast across the forest floor. I've hiked these woods many times in fog just like this, so it doesn't impede my sense of direction in the slightest but coupled with the night creeping in…it's ominous for sure. Before long, I hear the sounds of Valhalla's waterfall, the Widowmaker, pounding rock and earth in the distance. The uphill trudge begins to level out.

Slowing my pace, I keep toward the edge of the cliff as I near even closer to the falls. The wildlife grows quiet, coming to a stop. My hackles rise as I pause. Planting my back against a large oak tree, I attempt to breathe slow, then close my eyes and listen. Micah should either already be here or be coming in from the left of me at a ninety-degree angle to the falls. That was our usual entrance point to the bit of forest we cleared. I wait for several minutes but hear no footsteps. I start moving again, toward our spot hidden not a hundred yards away, tucked into the pitching pines.

The fog thickens the closer I am to the water's mist. It coats the atmosphere with an eerie ambiance. Swiping the gathered moisture from my brow, I step lightly, making sure no leaves or branches crunch under the weight of my boots.

Movement to the left catches my eye. Side-stepping a fallen tree, I tuck myself in between two pines as I watch. In the distance, still a good ways from me, the fog parts for a moment and I see Micah. He's in his usual hunting clothes, rifle across his back and would've blended in with nature had it not been for the black pack that's slung over one shoulder. The very backpack that I hope holds enough money for me to disappear…if the time comes for that. I don't come out to greet Micah as he makes his way east of where I stand, toward our fire pit in the small clearing. I stay right where I am and watch to make sure he's alone. Because even though he's my best friend, Nova is right. I need to be careful.

My very life depends on it.

I watch as he studies his surroundings, only seeing him every now and again when the fog parts enough to allow it. Right when I'm about to step from the cover of trees, the storm above rattles the sky with booming thunder that makes me flinch and pause. Rain streams down, pelting me and the ground. I wipe it from my bleary eyes. When I clear my vision, Micah is facing west of us. Weaving through the pines, keeping to the shadowed branches, I make my way closer to him. My heart racing suddenly. Wiping my eyes once more, I lose sight of him again. Craning my head around a spindly tree, I search but can't see him.

In the span of a heartbeat, bark slices across my cheek with its splintered shards creating a burst of pain to the right side of my face. I blink, breath stuttering in my chest, feet planted firmly as another rumble of thunder shakes the earth. I don't register what happened until the second heartbeat, and the sound that had accompanied that shredded bark makes me jolt.

A gunshot.

There's a clear gouge in the side of the tree beside me, long and dipped like a canoe, which alludes to a high-caliber bullet.

Someone's fucking shooting at me.

The thought drives me into motion. I duck behind a fallen oak just as another shot rings out. Looking ahead, my eyes dart this way and that, trying to gauge where Micah went. Footsteps sound in the distance, swift and pounding into the earth, not hiding their ascent in my direction. Leaping from the ground, I bolt toward the area Micah was in, darting in and out of trees to hopefully throw off any line of sight this guy has on me. Before I even make it to the spot I last saw Micah, another shot rings out…but this one *doesn't* miss.

White hot, searing pain blazes through my left thigh, like nothing I've ever felt. I stumble, a curse flying from my lips as I smash into the ground. Pine needles, leaves, and rock stab into my already lacerated cheek as my mouth gapes open, begging to release a scream, but I manage to hold it in. "*Fuck, fuck, fuck!*" I grit out in a whisper of panic through clenched teeth.

My hand moves to clasp the wound, and only slick, warm wetness meets my palm. Curling my body inward, I manage to look down at my leg. Blood soaks through the jeans where a jagged hole burrows into the lateral side of my thigh. Pulling myself into a sitting position, back against a log, I blink away the rain. Spots dot my vision. "*I have to survive*," I whisper to no one. I can't die out here. Nova…oh God, Nova. I need more time.

Boot steps falter somewhere nearby, and I freeze, body tense, readying for fight or flight. Some survivalist part of me shuts down the pain radiating throughout my leg, shuts down the fear slicing my conscious, shuts down everything that could possibly hold me back. Only the one thought rings true and gives me strength—the face in my head, her light shining through my dark. *Novalie.* I need more time…with *her.*

Lightning cracks the sky wide open illuminating a dark form on the ground, near the rotting trunk I've been leaning on. It's the backpack Micah was carrying. The boots nearby crack on a limb, and I can finally better gauge their distance from me. Lightning pops again, louder, more violent this time, and I see the glint of a rifle a few yards away. Thunder growls like the belly of a beast as I shift, crouched, ready to sprint. Lancing pain strikes through my leg, and a deep tissue burning sensation has my breath hitching.

Right now would've been a wonderful time to have a gun on me. But I sent Nova with hers, insisting she not go *anywhere* without it. I don't regret that. But it would have been nice to have it.

Cursing under my breath, I listen to the sky, to the wind whistling through the trees. The storm billows and groans, masking the noise I make limping to my feet. I wait for the lightning to show the way. A strike shoots downward this time, making contact somewhere in the mountains. Glints of metal flash a few yards to my left. I wait for the thunder, and when it rumbles the earth this time, I sling the pack onto my shoulder and lunge right, ignoring the protesting throb of my leg and the stickiness of the blood now racing downward.

I ignore everything as I sprint toward the river. A shot rings out, missing my head by inches, if the whirring sound that passed my ear was any indication. Feet pounding the ground behind me has me chancing glances over my shoulder, but I can't see him. Can't see Micah. Rage helps fuel my body. *Pure, undiluted rage.*

Time seems to slow. Dashing around trees, I push harder and faster, but my mind's adrift to a time long ago, lost in a memory.

"What do you want to do when you grow up?" I asked Micah, cracking open the stolen beer from his dad's garage stash.

"I don't know, dude, I'm sixteen," Micah said with a wry smile and then chugged half a beer, burping after. He held his chest with pride for his loud belch. "Why? What do you want to do?"

I leaned back against the rotted tires of the old rundown F150 and smiled. "I'm going to rebuild old cars and trucks."

Micah grabbed another beer, popped the top and finished a quarter of it before he looked me dead in the eyes and said, "I want to be you then. Do what you do. We could open a shop together."

I tapped my beer against his, making it slosh. Micah let out a string of curses that he could only do when no one was around or his mother would wash his mouth out with soap. Then I laughed and said, "Okay, you sure there's nothing else you want to do?"

"Nope. I like working on shit, and you like working on shit…plus you're like my only friend, so…"

I nodded. "Might as well work on shit together." I climbed up from the ground, dusted off my faded holy jeans and passed him a wrench. "Might as well start now." I tapped the fender of the truck for emphasis. Micah stood, grin splitting his face, and took the wrench as I added, "Plus, you're my only friend too."

Time barrels back into me, moving in a similar cadence with my heartbeats as another shot pierces the sound barrier.

I'm going to rip his fucking head off.

Anger swarms out of me like wasps with nothing to latch onto. Mud sloshes and splatters as it gathers in divots along the edge of the cliff. The next shot cracks through the limbs beside me, coming from the right. Looking ahead, there's no more trees to hide behind, nothing but a blank clearing for *far* too many yards. I could turn back. I could chance turning right and missing his trajectory. But Micah is more than just a good shot. He's one of the best marksmen I know. For whatever reason, he's not going to stop until he ends me.

In the few seconds it takes to make the decision, I whisper through panting breaths, "I'm sorry, Nova." My feet turn, angling toward the cliff's edge, arms moving, pushing momentum, strides lengthening. I hear footsteps, but the thundering now comes from the waterfall, not the sky, drowning out everything else.

Widowmaker.

What a fitting name we gave her all those years ago. My right foot hits the edge of ground that gives way to the cavernous river too far below, and I *launch* into the dark abyss, water misting my face, gravity taking hold.

Another shot slices the air, but I'm too far gone.

I fall.

CHAPTER 37

Novalie

My dad's aftershave clings to my clothing long after we part ways. It leaves painful stings of sorrow with each inhale I take. My cousins have yet to all make it to town, so we couldn't go through my uncle's final wishes just yet. Mel and I only stayed for a half hour before I couldn't take the environment a second longer.

Dad is a devastated mess. Him and his brother were extremely close. They did virtually everything together. I tried to comfort him, but how do you ease the pain from that kind of loss?

"Where was Ian today?" Mel asks, flipping her turn signal on as we near my parking garage.

I shrug, looking out the window as the rain leaves little droplets racing downward. "I heard Mom on the phone with him. Sounded like something important was going on at the station."

Mel hums. She pulls into a parking spot, squeezing her Bronco in between two equally large trucks, and cuts the engine. She doesn't move to get out, and when my hand reaches for the door handle, she stops me with her words.

"I know everything is a mess now and the last thing you want to do is have this conversation, but I need to ask you something."

Twisting in the seat to face her, I tilt my head. "Ask away."

Her hair is half up and half down. She rakes a pink fingernail through some unruly curls falling into her face. "I know I'm normally the comic relief friend, and also your ride-or-die girl, and I'd do anything for you, but this last week has been intense with you and Soren." She pauses, seeing me flinch at her words, then asks, "Are you sure you're making the right decisions here…getting close to him?"

My eyes widen. I open my mouth to scold her assumptions, but nothing comes out for several seconds. Mel clears her throat and adjusts her rose-colored dress straps. She looks away from me now, through her driver's side window.

I exhale and finally say, "I don't know how this happened, Mel." She slides her gaze back to mine. Pinching my nose with two fingers and scrunching my brow, I groan. "It all just crept up on me so fast."

I look up to see her hand gripping the steering wheel. "I want you to know that I do believe him. I think Soren's innocent, but getting involved with him…like this, it's scary." I watch her carefully, the way her shoulders sag, the way her eyes soften. "Nova…I can't watch you go through that kind of heartbreak again."

Her words slam into my chest like a battering ram, bringing back all my insecurities and tear-soaked-pillow nights. "This is different. He's different."

Her head tilts, brown eyes roving over my face. "I can see that. You're…better with him, more relaxed than I've ever seen you."

"Really?" I ask.

"Really," she replies. "Well, you know how I felt about Levi. It was no secret. My only concern now is for your sanity if he goes back to prison."

I sit up a little straighter, eyes drifting away from her as I let that possibility sink into my bones. "I won't let that happen, Mel. I won't stop fighting for his freedom."

She nods, lips pursing. "I know you want, and that's what worries me. You're one of those people who put everyone else's needs before their own." I open my mouth to retort, but she cuts me off. "Don't deny it, Nova. You are. You did it with Levi, you've done it protecting me, you used to do it for your parents. And now you're uprooting your peaceful existence for Soren."

"I…maybe you're right, but is that such a bad quality to have?"

"No." She smiles sweetly. "It's the best quality, as long as people don't take advantage of it…of you." Leaning back in the seat, I flop my head back and close my eyes, but her next words have me popping right back up. "Are you sleeping with him?"

My mouth opens, and I make an unintelligible sound before scoffing. "I…we—"

"I mean, I figured as much from the conversation the other night." Her lip pulls into a half-grin. "You see why this is scaring the living shit out of me, Nova? You are neck deep in a dangerous situation and now the hearts involved."

I reach for the doorknob again. "I know what I'm doing. I wanted this, just as much as him…and sure, I don't know where it all ends, but I know his heart, Mel. And his heart is pure."

She raises her hands in surrender as I pull the handle, but then shock has me frozen in place. Brows pinched, body tense, my breathing halted, I point to the left of the parking garage.

"My car," I whisper through a choked gasp, making Mel's head whip in that direction. "It's gone!"

"*Holy shit*," Mel mutters under her breath. "Let's not jump to conclusions here. What if he ran to a store?"

My eyes blaze with anger. "He's a convicted felon; he's not out lollygagging. *Ughhhh*," I growl out with frustration. "I would bet my life on it that he's meeting with Micah."

"Why on earth would he do that after what we told him?"

"Because! He's a pride-filled man! He's been quieter the last few days, and I could tell that the 'not knowing' was weighing on him. Micah was his best friend. It was probably tearing him apart." Some of the fire leaches out of my voice with that thought.

"So what now? We wait on him to come? See what he figured out?" she asks, eyes still pinned to the vacant parking spot. Overhead, the storm begins to rage outside, water whipping into the parking garage in sheets.

"No," I say quietly and smile. "After the last time he did this…I made sure I could find him if he did something this reckless again." One of her manicured brows raises. "I put an Apple tracker in my car." I grin ferally.

"You sneaky little shit…*I love it.*" She winks at me. "Alright then, let's go find him."

My heart is racing as she turns the key, while I frantically flip through my apps.

"Where the hell is he?" Mel asks, face scrunched as she tries to drive the last mile toward where the tracker's leading us, the storm making visibility scarce and the long drive slow and sketchy.

"Exactly where I thought. This *has* to be the area of mountains he told us about—the place he used to go to with Micah. There *Valhalla*," I say mockingly.

"I'll never understand men," Mel says, flipping the defrost on.

The fog is dense, thick enough to cut with a knife as we weave through the curvy mountain roads. My breath catches when I see just how close we are to the sheer drop-off on the right. We keep a watch for any cars coming up or down the mountain but see no one so far. Lightning cracks across the sky, making both of us startle. Mel gives me a wary look but then focuses back on the road. I watch my phone, eyes locked on the location of the tracker.

"It's here!" I yell, making Mel dart her eyes left and right.

"Where?" she asks.

"To the left…somewhere over here." I point in the general direction.

"There's nothing here," she says, confused, as she slows the Bronco down to a crawl, checking her rearview to make sure we're still alone on this mountain.

The rain is more like a sheet now, blocking out everything, but suddenly I see the shine of metal. "Right there! Slow down." She eases us to an almost-stop, and we see it. A hidden, barely visible area of depressed weeds and brush, just wide enough to fit a vehicle, but rugged enough that most wouldn't venture in with a car.

"Pull over to the side of the road," I tell her, already unbuckling my seat belt.

Mel parks far enough off the side not to get hit if someone does venture this way. Her voice rings out behind me, "*Hey, wait on me*," but I'm already out of the car, pulling my lavender cardigan around my shoulders. I was dressed for a family gathering to cover the last will and testament of my uncle, not this damn storm. And as Ren always liked to say…I never watch the news and therefore wasn't prepared for rain.

My flower dress plasters to my body almost instantly as the rain pelts into me in stinging strips. My hair clumps within seconds, and my wedge heels become slippery on my feet as I trudge around mud puddles and into the thick wooded area.

Mel is dashing to catch up, her rain jacket hood up and knee-high boots making it easier for her to move. I guess she *did* watch the news, I think as I wipe hair from my eyes. My footsteps squish and crackle through the wet leaves and sodden earth until they halt altogether at the sight of my Chevy. My car is tucked between two large oak trees, mostly hidden. I was lucky to have even caught a glimpse of something shinning and even then probably wouldn't have found it if it wasn't for that tracker.

"This isn't a trail, that's for sure," I say, looking around my car.

Mel opens the passenger door at the same time that I do the driver's side but we see nothing out of the ordinary other than Ren's discarded hoodie lying in the back seat. The keys are still dangling from the ignition with my little black and golden dragon keychains from one of my favorite fantasy series. Anger swells in me like a tide. "He's on this *fucking* mountain somewhere in this *fucking* storm because he's a *fucking* idiot," I rant.

Mel shuts the door, stands straight, and tucks her curls underneath the hood. "Well, what now? I love you and all…but I'm not going up this mountain…oh sorry, *fucking* mountain."

I roll my eyes at her and huff out a sigh. "You're right. We can't go after him." My voice rises to drown out the rain. "We could leave him a note—"

My words are chopped off with the buzz of Mel's cellphone. We look at each other in silent agreement and quickly get in my car. Pulling her hood away from her face, she then slips her phone from an inner pocket on her jacket. Her nose wrinkles with confusion. "It's your brother." She faces the phone toward me so that I can see the word pancake.

I tsk. "You still call him Pancake." A smile tips my lips as I grab the phone from her.

"He'll never live that one down." She grins. "You get slapped with a pancake by a girlfriend in front of the entire cafeteria in school…it kinda sticks with you."

A laugh bubbles out of me as I answer her phone. "Why are you calling my best friend Ian?"

"Nova." His voice is strained with a tinge of excitement. "Where are you? I tried your cell twice."

"It's in Mel's car, we were…" I look to Mel and she shrugs. "We were…shopping, and I left my phone."

"You need to check out the news. Some shit went down with the case you're researching. That book of yours just got spicier."

The hair on the back of my neck stands on end. I have to force myself to breathe. Mel is leaning forward now, checking me over, seeing my shock. I pull the cell from my face and hit speaker. "What're you talking about? *What happened?*"

"You didn't hear this from me. We're supposed to be keeping this quiet for now, but several units are heading to the mountains south of here. We got an anonymous tip that Soren Marshall was seen in the area."

Mel's hand hovers over her mouth, eyes wide. Then she moves it, mouthing quietly, "*We need to leave…now!*"

I'm nodding somehow, through numb senses. "Are you there?" Ian asks.

"Yeah…I'm here."

"That's not all." My shoulders tense before he adds, "It's wild. They're saying a hunter saw him fall over a cliff into a river. There's a separate team coming together for more of a…search and rescue mission."

Ian continues talking, but I can't hear a damn thing for the pounding in my pulse making my ears ring. Bile threatens to burn up my throat. Mel is yanking at my arm, waving for me to look at her. She snatches the phone from my rigid fingers. "Hey Pancake, we'll call you later okay, gotta run."

"Wait," Ian says, tone confused. "I—"

Mel hangs up the phone, shoving it into her jacket. "Look at me, Nova." My face moves of its own accord. "We have to go now," she says calmly. "You have to get this car off the mountain before the cops get here." I know she's right. Everything she is saying is *right,* but I can't move. "*NOW, NOVA*!" she yells, bringing me back to reality.

I follow her lead as she leaps from the car and sprints to hers, yelling over a shoulder, "I'll follow you."

Leaning back into the driver's seat, I crank the car as if on autopilot—my body and mind in two very different realities. Spinning in place with my first try, I angle the tires the opposite direction, slam it into reverse and sling mud everywhere as I barrel out of the forest, blocking all thoughts except getting my car out of here. I can't even let myself consider the fact that he might come back for it. It's too late for that, too late for anything.

I swing the car out onto the road, shift gears, slamming it into first and peel out of there with Mel hot on my tail. Something slides out from under the front seat and smacks my heel. Glancing down, I see Soren's burner phone. The battery lies a few inches from it. My heart twists painfully, the moisture now on my face no longer from the rain. I slam my palm into the steering wheel, cursing, raging. What the absolute fuck was he thinking? We were close…*so* close to his freedom I could taste it. If he'd just waited a little longer—just listened to me!

Somewhere in the distance, I hear sirens.

"Holy fucking hell," I mutter, tears flowing like a spout now. I sniffle, choking on the sobs. He *has* to be okay. He has to be! Because as pissed as I am that he did this…I'm really just *scared.* Scared of a life where he's no longer in it. How did we get here? How did I let myself fall so hard, so fast? I'm a *fool.* All my fears skitter through me at once—his capture, never seeing him bask in the sunlight as a free man, and worst of all…no, I can't…I *won't* entertain the last fear.

The sirens grow louder as the rain subsides to nothing more than a drizzle. The night sky opens up in blotches to let stars peek through where the clouds have rolled past. It's as if the very world is saying…it's over. The storm is over, and there's *nothing* I can do about it. Soren's eyes drift through my mind, just like this storm, leaving so much damage in its path.

We're no more than a mile from where we were parked when movement catches my eye. It's only a streak, a blur really, but enough that I hit my brakes and hope that Mel doesn't rear-end me. The movement halts, then moves fast. I make out the silhouette of a man climbing onto an ATV of some sort in the brush ahead. His head turns toward our oncoming headlights fast and then looks away. Too fast for me to see his features. I've slowed down, rolling past as I watch what I now recognize as a four-wheeler move from its hidden alcove, no headlights on. It darts into the forest and is gone…just like that.

A sour foreboding presses into my skull, leaving rancid rot to grow. Why would anyone be out here…in a storm…hunting? It's definitely not deer season yet. I don't think it's the season for hunting anything, but I could be wrong, and even if it was, no one would be out in the storm that was raging earlier.

Another sound worse than sirens whirrs above, and Mel beeps her horn behind me. I jump, startled, and suck in a breath. Looking up through the windshield, I see the light flitting through the sky. A helicopter. I take off at a much faster pace, leaving behind the stranger in the woods. Leaving behind Soren…leaving behind a part of me that I'll never get back.

CHAPTER 38

Novalie

A line of black vehicles, led by police cars, flies past us at break-neck speed. Mouth agape, I watch more and more of them zoom past. For a precious moment, I'm thankful that they aren't pulling us over. But that moment flits away. Flickering lights dot the night like strobes ahead of us. They're so blinding in their intensity that I have to squint the closer I get. I swallow the lump in my throat.

"Oh God," I whisper.

The police have formed a roadblock, and *we* are heading right for them. I glance in my rearview as if I can see Mel's face, but of course I can't. There's no other way to go but through this roadblock. Terror skates over me, making my hands flex around the steering wheel repeatedly. Using the hem of my cardigan, I rub at my face with fervor, trying to erase any sign of my misery to no avail.

I take several deep breaths and exhale forcefully as we close in on them. Uniformed officers flank the lone road that leads into the mountain pass. A few K-9 officers move along the highway, their dogs' heads lowered to the ground, scenting the earth.

My car rolls to a stop, and I put it in neutral.

I'm here in this moment, but it feels as if I'm watching it from a movie screen with bated breath. A light shines into my driver's side window, and I roll it down with jerky, uneven movements. My mouth fails to form words as I narrow my eyes and try to see past the blinding lights.

The officer moves the light enough that I can make out his boyish features—blond hair, acne-marked skin. He looks fresh from the academy. "Ma'am. I'm Officer Randall," he says, voice laced with his new authority. "We have a situation up here, and every vehicle coming and going must be searched. I need to see your license and have a quick look in your car."

I clear my parched throat, voice cracking as I ask, "What happened? Is everything okay?"

"I'm not at liberty to say the details, but you shouldn't be up here. There's a dangerous person on the loose." I nod slowly, in a daze. "What's your name?"

"Novalie Saw…" I almost give him my maiden name, the one I should give him, but my married name is on my license. "Novalie Rhodes. My license is with my friend behind me," I tell him, realizing that I left my purse in Mel's Bronco.

His brows wrinkle as he looks behind my car to Mel's. In the side mirror, I see she's already stepped out and another cop is searching her car.

"I need you to step out of the vehicle and open your trunk, please?" Officer Randall says.

Grunting with stiffness and fatigue that even the adrenaline can't cope with, I turn off the car and begin to slide out when my heel hits something on the floor. Panic seizes me. I'm not even sure that seeing that phone would throw up any red flags, but it strikes me with fear all the same. Thinking fast, I cough loudly and kick with my heel as I exit the vehicle, effectively knocking the phone under the seat.

Wrapping my arms around myself, I back away and watch as he sweeps his light throughout my car's interior and then takes my keys from the ignition. Walking to the back of the car, he opens the trunk, finding it empty. I glance at Mel, who's already handing my license over to the officer. I didn't even see her come over. Everything around me doesn't feel real.

"Are you alright, miss?" Officer Randall asks, handing my license. I nod, but he looks me over more carefully now. "What were you two doing up here? Why is your license in her car?"

I open my mouth, but Mel interjects. "She had one too many drinks the other night and left it in here." She laughs playfully, and I'm amazed at how absolutely controlled she is. "We came up here to take pictures for Instagram…didn't check the weather first though." She shrugs, her lie falling off her lips so easily.

He rolls his thin lips into his mouth and nods once. "Alright, ladies, get yourselves home. It's not safe up here tonight."

"Yes, sir," Mel says, and then she cocks her head at me as if saying, *get in the damn car and get out of here.*

"Nice car, by the way," the officer says, skimming the hood with his hand as he tips his hat to me and steps back.

Heart thudding away in my chest, I slump into the seat and drive through the cacophony of men readying themselves for a long night of searching. They fade into the rearview mirror as numbness blankets my mind.

Getting home, walking up the stairs, entering my house…it all relies on habitual motor skills because I am not here. I'm lost in a daze of grief and worry that claws and scrapes at my insides like razor blades. Melina has comforted me, held my hand, wiped away my tears, just as she did last December. She's a pillar of strength as usual—a veritable force to be reckoned with—while I am a fleeting feather floating in an endless wind.

The shower spray shocks my wet, clammy skin, and I suck in a breath. The steam fills my lungs and warms my bones as I wash my body in robotic motions. Mel left me in here to gather myself while she's watching the news from my living room couch. My eyes drift to the half-ripped shower curtain I've yet to replace. Soren put it back up for me after we…

If I close my eyes and try really hard, I can feel him here.

Half an hour later, I step out of the shower, wrapping a towel around my hair and another around my torso. While I brush my teeth, I notice a lone cotton ball on the floor where the glass container had shattered and pause. He's everywhere in this house, but also nowhere. Spitting, I rinse the toothbrush and turn off the sink, dropping my brush beside his. My feet pad softly across the floor to my dresser. I pull on some plain white panties and reach for a set of pajamas but stop and turn toward my closet instead. Walking in, I graze my fingers over Ren's shirts hanging in a small line. Taking a navy blue tee off the hanger, I slip it on, dropping the towel to the floor, then pull the one from my hair and flip my head over once to loosen the wet strands. When my head whips up, my eyes latch onto the box containing Levi's belongings. My eyes narrow, head tilting. It's turned with the label facing to the right. For anyone else, this wouldn't be concerning, but for me, I'm meticulous…OCD, as Ren would say. I know I didn't put it up there like that.

Reaching up, I lug the box down, almost tripping over my towel in the process, but manage to heft it over to the bed. As soon as I open it, my pulse hammers. My mouth falls open. My old journal is lying open to the last entry…the day of Levi's wake. But that's not what has my chest rising and falling fast. It's the choppy handwriting below that entry causing my state of shock.

Snatching the journal with lightning quickness, I lift the box off the bed to the floor and then scramble under the covers near my bedside lamp. My watery eyes devour the page while my vivid imagination pictures Ren sitting in here, back hunched over the parchment, face alight with a side smile. My heart swells.

Princess,

You said once that you don't write anymore, but on the off chance that you do, I'm leaving you this in hopes that it will find you at the time you need it most. First off, love isn't bullshit. Without it, what do we even live for? It's what drives good and evil in this world, but it drives us all the same. And yes, you'd do it all over again if you had the chance. We don't have hindsight, sweetheart. We can't predict whether the love we give will be reciprocated or ignored, but it's always worth the effort. And even though you were treated so poorly—even though you had your heart shattered, you still remained true to who you are. Look at everything you're doing for me. That takes a strong-minded person who has empathy and love in their heart. Your soft, kind nature is what draws people to you. Don't ever lose that.

Second of all, look at how much you've changed. I know what you're thinking—that I haven't known you very long, but I don't need to. Your journal tells me all I need to know. You went from being a people pleaser, a girl who did what her parents wanted, what her husband wanted, a girl who put her dreams on hold to stoke someone else's fire. And even though remnants of that life remain in the way you feel you need to be perfect, organized, poised...you have changed. You moved away, started your own business, and are slowly becoming the person you truly want to be. Let go of others' expectations. Live your life, Novalie. Live it well.

A sob racks my chest, and I have to blink away tears before continuing.

And last of all, princess, I'm sorry. Sorry for the part I'm playing in your life. You deserve so much more than this, and while I'm grateful for your change of heart, grateful that you believed in me, I was wrong. I should've never barged in here and taken over your life like I did. I scared you, made you cry. Anyways, just wanted you to know how sorry I truly am for that.

But...

I'll go back to your last journal entry. You said, "Would I choose to have known love in that way...just once, knowing what I know now? Was it worth it?" I can only give you my perspective on that one. Hell yes, I'd do it all over again. I'd make you cry, force your compliance, if it meant I'd get to experience this side of you one more time. Because you are an experience, Nova. I'd choose to do it all over again if it meant I could feel this kind of love.

Too soon? Yeah, probably, but time is not on my side, so I'll say it here on this paper and one day to your face. I love you, Novalie Annie Sawyer Rhodes. You are the experience of a lifetime, and if I end up back in prison or worse, please...live.

I hope this gives you a little insight into who you are. Everyone needs that sometimes when we lose ourselves in this crazy world.

With my entire fucking heart,
Love Soren Lee Marshall

P.S. From the time I first saw your picture until the moment I watched you on the balcony from the shadows looking at the moon, you've had me. Stop searching that moon at night for answers and instead, let it bring you the peace you deserve.

Tucking the journal into my chest as if someone may attempt to steal it from my clenched fingers, I slide under the covers, flip off the light, and breathe in and out. In and out. It's all I can do. When did he do this? I wonder. It's a vulnerable piece of him that I never expected to have. Some hidden part of my soul cracks, splinters into a thousand shards, ripping the air from the room, but I breathe.

In and out. In and out.

CHAPTER 39

Novalie

Gunshots rip through the air, and I watch as people jolt with each pull of the triggers. Fellow officers line up in a traditional formation to give honor to their fallen comrade. Franklin Jimmy Sawyer was recognized for the courage and bravery he exuded over his career. The Medal of Valor he had received years prior, a gilded, gleaming five-pointed star catching the sun. I watch numb as my father pays his last respects, my mother clutching his hand in comfort. It's one of the few times I've seen him cry. Jim's children gather around the coffin, sobbing uncontrollably.

I shift uncomfortably in my black heels as they punch into the soft grass, my long black skirt flowing in the light breeze. Melina keeps close to me, her arm resting in mine like an anchor. Brushing away a stray hair that's fallen from the bun atop my head, I eye our surroundings. My uncle's sprawling farmhouse lies in the distance, cold and uninhabited now, where it once held such beauty and warmth. The trees sway around us, rustling the leaves and whipping me with nervous energy. Because while everyone else is occupied with their sorrow, I'm filled with fear for what could be lurking in the wooded areas surrounding my family's cemetery.

It's been three days since the storm on the mountain. Three days since Soren went missing. In that time I've somehow managed to put one foot in front of the other, albeit leaden and mechanical. I'm now certain that whoever the man on the ATV was, he was the same to call in the anonymous tip to the cops. I'm also fairly certain I know who it was. *Micah Talon.* He had the same build. The same shape. And he's the only person who would've been there because I checked Soren's phone and recovered his last message sent that read, *Valhalla now.* He's still out there, and we have no idea how much he knows. Did Soren tell him about me? About where he's been staying? If so…I'm fucked.

Not to mention, Micah's mother has listed him as a missing person. No one has seen him since that night. The news has been littered with photos of him. Some reports are speculating that he helped Soren escape, while others are claiming his disappearance is unrelated.

Thankfully, Melina runs her own printing company and can take off whenever and manage things from afar, because she hasn't left my house and we keep our pistols with us at all times.

It takes me a moment to realize that the crowd is dispersing. I wait until there's a gap in the retreating bodies before I make my way over to my uncle's final resting place. A single tear leaks from the corner of my eye as I drop the rose, watching it land on the top of the coffin with a soft thud.

Suddenly, my mother is beside me. Her brown eyes, so different than my hazel ones in color but shaped identical, are down-turned with sorrow today. Her dyed blonde hair is swept up into a chignon. She wraps me in her arms, and a dam seems to break inside of me, splitting me down the middle. "It's going to be okay, honey," she whispers into my hair. "He's in a better place now."

She says all the things people say at funerals. They're in a better place. They're free of worry and pain. And while I hope those things are true, I know that Detective Sawyer would want to be here, doing what he loves. I nod into her embrace anyway, letting her provide the comfort she needs to sate her own mind.

She pulls away, holding me at arm's length, eyes scanning me, then a frown pulls at her cheeks. "You look gaunt, dear. Are you eating enough?" She squeezes my thin arms.

"I'm fine, Mom. Really," I tell her, fidgeting under her unrelenting stare.

She doesn't look convinced, and rightly so. She sighs, "Did you hear all the information from the will reading?"

I nod once. The last will and testament reading happened two days ago, but I was in no condition to join the fray. I felt it was more for his children and brother anyway. However, to everyone's shock, Jim was loaded. He had money set aside for each person in the family. His children got the land and house; his grandkids were left with enough money to send them each to college, and Mom and Dad were left a substantial amount too. He left me his entire library collection and other odd and end things he knew I loved growing up.

Mom purses her lips. "Uncle Jim seemed to have thought of everyone, didn't he? He was such a good man. I love you, honey. You need anything at all, you call us, okay. I'll keep your dad busy, but make sure you come see us more regularly. He needs that, you know."

"I know, Mom. Love you too." I hug her one last time, and as she turns to walk away, I grab her hand and squeeze it, stopping her. She turns back to me. "You two need to go on a vacation, get away from here." Her brow knits, so I add, "It's not safe around here after what happened to Jim. You two need to be careful."

Her face softens. "We'll be fine, dear. The police assured us that the investigation is thorough and that it was likely a disgruntled criminal that Jim sent to prison at some point during his career."

I hum in thought but say nothing as she turns and leaves me there on the hill surrounded by our dead relatives. Melina stands a few feet away, watching the woods as much as I was moments ago. A man and a woman catch my attention, heading my way, Bowen to the left of them and a younger woman tagging along behind. It takes me a moment to realize that it's Callon and Maisy Wolfe with their daughter Laya. A slow smile spreads across my damp cheeks.

Her case was one of the biggest Jim had ever worked on. He quite literally helped take down one of the largest underground sex trafficking rings in the nation because of her and Callon. It made national news at an unprecedented rate due to the fact that it was a senator here in North Carolina that ran it in his mountain mansion, selling women and even teens. It was unfathomable. Maisy survived with the help of Callon, and they found love along the way and a deep friendship with my uncle. I haven't laid eyes on them in years, seeing as they still live in Mexico.

Callon is as handsome as I remember him being when I was little. His hair has a few strands of gray now but is still mostly dark brown. He's still stocky like a man who works outside a lot, skin tanned. Maisy smiles at something Bowen says, and her green eyes crinkle around the edges. I was always envious of her long, wavy dark hair, but now it's made even more ravishing with two silvery white strips curling to frame her face. And Laya is a mix of the two of them. She has her daddy's vivid blue eyes and her mother's long dark curls. Light freckles dot the apples of her cheeks.

"Novalie." Bowen smiles as he nears me and then takes me into a hug. A feather tickles my face from where it protrudes from one of his long braids. One by one, they pull me in for hugs after Bo releases me.

"I'm so glad you could all make it here. I know how close you were to Uncle Jim."

Maisy's eyes soften. "We wouldn't have missed being here. He was such a good friend to us.

Callon wraps an arm around his wife, tucking her close to him. "Is there anything we can do to help the family?" he asks. "Do you need anything at all?"

I shake my head. "No, just the support of being here is more than enough. Thank you."

I spend some time catching up with them, with my cousin Laya, who Maisy and Callon thoughtfully named after Bowen's sister, who was murdered by the same people responsible for Maisy's kidnapping. She's grown into a beautiful woman who, at the young age of twenty-four, has started several foundations to help women who escape trafficking and women surviving domestic abuse. Bowen smiles and talks as if nothing is wrong, but I notice the way his eyes pin mine every now and again. He's waiting for a moment alone. It makes me antsy. I'm not entirely sure I'm prepared for anything he's discovered.

Our moment arises when everyone else says their goodbyes. Bo yells over to Callon as he's walking away, "I'll catch up with you in a minute." Cal nods to him. Bo turns back to me, and Melina closes the distance, coming to stand at my side.

Bo exhales. "I hate to bring any of this up today of all days, but I found something unusual this morning."

"What?" I ask, leaning closer.

Bo looks around to make sure we're alone and adjusts his western bowtie before whispering, "An IP address that has *consistently* been researching the case, photos of Soren and Victoria, just anything and everything related to them. It's not your average run-of-the-mill crime junkie search. This verges on obsessive. Especially over the last three days." He gives a self-satisfied smile. "I went a step further about two weeks ago and started a mock Facebook account dedicated to searching for the true killer of Victoria Styles." My brows raise in approval as he continues. "Like I expected, it became a beacon for all manner of crime lovers and also, like I expected, that one IP address continued to pursue the account."

I nibble on a broken fingernail before flexing my fingers and forcing myself to stop. "Where's it located? Do you know who this person is?"

He wobbles his head side to side. "Yes," he admits with a huff, and there's a hint of confusion in his eyes. "Yes, I know where it's coming from, and yes, I found the name of the person."

"There's a *but* in this…isn't there?" I ask.

He rolls his lips inward before replying. "It's registered to a Tahlia Grey."

Mel and I share a look of confusion, then I turn back to him. "And the location?" I press.

"That's the strange part. It's in California. La Jolla, a neighborhood out of San Diego."

"*What*?" Mel chimes in. "Who in California would have that much interest in a case from North Carolina?"

"My sentiments exactly," Bowen grumbles. He hands me a folded paper with the address and name inside. I tuck it into the pocket of my skirt. His hand moves to his shaven chin, scratching, and then he blows out another long breath. "It's probably nothing, but it does make you wonder."

Mel and I exchange a look of '*what the hell is going on*' before my eyes snap back to his. "What about that number I gave you?" I ask.

"I have a guy working on it. Sorry, with everything that's happened around here, I've been busy. Plus, I spent a few days with Molly and the kids before they went to visit Molly's parents out of state."

"Okay, no problem…I'll check this woman out."

"The hell you will," Bo snaps at me, making me rear back. "You're writing a book, Nova…it's not worth risking your life over. Stay as far away from whatever this is and take notes. Watch the news, shit like that."

My mouth opens to retort, but Mel beats me to it. "I won't let her out of my sight, Bo…you have my word." I glare daggers at her, but she ignores me.

Rolling my shoulders, I change my posture, and nod. "I'll take notes from the sidelines." The lie rolls too easily off my lips.

"Good," Bo says. "This is a very interesting case you've chosen to work on, but be careful, okay? Stay low. We still don't know if this shooting was related to Jim getting those case files. And if you need me for anything, never hesitate to call." He hands us both a business card reading, Bowen Innovations. He flips mine over. Written on the back is a cell number. "This is another of my personal lines, so to speak." Just the way he says it makes me wonder what all manner of illegal things this man does. "Use that one. I'll be in touch, ladies." Bo hugs both of us and takes off at a half jog, heading toward Callon and Maisy's 1970 Mustang.

"You know that I have absolutely no intentions of sitting around on this, right?" I say, spinning to Mel.

"Never thought you would." She grins. "What's the plan, supernova?"

"First, we get whatever's hidden in Uncle Jim's house, which I assume is in a clock. Second, we are going on a little road trip."

"*Little*…Nova, California, is not a little road trip," she whispers vehemently. "So please tell me that's not your plan."

"I have nothing to go on right now—no clue where Micah is, what he did," I have to pause at that and look away, "but this address…it's something." I pat my skirt, rattling the paper inside. "So, yes…that's the plan. Are you in or out?"

She cocks a brow at me. "I'm your ride-or-die, remember, but just know that I have *zero* plans of dying. I'm far too pretty and full of potential."

I roll my eyes. "You're full of something alright."

We watch the last of the crowd forming a line of cars leaving the long winding driveway. "That's the last of them," I say. We share a look of determination as we head for the house in the distance.

CHAPTER 40

Novalie

Melina is on my heels as I step onto the wrap-around porch. We had to wait a considerable amount of time for Jim's children to disperse. The entire family is meeting for dinner at Mom and Dad's, and they assume we'll be right behind them. I turn the knob, but unsurprisingly, it's locked.

"Well, shit," Mel says behind me.

"I didn't expect it to be left open for us," I say, peering over my shoulder at her. "But I stayed here a lot growing up and cannot count the times I got locked out when my aunt and uncle would forget to leave the door unlocked for me."

Mel watches me with interest as I walk the length of the porch. At the end, there's an old cement duck beside a planter. It's been there my whole life. It's weathered and cracked, and hardly any color remains. Shifting it to the side,

I find what I'm looking for and hold it up proudly. "Uncle Jim was set in his ways." I dangle the key. "He's had this same hide-a-key for ages. It's kind of the reason I use that frog as my hidey spot at the bookshop."

Mel grins as I shuffle back to her and unlock the door. It groans, swinging open, as we walk inside. The house is much the same as it was in my childhood, down to the paintings of racehorses, antiques, farmhouse décor, and original wood flooring. The only thing that's new is the sheet-rocked walls painted in a fair gray color. They used to be paneling.

I don't hesitate when I make my way over to the large oak grandfather clock that still sits in the same place it always did. Stopping in front of it, my outstretched finger traces the gold swirling designs embedded in the glass doors. Memories drench me with sadness, soaking my resolve. The clock hasn't been reset lately. The pendulum doesn't swing—the weights hang limp at the bottom, and the time is stuck at twelve o'clock on the dot. Reaching up onto my tiptoes, I pull out a key hidden behind the wooden designs and unlock the glass doors.

"This is kind of giving me the creeps; hurry up," Mel chimes in beside me.

I glare at her but reach up, angling my body until I can fit my hand behind the clock face. My fingertips and nails drag around for several seconds before I feel something. Pinching my fingers together, I grasp the corner of some type of parchment. Finally, I slip it free from the hiding spot, and my heels settle on the floor once more as Mel and I eye the brown envelope.

"Open it." She nudges my arm with hers.

"I am," I say even though I was definitely staring at it for far too long. I use a nail to slice open the envelope as I'm walking toward the kitchen table. Turning it upside down, I let the contents fall onto the polished surface. A photo of a man stares back at us, and beside it lies a folded piece of paper and a business card with a note pinned to it. It's a full-body photo. He's dressed in black from head to toe and has distinct cowboy boots on…tipped in silver.

"That guy looks really familiar," Mel says, picking up the picture first to get a closer look.

"He sure does…and I know why," I whisper.

Her eyes cut to mine. "Why?"

"Because that face has been on the news a lot lately." Her one brow raises and I nod. "That's Joe Sparks. He's the one who worked Soren's case in the beginning. The one that documented how combative he was. I'm almost certain he was also there the night Vicky and Soren argued at the bar."

Mel's mouth falls open before she gathers herself and asks, "Do you think Uncle Jim is telling you that *this* man might be involved?"

"I'm afraid so." I lean away from her as she continues to look at the photo. I lift and unfold the paper, quickly realizing what it is. "Mel, look at this," I say hastily. She peers over, reading as I confirm what her eyes are taking in. "This is a sworn affidavit, Mel." My heart begins to race as I read over it two more times to make sure I'm not crazy. "This is a sworn statement from the lab tech Serena Walter saying that the blood samples she collected that night were lost or tampered with and that there was sulfur boot casting done on a print in the snow that was never looked at."

"Why would they not analyze the boot print?" Mel picks the photo back up and narrows her eyes at Joe Sparks. "Unless it was his boots that left it there." She sneers.

"Exactly," I say quietly. "This is it, Mel...well, not it exactly, but this is real evidence that this case was botched!" My voice rises with rapidly growing anticipation. I throw my arms around her, almost toppling us over. "We can do this, Mel! We can clear his name."

She squeezes me back and, out of nowhere, tears leak down my face because I know that we have to do this alone. I know that this will only get worse before it gets better. But I don't care. Soren will have his vengeance...if only through me. I won't allow myself to lose hope. Because that's all I have left, and there are only a few strips of it remaining inside, stitching me together.

Releasing her, I grab the remaining thing my uncle left me, the business card and note. "This is for a literary agent," I whisper, showing it to Mel.

"What does the note say?" she asks.

Flipping the card over, I read it aloud.

This is a dear friend of mine, and she knows
all about you. She's ready when you are.
So when this is over...write the damn book.

With love,
Jim Sawyer

CHAPTER 41

Novalie

One week later…

Our bodies rock as the plane's tires make contact with the tarmac at San Diego International Airport. The atmosphere in here is filled with a frenzy of people smiling and laughing, a baby crying a few rows back, everyone traveling for work or play.

But not us. Mel is as silent as me for once.

After a week of putting our affairs in order, we bought tickets instead of driving across the country. My family and hers are under the assumption that we needed to get away. A girls' trip was a good excuse; it gave us the out we needed to track down this strange lead. But now that we're here, nothing feels right. Doubts bore holes in my psyche, creating divots in my unraveling future.

After the clock find at my uncle's house, suspicion escalated toward Joe more than anyone. Bowen shocked me to the core with his message the other day stating that the number I found in that storage unit was used the weeks prior to Vicky's death and could be traced to certain locations, including the police department. We are now positive Joe is the biggest player in this game of losers.

But…we were stumped as to how to proceed and decided to take a breather and check this out. We couldn't exactly go to the police anyway with nothing but theories and vague evidential findings. The picture of Joe Sparks fits with a cover-up at the police department, but not with everything. We needed more than a random photo, phone records that we couldn't prove, and that affidavit. And with no new leads and no news of Micah or…Soren, we booked flights.

"I can't believe we're actually doing this," Mel says, grabbing her carry-on.

I shrug and heft mine down as well. "If nothing else, we get a mini-vacation out of it," I say, but my voice lacks enthusiasm.

It's been eight days now since Soren went missing in those woods. I'm still holding onto the hope that he somehow made it to a safe place and that one day I'll see him again. One day I'll touch him again—feel his warmth.

In an exterior parking lot, we find our bland rental car waiting for us. I pull on my sunglasses, adjust my mauve-colored mini dress, and load my bag into the trunk. Hopping in, I grip the steering wheel and look to my right, just as Mel looks at me. The white camisole and flowy long baby blue skirt make her tan skin glow. "You ready for this?" I ask.

"Born ready." She waggles her eyebrows, making me smile. I flip my long waves of hair behind me and take off, just as she says, "I always wanted to see the West Coast, just never pictured we'd be doing it as undercover agents." She holds her hand poised like a gun beside her face.

"For real," I mutter under my breath. "This is all crazy…isn't it? Are we insane?"

She drops her hand. "Probably, but we wouldn't know, right? Insane people don't know they're insane," she retorts.

"Valid point." I laugh.

The city of San Diego looms around us with sprawling buildings reaching to the sky, lined by the bay. Military ships from the naval base hover in the distance. "Look," I point, "that's the Coronado Bridge," I say in awe, watching it arch into the sky with ships and boats passing underneath.

Mel's eyes widen as she takes it all in. "Maybe I can meet a sailor while we're out here, run away with him," she says dreamily.

"Stay focused," I say through a smile. "Uniformed men later, super important spy mission first."

She groans. "You take away all the fun," she says, her head whipping to the side as she eyes a group of sailors walking down the street. "And I mean *ALL* the fun," she huffs and then gives an appreciative sound in her throat as we drive by them.

No more than twenty minutes pass as we wind and weave along the curvy roads, leaving the big city behind. Cliffs begin to fall off beside us, ending in the ocean below that gives way to a magnificent view of the Pacific. Between those rocky structures are sandy areas lying full of fat and happy seals sunbathing. Mel squeals when she sees them.

"This place is gorgeous," I muse.

The small town of La Jolla is nestled among those cliffs and beaches. It's teeming with life. Little shops line the paved street as we slowly drive through. Palm trees sway in the breeze, and the very air feels cleansed by the rock faces and ocean. My GPS startles us as it directs me to turn left at the next light. All the beauty around me fades and becomes background noise the closer we get. I glance down nervously at the arrival time.

"Five minutes," I say. Mel's eyeing me as I glance her way. "What?"

"Can I ask you something…before we get here?"

"Sure." My brows crinkle.

"What if we find nothing today?" she asks plainly.

"Then we find nothing." I shrug, but she doesn't look convinced.

"It's just that…" she pauses, "you sort of lost yourself after Levi, and now threw yourself into Soren's battle wholeheartedly. You've been obsessed this week."

My face falls flat. "What are you saying?"

"I'm saying that if we keep finding nothing but dead ends…you need to learn to let go and do something just for yourself." I keep my eyes on the road as she continues. "Oh, come on, Nova, you know good and well that you're a people pleaser, and it's about time that someone catered to you for a change."

My shoulders slump a little as I chew on her words, but they taste bitter in my mouth. "I may have been that way with Levi, but Soren's different."

"I know he is. I'm just saying, live your life if this doesn't go anywhere. You can't spend your youth searching for a ghost."

The car swerves when I toss my head her way, but I straighten us out. "*Poor* choice of words, Mel," I grit out.

"Sorry, that wasn't how I meant it," she adds.

But it was. She's saying there's a strong possibility that Soren is…that he's…dead. And I could be left wondering, looking into crowds for his face. Always searching.

The GPS interrupts the heavy conversation, letting us know we're one mile from the location. The closer we get, the quieter the car becomes. I finally say what we are both likely thinking. "Whoever this is, they are hella rich."

"These are straight-up mansions on *cliffs* at the beach…*in California*." Mel puts her window down, curls blowing all around her. "They have to be worth millions upon millions."

"Without a doubt," I add. These are gated, manicured stucco houses with literal statues and fountains on the front lawns. Again, I mull over the last few days that led us here. We did some preliminary research on Tahlia Grey, but she's incredibly elusive. We found minimal information on her.

If I'm being honest, coming here was simply a distraction from the waiting game back at home.

My nerves have sweat gathering at the nape of my neck as we round a curve in the road; a dense forest now blankets the right side of us while the cliff is to our left. No more houses are close by as we near our destination.

"*There it is*." Mel jabs a finger in the direction she's looking, and I have to slow down the car to appreciate the view.

"Holy shit," my jaw hits the floor. While still a stucco-type exterior like the others we passed, this mansion is painted stark white, enormous, with two levels or three levels by the looks of the slopping grounds, but unlike the others this one is a modern build. From our angle on the road, we can see behind it to the plush deep green turf that surrounds a rectangle pool. A waterfall cascades from that one into a lower pool as if the house and everything built behind it was meant to move with the land, stepping down and down toward the sea.

I pull the car over when I see a large enough gap in the wooded area to our right. Not hiding it but not leaving us completely in view either. "What are you thinking?" Mel asks.

"I'm thinking we need to watch and see who comes and goes from this place. We can't waltz up to the door and say, 'Hey, heard you were obsessed with the Marshall case.'"

"True, although that would be hilarious and worth the shock factor," Mel says as she gets out of the car, stretching her arms.

I get out too and reach into my purse, pulling out two sets of binoculars. Mel stops mid-stretch, one of her arms still pulled across her body. "When did you get those?"

I smirk and wiggle them in the air. "I swiped them from my uncle's house when you were in the bathroom."

"Well, this makes it official." She comes over, taking one from me.

"Makes what official?" I ask.

"We're criminals." When I wrinkle my nose at her, she adds, "Trespassing, stalking—those are criminal behaviors, Nova…in case you've forgotten."

"*Okay*, *okay*, whatever, just come on," I say through the half-smile I'm trying to hide and wave her to follow me to some nearby bushes that flank the property. I point toward the front of the house and circular drive and then the back that leads to the ocean. "We're uphill, which gives us an unobstructed view of the front and back of this house from here. This is perfect."

"So, we just sit here all day and watch? I should've brought snacks," Mel complains.

"You ate a shit-ton on the plane…you're fine," I grumble back.

"We could've at least brought some spiked drinks."

I glare at her before sitting cross-legged on the ground. I pull the binoculars to my eyes and wait.

CHAPTER 42

Novalie

Shifting on tingling legs, I stretch them out behind me and lay flat on the grass where we're tucked between two tall bushes—our discarded shoes tucked under the bush. Mel mumbles something about the heat and how hungry she is. It's been a good hour and we've yet to see any movement. With the binoculars, I'm able to get a close-up view of every inch of the sprawling estate. That Olympic-size pool in the back doesn't just drop down to another but is also surrounded by a manmade stream. The cobbled walkway that weaves its way down to the sea begins right at the end of the last patio behind the pools. Flowers of brilliant colors pop from every corner and only end at the sand dunes where the walkway meets a deck that drops off even more into a set of stairs.

"We need a better plan," Mel gripes. "Even *if* we see this person, what good will that do?"

"I don't know Mel!" I whisper forcefully. "This is my first time doing this kind of thing too, you know. I…" Just as I'm about to go into a rant, I stop, my words dead and lifeless on my tongue.

Mel hunkers down beside me, bringing her binoculars back to her eyes. "What…what do you see?"

"A woman," I whisper. "Right there." I grab Mel's head, turning her toward what I see.

Exiting the back of the house is a tall, slim woman sporting a white thong bikini. Her hair is dark, almost black, and cut into a bob. She pads over to the pool, holding a glass of something in her left hand and a phone in the other to her ear. She bends her knees to dip a foot into the blue water. A man comes out a moment later, older than her by the looks of it. While still physically fit, his hair has gone more white than gray. He's wearing an expensive-looking suit that he's buttoning as he creeps up behind the woman to run his hand along her ass.

"Ugh, gross." My nose curls at the sight. "This could get R-rated fast."

Mel giggles. "For real. Damn, I feel like a creeper. If they start dropping clothes…I'm out. You can see everything with these things." She taps a fingernail on her black binoculars.

"We're not creepers. We're spies, remember."

"Uh huh, keep telling yourself that." She makes a sound of interest. "I can even see her tattoo from here."

I squint my eyes but don't see it. I continue watching them. The man caresses her from the back of her neck to her lower spine. She bats his hand away and gestures to the phone. Her body shifts more facing us as she talks to whomever is on the line as her gentleman friend kisses her cheek and waves bye to her. We follow his movements until they disappear behind the right side of the house. Not long after, we see a *very* expensive McLaren leaving the drive.

Several minutes pass, but nothing stands out to us. I'm beginning to regret this trip, beginning to feel like the creepers we are when the woman shifts. Her hands move as she speaks, and just as her left arm is lifted to swig from her glass, I gasp aloud in shock. My mouth goes dry as I try to swallow what I'm seeing.

The tattoo.

And not just any tattoo. A butterfly on her ribs, one I've only seen once before.

The binoculars hit the ground. I shuffle back onto my ass. Mumbled incoherent thoughts trail from my lips. Mel is grabbing at me. "*What's wrong, Nova?*" she's asking. I hear her, but everything is fuzzy, my ears ringing as my heart tries to catch up with my brain.

Mel grabs my shoulders, shaking them. "Nova! *Look at me.* What's wrong?"

My chest rises and falls fast. I feel like I'm hyperventilating. "Tha…that's Vicky."

Mel's grip relaxes as she cocks her head in confusion. "No…no, no, no, that can't be."

"It's her!" I say a bit too loud. "That's her tattoo. I remember it from the picture I gave Ren."

Mel shakes her head. "Do you know how many butterfly tattoos there are on women her age? It *can't* be her Nova. She's dead, remember."

I push away from her, grab the binoculars and shove them into her hands. "*Look again*! You watch the news…I don't, but I saw that picture. The hair is different, but that. Is. *Her.*"

Mel snatches them from me, placing them to her eyes, but then sighs, "She's gone."

"*What?* No…she was just there." I grab mine off the ground, pressing them into my face and see…*nothing*. The woman's no longer by the pool. Our heads swivel as we try to relocate her.

"It's her, Melina. *I know it.* We need to get out of here. I need to call my brother; maybe he can help." I spit out words frantically. "This changes everything. Mel, you have to believe me…it's *her.*"

Mel's voice beside me cracks with emotion, startling me. "I believe you," she whispers in such a tiny voice.

I snap my head to hers, and my heart slams against my chest walls with the force of a thousand hammers. Her face is pale, her big brown eyes glassy.

A gun is aimed at her skull by a man in a black suit. I'm frozen in place, mouth open without a voice. My hands begin to tremble as I lose grip on the binoculars and they thud to the ground.

The man tsks. "What're you two doing trespassing on Mrs. Grey's property, huh?" I close and then reopen my mouth to answer, but he shakes his head, a clear indication not to speak. With his other hand, he presses a button on the earpiece he's wearing. "You want me to call the cops? Run them off? Rough them up a little?" the man says with a grin. His light brown hair is cropped short, and his face is cleanly shaved. He has a cleft lip scar and looks boyish with a detectable amount of arrogance in his stance.

"Bring them to me," a female voice chirps on the other end of the line, sounding…*bored.*

"Sure thing, Mrs. Grey." He motions with his hand for me to stand, while he yanks Melina from the ground.

"Don't *fucking* hurt her!" I snarl, finally finding my voice.

His brows raise. "Walk," is all he says as he shoves her forward and gestures for me to get in front.

I lace my arm in hers and hold on for dear life. I glance at her, the shock worn off her face and replaced with absolute rage. *There she is*…I think. My strong, stubborn friend who can handle anything. Our eyes collide, but we remain mute due to the wall of muscle a step behind us.

Tension gathers in my shoulders the closer we get to the house. My fight-or-flight response is surging for me to run. Just keep breathing, I tell myself, trying to keep my emotions in check. They can't possibly know who we are. We can simply talk our way out of this.

My eyes flit around us as if a solution will pop out of nowhere, but there's no solution. I can't help but take in some of the overtly grand displays of wealth out here. Everything is immaculate. I don't think a single blade of grass is longer than the other. Soren would hate it. And even with all the fear coursing through me, the thought of him de-organizing my cabinets almost brings a smile to my face.

But then reality settles over me like a black shroud because we are standing at her front door.

The security guy opens the massive, intricately designed door, which swings inward with a groan. He ushers us forward and all but slams it closed behind us. My bare feet make no noise on the marbled tile floor.

A voice trickles through the foyer. "*Bring them in here*," almost echoing in the space that has a literal koi pond in the center—colorful fish flitter around the five foot tall statue of a mermaid that looks as if she's bursting from the water.

"Who has a pond inside their house?" Mel wrinkles her nose at the ridiculous display. The security guy shushes Mel.

Further inside, we're pushed into a room to our left. I snap my head back to the man. "Touch either of us again and you'll regret it." His eyes skate down my slight form, and he smirks.

Facing the direction Mel's eyes are pinned on, I realize we're in some sort of formal dining room with a table long enough to hold twenty people or more and a layered crystal chandelier dangling from the center of the pitched ceiling. I get only a glimpse of the ornate foreign decor and paintings before my eyes lock on the female with her hip braced against the table.

Now, seeing her up close, there's absolutely *no* denying it. Melina must realize it too because her mouth is hanging open as she studies her. Victoria has a white silk robe on that only reaches mid-thigh. It's left open in the front for a moment, and my eyes lock on the tattoo before she wraps it around her torso and ties it.

She tilts her head in a catty way, taking us in as much as we do her. Her feminine but strong voice startles me when she speaks. "Are you two with the press?"

Mel and I share a look, one that seems to say, '*Let's not give anything away as to why we are here.*' Then, I shake my head at her. "No."

"Then who are you? Names…now," she commands, managing to still sound bored. "I don't have time to dillydally with you. I can just as easily call the police and have you arrested for trespassing."

I open my mouth to speak, but Mel lays a hand on my arm and beats me to it. "Yes, we're with the press. I'm Violet and this is," her head swivels to mine and back to Victoria,

"Imogen. I'm sorry my friend lied. It's our first gig, and we were really trying to impress the boss."

Keeping my expression neutral is a feat after listening to Mel just give us the names of two characters from the book series we're reading, but I manage.

Victoria rolls her eyes. "Vultures. That's what you are." She raises the crystal glass and sips the pink concoction inside, pursing her pink lips after. Her icy blue eyes rake down my body, and it feels akin to razor blades. "You're both fools if you think spying on us in our personal lives will gain you any insight into the political world. When we're here, that world disappears. Do you not have any common decency? Integrity? This is our home."

I can't help my brows stitching together at her words. *Political world?* The white-haired man…maybe he's a politician.

Her eyes suddenly take in our state of dress more closely, head cocking to the side, her dyed brown hair swishing with the motion. She stands fully and pads toward us slowly, like a cat stalking mice. "Where are your cameras? If you're truly with the press."

Mel stiffens beside me, but right then my phone chimes in my dress pocket with a message. I don't reach for it as Victoria comes to stand before us. She looks over my head to her security guy and nods once. He holds me with one hand and before I can stop him, he's snatched my phone.

I thrash out of his grip, and he freely lets me go, causing me to stumble a few steps. "Hey!" I yell at him. "You can't do that!"

Victoria ignores me and opens her manicured hand. "The phone, Talbert," she says. He drops my cell into her waiting palm. "Imogen…was it? We shall see." She raises the phone to my face to unlock it.

I take a step forward, bitter anger seeping out of my expression, but a hand stops me. The security guy, Talbert, squeezes my shoulder in a painful grip.

Victoria grins happily, sleuthing through my phone, proud of herself. "Who's Ian? She muses with a raised brow.

My brother, he must've messaged me, but why? A strange foreboding forms in my gut. It's like knowing you are about to crash before it happens. I feel like I'm in a Tesla on a winding road, and Victoria is in my lane driving a semi-truck. My stomach twists into knots as Mel and I watch Victoria's face go from cocky to shocked. Color leaches from her skin, leaving the already alabaster tone somehow whiter. Her breathing rate increases, her mouth opening to form words that seem lost to her. Her eyes flit from left to right as if she's reading whatever my brother said over and over again.

Suddenly, her eyes snap to mine, narrowing. My fingers fist into the fabric of my dress, bunching the material. I see Mel's cold stare on Victoria as she levels me with one of her own.

Her voice drops low and drips with accusation. "*Who* are you two and *what* are you doing here?"

Squaring my shoulders, I scoff at her, making Mel cut her eyes to me and then throw all pretenses of being reporters out the window. "The real question is, who are you? Tahlia Grey…*or* should I say…Victoria Marshall?"

She doesn't show shock this time, likely because of whatever was on my phone. She smiles condescendingly, catching us off guard as she backs away, her bare feet making no noise on the floor. She sips her drink and shakes her head in awe, leaning a hip once more against the table. "What's your connection to Soren?" She waves the glass between us, making the ice tink against the sides. "There must be one for you to have come all this way?"

Neither of us speaks.

She picks the phone back up and begins reading the message. "Nova." She glances into my eyes briefly, letting me know she has my name, then continues. "Why are you not answering my calls? You were all over this case and just left…for a girls' trip? Really? That guy Soren is still missing, but they found a hat a good ways down the river, caught in some rocks. I saw it in evidence." She stops reading to look at me and smirk. "The next part Ian has typed in all caps." She says, smiling, "YOU WANT TO TELL ME WHY IT'S YOUR HAT THEY HAVE!" A humorless laugh trills out of her as she gets to the end of the text message. "I know that hat. I remember when you put your initials on the inside and how you always did that little lightning thing beside your S's. What the hell is going on, Nova? Call me back now!"

She's studying me, and I'm sure she can see the devastation that just washed over my features. Out of nowhere, a lump forms in my throat. They found my hat in the river. Did he really jump off that waterfall? It's confirmation that I didn't want to hear. I shudder and hold back the tears threatening to bloom.

Victoria tilts her head in that weird feline way she has about her. "Is that sorrow I see in your eyes?" Her brow wrinkles in distaste. "Nova was it?" she asks without expecting a response. "Do you have some sort of feelings for my husband? How on earth did that come about…I wonder."

Cold washes over me, sending chills straight to my bones with her admission. I swallow hard and bite down on my inner lip, tasting copper. Rage coils inside me, but I can't hold it back a second longer. "He's not your husband and never should've been! How could you do this to him? To anyone, for that matter? Why didn't you leave him, get divorced?" The floodgates open in me, and the need for answers is all-consuming.

My raised tone fails to get under her skin. She shrugs nonchalantly and looks back at Talbert. "I thought you handled my affairs." Her tone is laced with the promise of punishment.

"*I did*," he says firmly. "There was only one person requesting evidence on that case and drudging it back up, and it wasn't these two."

Everything clicks into place. Into a dark place. Whoever this Talbert is to her, he either killed my uncle or had him killed. Uncle Jim had the picture of Joe though…so maybe…

Victoria almost growls, stopping my train of thought. "You obviously didn't," she spits at him.

She lets her eyes fall back to us. "What to do with you two?" She says it so calm, collected, while tapping a French-manicured nail on the side of her glass.

The hairs on the back of my neck stand on end. I talk, if only to give us time to figure a way out of this. "At least tell me why you did it?" I go straight for the heart.

"I deserved a better life than a greasy mechanic could ever give me. I was *owed* it." She sips from her glass, looking self-satisfied. "If you want something bad enough, you'll do anything to get it."

"So, money," I say plainly, then grit my teeth before adding, "And no. Decent people do not even consider something as atrocious as what you did. And that greasy mechanic is the best thing you ever had. The best thing you'll *never* have. You were just too *fucking* stupid and self-absorbed to see it."

She smiles eerily, then asks, "How do you know Soren girl?"

This makes me fidget. Taking in a long breath, I say through the exhale, "I was helping him hide, helping him find a way to clear his name." I laid the truth on her. Because why hide it at this point. A moment of shock crosses her face but fades just as fast. My brows draw together in thought. "Was it really your blood all over him that night? And whose bones were found?" I ask, hoping she will keep talking because I have no fucking clue how we will walk out of this place…*alive.*

She glares at me and then laughs. "Yes, it was my blood. I'd been slowly taking my own for weeks and keeping it stored somewhere safe. And the bones…she lifts her right hand, wriggling her fingers at us. "I did leave this one…though the others…came from elsewhere."

Bile rises in my throat as I finally notice the tip of her ring finger…that's *missing.* "You're insane," I whisper.

Her time working at the hospital. It must be how she stored the blood and maybe numbed her finger in order to…I forcefully stop that train of thought before I vomit.

"Why couldn't you leave him?" I ask with clear sorrow dragging down my voice. "Why go through all that trouble?"

She chugs the rest of her glass and sits it down gently on the table before standing and walking within a few feet of us. She rakes her eyes over me scathingly. "Soren was never going to let me leave with the money, and his goody-two-shoes nature and pride made it all even harder to get around. Not to mention the prenup I was forced to sign. I was *sick* of living modestly. I needed to *erase* that life and start anew. I wasn't a killer…*back then*, but man I wish I would've just poisoned him."

She says it so casually that goosebumps pimple my skin. And I don't miss the way she emphasized that she wasn't a killer…*back then.*

More of the pieces fall into place. I decide to lay it all out there and see what she says, because I know deep down, she's not going to let us leave here today. "Let me get this straight." I clear my throat. "You or Micah took Soren's dad's collectibles from the safe-deposit box beforehand. You must've paid off whoever helped you. You had a lover…" I look into her eyes, feeling the rightness in my words, "someone you could pay to wipe away the camera footage. Someone you could manipulate."

My brows wrinkle as I play through the possibilities.

"The detective, Joe Sparks…maybe he wiped the camera footage," I appraise her, but she gives nothing away. "You were able to fake your death with the blood and even had people at the bar see you arguing with Soren to make it more believable that he killed you. You made accusations about him being violent along with ones against your ex…Jace Farrow." Her face is still unreadable as I continue. "The police had your blood covering Soren…your finger." I grimace. "They had bones that were too charred for DNA. They had enough hear-say and conjured up a motive to make Soren responsible."

I stop when she claps her hands once. "And here I thought you were just a pretty face. There's actually a brain in there too. Although your version isn't completely accurate…it's close enough."

My face contorts. "You put Soren through absolute *hell*," I say through clenched teeth. "You had my uncle *murdered*." She is taken aback by that knowledge, but I don't relent. You took away years that Soren will *never* get back and years that my family has to live on with my uncle in the *fucking* ground. You *won't* get away with this."

"Oh, but I will and *have*. My problem sorted itself out the moment you walked onto my property." Mel's jaw flexes in anger, and I openly glare at her. Why is she so fucking quiet? She hasn't spoken this whole time. Then, I snap my attention back to Vicky when my phone chimes, and she reads whatever is on the screen with a devilish grin. "And *bonus*!" She beams with a brilliant, devilish smile. "My other problem worked itself out too. Ian…whoever that is, says that they're likely declaring Soren deceased soon." Her eyes flit above our heads to pass a longing look at Talbert.

I sway on my feet. The room suddenly seems so small, closing in on me, making it hard to breathe. Mel steadies me. "Everything will be fine, Nova." She finally deigns to speak to me. Everything is not fine! It's anything but fine. Soren…he's…no, he can't be.

Victoria says slowly, with the feral smile of a madwoman, "No, everything will, most certainly not be *fine* for you two."

CHAPTER 43

Melina

My body is angled just enough that no one notices my hand slipping into the pocket of my skirt. On my Apple phone, when the passcode entry screen comes up, so does the emergency tab. I'm not certain, not even twenty percent certain, but I'm praying I've activated it and that a dispatcher is on the other end. Although there is the chance that I didn't hit the emergency at all and simply locked myself out of the damn phone.

But if it is on…we'll have help here soon enough. I've had it on for almost the entire conversation…in theory, anyway. Inwardly, I groan. We need a Plan B in case I didn't in fact reach the police.

Victoria says something, bringing me back to the conversation. "No, everything will most certainly not be *fine* for you two." I see everything playing out in slow motion. It all happens so fast.

Too fast.

Vicky's eyes meet Talbert's, and she nods once. "Handle this." Victoria turns on her heel as if we're simply trash she's asking him to take out. She *almost* makes it to the door.

I spare a look at Nova as she does the same to me. Her brows are drawn together in a deep scowl. A silent but clear communication falls between us, and I see in her eyes the same void as the day she protected me in school.

We fight. We have no choice.

I tip forward and slam my elbow backward as hard as I can, making contact with Talbert's ribs and giving my friend the time she needs to run. My arm jolts with the shock, and pain zings through it, but I don't have time to even flinch.

Nova's eyes are wild. It's the look she gets when her cutesy nature is stripped away and replaced with pure protective Mama Bear rage. The look of someone who loses herself completely and becomes more animal than woman. Although she's several inches shorter than Vicky and smaller in all ways, she lunges forward, arms pumping as she runs, catching Victoria by surprise as she slams her slight body into hers, toppling them both to the ground near the doorway. I manage to duck and shift back just as Talbert tries to grab hold of me. From the corner of my eye, I see Nova on top of Vicky, punching her over and over. Vicky rolls, pinning Nova down momentarily before Nova manages to elbow her in the cheek. They fall apart, and then Nova is on her again as they tumble through the doorway and out of sight.

I scramble away from Talbert, darting around the edge of the table. His gun is now out and aiming wildly at me. A shot rings out, bursting the window right beside me. Glass flies in tiny stabbing shards against my skin. My eyes widen when I realize he actually shot at me…the bastard shot at me!

He comes forward, long strides, as I run toward the opposite door—the one Nova and Vicky went through.

Glass shatters from somewhere inside the house, making me flinch, making me misstep at just the wrong time. The next shot sounds from behind me. White-hot pain stabs through my side.

My feet falter.

I stumble, crashing to the ground on my knees. They sing with pain, but it's meek compared to my side. Head bent, heaving in a breath, I press my hand to the right side of my abdomen, feeling the warmth of my lifeblood seep through my fingers. Commotion is happening all around, but it's muffled by my ringing ears. I shake my head to clear it, realizing it was likely the gunshot that has my ears ringing.

Something's happening outside, but I can't make it out. I hear a feral yell and the splash of water through that broken window.

Talbert's shiny black shoes come into view where I still sit on my knees, head lowered. Blood coats the floor at my knees as I wait for the final shot. The fatal shot. I can't even force my body to move, the pain is so bad.

"I love you, supernova," I say aloud. "Shine bright. Give 'em hell."

The gunshot merges with the tremors already racking my body. I suck in my last breath as a tear stitches its way down my cheek.

CHAPTER 44

Novalie

Victoria bolts to miss me as I give chase. My steps falter for a second when I hear a gunshot. I can't turn back, though. I have to stop her. I press on, passing by tall glass doors that lead out toward the pool. Vicky lifts a vase from its black marble perch, turns and slings it at me. I duck just in time for it to miss my head. It smashes straight through those glass doors. I bend at the waist, covering my head as the shards fly in all directions.

Then…I hear it again…a gunshot.

My momentum and rage are momentarily stunned into submission as my only concern becomes Melina. Heart squeezing in my chest, I turn my head, about to run back the way I came when Victoria *slams* into me.

We fall through the now-shattered doors, rolling into the glass, bits embedding into my skin. Our bodies are jostled apart long enough for me to stand up. My eyes flit in Mel's direction and back to Victoria.

Blood dots her robe in speckles from our tussle. It hangs barely on her shoulders; blood leaks from her nose that I'm sure I've broken. Somehow, she still manages to stand tall and exude confidence. With a haughty raise of her chin, she fixes her bikini top that was skewed and almost baring her breast. She cracks her neck to the side and then spits blood between us. "You surprise me." Her eyes drag down my tangled hair, bloodied lip, to my torn dress and bare feet. "You're scrappier than I anticipated."

My lip tugs into a vicious smile, and I don't even flinch as it splits further, blood trickles from the wound down to my chin. "You have no idea the lengths I will go to for the ones I love."

She laughs chillingly. "And you've found love with Soren. Tragic. You fell in love with a convict. Seems desperate. Too bad he's six feet under. Maybe you can write letters to another lost soul rotting away in prison, find you another inmate to fuck like the trash you are."

My smile never dissipates. "You have zero attributes to love, nothing inside you worth wanting, worth dying for. And all the money and material things handed to you will never sate your greed. And when your beauty fades and," my eyes flick down to her bikini bottom, "your *way* of manipulating men is no longer appealing, you'll only have yourself to stare at in the mirror. Old, withered away, with no one to love you…not even yourself."

She bares her teeth at me, fist clenching. I launch myself at her, vaguely aware of another gunshot somewhere. She doesn't have time to move before my body hits hers. My arms snake around her, and I plunge us into the pool.

Air bubbles up from my nose and her open mouth as I push and fight and pull her toward the bottom of the deep end. In my head, there's no warning bells that scream stop. It's like red has taken over my vision and everything around me blacks out in a crimson haze. Her hands claw at me as I grip her neck and hold her below the surface. Blood from our combined wounds makes the blue water murky—a coppery hue. Her eyes widen when she begins to understand that I'm *not* going to stop. For Soren and for my uncle. This is for them and for us…because she had no intentions of letting us live today. We were dead the moment we stepped foot onto this gaudy land.

My chest hitches, jerking with the need to inhale as we roll and fight for purchase. A sharp pain sears my side but mixes with all the other injuries. A dark form dives into the water beside us, shocking me enough that I lose focus. Victoria kicks away from me. I snatch her legs, nails biting into flesh, but she breaks the contact. Unable to hold my breath a second longer, dots blur my vision as I inhale, no longer able to hold my breath.

Everything grows dim, fades with the sharp sting of water that fills my lungs. I choke, losing my grasp on reality. My fingers flex but grow limp, arms becoming weightless. The brain is a magnificent machine, capable of protecting you from horrors and pain. Somehow, my mind has shut down to what's really happening, and all I can picture is Soren's handsome face. All I can imagine is him soaring over the waterfall.

If we drown together, can we swim in the heavens side by side? My closed eyelids twitch, lip curving one last time into a wistful smile as I drift away on a phantom current with Soren.

CHAPTER 45

Melina

The sound of the gunshot echoes, and the echo gives me pause. I expected silence—lights out, not an echo. I blink my eyes, noises inside the house and outside collide and I'm not sure what's going on. Talbert's shiny black shoes are now speckled with blood as they stumble backward.

Suddenly, his body slams onto the floor inches from me. His mouth is hung open at an odd angle as he groans, stretching the scar that moves from his nose to lip. His guttural cry comes next as he clutches his knee that looks to be...*blown off.*

My eyes widen at the gaping wound. *What the hell?* How am I alive?

I take one shallow breath after another. Forcing the air to keep coming. Why do I feel like I'm *drowning?* My eyes burn as tears brim my lashes. The pain in my side is duller now, and I know that's not a good sign.

"Are you okay?" A man bends in front of me, grasping my shoulders, but I don't even flinch. I simply shake my head lazily. He has haphazard sandy blond hair and a square jaw with blond stubble. His brown eyes dart over my features, with thick lashes framing them. He tracks my injuries down to where my hand rests at my side. Gently, he strokes away a curl from my face with a calloused thumb and dips his head to level his eyes with mine.

He has really *beautiful* eyes.

"You're really hot," I mumble, not sure why I said that. Must be the blood loss.

His brows raise. "You have a sense of humor…which is a *good* sign, but your wound is bad. I need to get you some help, okay?" He proceeds to rip the hem of his white T-shirt and rolls it into a thick ball before lifting my hand so that he can place the cloth there. "Hold pressure here. I'm going to pick you up now."

My eyes fall closed, but then he skims his knuckles along my cheek, making them come alive again. I hear a second voice but can't register it because pain rips into me all over again as the man's arms lift me from the ground.

"I have to get her out of here. Go find Nova," the stranger says.

"Nova," I say, voice cold and weak suddenly. "She's outside."

The stranger turns us, heading for a door, and I see the face that belongs to the other voice. My brows manage a furrow in my weakened state. "How?" I whisper.

"It's a long story, Mel. We've got you now. You're going to be okay," he says.

A choked sob breaks free in my chest.

I don't understand.

The stranger holding me moves us toward the doorway, talking softly into my ear. "You're going to be fine. My name's Micah. I won't let anything else happen to you."

Soren…

Micah?

CHAPTER 46

Soren

Eight days ago…

They say your life flashes before your eyes when you face death head-on. That's bullshit. You don't replay your entire life—all the memories, good and bad…*no.* Only the most pressing people in your life stay with you, not even the moments with them, just an overwhelming feeling of loss before it happens. You know you're going to die, and they'll grieve for you. And if you're truly in love, guilt for leaving them is the real kicker.

That's all that I feel as I fall…guilt. No fear. I'm not scared as my stomach drops and the world below me is a black raging river waiting to wash my bones away. I wish I'd never stepped foot in Novalie's life. That's how much I love her. Enough to wish I'd never met her so that she could live on in peace…so she wouldn't grieve my loss.

At the last second, I suck in a breath, bend my knees slightly for impact, and curl my fingers around the backpack's straps. My arm grazes a boulder as my body crashes into the frigid rapids. I sink, clothes snagging on rocks as the current quickly proceeds to drag me under.

Cold slices into my bones like razors.

I reach for purchase, fingers slipping—catching on the jagged edges of stone.

My boots knock into the sandy riverbed below, and I kick hard, changing my body's trajectory skyward. My chest burns right before warm night air shoots into my lungs the moment my head breaks the surface. I gasp, choking, spitting out sprays of water.

Looking around as I float with the quickening current, it's hard to make out anything. The fog is still thick, and night has fallen. The rapids shift me violently as I try but fail to find purchase.

My back slams into something, knocking the breath clean out of me, the force of it causing me to roll sideways. I catch a glimpse of the fallen tree right before the water sends me past its outstretched branches. I give one last fight against the push of the water, reaching. My fingers curl around a branch, and I pull—breath heaving, body shaking with the effort. But eventually I drag myself onto the tree and crawl one limb at a time to the bank's edge.

When I feel dirt and weeds against my palms and knees, I exhale roughly. Dropping the pack, I fall against the earth, coughing up the remainder of moisture from my lungs, and go limp, shuddering with exhaustion. An unusual warmth spreads along my outer thigh, but I pay it no mind.

I'm not sure how long I lay in that position. The forest's chorus of sounds lulled me into oblivion.

My eyes feel leaden as I come in and out of reality. It's not until I hear the sound of twigs snapping that I'm slapped with the reminder that I'm being chased. I hear the footsteps coming closer and closer. I stay as still as death itself, but now that I'm out of that river…death *can't* have me.

A renewed sense of urgency rocks my soul.

Very carefully, I raise myself to a crouch. My leg barks in pain as I reach into my pocket, finding the knife I took from Nova's. I flick it open and shakily slip behind the nearest outcropping of rocks. The steps falter, shifting near the log that just saved my life. At first, I can only make out a shadow of a man, but then the fog begins to lift and I see him.

I see Micah, his rifle still slung across his back.

A burning, seething rage rips at my insides.

Creeping from the shadows, I stalk forward like an animal. Micah tenses. He's always been one with the wilderness and a better hunter than me. He senses me before he sees me, but by then it's too late. I smash into him, sending us both crashing to the ground. One of my hands is already positioned, blade to his throat, before we even stop rolling. My knees burrow into his back, holding him in place, and my other hand has his right arm pinned painfully behind him.

Micah's voice growls out, half pissed and half panicked. "*Soren*, stop, *please*! What the hell are you doing? *That wasn't me shooting at you!*"

I lean closer, teeth bared. "Who *the fuck* else would it be?" The blade sinks in just a touch, causing him to thrash under me. He wrenches and wiggles in my grip.

"*Wait!* Wait, Soren, it wasn't *me*. I had *no* idea I was being followed. You know me!" he pleads.

I lean in close, water from my hair dripping over him. "And why should I believe that, when you were the *only* one I saw out here with a *fucking* rifle? The only one who knew where to meet me…and the only one who talked to Victoria the night she died." I let that last part marinate in his brain. He's unnaturally still as he thinks through what I just said.

A breath rushes out of him, stirring up dust from the ground. "This looks worse than it is. I came by that night to have beers as usual. That was my hangout. *You know that.* Vicky saw me come in and stopped me. She said tonight wasn't a good night to talk with you cause y'all were having a fight. I left. I swear. I didn't even think much of it after she passed because you two always had issues." He yanks again, but I hold firm and dig the knife in deeper.

"How do I know I can trust you? Huh? I can't trust *anyone*!" My words are spat out through clenched teeth.

"Take my rifle and ammo. Fucking shoot me if I act up. I don't know. Just get the fuck off me. I'm not your enemy here."

Indecision rears its ugly head. Memories flash through me. Memories of our childhood. Memories of the man I once knew. Shaking my head, knowing this could be a mistake, I check his sides and boots for any other weapons, but find none. I take my knees off his back and release my hold on him, pulling the blade away. Before he can get to his feet with a groan, I snatch the rifle and ammo pack, making him fall sideways when it pulls off his shoulder.

"You're a real fucking *dick,* Marshall." Micah spits on the ground as he shuffles away and stands fully.

"I have reason to be Talon!" My voice matches his own. We only call each other by our last names when we're pissed, and we are both fuses ready to ignite and blow the forest sky high right about now. I check to see if the rifle is loaded and then aim it right at him.

Micah raises his hands, looking down the barrel. He eyes me closely, gaze falling on the oozing wounds littering my body, and then shocks me to my core with his next words.

"I have him."

Eyes narrowed, brows drawn tight together, I take a step forward with the rifle. "Who? What are you talking about?"

His hands drop with defeat, but there's a hint of pride that follows his response. "I knocked out the guy that shot at you." His eyes find my oozing leg again. "The one that *shot* you. He's tied up…near the top of Widowmaker's Peak."

A huffed breath leaves me in disbelief. The gun doesn't waver as I give a cynical laugh. "You expect me to buy this bullshit?"

I watch as Micah shrugs with frustration and then reaches for his pocket, and in an instant I move a step closer, rifle aimed for the head.

The moonlight shows the anger pinching his face and the hard contours of his jaw. "I was getting a cigarette…you *dick.*"

I cock my head and nod, allowing him to make a move one way or the other. My finger itches on the trigger. He slips a pack of Marlboro Lights from his pocket and flicks a Zippo.

After a few seconds, I lower the gun a few tics and nod to the pack. "When did you start back?"

"About the time my best friend was sent away to prison and refused my visitations," Micah says, exhaling a cloud of smoke.

"I had my reasons," I mumble.

"I'm sure you did." He rolls his eyes. "Can you put the fucking gun away?"

I watch him carefully, not lowering the weapon completely. "What's in the bag you left me?" I ask, gauging his response.

"Money…just like I said I'd bring you. From my account," he retorts.

In this moment, he looks like my best friend; he talks like my best friend. A part of me that knows him inside and out screams to listen, but another part shouts to be wary.

"Okay Micah. Another question. What happened to the contents of my safe-deposit box?"

He waves a hand in anger, smoke streaking about him. "I don't fucking know! After you were taken away, I handled the business *alone* until I couldn't anymore. I didn't touch your assets, and your half of the business money is right where I said it'd be in my safe…all but the amount I sent to your prison account."

His face is demanding, honest as it used to be. But am I a fool if I trust him now?

"Look," Micah says, kicking a rock with his boot. "I saw the guy. A blur moving through the woods right before I heard the shot. He must not have seen me and got focused on you, cause he got sloppy. He never saw me coming. I followed him to the falls. When he was close, looking over the edge, I knocked him out cold with the butt of my rifle and tied him to a tree." He takes a drag off his cigarette and watches me lower the gun completely. "I came looking for you right after."

"Lead me to him...*now.*" I leave no room for argument.

He flicks the cigarette onto the ground and puts it out with the toe of his boot. "Follow me." He turns and begins the walk back up the mountain. Every fucking step is agony. My leg seems to have a heartbeat of its own. But I keep going, making sure that Micah stays a few feet ahead of me...just in case.

The track up the mountain was silent other than the crush of leaves and twigs and the rush of water. It takes considerable effort to feign strength when my body is trying to crash. We eventually reach the landing, and the ground flattens. My breath is more labored than I'd like.

Micah's voice has me shifting my stance and bringing the gun back toward him as he says, "Here, he's right here." I watch him point toward a small oak tree.

I almost drop the fucking gun.

Part of me didn't believe a word he was saying...but there he is. The man who shot me—he's tied to the tree, dressed in all black, some sort of cloth shoved in his mouth.

He has a face I remember clearly.

How could I forget the man who put me away? Joe Sparks watches me, eyes as big as saucers. He immediately starts to flail, to pull and wrench at his bindings to no avail. He mumbles through his gag.

My shoulders sag. It's relief that streams through me—pure relief that my friend wasn't lying. I didn't realize how badly I needed that confirmation until this second. How badly I needed my best friend on my side. After losing so much...I still have him.

The gun drops, and I slip the strap over my shoulder. "This is Joe Sparks," I tell Micah without taking my eyes off the detective.

Micah's eyes shift uncomfortably, and then he's pacing. "Oh, fuck…Soren. *Fuck*! I knocked out a fucking detective?" It's a question and yet not. His anxious footing stops, and he pins me with a look of sympathy…some of the pieces clicking into place. "He…he was the one on your case."

I nod as I watch the bound man squirm. Before I can even decide where to go from here, anger washes over me. I rear back and punch Joe with everything I have. Bone cracks in his nose, and blood sprays left and right. He groans, eyes pinched together as he fights for release. I hit him again.

And again.

And again.

Until hands grip my shoulders, dragging me back. Panting, seething, I shake off Micah's hands, but he grips me again. I almost turn my rage on him, but his words are a plea. "*Stop*! You need him. He's the key to ending this."

I watch, chest rising and falling fast as Micah crouches before a wheezing Joe as he struggles to breathe through the blood gushing from his nose. Micah sifts through his pockets, pulling out random items until his hand stills and a smile pulls at his cheek. "Here we go." He pulls out a cellphone slowly, looking my way and waving it. "Let's see who he's been talking to, shall we?"

Joe's pleas grow wilder behind the cloth, and that tells me all I need to know. "Let's," I say.

Micah tosses me the phone. I hold it in front of Joe's face, unlocking it. The light of the phone illuminates our surroundings, and I can see more clearly the blood seeping from Joe's head. Micah must've gotten him pretty good. Smiling, I scroll through his last calls and messages.

My brows furrow deeply. The last call looks to have been a few hours ago…maybe even right before he had time to get up this mountain. It doesn't have a name associated with the number. I hold it in his face, yank down the gag, demanding, "Who does this number belong to?"

Joe gasps for breath, coughing, body shaking. His eyes are determined, cold as he grinds his teeth, a clear sign that he has no intention of telling us. Before I can react, Micah punches Joe from the side. His head whips left, more blood dribbling down his chin.

He spits and sputters, eyes wild as he looks between us. "I can't."

"Can't what? Tell us?" I inquire.

He shakes his head. I stand and kick out, landing a blow to his ribs. His cries pierce the night's calm around us. He chokes, trying to get just one breath into his lungs, but when he looks up at me…his eyes don't falter.

"He's not going to tell us anything," I say calmly.

"Guess we have to kill him." Micah shrugs beside me.

Joe's eyes bug out of his head as he flits his gaze back and forth between us. "You don't understand…I can't…I just can…"

Before he can finish, I shove the cloth back into his mouth forcefully, making him gag. Wiping his blood off my hand, I limp over to a log and grunt as I sit. Tearing my shirt at the bottom, I begin wrapping my gunshot wound.

Micah watches me. "You going to be okay?"

I growl as I cinch the cloth tight, unleashing an ungodly amount of pain throbbing through my thigh. "I'll be fine,"

I pant. Once it's tight, I stare at Joe as I smile and call the number.

Swiping away sweat and damp hair from my eyes, we listen to it ring.

Once.

Twice.

Micah moves closer to me, and Joe shakes his head violently, the bark of the tree scraping his scalp.

Three times.

Four.

A voice sounds from the other end. "Is it done?"

A wave of shock falls over me like a cloak, blotting out everything around us. The woods become fuzzy. The phone loosens and almost falls from my grip, but my fingers clench automatically. I'm hardly aware of Joe sputtering nonsense behind the gag. Hardly aware of Micah's wide eyes, his hands dragging through his hair.

"What the fuck, Joe! *Answer me*! Is. It. Done?" the feminine voice trills again.

My mouth opens to speak. Nausea roils inside me, but I swallow it down. Just as I'm about to say something…anything…Micah snatches the phone from my grip and smashes the phone against a tree.

"*What the fuck are you doing*!" I scream at him, stumbling back to my feet.

Micah shakes his head as I try to come for him. "You can't let her know you're alive, Ren…think, man…*think*."

But I can't think. My head swims, and the nausea wins after all. I stumble to the ground and vomit. Heaves rack me with what little remains in my stomach…mostly water from the river. "It was her. This…this can't be," I mumble once the retching subsides.

Micah lays a hand on my back but doesn't say anything.

Rocking back to my knees, I loll my head, looking up to him through watery lashes. "Vicky's alive," I choke out.

CHAPTER 47

Soren

Four days ago…

A strange calm has overtaken my body and mind—a finality building inside that is long overdue.

When the shock wore off and the daunting prospect of what I was facing settled that night on the mountain, a cacophony of memories flooded me—memories and new perspectives. We eventually got Joe to talk…after more *persuasive* techniques.

We left him alive that night…to be found later by the flood of cops that cascaded over the mountain after an 'anonymous' call came in. Micah had no choice but to leave his truck. I'm sure it was found too. He'd stashed a four-wheeler nearby that I knew nothing about. He'd hidden it for me to use in case I needed it…turns out it was our only escape. Happy accidents…as Nova would say.

If they found his truck, then he's now either deemed missing or an accomplice. Either way, he's in this now.

We have no clue what Joe may or may not have told the police. We can only hope that he wants his secrets hidden enough to keep his mouth shut. I wasn't about to have blood on my hands after everything. I needed him alive at the end of this.

We hid out for days near a burned-up cabin that we found in the woods. It had enough shelter and even a well, that we made do. With nowhere to turn, all seemed lost. We had no way of knowing where that number came from—where Victoria was now—but we knew she was *alive.*

Her words stuck in my brain like sap from a tree. "*Is it done?*"

It's a hard pill to swallow, knowing the person who ruined your life is someone you once shared vows with. All her petty scheming, grandiose sense of wealth, her narcissistic behavior…none of it was enough to make me truly believe she could do something so heinous.

I should've seen the warning signs. For someone who reads people so well, I was blind to her determination. The way she walked around as if everyone around her were worker ants and she was the queen. The way nothing was ever good enough. She always wanted more and *more.* It was like she felt she deserved to be worshipped. All the hours I put into work, into our home, into our relationship, just for her to turn up her nose at my grease-stained hands when I'd come home after a long day at the shop.

Just thinking about it now makes me want to puke all over again.

A few days in the woods and I couldn't take it anymore. The unknown was *killing* me. What were the news reports saying? What was Novalie going through? Her face became a beacon—a light in the dark for me to find, just like my prison days. Hope formed out of the nothingness. Something urged me to go to her, to hold her, to make sure she was okay, because through it all, that's all that mattered to me. Yes, I wanted the truth. I wanted justice, but the worry for her was even stronger than that.

It took some convincing. A whole hell-of-a-lot of convincing to get Micah to agree, but he eventually caved, and we made the long trek through the mountains until we were closing in on the city. Between stolen disguises of ragged clothes and hats, we blended in with the homeless and downtrodden. It was touch and go for sure. Every siren would have our backs rigged with fear and adrenaline.

Fate or luck has brought us this far. I stare through the cracked, filthy window of the rundown building facing Nova's shop. The streets are eerily quiet this evening as the sun sinks in the sky and the moon begins its glow. Very few bystanders meander past.

Her shop is closed. All the lights are off.

"What now?" Micah asks, coming up from behind me to look up at the balcony I'm staring at.

Shaking my head, I lean with one hand on the wall. My leg stings with every move, but it's much better than it was a few days ago. I was lucky that the bullet went clean in and out the side of my thigh. It's red, and there's always the possibility of infection, but I can't focus on that right now.

"I need to see her," I say.

"That's probably not a good idea right now. It's best if everyone thinks you're dead or long gone. What if she's talked about you to someone? What if the cops already know about your squatting there?"

I cut angry eyes at him. "She would never."

He throws up his hands. "Okay. I trust you, but we need to be careful. Once you see her and make sure she's fine…we have to leave here."

I stare him down, shoulders sagging eventually. He's right. We can't stay here and put her in any more danger. She's already lost her uncle because of me. We have no way of finding Victoria, and until we do…she's safer without me.

Movement has me snapping my attention to her balcony, bracing arms on either side of the window. My fucking heart squeezes painfully when I watch her fall into a chair. She brings her knees to her chest, wrapping arms around them and stares at the moon. I have to choke down the lump in my throat.

"That her?" Micah asks.

I nod. A ragged exhale shudders through my lips when I watch her shoulders shake. She's crying. I push off the wall and head for the exit.

A hand stops me, gripping my shoulder. "Soren, you can't go to her…not yet. We need to finish this, remember. Keep her out of it…keep her safe."

My shoulders rise with the rapid pace my torn heart is creating. I shrug him off but don't take another step toward the door. Reluctantly, my feet move back to the window. Swallowing hard, I watch her for the next half-hour until I'm sure there's no more tears. My heart fractures into a million pieces.

"You love her," Micah says quietly. I feel his eyes on me without seeing them.

My voice is gritty when I answer. "I do."

He blows out a hushed breath, but says nothing more, only pats my shoulder and gives it one squeeze.

I don't stop watching until Melina retrieves her. Until all the lights go out. Just as I'm about to turn and get rest myself, a shadow moves inside the shop, only illuminated briefly by the moon glaring on the glass window with all the hanging vines.

My head tilts. Micah pushes up beside me, watching too as a slight form in baggy pajamas comes out of the front entrance door. I can tell it's Nova right away, hair in a big messy bun. She looks left and right before slipping something into the mouth of the cement frog planter with the huge fern hanging haphazardly over the sides.

"Did she just put something in that frog?" Micah asks, confused.

I snort, taking him off guard. A smile tugs at the corner of my mouth. "Yes…yes, she did."

CHAPTER 48

Soren

One hour ago…

A stolen car, an escaped convict, a missing person…what could go wrong? The eighty-five Firebird soars down the highway as we make our way into San Diego. I have to admit, I always wanted to visit Cali—to see the Pacific Ocean, to ride the coast up and find the Redwood trees.

But that's not in the cards for us.

No, we're headed straight for hell or for me…prison, which is one and the same.

I can't help the shit-eating grin that's plastered on my face.

We know *exactly* where Victoria is.

Thanks to my girl's soft heart, we can find her and try to end this.

Nova had been slipping letters to me in the spot where she told me once to look if we ever got separated or needed to communicate. That damn frog.

Micah ignores me as I re-read each letter she's placed there since the day I left to meet him on the mountain. She wrote one a day, every day…telling me about everything that's happened. About the funeral, about finding that photo of Joe, about the information Bo had given her and about a strange woman obsessed with the case in California. She even went as far as to leave the woman's address.

The last letter is wrinkled and creased from the amount of times I've read through it. I open it again, flattening out the page. It's short but holds the entirety of my heart. It's the one from the night Micah and I saw her place it in her hidey spot.

Soren,

Yesterday is heavy on my mind. I still can't believe Uncle Jim is gone. I can't believe you're gone. Greif is a fickle thing, sharp and jagged. Part of my soul still feels you. Shouldn't I feel it...your death? Maybe I'm just not accepting it, or maybe we're connected enough that I would feel the break. Wouldn't I feel it if the connection was shattered?

The news reports are vague, and I feel a deep sense of foreboding. They're hiding something. The police are keeping tight-lipped. No news is supposed to be good news, right? I'll hold on. I won't let go of you. You're out there somewhere.

I read your entry in my journal, by the way.

You're right. I know now that I would do it all over again because it led me to you. You made me see my true reflection, and I'm no longer scared to be her. And yes, I still look at that moon, but now it's not because I'm lost. It's because I'm picturing you looking at the same moon somewhere.

You said I'm yours once. Come back to me, Soren.

With my entire fucking heart, I love you, Soren Lee Marshall.

Folding the note, I place it in my jean pocket and roll down the old window to let the warm air rush over me.

"*Come back to me, Soren.*"

Her words replay over and over.

Not long after finding that note from her, a plan formed. I knew Micah's house would be watched carefully, so we opted to check out his parents' house instead. Thankfully, finding it empty. We used their old hide-a-key to get in after watching the two of them leave together. We took turns showering and watching for headlights. Then ate and packed bags of clothes and supplies. We took two pistols from his dad's safe and then stole the old Firebird his parents rarely drove anymore, snagged a tag from his dad's beat-around truck to put on it, and hauled ass. Micah left a note for them, begging them to trust him and not to tell a soul that he'd been there. He promised to explain everything in a few days.

We played the news while we were at his parents' house and…it's gotten worse than we suspected. Micah is now a missing person; people are out searching for him…including his parents.

As if he can read my mind, Micah takes a hit off his cigarette and says softly, "Mom and Dad looked awful on the news."

I hum in agreement. "It'll all be over soon. They'll forgive you for getting involved."

"Maybe…maybe not." He flicks the cigarette out the window and runs a hand through his unruly sandy hair. "Let's just hope they found my note and keep quiet."

Trying to make light of the situation, I say, "Look at it this way, your mom always wanted you to travel, and this car really needed to be driven."

He raises a brow, one hand on the steering wheel and the other changing radio stations until a Def Leppard song comes on. "I don't think this is what Mom had in mind."

We've paid hardly any attention to the sights around us as we traveled. The closer we got each day, apprehension and unease filled the car like poison—infecting our minds. But we are here finally. After days of driving…we are here. Twisting, winding roads lead us through a picturesque city perched off the ocean, then past cliffs that fall away into the Pacific.

With mere minutes to spare before laying eyes on what is possibly my ex-wife's new life, doubt starts to creep along my insides. What if it's not her? We can't be sure. What if this is yet another bump in the road that is my fucked-up life? What's waiting for us around the bend?

I clench my hands so hard a knuckle pops. Micah's shoulders tense as we near the property.

The astonishing beauty of this place would bring most people to their knees with mouths hanging open in envy…but not us. Only one thing has my undivided attention.

Not in a million fucking years would I have imagined seeing what I am seeing.

Micah slows down, but not enough to make us obvious. "What the fuck? *Who's that*?" he says under his breath.

My heart wrenches inside my chest and feels like it's going to rip in two at the figures moving toward the house. I can't make sense of it. It's not possible.

"Stop the car, Micah," I whisper, voice low and commanding. When he doesn't listen, I yell, "*Stop the fucking car, Micah*!"

"Okay! Shit, hold on." He passes the house far enough to hide us and jerks the car off to the side of the road, dirt flying around the windows as I slam a hand against the dash bracing myself. "What…who was that?" he asks again.

I'm reaching for the handle and out of the car in seconds. I lean into the open window. "That's Nova and Melina!"

I don't have to say more before Micah is on my heels, coming after me. "Why are they here? What the hell is going on?"

My head shakes even as a forced laugh without any humor attached leaves my chest. I glance back, seeing Micah shoulder his hunting rifle and place a pistol in the back of his jeans.

"Did I ever tell you how persistent Novalie can be? I'm going to fucking throttle her," I grumble.

Micah is beside me now as we approach the property's edge. We watch, hidden behind foliage, as the girls are ushered to the front door of the house by a man dressed in a black suit.

"You *did* ask her to help you solve the case," Micah says dryly, peering up through a bush. "Looks like she's finishing what y'all started."

A growl rumbles in my chest as I see the door to the house close. I give Micah a withering look. He's right, and I should've known exactly what Nova would do. With me gone and Sawyer gone…she went after the only lead she had. But does she even fucking realize the danger she's in?

I'm off the ground, feet moving before I can think through the consequences. Micah doesn't try to stop me this time. I hear his footsteps fall in sync with mine. We move to the side of the house, creeping in and out of shadowed areas.

For several minutes, we listen and wait.

That is…until the *first* gunshot.

Panic seizes us both and then fades to adrenaline. We rush the house, exploding through the door. Hearing an obvious gunshot has my cares about being seen the farthest thing from my mind. Fear and urgency have taken over.

I *have* to get to Nova. Nothing else matters.

Another shot rattles through the house not long after, giving away the direction it came from. We run, feet pounding the marbled floors, and without stopping, I slam my shoulder into the door where the noise of a fight is ensuing.

Micah almost crashes into me as I come to an abrupt stop.

Melina is on the floor, on her knees, and there's *so* much blood. Her head hangs low, curls dangling around her.

Something in me cracks wide open.

CHAPTER 49

Soren

Present Time

I don't have time to process. My pistol is out and aimed toward the head of the man in a black suit, but a shot pierces my ears before I pull the trigger. My eyes cut left to see Micah, pistol out, and still aimed. The man who was standing before Melina is down on the floor, clutching his knee.

Micah moves forward toward her, but whispers to me first, "*No killing*...you need to come out of this clean, remember." I watch as he bends and surveys her carefully, talking softly. I can't hear the exchange between them. He lifts her, clutching her to his chest and I watch her face twist in pain.

"I have to get her out of here. Go find Nova," Micah says, nodding toward the other door.

"Nova…she's…outside." Melina's voice is so damaged that I want to shoot the fucker in the head that's still writhing on the ground.

Melina finally lifts her head weakly, catching sight of me. "How?" she croaks out.

"It's a long story, Mel. We've got you now. You're going to be okay," I tell her.

I nod to Micah. Walking over the man on the floor, I flip my gun in my hand and smash his head with the butt of it. He's out cold before his face smacks the floor. Taking his gun, I slip it into my jeans and check for more weapons, finding none.

I gasp an inhale when I hear an all too familiar sound…*sirens.* They're distant…but that's definitely fucking sirens. "No, no, no…not yet," I whisper under my breath.

I lurch to my feet and run through the doors, my eyes tracking dots of blood toward the right. Some are smeared by a bare foot. My heart rises into my throat when I round the corner and see the glass doors shattered. My brows draw together.

Holding the pistol by my head, I move *carefully*, silently clearing the area. Peeking my head around a jagged shard of glass still clinging to the frame, I see no one. There was an obvious struggle on the ground due to the amount of blood, but she's…not here. Where the fuck is she?

I walk, one foot over the other, glass crunching under my boots, following the trail, before my eyes finally see it. The slight ripple of discolored water waves and churns near the center of a massive pool. Sweat trickles down my temple. Panic like I've never known threatens to choke the life from me. I'm moving without conscious thought, boots pounding the concrete. The pain in my thigh becomes a distant memory as I lunge toward the water.

In the last two strides…I see bodies…more than one. They're twisting like snakes, forms blurred out by the undulating water churning and bloody.

Dropping the pistol alongside the pool, I dive, body airborne as I suck in a breath.

Warm saltwater bursts over me as I shoot like a rocket toward the flailing limbs of two figures. The bloodied water makes it hard to see, but my body…my *entire being* knows Novalie the moment I'm close. The feet of the other woman kick away just as my arms find purchase. I wrap them around her tiny waist. Her body goes limp in my arms as I kick hard off the bottom and launch us up. Sunlight bounces off the ripples almost blindingly as I push us fast toward the surface.

We break through, water cascading over our heads and streaming down her face. Gulping in a strangled breath, my voice permeates the air. "*Nova*!" I yell, but she doesn't respond. Her eyes are closed, skin pale white. Her hair is plastered to her face, and her lips have taken on a sickly shade of blue.

I swim with her clutched against me, gasping in air, more from fear than exertion. When we near the shallow end, I stand and lift her into my arms and wade toward the side, trudging through the water. "*Nova…Nova…*come on, baby. Come back to me. I came back to you…now come back to *me*!"

The moment my feet hit solid ground, I lay her carefully onto her back. Water droplets drip in a steady stream from me to her…or are they my tears? I don't know. I place my cheek to her mouth and then my ear to her chest but hear nothing…I stop breathing completely as I listen, but she makes no sounds. The concrete is quickly coated with blood-streaked water.

The sirens are closing in, some sounding far too fucking close. My whole body trembles as I tip her head back, chin up, and place my mouth over hers.

I breathe into her. Once. Then twice. Watching her chest rise each time before placing my hands on her sternum. I press into her. Over and over again, I pump her heart. Guttural sounds of agony that I don't even recognize flow from my lips.

I don't stop. I can't stop. She *has* to live. This woman has given me more than I ever bargained for. She relinquished the rigid control of her life and allowed me to wreck it completely. But in turn…she wrecked me. Down to my very fucking core…she's wrecked me.

Movement catches my eye at the far end of the long pool. A woman stands there, soaked and bloodied, dark bobbed hair stuck to her head as she watches me force Novalie's heart to pump. I can't see her expression through my watery lashes, but I know it's *her*.

I know it's Victoria.

Baring my teeth, I give a guttural yell as I press down thythmically into the chest of the woman I love and seethe toward the one I *fucking* hate. All this is because of her. All the time that was stripped from me, the damage she's now caused Nova and her family…it's all too much. Undiluted rage bursts through as my voice carries to her in a haggard yell, "*If she fucking dies, so do you! You better fucking pray she lives!*"

My vision clears enough to see Vicky. Her eyes are wide and I'm not sure if it's shock or wonder, but something blankets her features as she watches my rapidly failing attempt to save Nova.

Bending, I breathe into her again and again. Giving her my life with each exhale. And I'd gladly hand it over to her. I'd gladly trade my soul for hers. She deserves nothing less.

She doesn't breathe though.

Rising up, a tear leaks down my cheek as I continue CPR. My attention has narrowed to the woman beneath me. Victoria's silhouette is still there, though. I chance a glance her way. She hasn't moved her body, but her head is moving between my actions and the oncoming wave of police that have closed in on the house—no doubt realizing her long reign of lies and deception has reached a finality.

Suddenly she's moving, walking slowly and calculated around the pool. The closer she gets, I see that her body is an array of scratches, bruises, and the robe she wears is tattered—floating in the breeze.

I watch Vicky as I beg God to save Nova. I plead quietly as I work her heart. Bending, I breathe into her lungs one more long exhale.

This time…*she coughs.*

My eyes divert from Victoria and land on Nova. Her forehead creases the slightest bit with movement, making my heart explode inside. A garbled sound rushes through her, and I shift her body on instinct to the side as water spurts and sloshes from her parted blue-gray lips. "That's it, baby. Breathe for me. *Breath. Come on.*" My fingers part her hair and pull it away from her face as she gags and releases the trapped water from her lungs.

Nova's eyes finally open and break my heart into a million shattered pieces as she wails and flails herself into my arms weakly. I hold her against me, rocking, kissing the side of her head, her face, her hair. "You fucking scared me, woman," I cry into her hair.

Another choked sob shakes her body as she clutches me so hard against her that I'm not sure where one of us begins and the other ends. She pulls back to look at me, running her delicate fingers through my hair and over my cheek. She frowns at the tears leaking from my eyes. "You're crying," she says, her voice cracking, making my chest shake with the effort it takes not to completely break down.

Placing her head between my collar and jaw, I squeeze her again, not releasing her, not giving her an inch. Her voice melts me entirely against my skin when she says softly, "I thought I drowned and we were together…in water."

"You're alive, princess. With me. We're together now," I tell her.

"I think I was always waiting for you. You're my happy accident, Ren," she whispers, her voice too low…too weak. "I'll love you long after I'm gone, but I'll wait for you."

I open my mouth to respond, a sick, pained feeling sinking into my gut, but I don't get the chance to decipher what she's saying. Victoria is slinking this way. I can feel it before I see it. The shift in the atmosphere. I raise my head just as she bends and picks something up off the ground. The blood drains from my face as the glint of metal catches the sun when she stands fully again. My discarded pistol that I'd dropped by the pool, white-knuckle-gripped in her bony hand.

Slowly, I reach for the one still tucked into my sodden jeans. The one I took from the man in the black suit.

Vicky's icy blue gaze cut me down from my face to my grip on Nova, who's shaking in my arms. "Don't reach for that gun, Soren," she growls.

I give her the same once-over she gave me, my hand suddenly pausing on the cold metal at my back. Nova's gone rigid in my arms, fingers tightening into the fabric of my wet shirt. Her hold on me releases enough to shift her head toward the voice.

Up this close, I can see that Vicky's nose is fucked—broken and slightly crooked. And through her parted lips…a chipped tooth. I smirk despite the precarious situation. "You look like shit." My eyes drop to her mouth.

One perfectly trimmed brow raises at that—a line of blood dribbles down from it. She flicks her tongue up in a hooked motion, testing the area of her jagged tooth. A small sliver of shock comes over her but is quickly erased by indifference. She looks pointedly at my neck and tattooed arms wrapped around Nova with a fierce grip. "I could say the same to you. Prison life has made you…*grungy*."

I give her a deadpan look. "It's over for you. The police are here. It's only a matter of minutes before they find us…*you're done*."

"No." She smiles a little. "I'm only getting started." She sighs dramatically and waves the gun to her surroundings, then aims it back to me. "*You* are trespassing on private property." A wicked gleam lights up her eyes as she forms the plot in her mind. "I'm Tahlia Grey. And the only people that know otherwise…"

She shrugs and lets the threat hang in the air for a brief second. Her head pivots, hearing the voices of men, sounding as if they've just arrived on the scene inside the house. Bringing all her focus back to me, she laughs a low trilling sound that makes me ill. Her eyes now fall on Nova. "Was all this worth it, girl? Was *he* worth it…your life?"

My brows draw together, my hand still resting on the pistol grip at my back. "I'll *never* let you hurt her." My venom-laced voice is low and full of promise.

Vicky winks, drawing even more confusion and menace from me as she says, "*Too late.*"

Vicky grins as if she's on cloud nine. I don't understand. I don't want to tear my eyes away from the threat of that gun in Victoria's hands, but I do…just for a moment. One look at Nova's face and the world crashes around me.

How had I not noticed that her lips are *still* blue, her face still white as snow, her eyes that have grown distant? Her normal biting tongue has been silent—nonexistent, even. A sob racks my chest as I pull her back to me, clutching her head with my free hand.

The blood from the pool. It was far *too* much for scratches and small wounds to have made. The wet concrete around us is streaked with red hues. "What did you do?" My choked whisper cracks from my chest.

Victoria holds up her opposite hand, which I didn't register before. It's awash in red—blood still streaming from a gash there. "I *plunged* a rather large piece of glass into her side," she says matter-of-factly. "You should probably say your goodbyes."

My heart hitches deep inside me—stuttering in disbelief. My very soul detonates. Victoria says something else, but I can't hear her through the pounding in my skull. Nova's losing too much blood. *Oh God.*

Did she know she was bleeding out? Did she know she was…she said she'd…wait for me.

"I can see you warring with yourself." Vicky laughs lightly. "Let me make it nice and easy for you…end the battle, so to speak."

Time doesn't slow down—doesn't give me the briefest of moments to say the words I need to say to Novalie. It doesn't give me the moment to kiss her one last time. Vicky's arm and gun rise together. In a flash, I'm pulling mine from behind. Shifting fast onto my knees, with Nova slumped over half behind my body that I'm desperately trying to shield her with.

The shot that rings out seems to ripple through the very earth itself.

My finger rests on the trigger, never squeezed.

Victoria's scream pierces my eardrums as she hits the concrete with a sickening thud. Blood immediately pools around her knee that's been ripped through by a bullet. My gun is still aimed at her, while hers has fallen uselessly several feet away.

I don't have to look to see who made that shot, but I do anyway. He never misses. It's why I should've known it wasn't him on that mountain shooting at me. Best hunter I know. And for some reason, really likes to incapacitate by taking out knees today.

Micah stands off in the distance, shadowed by a tall cypress tree. His rifle is still raised as he looks through his scope. As if realizing I'm okay, he begins slowly lowering it. A blur of blue-clad figures emerges from our surroundings. Several aim weapons toward Micah, but his eyes never leave mine. He rolls his lips inward and nods once.

Without words, I understand him completely. He has my back…I have his.

I shake my head at my friend, even though he can't see the pain and gratitude overtaking me. I watch as he raises his hands, laces them behind his head, and drops to his knees. Police take him to the ground all while hearing the ones closet to me yelling for me to drop my weapon. I'm vaguely aware of Victoria screeching to the cops to help her, that she's been attacked.

I finally let my arms drop. The gun falls to the ground, but I don't lace my hands behind my head. No. I turn and scoop Nova into my arms, placing her on my lap. Frantically, I rock her in my arms and whisper over and over, "I love you…come back to me…I love you…come back to me."

I can feel her weakening heartbeat with her chest formed so tightly to mine. My hands roam her abdomen until I feel the source of the blood flow and press my hand there firmly. "*She needs help*," I cry, voice punctured and weary. "She needs help…*please*."

Police surround me. One kicks my pistol out of reach before coming closer. "Get down on the ground, place your hands behind your head, son. Let the girl go."

I shake my head. I can't let her go. I can't. I won't.

The man hesitates when he sees the blood covering the ground. "Get the medics back here!" he yells, then directs me again, "You need to let her go now. We have help for her. Let her go."

A pained cry roars from my chest as I release my hold and begrudgingly allow the officer to take her from me. Her head lolls to the side, lips still parted. Her serene, beautiful face begins to disappear as I'm thrown to the ground, face scraped against the rough concrete.

With my cheek smushed to the ground, hands wrenched together painfully, I watch as they lift Nova onto the gurney. I pay no mind to Victoria's screams as she rants and rages. I'm jerked upright with the force of two men. I don't speak as they read me my rights. My lips form a tight line, knowing that anything said will most *definitely* be held against me.

Been there…done that.

The last time I was arrested, I resisted. I laid Detective Sparks on his ass with one punch. Which is something I'd gladly repeat over and over again, but not today. Not here and now. This time, I will fight for myself harder, fight for my freedom with everything I have because that's what Nova would want. Because that's what she sacrificed for, what Micah has now sacrificed for.

My feet stumble as they all but drag me toward an awaiting patrol car. Chaos ensues all around. Sirens, flashing lights, people running wild. To my right, I hear Micah yelling at an EMS worker. "*Is Melina okay*?" The cop who has him shakes him and then forces his body to bend and fall into the back of the car. Even with the door slammed shut, I can hear Micah's angry yells. Wherever Melina is…I can only hope and pray she's okay.

In the distance, lurking news reporters are gathered with policemen shooing them back. An ambulance on my left has the unconscious man in the black suit strapped in. Sweat now coats the back of my tee mixed with the pool water as the heat bears down on us. Turning my focus back to the gurney ahead, I keep my eyes trained on the medics as they lift it and position it inside the ambulance. They swarm around Novalie's lifeless form.

The cop behind me shoves me forward. I didn't even realize my feet had paused. Grinding my teeth, I chew back the words and violence that my mind is craving to dish out. He's a good five inches shorter than me and rotund. I'd have him on his ass in a second flat. Ignoring his persistence, I don't move. The doors of the ambulance start to close, and I snap out of my head.

Yanking away from the officer, arms handcuffed behind me, I run the last few paces it takes to reach the truck. Sliding to a halt and startling the medics, I plead just as the rotund officer and another lanky cop get ahold of me. "Tell her, Soren says come back to him. Tell her I love her! She's my happy accident!" The petite medic with a cherub face surveys me with pity in her dark eyes. "Just tell her…please!" I beg again as they pull me away. Every fucking step from Nova stabs holes in me—draining me of life.

The medic's head tilts, lips drawn tight, but she agrees. "I'll tell her…Soren, was it?" When I nod, she does too.

My body jostles and weaves as they drag me backward. I can feel the veins in my neck bulging from the strain of fighting against their pull. Tail lights illuminate on the back of the ambulance and in the span of a breath, they take off—my whole world going with them.

My knees buckle, and I hit the ground as my mind fractures into sheer agony.

CHAPTER 50

Soren

The fissure in the ceiling seems wider than before or is it longer…or is it just the fact that I've been staring at it for days now. Seven days, two hours, and forty-five minutes…that's how long it's been since I was arrested on Victoria's property. That's how long it's been since I've laid eyes on Nova.

No one will tell me a damn thing. Although, who would be able to tell me? Nova and Melina were rushed to the ER, Micah was incarcerated in California alongside me, and Victoria was damn sure going to lie through her chipped fucking tooth. Not to mention, I've been refused visitors and am currently being monitored day and night. I guess escaping once did land me on a shit list with the warden because I was put in isolation for four excruciating days until someone pulled strings to get me out. Whoever it was, the guards wouldn't say.

I study the crack in the ceiling some more before reaching under my bunk and pulling out the wrinkled old newspaper from earlier this year. I was immediately shipped back to North Carolina after the arrest out west and found myself in an all too familiar cell. At least I have it all to myself. I was floored to find the news clipping still tucked neatly into the metal framing under the bed.

Nova's eyes stare back at me, the same ones that held fear and anger when we'd first met, and rightly so. But also the same ones that softened under my touch. These eyes, though. It was from a time in her life when she felt utterly alone. What she couldn't possibly realize is that her lonely eyes were the only thing that kept me going in this shit-hole.

Even back then, when my plans for escape were infantile, I'd sit and stare at her. Always wondering what created such down-turned eyes full of distance and pain. Good God, she was the most beautifully wounded thing I'd ever seen. It was the mere prospect of seeing her that shoved me forward—that fueled my every waking hour. I knew it could take years for it to pan out, but I didn't care. I'd do whatever it took to get the hell out of this prison and into her life.

While convincing her to enlist her uncle was the ultimate goal and reason for my initial infatuation…it was far from the *only* reason. If I'm being honest, I became a little obsessed with the idea of her…fixated on what might happen when we'd eventually meet.

I was woefully unprepared for the reality of seeing her in the flesh. It was like taking off your shoes and dipping your feet into the ocean for the first time, like a crisp morning breath of fresh mountain air, like riding a bike with your arms outstretched and the wind whipping your face. She felt like that and more.

There's something wholesome about her…like coming home.

When I can't take the pain a second longer, I put the news clipping away and drift off into another fitful sleep surrounded by the sounds of broken men.

Sometime later, the clang of a metal lock reverberates through the small space, waking me instantly, followed by the voice of my not-so-pleasant guard.

"On your feet, Marshall. You've got a visitor," Harry says.

I stand fast, turning toward him. His bronze face is contorted this morning, and his dark eyes are creased around the edges as if he's completely against whatever meeting this is. I can't blame the guy for hating me. It was his friends that I bested when I escaped.

Straightening and stretching, I ask, "Who is it? Thought I couldn't have visitors."

His muscled shoulders tense almost imperceptibly. "I was told to bring you to him…nothing more."

"Uh huh," I mutter. That's been the bullshit I've heard all week. Everyone has refused to tell me anything that's happening on the outside.

Raking a hand through my unruly hair, I turn my back on him. "Give me a sec." He doesn't balk me on it as I go over to relieve myself and then proceed to brush my teeth and splash my weary face with a spray of icy water.

Turning, I see his back is to me, and for some reason I feel the need to have Nova with me. I pull that article from under the bed and tuck it into the pocket of my orange jumpsuit before saying, "I'm ready."

Minutes later, I'm handcuffed to a chair in a small, bland gray room that looks like it was meant for interrogations. Fluorescent lights flicker, making my skin crawl. Harry stands, chest out as always, like a fucking bird trying to get the attention of females. Cocky bastard. His face gives nothing away. Sweat begins dampening the back of my neck in this stagnate room with no apparent ventilation.

The healing wound on my thigh thrums a little with the slightest pain. A dull reminder of everything I've been through. It was thankfully not infected.

Movement by the door and quieted voices catch my ears. A fucking ghost walks through the door…or at least I think it is. With pinched brows and mouth agape, I cock my head to the side, analyzing the man who's partially turned, still talking to someone outside the door.

Detective Sawyer?

My mind is a cacophony of questions as I sit straight in the seat. I'd only seen him once through the doorframe in Nova's bedroom when I hid that day, other than news reports from his hero days.

Suddenly, the man turns to face me fully, and part of me realizes instantly my error, while another part still questions it. This isn't Jim Sawyer…but damn he looks so much like him. An ache forms in my heart when I notice his multicolored hazel eyes pinning me with a mix of emotions. They're her eyes. Nova's.

This is her father.

Baron Sawyer walks slowly, dragging his eyes over me. It's hard to miss the grit of his teeth—jaw flexing. His white hair is much like his late brother's—same build too, except Baron is a little thicker around the middle.

"Soren Lee Marshall," he says firmly.

"Yes sir. That's me. And you're…Nova's father," I reply, keeping a mask of indifference on my face just in case this is about to be a very fucking bad day for me.

"You've caused quite the uproar around here." He sucks his teeth.

"Yes, sir. I suppose I have."

"Do you know why I'm here?" he asks.

A frown pulls at my face, and something inside my chest stabs with pain that writhes up my throat. "Is it Nova?" I drop my eyes, finding it extremely fucking hard to breathe suddenly. "Is she…" I can't even finish the damn words with the lump that's closed off my airway.

"Is she *dead?*" he repeats vehemently.

I exhale deeply. "Yes…is she dead?" I raise my eyes back to him pleadingly. Unspent tears surely make my eyes glassy.

He stares at me for far too many seconds before he curses under his breath. "Well shit. You really do care for her, don't you?"

This has me taken aback, but I answer all the same. "Yes, sir. I love her." I say it, leaving no fucking room for doubt.

He shakes his head, rolling his thin lips into his mouth before bringing that almost irritated gaze back to mine. "You know…I came in here determined to loathe the sight of you. You're part of the reason my brother is six feet in the ground." His Adam's apple bobs with that. "You dragged my daughter through your mess of shit and almost got her killed…and Melina."

I breathe for the first time in a week…really fucking breathe. Air goes to and from my lungs as a stray tear drags slowly down my scruffy cheek. "*Almost*…so she's alive then?"

He squares his shoulders, crosses his arms, and finally sighs. "She's alive."

My head bobs repeatedly with his words as my face crumples and I have to fight to stay upright. She's alive. My girl is alive. "Thank you," I manage to croak out.

Confusion shows in his forehead. "For what?"

"For telling me. No one would tell me anything."

He nods once. "That was part of the reason I came."

Composing myself, I clear my throat. "And the other reason?"

Baron looks behind him to the guard Harry and nods. Without speaking, Harry stomps over to me and…I can't believe my eyes as he unlocks the cuffs on my hands and feet. They clang loudly as the metal hits the floor.

Bringing my hands in front of me, I stretch my fingers and rub my sore wrists. "What is this?" I ask with uncertainty.

Baron waves Harry away, and once we're alone, he moves closer to me and leans down to plant his hands on the table in front of me. Looming over it, he says matter-of-factly, "You're free, Mr. Marshall."

My head shakes in disbelief, eyes scanning him as if it's some sick joke. "You're serious?"

"As a heart attack, now get up and follow me before I find a reason to change this outcome."

Without hesitation, I stand, following him from the room. Brows drawn together tight, I eye everyone we pass with suspicion, my body and mind not allowing my soul to feel the slightest happiness…not yet. It's all too unreal. Guards stare in awe, some even…*smiling* at me and tipping their heads. "How?" I demand, voice like gravel. "Was it Victoria…did she confess?" Before he can answer, I ask the more pertinent question, "Where's Novalie?"

He's a step in front of me and answers over his shoulder. "You have several people to thank for this. Victoria *not* being one of them." He waves me to follow down another long hall. "While I can't condone everything that's transpired…for obvious reasons, I was…coerced into taking on your case."

When I refrain from talking because words have fled my mind, he adds, "Let's just say that many factors played into this circus." He stops at the last set of double doors and turns to me. "And it *is* a damn circus out here…I suggest you get prepared."

Swallowing hard, I nod twice.

"Go in here and get dressed." He motions to a door to our right. "Some of your belongings were left for you. Then come through these doors. I'll be waiting for you."

Doing as he says, I find a pile of clean clothes stacked on a chair in the empty room. Black tee, dark jeans, and boots, along with other necessities. I dress quickly, then do my best to run my fingers through my hair, pushing it back. Before I leave the room, I tuck the clipping of Nova into my jean pocket and then meet Baron through the double doors.

Inside, the entryway is large and open. Only three people stand inside. The warden, and two officers. Their faces awash with…what I swear looks like guilt. They move forward as one, the warden handing over a packet of documents to Baron, his dyed brown hair mussed as if he's drug a hand through it repeatedly. His beady eyes look up at me from his short stature.

"The court has issued an order to vacate the original conviction, Mr. Marshall…you're a free man. How does it feel?" He reaches out a hand, withered and aged.

I hesitate, remembering all the hell this man put me through, but finally reach out and take his, squeezing it hard with a firm shake. "Feels like…" I pause. What does it feel like? Victory, elation, fear, confusion…all the above. I think about Nova and how she made me feel. Her lonely eyes. "Feels like coming home," I finally say gruffly.

The man has good enough sense to let go of my hand and avert his eyes.

Baron shakes the packet at him. "I'll be in touch," is all he says before he ushers me toward the exit doors of the prison.

Sunlight warms my skin the moment the doors close behind me. Ignoring the chaos around us that hits my ears instantly, I lean back my head and let it wash over my face. My chest rises with the deep inhale I take—my first breath of freedom. When my head drops back to take in our surroundings, I'm stunned and frozen in place. Beyond the drive, past the final barbed gates, a veritable sea of people are gathered. News vans, crowds with picket signs held high, too far away for me to read. My head swivels, taking it in.

Baron waves to someone, a woman and a younger gentleman settled in front of the crowd off to themselves and protected by police officers. A man to her left throws his arm over her shoulders and squeezes. I recognize his long black braids instantly. It's Bowen and based on the loving look Baron throws at the other two, it must be Nova's mom and brother.

In a moment of pure, undiluted bliss, they all disappear as someone else catches my attention.

A blacked-out car sits inside the gates directly in front of us. Tinted windows block out everything inside. But auburn hair catches the rays of the sun as *she* climbs out of the back door. It flows around her in the breeze, and her light green dress billows around her.

My feet are moving slow at first and then faster and faster. Baron says something from behind me, but I don't stop moving, don't hear a damn word of it. Closer and closer, I make my way to her. She doesn't run for me…just stands there, hands clasped over her mouth. Tears pour in thick streams down her cheeks.

"Nova!" I yell as I slow to a jog and then finally slide to a stop in front of her. Her hand dropping onto her side is the only thing that keeps me from yanking her to me. My chest shakes with the effort to breathe. "You came back."

She sniffles through a sob. "Always."

My eyes flit to her hand on her side, and ever so slowly I step forward, reaching with trembling, calloused hands. I cup her face. Closing the distance between us, I lower myself to her, pressing my forehead to hers. "I have no words." I exhale deeply, our breaths intertwining.

Her whole body is shaking, her voice a destroyed whisper, but she somehow manages sarcasm. "That's a first."

A deep chuckle comes out of me.

Breaking the moment, a voice from my left startles me and then punches me in the gut. "We gotta go, lover boy.

Crowd's getting crazy out there," Micah says, standing on the other side of the car, his sandy hair flitting in the wind, and a very *oddly*, serene looking Melina standing alongside him.

I shake my head, unable to believe what I'm seeing, what I'm feeling. I choke back emotion and nod to him, still at a complete fucking loss for words. My best friend is alive. Melina is okay. My eyes find the gorgeous creature looking up at me, lashes wet and clumped. My princess is here…with *me.*

Without a fucking care of who's around and who's seeing this, I grip her chin, tilting her head, and fit my mouth over hers. The crowd erupts in whoops and hollers, but then the world fractures and disappears entirely—fragmented and forgotten. Small plump lips caress my own, and the taste of her threatens to bring me to my knees when her tongue meets mine.

Pulling her into me more firmly, I break the kiss just long enough to bend and lift her into my arms, cradling her to me, then my mouth finds hers again and I'm home.

I'm home.

Epilogue

Novalie

Where do I begin? Love is not, in fact, bullshit. It's a lot of things...annoying at times, thrilling, heartbreaking, and even lonely, but never bullshit. After everything I've been through...I can attest to that. Let's go back to the beginning of that statement. The day I had to throw a wake for my deceased husband. In that moment, I was sure that I'd never love again and that it wasn't worth the pain. What if you lose the one you love? What if they treat you poorly? What if the love is not reciprocated? Those were just a few of the questions that I thought I had an answer for. Just don't love. If you don't love, you can't be hurt.

The better answer to those questions is, love every chance you get, but protect your heart from those who take advantage of it.

Would I do it all over again? I'd asked that question of myself. The new me...this version of me has only one answer.

Hell yes!

"You gonna put that journal away anytime soon? We have shit to do," Melina asks annoyingly, cocking her head at me, making a brown curl bounce that fell loose from her bun.

"Yeah, yeah. I'm coming." Closing the leather-bound journal, I place it in the side drawer in my bedroom. Then, I give my bestie a once-over. "You look really hot in that," I muse. Her black jeans are tight and formed to her curvy figure; the snug green tank top leaves almost nothing to the imagination.

She tugs on her hiking boots, grinning. My brows raise. "What's that grin for…and the clothes that look like extra skin? Wouldn't happen to be because of a certain outdoorsman that's going with us today, is it?"

She tries but fails to hide her smile. "No way, he's too quiet and broody."

I hum under my breath. Not buying it for a second. "Sure, but I see the way you two eye-fuck each other."

She feigns shock and then rolls her eyes like a petulant child. "You're grasping at straws. We're not even friends…I barely know him, really."

This time I roll my eyes but refrain from stating the obvious tension that radiates between her and Micah.

It's been two months since we picked up Soren from prison. Things are still sketchy and unknown, but every day is bringing us near closure. Some days I relive it in my mind and still can't believe it. Between the four of us, the cops on the scene that day at Victoria's, and a confession from not only Joe Sparks but also from her security guard Talbert, we've pieced together what actually happened.

Melina's quiet nature when Victoria and I were verbally going at it now makes much more sense. She'd silently alerted the police with her phone. After everything went down. Micah had carried Melina outside. She'd had him get her phone from her pocket and check it. Sure enough, a dispatcher was still on the line. Once he bandaged her side enough to slow the bleeding, he'd left her alert and in a position to flag down the police. He, on the other hand, had slinked around the house with his rifle. He said he had the most nagging, uneasy feeling and listened to it. Micah possibly saved Soren's life that day; we'll never know for sure which bullet would've hit its mark first if Victoria and Soren would've pulled those triggers.

Do we care whether she lives? Not a fucking chance, but there's a sick and wonderful feeling of vindication knowing her ass will rot in prison and have to think about us every single day.

Joe Sparks was found in the woods the same day that Soren and Micah left him tied to a tree, beaten. They placed the anonymous call that saved his miserable life. He never confessed a thing until Talbert came forward. Then, the hypothetical floodgates opened. Talbert didn't meet Vicky until three years later. She'd already snagged her rich old man in California at the time, but began a heavy affair with Talbert and, according to his words, on a night full of drinks and debauchery, she confessed everything to him. One of the worst being, she married Soren knowing beforehand about his and his father's collection.

In an odd turn of events, she'd learned about his impressive collection from none other than Jace Farrow.

Jace knew of Soren's father through his own dad. The two old men traded produce back in the day. During a casual conversation with Vicky, Jace mentioned the collector cards and comics because he was fascinated by them. She researched the Marshall family and found an unsuspecting Soren, who owned a mechanic's shop. The irony of it is almost poetic. She left Jace because he was a dead end and would never make her wealthy and pampered. Jace ends up just that…very wealthy with a pampered wife and three lovely children.

She *never* loved Soren. Not one day. She stayed long enough to leave with everything but found that impossible with the securities Soren had in place. He was smart enough to keep her off his personal and work accounts. The prenup kept her from taking it to court, and so her plan formed to take the comics and cards. It was the only thing she had her name on.

It appears that Joe, who's been married for nearly twenty years, was having an affair with Victoria around the time she formed her plot to fake her death. She wasn't going to include him in the ruse but needed him in the end to help clear some pertinent camera footage in the bank. He was also the one to visit the storage unit once…apparently to remove some incriminating…and rather indecent photos that she had stashed of her and Joe.

The contents of that safe-deposit box were more than just a small fortune. She paid off Joe and swore him to secrecy. It was his boot print that the lab tech swore on an affidavit about and him who botched Soren's lab work. We know now that Soren was drugged that night, but that part will never be proven. Joe also helped secure the bones needed to burn from a local graveyard. And her finger…that was all her.

Still makes me want to gag.

I'll admit, they had a good plan. And no one would've ever been the wiser if it hadn't been for Soren's grand escape.

Joe did kill my uncle. The order came straight from Victoria, but Talbert was tasked with making sure it went down. Joe received a life sentence for murder, being an accomplice, defacing a grave, destruction of human remains, amongst other charges. Talbert got thirty years for his role and the attempted murder of Melina. Victoria, on the other hand, received the death penalty in North Carolina. She's appealing, but with my father on the case…she's not likely to make any headway.

Soren had the opportunity to speak with her face to face but declined. He was content with imagining her in that cell and utterly miserable. He said he's found peace and didn't need to see her face ever again.

We found out later that the surgery on her knee couldn't fix all the damage, and now she walks with a cane. A picture of her in the local paper showed a shell of the immaculate woman from California. Her stringy hair was growing out, sandy blonde down the center, making her look akin to a skunk. Her chipped tooth and crooked nose had me smiling from ear to ear.

Melina likes to send her letters every once in a while. Not letters really, as there's *no* writing involved, only a traced drawing of Melina's hand, middle finger raised. What I wouldn't give to see her face when she opens those.

I've joined in the fray. Now sending our hands side by side flipping the bitch off.

My uncle had Joe figured out rather quickly. He was an amazing detective. Recently, I took Soren out to his house to pay his respects, and I swear the very wind whispered that day. An overwhelming feeling of peace sank into my bones. It's like I could feel his love in the air.

Standing, I walk over to the mirror, checking my reflection. Bootcut Levi's, hiking boots, and a lavender tank. Not my usual frills and heels, but it appears that we will be climbing a damn mountain today. So, boots it is.

Before we head out the door, I pause to look at the picture hidden on the bookshelf of Soren's arms around me. I'd never seen it—never once noticed it before, but as soon as I stepped foot back in this house, it was like a beacon calling me forward. My heart had swelled, damn near bursting with emotion that day.

Now, sitting beside it, is the very worn news article that Soren framed. His influence has not only changed my perspective on life but changed my surroundings. He was right. Before him, I was refusing to live. I just existed. Nothing I loved adorned the walls. It was like living in a magazine, but now he's ruffled the very fabric of my life. The cabinets, to my dismay, are unorganized. Which he finds entirely too amusing. Pictures of us, Mel, and Micah, and my parents and brother, have replaced the fake landscape paintings.

Slowly…so slowly, this place has become a home because of him.

A few hours later, sweat beads on my brow as we trudge through the woods. Soren clasps my hand in his firmly, helping me navigate the rugged terrain. Soren had Micah and Melina split off from us an hour ago…saying he had something to show me before we go up the mountain to the guys at Valhalla.

"How much farther?" I ask, swatting a limb that tickled my arm.

"Almost there, princess. What? Does the outdoors not suit you?" His grin is infuriatingly handsome.

I make a derisive sound. "I'm perfectly suited for the wilderness," I lie.

He chuckles lightly. "You're more suited for coffee shops and frilly dresses."

"Are you saying I'm too…*soft*?"

His thumb caresses my hand, causing goosebumps embarrassingly fast. "Yes, that's what I'm saying, but it's not a bad thing. I find that I like your soft…nature."

My cheeks warm at his deep voice and pointed words. The rush of water around us drowns out the noises of the forest as we finally reach the river. My eyes round, mouth dropping open in awe at the sight. We're standing below the massive waterfall. The one Soren told me so much about. The one they call Widowmaker. The very one he launched himself off of.

"Holy hell," I whisper. Chills snake down my vertebrae and still my breath. "I can't believe you jumped from up there." My head falls back to take in the sheer rise of the falls.

He drops my hand, pointing to the top. "Valhalla is up there." He smiles thoughtfully and then turns to face me. "You were the last thing I thought of that night…your face…the guilt I felt for causing you so much pain."

Reaching up, I stroke a thumb over his short, bearded cheek, the coarse black hair thick under my touch. "Don't. Don't go back there," I tell him. "I have you here, in the flesh, and it was all worth it. Now show me what it is you were dying to show me."

A surprising, sexy drag of his eyes down my body has me questioning his intentions as his deep voice rolls over me. "Clothes are not optional here. Strip for me." My mouth forms a retort, but he just shakes his head, stopping me. "No, no, little princess. For me to show you, I need you to cross the river with me…now clothes off."

Swallowing my nerves, I back away from him and lean around to view the water rushing past. "Are you sure it's safe?"

"I've got you. Don't worry."

Holding my chin high, I drop my pack on the ground and give a determined look before dragging my shirt over my head slowly. His hooded eyes trail every inch as I slip off my boots, socks, and jeans next, leaving me in only my black panties and lacy bra. "This is water approved, right?" I ask, purposefully fingering the lace around the curve of my breast.

He licks his bottom lip, dampening the area and drawing my eyes there. "Perfectly," he replies gutturally. His gaze drops to the scar along the side of my abdomen where Vicky stabbed me under the water.

A flash of anger creeps in before I shake my head. "*Don't.* Don't let her taint this day."

His throat works as he masks his former rage. Thankfully, the rancid bitch had only gotten my spleen. And thankfully again, that's something I *can* live without.

I gesture to his clothes. "Your turn, pervert." I smirk, and he can't hold back his side-smile. My mouth dries out completely when his shirt is ripped over his head, muscles rippling with the motion, tattoos coiling. His sweat-dampened skin glistens in the few rays that make it through the trees. The deep V leading to his…*oh good Lord.* I have to tell myself to breathe as he drops his pants and boots alongside mine. His black boxers do little to hide the bulge already forming there.

Holy hell. The man is perfection.

"You blush so prettily, princess." His thick thigh muscles shift when he steps forward. My eyes snap back to his, but I don't get the chance to reply as he takes my small hand in his too-large one and leads me to the river's edge.

I wince as my tender feet pad over stones and sticks. When the cold mountain water meets my toes, I freeze. "I can't do this."

"Yes you can. There's a deep pool here that isn't as rough, then there's several rocks to help us over." He ushers me forward.

"But why can't you just show me from here? Point it out…I'm sure it's lovely," I say shakily.

He bites back a smile. "You're ruining the surprise…you can't get to it from here or see it."

Pursing my lips, I grimace. "I don't think I can."

Soren moves fast, too fast for me to object, and lifts me into his arms, cradling me to his chest just like the day I got him back. Our heated skin together brings the slightest bit of comfort before it dissipates as he wades into the water. "I've got you. Calm down."

"Easy for you to say," I grumble as the rush of frigid water laps over my feet, rising to meet my stomach as Ren pushes us toward an outstretched stone. Lifting me high, he sets me atop it before climbing up himself.

We climb over them and wade into another section of rapids before finally reaching the bank. Without words, he pulls me up and directs me to follow him toward the falls. The misting spray of water grows thick as we round the edge.

"Wait…are we going behind it?" I ask breathily.

He has a wicked grin as he glances back at me and then disappears behind the wall of water, pulling me with him.

"*Soren,*" I say, giggling, but the giddy laughter dies away. "Oh…oh wow. I wasn't expecting this," I admit, shifting my body in circles, taking in the wall of stone on one side and the barrier of the water on the other.

"You like it?" he asks, trailing his hand through the water. It parts with his fingers.

"Are you kidding? It's breathtaking." On the opposite side, it's blocked with boulders and vegetation, definitely not passable. A rainbow glints off one of the smooth stones from the mist. "Did you and Micah find this place?"

He shakes his head. "Nah. Actually, this is the first time I've been in here."

My eyes snap to him. "You've never been here? I thought it was safe? How did you know it was *safe,* Ren?" I pepper him with questions. "What if we'd gotten washed down the godforsaken river?"

He just smiles, shrugging. "I was like eighty percent sure we could make it across right there." I give him a scathing look, which he mocks. "Bowen told me about it." My interest piques at that as he continues. "Turns out he knew these woods well. This was the same place Callon had brought Maisy when they were in hiding."

"No way?" My mouth curves into a smile.

"Yeah, and not just that. The burned-up cabin they lived in is not too far from here."

Rolling my fingers across the stone, I study this place with new eyes. "I wonder if this is where they fell in love?" I say wistfully.

I don't realize Ren is beside me until his clean male scent washes over me. His body brushes against my back as he braces one hand against the rock face and snakes the other around my waist. His hot, minty breath feathers over my ear. "Maybe this is where they made love?"

Shivers scatter all over my skin, making me tremble. His hand splays on my abdomen, moving north first, and with one hand my front-clasp bra is released. "Ah," I say hoarsely, "so this was your plan, huh? Get me out here alone and take advantage of me."

He lets the bra drop before his hand moves south, dipping into the band of my panties. His chest rumbles against me with a slight laugh. "You can't take advantage of the willing princess. And I don't see you putting up a fight."

His fingers dip lower and slide right through me, cupping me. My breath hitches somewhere in my throat as he drags his thick fingers over my center and then makes slow, agonizing circles. "*Soren.*" My tone is pleading. I can feel his thick length pressing into my back. My eyes pinch shut.

So fast, he spins me to him, taking my mouth with a feverish kiss and lifting me until my legs are snug around his waist. My hands move to grip his shoulders, then thread into his hair as his tongue delves into my mouth, claiming me, my breasts firmly against his warm chest. He presses me into the stone gently with me perched against him; He breaks the kiss long enough to look into my eyes, holding my stare, as he releases his hands, letting me rest against the stone and his waist…and I feel the fabric of my underwear rip on either side.

My eyes narrow playfully. "You now owe me a Kindle, a pair of *vintage* leather Mary Janes, a shower curtain, and panti—"

The bastard nips my jaw to shut me up. And *fuck him*…it worked.

"Right now you are *mine,* and I tell you what to do, little princess. So stop talking." He stuns me again as he licks over the bite mark.

My entire body burns at his words. I should cut him down. Rant about the patriarchy or some shit, but *no, no, no*…what do *I* do? I *blush*, heat rushing through me and landing between my legs like some simpering virgin.

His shit-eating grin almost brings me out of my embarrassing submissive state, but then he's holding me with one arm and positioning himself with the other. When he rubs his length over my core, I moan aloud.

His jaw clenches as he watches my reaction. "I want you to scream for me," he demands. His teeth flash when he all but growls the words at me. It's as if holding back a moment longer will shatter him. And when I nod…he doesn't hold back any longer. With one powerful thrust, he buries himself inside me, stretching me, filling me to a point of sheer ecstasy. His groan mixed with a strangled sound from me echoes in the hollow space.

Holding me there, he revels in the moment, in how deeply seated he is. We are one. He drags his nose over the column of my neck to my hair and inhales as if my scent gives him life itself.

Then his lips claim mine again. It's not slow, not in the slightest. It's all tongues, teeth, and panting breaths. He guides me into a rhythm atop him that only grows more and more chaotic as we devour each other, body and soul.

The coiling, writhing ache deep in my belly grows frantic with each angled thrust. His mouth moves, and without warning, teeth are clamping lightly over the peak of one breast. The pain and pleasure collide and have me doing exactly what he told me to.

I scream out his name, "*Soren*!"

His chest rumbles with pleasure when he hears my lips pleading out his name. And then I can't hold back any longer. When his tongue laps at my aching breast, my legs begin to shake, my climax reaching, body begging for release.

"Come with me," Soren says in a still demanding tone. "Give me all of you."

His words are my undoing, like detonating a bomb. I toss back my head, leaning it into the rock face, and cry out with the force of the spasms that rack my body. Wave after wave threatens to pull me under as his pounding slows. I feel him tense right before he releases an animalistic sound and buries into me, pulsating. He braces us up with one hand and holds me with the other. Our chests rise and then fall faster than the water around us, breaths mingling as he rests his forehead against mine.

Our eyes stay locked on each other. Really seeing each other from the inside out. Reaching up my hand, I smooth back his damp hair and then pull his face to me for another long, sensuous kiss.

When I pull away, his eyes drop to the moisture on my swollen lips. "This is what I want every day, for the rest of my life."

"Sex," I say, my cheek dimpling. He snorts and nips my jaw again, making me curse. "*Dammit, Soren.*"

"Stop talking, woman." He uses his sexy voice to distract me and bend me to his will. And again it fucking works. *Ugh.* "And yes, sex too," he says, giving me that panty-dropping side-smile that he clearly doesn't need to give me because he's still inside me. "I want to wake up to you every morning, look into those eyes that haunted me for so long."

Soren had explained what that simple picture of me in the paper had been for him. In the beginning, a means to an end, then somewhere along the line…things changed. He became fixated on me and intrigued by my solemn face. He was worried that I'd bolt at the thought of his premeditated fixation on me, but I didn't. We were meant to meet. That's devastatingly clear now.

I nod, realizing I had been far too quiet after his words, then lean in for a quick kiss. Pulling back, I whisper on his lips, "You have me. Every day, from now until my heart stops beating…and then maybe even after that."

He angles his head to one side and then the other, planting small kisses along my cheeks before he lowers my trembly legs to the ground. I hold on to him for support, hands around his waist as he leans over me, pinning me with those stormy eyes.

I'm quiet, contemplative for several seconds when he asks, "What're you thinking?"

Inhaling deeply through my nose, I take a beat to appreciate this perfect moment in time. The stunning location, the clean mountain air, the love…and bane of my existence looming over me. Finally I say, "Maybe our souls knew each other in another life or maybe they were fated in this one. Too many coincidences brought us together for it to be chance."

He flicks my nose in that annoying yet adorable way, making me scowl. "No. You were right before."

My brow rises. "I like the sound of that…but right how?"

His brows rise and drop quick as if he's replaying the memory. "We are simply a happy accident."

A smile plays at the corner of my lips as I suddenly recall waking in the hospital to find out that I'd almost died twice, even coded on the surgery table. That's not why I'm smiling. I'm smiling because as shocking as that was, it was even more so when a woman claiming to be the medic from the ambulance demanded to see me. No one would let her in, but I could hear her pleas out in the hall of the recovery room. She was saying, "*Tell her that Soren said come back to him. He loves her! She is his happy accident. Just tell her!*"

I'd blocked it out or lost the vague memory, likely due to the amount of painkillers they had me on, but now it slams back into me with the force of a thousand suns.

"I like that," I say quietly.

Soren's finger grazes my cheek, trapping a stray tear there that I had no idea had fallen. "I love you. You know that? More than anything. I'll always come back to you, Nova. Even the afterlife or the devil himself couldn't keep me from you," he says softly.

"I know. I love you, too," I say, whispering through the breeze that swishes the trees in the distance. Our mouths fall back together, but this time without the frenzy. This was love and connection at its purest level.

He's my happy accident that, if given the chance, I'd do all over again...and again...and again.

He breaks away, his gaze questioning before he whispers against my lips, "What does the future hold for Novalie Annie Sawyer?"

My cheek pulls with the sly side smile I'm giving him.

"I'm going to do what my uncle said...*write the damn book*."

THE END

Turn the page for a bonus chapter.

Dear Victoria,

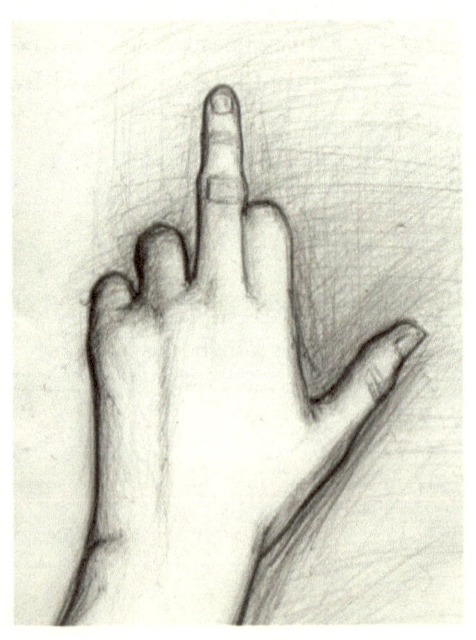

Mel

BONUS CHAPTER

Melina

"This is *bullshit,* and those two are fired from the friends department." I push a sweat-damp curl behind my ear, glowering at Micah. He doesn't even deign to look my way or acknowledge my complaining as he carries several large logs over to the fire. "Hey, mountain man…I'm talking to you."

His face screws up in a scowl that only seems to accentuate his jawline. Which pisses me off. I mock his face behind his back as he turns and kneels to ramble through his pack, pulling out various tools and what looks like a fire starter.

"You not gonna strike rocks together like a good boy scout," I mumble.

His shoulders tense in the camo shirt he's wearing, hands pausing momentarily, but then he continues as if he's trying really fucking hard to ignore my jabs. Which, of course, only fuels my fire. "Squirrel got your tongue?"

He lifts his trucker hat, raking a hand through his unruly shoulder-length sandy hair in frustration before putting it on backward. "It's cat…not squirrel. And do you ever shut up?" he snaps.

"You're a mountain man…hence the squirrel. And no, not particularly. Do you ever talk? Or is your range of vocabulary minuscule?" When his head shakes, I add with a flourish, "You were in special classes in school, huh?"

He stands, turning to face me…intimidatingly large and muscly for anyone other than me. I tend to like a challenge though. His deep brown eyes seem even darker with the thick brows pinched together, shadowing his features. "Anyone ever tell you, you were a pain in the ass?"

My shoulders jerk with the huff of breath I blow. "Among other compliments, yes." When he takes a calming breath, I smile sweetly. "What's your deal?" I ask flatly. "You've hardly said five words the entire hike up this hellscape of a mountain."

He shifts back to his task, dropping a fire starter into the pile of wood. Pulling out a lighter and a cigarette, he lights his smoke first and then the fire starter before flicking his Zippo shut on his green tactical pants.

For some odd fucking reason…that was sexy.

Exhaling a cloud of smoke, he grumbles, "I've been told I'm a man of few words."

"So…it *was* special classes?" I say again, biting back a laugh when he curses under his breath. Before he can retort,

I say, "You talk to Ren all the time. Y'all are like two clucking hens."

He takes another drag. "We've been together a long…long time. I'm not much of a conversationalist with people I barely know."

"You've known me for what…like *two* months now," I point out.

He feigns exhaustion. "Two very…*very* long months."

A small part of me wants to be offended, but a larger part of me knows I'm not going to be. "You're welcome," I say through a sigh. I'm pretty sure that an 'almost smile' pulls at his cheek.

Standing up, I pull my shirt over my head and toss it to the ground, eliciting a shocked look from Micah. I frown, looking down at my red bikini top, then back to him. "What? It's hot as hell. It is fucking August in the south, you know?"

"Besides being a pain in my ass, you have a filthy mouth." He flicks his cigarette into the fire.

"Again, *you're welcome.*" I grin.

"It's not a compliment *or* a thank you, Melina," he says dryly.

"I beg to differ."

He turns to face me fully. "Oh? How so?" He crosses his arms over his broad chest. And is that…is that his veins bulging in his forearms. Ugh. Why does he have to be so pretty? All the assholes are pretty.

Then I remember that I'm an asshole and smile. "Because I'm not ashamed of my filthy mouth or vulgar nature. It makes me *real…honest.* You get what you get with me…nothing is salt-coated."

He laughs, and it catches me off guard, his deep rumble somehow making its way to my freaking toes. "What's so funny?" I ask, crossing my own arms now.

"*Salt* coated?" He reigns in another smile. "Don't you mean *sugar* coated?"

"No, I meant what I said." My lips purse outward as I try to stand taller. "Sugar is decidedly trash. It's bad for you. Salt, on the other hand, is necessary for the body and therefore the better option to coat something in."

His mouth opens slightly as if he's completely lost for words. "You just make things up…don't you? You can't change a saying that's been around forever."

"Sure you can." I walk closer to him, studying the fire he's made. "Free will and all. You can virtually do anything."

"That's…" he stops and seems to reconsider his words. "That's a terrible way to look at life, Melina. You have free will, sure, but rules are in place for a reason. What if *everyone* did *everything* that crossed their minds?" I hum and shrug as if it's not a bad idea. He shakes his head and walks away toward the woods. Apparently done with the conversation. Over his shoulder, he says, "I'm gathering more wood. If we're staying the night, we'll need it." I hear him grumble about Soren's cooking or something to that effect as he disappears.

Bending down to his pack, I begin rifling through it. I'm nosy, but also just plain ol' hungry, and at this point, I'm not so sure that Nova and Ren are coming back. I push aside more camping tools, spare clothing, a rather large, sheathed knife, and finally see a granola bar peeking out. When I reach for it, my thumb catches on the point of something sharp.

"Owww, what the fuck?" When I yank my hand back, the tip of my right thumb impaled by a fishhook. The ridiculous glimmering fake minnow dangles from my hand as I raise it in the air to inspect the barb. Blood dribbles down the base of my thumb and then quickens, reaching my forearm.

"I was gone less than two minutes. What have you done?" Micah's voice grits out. He drops the wood, letting it crash to the ground, and bounds over to me.

"It's *your* fault. Who has a fishing hook just lying around, jumbled up with everything else? Why was it just thrown in your bag?"

His lips form a thin line as he grabs my hand and jerks it to him. "Key fucking words there, Melina…my bag…*mine.* Why were you digging around in it?"

"I was hungry."

"We'll be cooking soon. Do you need to be told like a petulant child that you shouldn't snack before dinner?" His voice is biting and sharp.

I try to yank my arm away, but he holds firm. "Petulant…big word for you. Now…*let me go.*"

"No. Sit down," he commands.

"*No,*" I say back to him as I narrow my eyes in anger.

Before I realize what has happened, he's knocked into my knees just right to make them give way. With his arm around me, he guides my almost fall and forces me onto my ass.

My eyes widen, and for once…I'm speechless. Did he just…put me on my ass? He ignores my frozen face and sits beside me, pulling his bag over with his free hand. He yanks out a pair of pliers and a first-aid kit.

My voice makes a gallant return. "You're not fucking touching me with those pliers! I bet they're not even clean. You're going to cause my fucking hand to rot off."

"Melina, I need you to really *attempt* to shut the fuck up. I'm helping you get this out if I have to tie you up and force your compliance."

My eyes shift to the side as my mind takes a dive into the damn gutter. I mean…headfirst into the gutter. I glance back at him to see that his eyes are already on mine. "What?" I ask, trying to imagine anything other than him tying me up right now.

His brows draw together. "Where did your mind just go?"

"No, where…why do you ask?" I reply a bit too fast.

"You're blushing, and you just…looked lost in thought." When I don't reply, he says, "Just hold still. It'll only hurt for a second."

Annnddd there went my mind again. Maybe I'm ovulating, and he's just the closest barbarian triggering my woman parts. It's his scent…that's probably it. His stupid man smell that somehow still smells like the shower after hiking up this godforsaken mountain.

"You just did it again," he muses with a smile.

"No, I…" I choose not to lie. I did kind of brag earlier about being honest and real. "Okay, yeah. My mind has been a cesspool lately. It's been a dry year."

He drops the bottle of alcohol that I never even saw him pull out and quickly grabs it and starts disinfecting the pliers. "Dry year?" His voice lifts in question. "You mean *sex*. You haven't had sex in a while." His voice is low and so very cute and uncertain.

He's probably just distracting me, because the pliers are clean and he's aiming them near my thumb, pointy ends open like a mouth. I turn my head to avoid watching. "Yeah, what else would I mean by that?" I ask bitterly.

He takes my hand in his, and I flinch on instinct. His calloused fingers inspect the area from what it feels like, but for me it sends whole other feelings fleeing through my body. His voice is soft and understanding when he says, "I get that. It's not been a record year for me either."

My brows raise at that. "Really. No women out there dying to be ridden by a mountain man with vocab issues?"

"Dear God, Mel, do you ever take anything seriously?"

I think about that for a moment. "Yes, of course. Dire situations call for it, but ninety-nine percent of the time…no." A ripping sensation makes me squeal, pulling at my arm to no avail. Micah holds me firm as I sling my head back to him, curls flinging around my face. "Shit Micah! That hurt!" I frantically look to my thumb, half expecting the end to be missing. He's already dousing it with alcohol before I can muster another yelp.

"Stop being a baby," he growls, pulling out a gauze and holding it over the wound tightly. I try to drag my arm away again with a curse, but he doesn't allow it. "It's just a little pressure."

Not going back to the gutter…*not* going back to the gutter. I chant in my head. "You're *more* of an asshole than I first realized," I say, even though my finger feels a hundred times better without the plastic fish hanging from it. But he doesn't need to know that. He looks at me with an expression I can't place. "What?" I ask.

"You didn't seem to think any negative thoughts about me when we first met. Let's see…what did you call me?"

My face heats, but he pays it no mind. "I believe you called me *hot*."

I make a dismissive sound in my throat. "I was *dying*…remember. Probably hallucinating." I point with my free hand to the scar the bullet left through my abdomen in almost the exact spot as Novalie's. Although hers caused her to lose a whole organ. For me, the bullet caused some internal bleeding, but all my parts are still there. Cup half full, I guess.

He smirks, shaking his head as he wraps a bandage around my thumb. "Nah, you thought I was hot."

Again, my brain stalls and then demands honesty…realness. "Well, since you saved my life, I guess I can admit that you're…*hot*." I say the last word distastefully.

"Wow, such an ego builder. Don't think I've ever had such a shitty compliment." He holds my hand in his, checking the bandage one last time.

"Get used to it with that face," I say smarmily.

He drops my hand with a deadpan look blanketing his face. "You really say whatever comes into your head, don't you?"

"And do whatever I want also," I say confidently. But that confidence falters when I suddenly realize just how close we've gotten. Micah is shoulder to shoulder with me, the barest of my skin brushing his shirt, but our faces are only inches apart. Tamping down the blasted butterflies that keep flitting their fucking wings in my tummy, I say, "Free will remember."

He licks his lower lip and then drags his teeth over it. It should be a normal bodily reaction to wet your mouth, but it's sinful coming from those full lips. His face is shaved clean, but I can tell that if I reached out and touched his hardened jaw, a few days' worth of scruff would meet my fingers.

"Is that right?" he asks.

It takes me a few seconds to remember what the hell I said prior to his response. Oh yeah, free will. "That's right," I say, barely recognizing my voice that's dropped to a whisper.

He angles his head, dragging those dark eyes over my lips and up to meet my gaze. "Tell me, *Melina.* What do you want to do right this second?"

Why did his voice become even hotter when he said my name like that?

I debate for one second, then two, then three…before saying, *fuck it.* Leaning in to him, I place my lips over his, parting his mouth with my tongue brazenly. His whole body stills, but then his tongue laves into mine with a guttural groan radiating from his chest.

Fireworks, explosions, something for sure explodes inside me. The butterflies are demolished in the inferno that is my body, replaced by embers. My hands, bandage and all, cup around his head, threading into his hair as I angle my face and kiss him long and deep. His hat falls to the ground.

This man tastes like nothing I've ever had before. Or maybe it's the electricity sparking through me that's tinging the moment, but I could kiss him forever. His hands have managed to reach my hips, settling into the curves and squeezing. In a blink, he's somehow drug me onto his lap as we rock on the ground. Sticks dig into my knees, poking into my jeans to meet skin, but I don't stop kissing him.

That is…not until I hear the crack of a branch somewhere nearby. I'm off his lap and stumbling to stand fast. He's awkwardly doing the same when Soren walks out of the tree line, Nova on his heels.

"Sorry it took so long," Nova says before she's even reached us.

My chest is still acting like a damn fool, rising fast with every breath, flitting wildly like a hummingbird's wings. I shift my eyes to Micah, watching his throat work as he tries but fails to keep his eyes from me. "It's okay!" I yell over to her. Then I lower my voice so that only Micah can hear me. "*What was that?*" I ask as if he's completely to blame for that interaction.

"That was me proving a point." He smirks.

"What point might that be?" I whisper forcefully.

"You talk a big game, but deep down…you're as malleable as putty."

My face burns with heat. I'm going to *kill* this man and enjoy every second of it.

Acknowledgments

Where. To. Start…

Well, let's start here. If you were a fan of Finding Maisy, then thank you first and foremost. You've been with me since the beginning, and that warms my heart. Finding Maisy was my first novel and still holds a special place in my soul. Happy accidents, while it is a standalone, contains some of the characters from my first book. Therefore, it was a thrill to bring to life those familiar names. I hope that each of you who has followed me from the start enjoys finding the Easter eggs in each book that relate to another. It's my little *Elledgeverse*, so to speak.

Next, a big shout-out to my editor from day one, Maryssa Gammon of Pocket Editing! She's my rockstar from behind the scenes…like the Wizard of Oz. You've never failed to take on my projects on short notice and always have friendly words for me. Thanks for being awesome ;)

I definitely can't leave out my work family at Cherokee Medical Center for following my writing, listening to me plot, and making work…not feel like *work*. Our abundance of giggles and immature banter is the glue that holds the Radiology Department together. Love you guys!

Special thanks to my coworker and friend Schae Clark for taking the time to proofread Happy Accidents with me. She has a knack for fast reading and catching plot errors. She is the president of our completely *'normal and demure'* book club…the Cliterature Club. Thank you for all the laughs.

As always, I can't leave out my wonderful, crazy family. My daughter and son-in-law—Megan and Caleb—for being supportive, Cameron Shay for talking books with me anytime I need to vent, to my twins Emily and Amelia for showing me that I need to let go and see the fun in every day. I can't leave out the newest edition to the family…Megan and Caleb blessed me with my first grandchild on December 4, 2025, and even though she is but a few days old, thank you Evelyn Marie for bringing such unbridled joy into our hearts.

Last, but first for me. Thank you to my husband, Mitchell Elledge. You are my muse for what real men should be. I've loved you since 1999, and that's not nearly long enough.

www.ingramcontent.com/pod-product-compliance
Lightning Source LLC
LaVergne TN
LVHW090547110826
845146LV00001B/45

* 9 7 9 8 9 9 1 9 3 8 1 4 3 *